Our earth is abundant with possibilities for people to live in peace everywhere. Yet, as fear and violence from conflict around the world overwhelm our headlines, many of our thoughts are invaded with confusion, discouragement, even disillusionment over root causes of war and the populations who engage in the treachery and brutality.

Though we may not always be able to comprehend the atrocities occurring worldwide, we all know the face of a child, so innocent, and so unsuspecting until war invades his world and turns the joy that every child should know each day into a nightmare.

War Child tries to speak directly to the experiences of children of war by offering them tangible hope and the possibility of recovering their lives.

War Child was created in response to 1993 headlines that first reported on the horrors of ethnic cleansing taking place in Bosnia and the former Yugoslavia. Massacres of inconceivable proportions made an unprecedented impact upon millions, shocking and devastating them with detailed reports of endless brutalities.

Two individuals, deeply affected by what they saw and read responded. Their efforts laid the groundwork for the founding of War Child, their goal, first in the U.K. and then worldwide.

Today, War Child offices around the world have each established an independent presence. United in their missions, each War Child office has initiated aid programs that attend to the profound needs of children. With one of the lowest administrative cost ratios among all humanitarian agencies, we have established emergency food aid, medical and psychosocial rehabilitation programs for orphans and education programs that enroll children in schools and provide teachers with training.

This year, for the first time, War Child USA is proud to have provided that opportunity to children in Sierra Leone, West Africa, the poorest country on Earth, and once described as the worst place to be a child.

In all of its endeavors, War Child has joined in the struggle to reclaim the childhoods stolen by war. By offering programs that feed the bodies, minds and hearts of children, we believe we are providing a means for overcoming their sorrow and grief and for knowing joy every day, in some small way.

Wherever children are suffering we will go there to help.

Thank you for selecting this new collection of stories to read and to recommend to your friends.

If you would like to make a donation to War Child USA, please visit www.warchildusa.org.

Betsy Small-Campbell, Director of Development and Programs, War Child USA

Greg Spitzfaden, Chairman, Board of Trustees, War Child USA

From No Strings

Miss Piggy, Fozzie Bear and the Muppets are household names, but in 2003, longtime Muppet designer and producer Michael K. Frith, and his wife and puppeteer, Kathryn Mullen, decided to use their years of Muppet expertise and experience to do something more serious.

Their idea was to teach children affected by war about the dangers of unexploded land mines using live puppetry and video. With help from staff and volunteers drawn from some of the world's best-known aid agencies—including War Child, GOAL and HAAD—No Strings was born.

Their first project involves land mine awareness for children in Afghanistan, created in partnership with OMAR (Organization of Mine Clearance and Afghan Rehabilitation)—and money raised from the sale of *Girls' Night Out* will fund completion and distribution of the first forty-minute video, which is being translated into the two main languages of Afghanistan. UNICEF have already agreed to field-test the video, and No Strings hopes to distribute it throughout local schools, television stations and cinemas.

Money from *Girls' Night Out* will also help fund HIV awareness videos for Africa.

To see photographs of the No Strings puppets, and recent press coverage in the *New York Times* and *The Independent* (UK) please visit www.nostrings.org.uk.

Thank you from everyone at No Strings for buying *Girls' Night Out*. Although No Strings has had massive support so far, it is still very new—and exists on a tiny budget. Contributions from *Girls' Night Out* will help to get the charity off the ground.

Meg Cabot

Elizabeth Buchan

Cecilia Ahern

Marian Keyes

Lolly Winston

Emma McLaughlin & Nicola Kraus

girls' night out

Kristin Gore

Emily Giffin

Alisa Valdes-Rodriguez

Tilly Bagshawe

Edited by Carole Matthews, Sarah Mlynowski, Chris Manby

RED
DRESS
INK
™

First edition June 2006

GIRLS' NIGHT OUT

A Red Dress Ink novel

ISBN 0-373-89579-8

© 2006 by Harlequin Enterprises S.A.

© 2006 individual stories remain with the authors

Author Photo credits listed as follows:

Cecilia Ahern © Kieran Harnett
Maggie Alderson © Derek Henderson
Tilly Bagshawe © Michael Pilkington
Elizabeth Buchan © Mary Duncan
Meg Cabot © Ali Smith
Laura Caldwell © Anthony Parmalee
Lynda Curnyn © Julie Ann Coney
Kathleen DeMarco © Emory Van Cleve
Nick Earls © Mick Toal
Kristin Gore © Tipper Gore
Emily Giffin © Sebastian Thaw
Robyn Harding © Garry Sarre
Lauren Henderson © Mike McGregor
Imogen Edwards-Jones © Joth Shakerly
Marian Keyes © Mark McCall
Nicola Kraus and Emma McLaughlin © Leonard Lewis
Chris Manby © Michael Pilkington
Carole Matthews © Angus Muir
Anna Maxted © Colin Thomas
Lynn Messina © Chris Catanese
Pamela Ribon © Thomas Hargis
Lolly Winston © Lisa Pongrace

www.RedDressInk.com

Printed in U.S.A.

Dear *Girls' Night Out* Reader,

First of all, a big thank you for buying this book—the second of the Girls' Night In series in the U.S.A.—which has been especially put together for humanitarian organizations War Child and No Strings. If we could give you all a big hug we would. Be happy to know that the royalties from every copy of *Girls' Night Out* sold go directly to these terrific charities to enable them to continue their valuable work throughout the world.

Since it was first conceived over a bottle of chardonnay in London's Groucho Club back in 1999, the Girls' Night In series has raised almost two million dollars around the world—with editions published in the U.S.A., U.K., Australia, Canada, The Netherlands, Germany... You name a place, we're there. None of the authors or editors received any money for their stories—they all contributed out of the goodness of their hearts and we're very grateful to them. We didn't even have to beg. Although we did ply one or two with very colorful cocktails. Sometimes a writer has to have a night out, too! The three of us have enjoyed working with every one of the contributors—they're all superstars. As authors we're always encouraged to write from the heart—it's amazing to see what can happen when we do.

The money generated by *Girls' Night In* has made a real difference to children with extraordinarily difficult lives. But we couldn't have raised it without you, the readers. You've sent the books to the top of the bestseller charts across the globe. So, pour yourself a glass of something chilled, curl up on the sofa with your book and think of how much good you've done by having a great night in.

XXX

Carole, Sarah & Chris
www.girlsnightin.info

ACKNOWLEDGMENTS

A big thanks to all the people who have made the Girls' Night In series work so well:

The fabulous authors who've generously contributed the wonderful stories that make up this book.

Our amazing U.S. editor, Farrin Jacobs. The great team at Red Dress Ink, including Margaret Marbury, Tara Kelly, Margie Miller, Rebecca Soukis, Selina McLemore, Sarah Rundle and Amy Jones. Also thanks to U.K. editor Katie Espiner at HarperCollins, Susan McLeish at Penguin Australia and Andrea Crozier at Penguin Canada.

Our fantastic American agent, Laura Dail. Plus our founding agent in Australia, Fiona Inglis, Tara Wynne and all at Curtis Brown Australia and Curtis Brown U.K.

To the people at War Child and No Strings for giving us the reason to do this.

Editors around the globe: Jessica Adams, Maggie Alderson, Nick Earls, Imogen Edwards-Jones.

James Williams, for the Web site.

And, above all, you, for buying this book and helping to change the life of a child.

Carole Matthews
Sarah Mlynowski
Chris Manby

CONTENTS

Marian Keyes is an Irish novelist who was first published in 1995, and has been credited with starting the chick-lit genre. Her seven novels are all comedies about serious issues: *Watermelon, Lucy Sullivan Is Getting Married, Rachel's Holiday, Last Chance Saloon, Sushi for Beginners, Angels* and *The Other Side of the Story.* These titles have become international bestsellers, have been published in thirty-one languages and have sold eleven million copies. She has also published two collections of humorous journalism: *Under the Duvet* and *Cracks in My Foundation.* Two of her novels have been filmed for TV, and two for the cinema.

Wishing Carefully
Marian Keyes

Be careful what you wish for, they say. So when Siobhan came back from Australia with an Aboriginal dreaming bowl and invited us all to place a wish in it, I'm ashamed to say I asked for a fairy-tale romance. It wasn't the kind of thing I would normally do but I was a bit wounded at the time. Even while I was folding up the note to put in the bowl, I hated Mark for turning me into the sort of person who made such pathetic wishes.

Naturally enough, I told everyone that I'd wished for peace in the Middle East. The only person I told the truth to was Siobhan—who confessed that she already knew, that after everyone had left she'd unfolded the notes and read them all. She was quick to reassure me that I wasn't alone; the person who'd claimed he'd wished for his mother's arthritis to improve had in fact wished for a silver SL320 Merc with many optional extras, including heated leather seats and a CD player.

"It's just a bit of fun," Siobhan said, but I was keen to have faith in the future, and hoped my wish would come true. In a way it did.

Would you believe it, less than a week later I met a man. Not just any man, but a fireman. The job alone was sexy, and he was gorgeous—arms the size of my thighs, huge barrel chest all the better to crush me against. The only thing was...he was shorter than I expected firemen to be—but never mind, I was off tall men.

And he was a kind and caring person; only a kind and caring person would put their life at risk entering burning buildings to rescue sleeping children and climbing up trees to bring home beloved cats.

We hit it off, he asked me out, Siobhan smiled proudly from the sidelines as if it was all her doing and suddenly I was in great form. I embarked on the round of shopping and ablutions that a first date calls for and Saturday night couldn't come fast enough.

But on Saturday afternoon my phone rang. It was my hero and he was yawning so hard his jaw cracked. "I'm sorry, Kate, out on a job last night, just got back, need some sleep, on a shift again tomorrow."

Another huge big yawn.

What could I say? Huffiness simply wasn't an option—no sniping about freshly done nails, new sandals, having turned down four other invitations and now what was I supposed to do, spend my Saturday night cleaning the bathroom? (Like I'd done every previous Saturday for the past month.) Instead I had to sympathize, even praise, and for the first time I saw the downside of having a boyfriend who saved lives for a living.

★ ★ ★

We rearranged for Thursday night and he promised he'd be wide awake and full of beans. I came to work on Thursday in my going-out clothes and Mark watched me click-clacking in my high sandals to the photocopier, but said nothing.

But that afternoon—minutes after I'd got back from spending my lunch hour getting my hair blow-dried—my fireman rang. He'd just returned home after a fifteen-hour stint dousing a huge conflagration in a rubber-goods warehouse.

"I'm sorry, Kate." A five-second yodelly yawn followed. "I really need some zeds, I'm so sleepy."

The disappointment was intense and as I thought of my good hair and my inappropriate clothes, I swallowed, braced myself—then went for it.

Brazenly, I said, "I could come over and keep you company."

He was shocked. To the core. He made interfering with a fireman's sleep sound like a criminal offense and as I hung up I suspected I wouldn't be hearing from him again.

But there was no time to be miserable because within days I'd met Charlie—at a party where he walked straight over to me, pointed a finger and said, "You, babe, are the woman I'm going to marry."

"What a fool," Siobhan murmured, and even while one part of my brain was agreeing with her, another part found his confidence strangely alluring.

"The name's Charlie," he said. "Remember it because you'll be screaming it later."

"I don't think so," I replied, and he just laughed and said he wouldn't take no for an answer.

★ ★ ★

Over the next two weeks he pursued me rapaciously and he seemed so sure he'd win me over that in the end he managed to convince me of it, too.

When I finally agreed to go out with him, he promised he'd show me the best night of my life and I must admit I was intrigued.

First he took me to a party, but he made us leave after fifteen minutes because he was bored, then he took me to a bar, which I'd read about but hadn't been to, but we were barely there half an hour before he wanted to be off again. Two more parties and a club followed—he had the shortest attention span of anyone I'd ever met and in a way all that variety was exciting.

There were three or four more nights like that and at the time I thought of myself as glamorous, but now what I remember most is the number of times I had to gulp back the drink which had just arrived, while Charlie eyed the exit and tapped his foot impatiently.

So convincing was Charlie's wide-boy swagger that it took me some time to notice that he was shorter than me. A lot shorter when I wore my boots. And when he couldn't sit through a film—and we're not talking *Dances With Wolves* or *Heaven's Gate* here, only a normal ninety-minute one—his attention deficit disorder began to annoy me.

Worse still, he always seemed to have a cold and his constant sniffing was driving me mad. *Mad.* As soon as one sniff was over, I was tensing my shoulders in irritation against the next one. Occasionally he sneezed and he baffled me by treating it like a major disaster.

Then I discovered the cause of the constant sniffing—and the short attention span—when I accidentally walked into his bathroom and found him crouched over the edge of the sink, a rolled-up fiver at his nostril.

It wasn't the cocaine itself that shocked me. It was that he was taking it for a Saturday afternoon's shopping. And that he'd been snorting it all this time and he'd never once offered me any. Marching orders were swiftly dispatched and not even him prostrating himself and swearing that we'd get a video and Chinese take-away and stay in for an entire evening made any difference.

The disappointment of Charlie set me back, and I was missing Mark a little too much for my liking, so to take my mind off things I decided to throw a party, which is where I met Owen.

The moment we made eye contact he began to blush and I'd never seen anything like it. It roared up his neck and face like red-hot lava, rushing to the farthest reaches of his head, then kind of "pinged" on the outer edges of his ears. For some reason I thought of an advertising slogan: Come home to a real fire.

Flustered, he turned around and bumped into a bottle of red wine with such violence it splashed Siobhan's dress and my pale-gold curtains and the only reason I didn't start shrieking like a termagant was because I felt attracted to him.

Owen was, quite simply, the shyest man I'd ever met, but after the cocaine-fueled arrogance of Charlie, I liked his self-effacing charm.

And though he was short, he was very good-looking—a neat, handsome little package.

He asked if he could take me for a drink sometime and when I said yes, he was so pleased that he knocked over and smashed my good flower vase into smithereens.

Our first date wasn't much better. He came to pick me up, said, "You've lovely eyes. Even though they're quite close together," then swept the phone off the wall with such force that it never worked properly again.

I urged myself to give it time, that he would eventually relax with me. But each outing was as bad as the first time—the blush that could be seen from outer space, the stammering compliment that managed to be an insult, then the ceremonial knocking over and breaking of something.

I had to end it with him before he'd destroyed all that I owned.

And into the breach stepped Shane, a friend of Siobhan's youngest brother. He was too young for me but I didn't care. He was cute-looking—another dinky one, actually, I was having quite a run of short men asking me out—and he was sweet.

He took me to Brittas Bay to fly kites, which might have been fun had he not told me that we were going to an art exhibit and had I not dressed accordingly. Shane claimed to have no memory, no memory at *all* of telling me about the exhibit. Then he raced off down the beach with his big yellow kite and I almost ended up flat on my back as I chased after him and my four-inch heels sank into the sand.

Eventually the kite-flying torment ended and we went to the pub and the real date began. But within minutes, Shane disclosed that he thought: a) Jack Nicholson and Jack Nicklaus were related; b) that flour was made from flowers; c) that the Mona Lisa's real name was Muriel.

At the Muriel bit I sighed heavily; this was awful. And thick and all as he was, Shane said, "You're not really into this, are you, Kate? Some guy wrecked your head, yeah? Siobhan said."

I sighed again; Siobhan was so indiscreet. But all of a sudden the idea of spilling the beans about Mark to this dim, sympathetic boy was enticing.

"It was great for ages and I don't really know what happened but in the end he just rode roughshod over me."

"He rode who?" Shane was all indignation.

That was it! But Shane was mad keen to see me again. "We could go to this exhibition you keep talking about," he beamed.

Gently I turned him down. I couldn't see him again. He was simply much, much, much too stupid.

Then I was depressed. I'd gone out with so many men and I was still thinking about Mark. I saw him at work but we never spoke. He'd been smiling a bit at me lately—probably because he thought enough time had elapsed for us to start behaving like civilized people again. Well, he could think again.

I squared my shoulders and told myself it would all be fine eventually. I thought the good times had finally arrived when I met a short, clever doctor who kept trying to get me into bed by tugging at my clothes and saying, "Let me through, I'm a doctor." It was funny the first time he said it, though not funny enough for me to sleep with him. Quite funny the second time, too. By the fifth time I was worried. Was this what counted as a sense of humour with him? Unfortunately it was and I stopped letting him through.

It was Siobhan who twigged what was happening.

"Hiho," she greeted me with. "How are you enjoying your fairy-tale romance?"

"Still waiting for it," I said glumly.

"What are you talking about? You're slap-bang in the middle of it. You're Snow White and you're working your way through the Seven Dwarfs."

I told her she was off her rocker and that I wasn't going to play, but she insisted. "They've all been very short, haven't they? Haven't they? And their personalities fit. The fireman who couldn't get out of bed? Sleepy, obviously. Charlie the coke fiend is Sneezy, of course."

"There wasn't much sneezing, mostly sniffing," I said, but Siobhan was undeterred.

"Poor shy Owen is an open-and-shut Bashful. Shane is Dopey—the funny thing is that's what his friends call him anyway. And the doctor? Well, Doc, obviously."

"So which ones haven't I done?' It's impossible to remember the names of all seven of them.

"Grumpy and Happy."

Mark asked if I'd meet him for a drink after work. With a heavy heart I agreed. It had been five months now, I supposed he was entitled to his stuff back.

But we'd barely sat down when he blurted out, "I'm sorry, Kate. I was such a grumpy bastard."

As soon as I heard the word *grumpy* my heart almost stopped in my chest. But Mark couldn't be Grumpy! He was too tall!

"You were right not to put up with me. I've had plenty of time to think and, Kate, I feel small. I feel so very, very small."

"Small?" I repeated.

"Small. Tiny." He held up his thumb and first finger, barely leaving a gap. "This small." Then he told me he loved me, that he was miserable without me and asked if there was any chance that I'd take him back.

"I know I don't deserve it." He hung his head. "But if you'd give me just one chance I'll make it up to you and I'll do everything I can to make you happy. If you come back to me, Kate, I'll be happy. I'll be so happy."

Lynda Curnyn is the author of four bestselling novels for Red Dress Ink, *Confessions of an Ex-Girlfriend*, *Engaging Men*, *Bombshell* and *Killer Summer*. She is currently at work on her fifth book, *My Inner Brunette*, due out in spring 2007, which will feature characters from "Some Girls."

Lynda lives, fearlessly single, in New York City. Say hello at www.lyndacurnyn.com.

Some Girls
Lynda Curnyn

We could party all night. After all, no one is waiting at home for us. But we don't. We know what the morning after feels like and we've had enough of them.

Our apartments are covered in artifacts collected from the countries we've traveled to and remnants of the men we've discarded. We paint our living rooms lime green and hot pink and no one complains.

Who's going to complain?

We spend way too much money on the upkeep of our hair, our nails, our feet. While away our weekend afternoons in cafés, downing Bloody Marys as if it's our God-given right. And it is. We work hard all week. We owe it to ourselves.

We are nearing forty.

We tell people when they ask (and they always ask) that we're waiting for the right one and if there is no right one, we're happy to be single. In the best moments, when the walls are painted just right and the weekend calendar is scribbled full, we believe this to be true.

On other days, we worry.

"What're we doing?" Liv asks, shifting restlessly over her Bloody Mary, our first of the day. We're at Raphaella's, one of our regular brunch spots. The usual crowd is here—Liv, Sidney, Nadine. Everyone, that is, except Kate.

"What do you mean, what're we doing?" Sidney replies, her gaze moving to the window and narrowing on Clyde, her well-muscled mutt, who stares dolefully at us from the sidewalk. "Having brunch," she says, leaning close to the glass to glance down the street. "If Kate ever gets here."

Liv shakes her head. "I don't mean now. I mean, in general."

"It's too early for this, Liv," Sidney replies, although really it's already 1:00 p.m.

We haven't had this conversation in a while. The one in which Liv questions our existence. Not since we lived together on East Twelfth Street in a renovated three-bedroom with Kate. Nadine wasn't technically a roommate, but she took refuge on our sofa whenever she was too drunk or too disillusioned over some man, which was often. We lasted in that rambling old apartment until we were nearly thirty, then Sidney decided she needed a live/work space for her growing industrial-design business rather than a live-and-try-to-let-others-live space. Liv wanted to hang on to the place, but it was Kate who finally decided it was time to move on. "Staying here after Sid is gone would be like Led Zeppelin continuing to tour after John Bonham died." Though Liv liked the analogy, she was never fond of change.

Now everything is about to change.

Kate is having a baby.

Not that she planned on having a baby. We aren't really planners when it comes to our personal lives. Besides, we aren't really sure where we stand on the children issue. Having children is what other people do.

Now Kate is two months pregnant by the man she's been dating for four.

We can barely wrap our minds around it.

As far as we're concerned, the baby doesn't exist. In fact, we were more than willing to believe some mistake had been made, until Kate showed us the sonogram. Even then, we couldn't be sure whether the fuzzy, grayish form pictured there would ever be someone we could take to brunch with us.

A whine pierces us through the window and we look out to see Clyde wagging his tail, signaling Kate's arrival.

"Sorry I'm late," she says, bringing in a gust of the coming winter with her. "Still can't get used to New Jersey transit, you know?"

We can't get used to the fact that Kate has been spending her weekends in New Jersey. At Steven's. Up until three weeks ago, their relationship had taken place exclusively on the island of Manhattan, mostly because that was the way Kate wanted things. And when it came to relationships, Kate always got the upper hand.

Now she felt obliged to make regular treks to New Jersey.

We're starting to fear the worst.

"So what's going on?" Sidney says the minute Kate sits down, reminding us that it was Kate who called for brunch today, even booked it a week in advance, which was something, since we never booked anything in advance.

"Food, I hope," Kate says, waving down the waitress. It's

a delaying tactic, we know. She hasn't even looked at the menu yet.

Sidney's eyes narrow as if she's holding back some biting remark. It's not that she doesn't love Kate. In fact, she might love Kate a little too much. They've known each other the longest, having grown up together, which somehow gives Sidney the sense that she has a say over Kate's life. And perhaps it's the realization that she doesn't that has made her so angry at Kate as of late. Probably ever since Kate dropped the news on us while trying on pants at a sample sale.

"I'm pregnant," she announced, as if she'd just discovered it the moment the zipper wouldn't go up.

We were stunned into silence.

Except for the breath that whooshed out of Liv, her hand moving fretfully to her abdomen, perhaps because she just remembered she has ovaries.

"What are you going to do?" Sidney finally demanded.

But Kate only shook her head, busying herself with the buckle on her pants.

Judging by the unease on Kate's face now that the waitress has disappeared with our orders, the time has come for answers.

"So?" Sidney says, her fierce green gaze on Kate.

Kate raises her chin. "I'm moving in with Steven."

We let this wash over us. We knew it was coming. Well, we knew something was coming. We just weren't sure what.

"Kate, you don't have to get married in this day and age," Sidney begins.

"We're not," Kate answers quickly. "At least, not...not right away." She lowers her eyes, probably to avoid our gaze. But she doesn't have to look at us to know what we're thinking.

We're remembering how we tried to warn her away from him. He was too old, we said, though forty-six was probably within our upper limit. He was too divorced, too encumbered. He had a child, a boy, just six years old, with his first wife. We thought this reason enough for Kate not to date him, but she just laughed. "So he spends his weekends with the kid. It's not like I want a man around 24/7 anyway."

Now she's moving in with him.

"Where will you live?" Liv asks.

Kate meets her gaze. "New Jersey."

"New Jersey?" we echo.

"It's just across the water," Kate says, pretending it's merely the Hudson River that's been keeping us from fleeing there in the name of lower rents and larger living space.

"You guys will have to come out and visit."

Our stomachs lurch at the thought. Still, we smile as if everything will be fine. As if it does not bother us that seeing Kate in the future will involve more planning, possibly even an overnight bag.

But we're thinking: no more lazy Sunday afternoons. No more spontaneous nights out.

No more us.

When the e-mail goes out from Sidney the following week, requesting our presence at her place on Friday for game night, it feels like a test of loyalty.

Which is probably why we breathe a sigh of relief when Kate's reply finally comes, later than the rest of ours, declaring that she's in.

The temperature drops by week's end, making us feel resentful of Sidney as we hunch our shoulders against the wind, hurrying to her apartment on Thompson. Somehow game night is always at Sidney's and we wonder how she has deceived us into abandoning our cozy homes for her convenience once more. "I have more space," she argues when we grumble in her foyer. This would be a legitimate argument if we had more players. But as usual it's only the four of us. Five, if you count Clyde, and Sidney always counted Clyde.

"It's beautiful, Sidney," we say, understanding why we have been summoned here tonight as we stand huddled together in her bathroom, examining the tile she has just laid. Someone has to bear witness to Sidney's latest efforts on the ever-evolving project that is her apartment. Just over a year ago, she signed a long-term lease on a run-down storefront on Thompson Street that she is quickly converting to the kind of expansive loft space in which most single-and-under-a-certain-income New Yorkers only dream of living. Only, Sidney is living in it at a quarter of the usual rent.

At first, we tried to warn her against the move. We couldn't fathom why she would want to put all that work into a place she would one day have to give up. But Sidney isn't the type to think of tomorrow.

Now as we stood beneath the towering certainty of her twenty-foot ceilings, watching the way the streetlights spilled across her freshly sanded floors, we couldn't help but feel the familiar stir of admiration. Maybe even a touch of envy.

Could you blame us?

"Margaritas okay?" Sidney says, stepping into her cavernous kitchen.

We nod eagerly. We really don't have a choice. Tequila is the only thing Sidney drinks and therefore, the only thing Sidney keeps in her liquor cabinet.

"I'll just have water, Sid," Kate says. "Or ginger ale, if you have it," she adds.

Our eyes drop to Kate's still-slender stomach. *Right.*

"Me, too," Liv says. "For solidarity," she explains when we all turn to gawk at her. "With Kate."

Nadine lets out a dramatic sigh. "Come on, really? We're not drinking?"

"Drink, for God's sake," Kate says. "*Someone* has to."

"That's right," Sidney says, her gaze on Kate. "No reason we should all suffer."

"I wouldn't call it suffering, Sid," Kate replies, eyes narrowed.

"Okay, okay," Liv says, waving her hands in the air as if she could bat away the sudden tension. "I'll drink if I have to." Then she laughs at her own joke, mostly because no one else does.

Once we settle ourselves on pillows around the low coffee table in the living room, watching Sidney struggle to keep Clyde's considerable snout out of the bean dip as she sets up the Scrabble board, it almost feels like old times.

Except Kate is talking breast pumps.

We're not even sure how we got on this subject. Maybe it started when Sidney asked Kate if she planned on going back to work after the baby.

The question seemed to offend Kate. "Of course," she replied, then went on to talk about day care and the virtues of breast milk and all kinds of things we had not even begun to contemplate.

It's almost as if she's been researching this baby business behind our backs, paving the road for parenthood, all the while swearing allegiance to the single life we shared.

And apparently she isn't the only one.

"Do you realize that if I want to have a baby, I'd have to meet someone, fall in love with him, or at the very least, convince him to give up a sperm, all within the next two to three years?" Liv says, breaking the silence we had fallen into once Kate finished her discourse.

"There's always in vitro," Nadine offers, reclining on one of the pillows.

Liv shakes her head. "Forgive me for being old-fashioned, but I'd like to at least know the father of my future children. Maybe even be in love with him."

"You have time," Kate replies. "When you meet the right one, you just know. Then everything else falls into place."

We've heard this kind of thing before. We just never expected to hear it from Kate. We look at her, wondering if that's the way it happened for her. Wondering if, in fact, Steven would be the husband she would choose if she had more time, more options.

And if he is, then why isn't she marrying him?

"If I don't meet someone by the time I'm forty," Nadine says, eyes dreamily on the ceiling, "I'm going to ask Meyer to father my child."

"Meyer?" we exclaim with disbelief.

"Maybe you guys should try having dinner first," Sidney adds with a sly smile. The fact that Nadine has yet to exchange more than bodily fluids with the man she has been sleeping with for over a year has become an old joke with us. Except none of us are laughing now.

Nadine shrugs. "I already have him on the shortlist."

"Shortlist?" we echo.

"Of potential donors," she says, as if the answer was obvious.

We're not sure what alarms us more. That Nadine would consider having a baby with a man we only know by last name, or that she is actually considering a baby—by any means.

Is this what we've come to?

"That's insane," Sidney says, bringing us back to our senses.

Until her next words.

"Why would you go that route, when there're plenty of babies in this world who need homes?"

We swallow hard, watching as her hand comes to rest on Clyde's head, wondering if the dog she rescued from an NYC shelter is just a substitute for something else. Or a precursor.

Our glance falls on Kate, as if she is somehow to blame for our current uneasiness.

"Well, I'd rather have a baby than adopt," Nadine continues. "And if I'm going to have a baby, I'd rather do it the way Kate did it."

Kate looks at her. "What's that supposed to mean?"

"What Nadine means," Sidney says, "is that she'd rather get knocked up by someone she knows than someone she doesn't."

"You act as if I did it on purpose."

Sidney merely shrugs, picking up her drink. "Maybe I just don't believe in accidents. Or maybe I just don't believe a thirty-eight-year-old woman gets pregnant by *accident*. I mean, come on, Kate, we all made it this far in life without getting knocked up."

Kate has no reply for this, which only makes her seem guilty in our eyes.

On Saturdays we like to sleep in, as much as we can sleep in after so many years of nine to five. Yet here we are, on the first snowy day of December, on the way to Kate's apartment to help her pack.

We might have our differences but we will never abandon each other. In all this madness, that thought, at least, is reassuring.

We smile when she opens the door, despite the lack of caffeine in our systems. She looks tired. Beaten in a way Kate never looks.

We're immediately worried.

"What's wrong?" we demand.

"Nothing, I just—"

Tears fill her eyes.

An answering sob rises in our throats.

And then we're hugging, hanging on to one another among a sea of boxes, the wreckage of Kate's apartment.

"It's okay," she says, detangling herself. "I'm okay." She sniffs. "Crazy hormones," she explains, one hand going to her slender stomach. Her glance settles on the kitchen, which is still intact, right down to the pretty row of painted plates that line one wall. "I'm going to miss this place. I'm gonna miss…you guys." Her voice cracks and now there are tears in all our eyes.

"It's just across the water," we echo, our voices bouncing eerily around the half-empty apartment.

We've come today because Kate is our friend. And because she's our friend, we want to know why Steven isn't here.

"He's got Timmy today," Kate says, referring to Steven's son. "He's coming tomorrow, with the movers." Then she smiles shyly. "Anyway, I just wanted to be here with you guys, you know? One last time."

We understand. We wanted to be with Kate. To support her as she moved on to this new phase of her life.

And of course, to take whatever she wasn't bringing with her.

"You're throwing this out?" Sidney asks, holding up what appears to be the chipped base of an old lamp.

We're in the living room, attempting to fit the last thirty-eight years of Kate's life into boxes.

Kate looks up, smiles. This is one of many items Sidney has scavenged from the growing heap of garbage. "You can have it, Sid. But what you are going to do with it..."

"Are you kidding me?" Sidney says, tucking the lamp base into the corner she has set aside for her "treasures," which include a brass towel rack, a tarnished pewter vase, a torn curtain, three ceiling hooks and an old fan. Although we're ready to dismiss it all as trash, we're certain that Sidney will transform each item into something that will make us wistful the next time we're in her apartment.

"Oh my, Kate, where did you get this ashtray?" Liv says, holding up a small white dish pulled from the glass cabinet she is clearing. Squinting at it, she reads, "Veronica and Edward, June 9, 1964." She looks up. "Veronica and Edward—don't tell me this is from your parents' wedding?"

Kate nods. "And that's about all that's left from my parents' marriage." She stares into the box she's just packed before grabbing a tape gun to seal it.

"At least your parents had a wedding," Sidney says, frowning, as she often did, when she thought of her perpetually single mother, the father she barely knew.

"Yeah, well, a lot of good it did them," Kate replies. "They didn't even make it to my fifth birthday." Then she shrugs. "I guess there's no reason to save it. No one even smokes anymore."

"You can't throw it away," Liv protests.

"I haven't yet," Kate replies.

A silence falls among us, except for the sound of newspaper crumpling as Liv wraps the tray and places it carefully in the box on the floor beside her.

Sidney's voice cuts into the quiet. "So what's it gonna be, Kate? Have you set a date?"

Alarm crosses Kate's face. "A date?"

"For the wedding."

She shakes her head. "One thing at a time. What's the rush?"

Her hand moves to her stomach, as if she just remembered what the rush was.

We look at one another.

"Come on, who am I talking to here?" Kate says, as if remembering herself. "If I'm gonna do the whole wedding thing, I at least want to look good in my dress."

"The baby can be the flower girl!" Nadine says.

No one brings up the fact that Kate hasn't found out the baby's sex. We've already decided it's going to be a girl.

"And Steven is on board with all this?" Sidney asks, eyebrow raised as if she already knows the answer.

"Steven has accepted it," Kate says carefully.

We think: what else can he do? He's not the kind of man to abandon his responsibilities. According to Kate, he never misses a weekend with his son, though until recently we wondered why this was a virtue since it meant less time with Kate. He was a good father, a good provider, Kate assured us. Solid, steady, secure. The kind of man our mothers would want us to marry.

So why are we so worried?

★ ★ ★

The last of the day's light begins to slant through the windows in Kate's bedroom, nearly blinding us as we pluck the remaining books from her shelves, pack the few pieces of clothing left in the closet into bags.

"Kate, is there any reason why you're saving these sunglasses?" Liv holds up a bent pair of aviator shades for our perusal. But Kate has slipped from the room.

It's only the muffled sob from the kitchen that makes us realize where she's gone.

"What am I doing?" she says when we find her, huddled over the kitchen table.

For a moment, she seems lost. Then she looks up at us, her gaze surprisingly clear. "I sometimes think the reason Steven and I get along so well is that he lives in another state." She shakes her head, her eyes widening, filling. "God, what's going to happen to us now?"

We have no idea. But we know enough to tell her the things she needs to hear. That Steven is a good man. That New Jersey isn't so far. That life as we know it will not change so drastically.

But we aren't sure of anything.

"Well," she says, her gaze beyond us, at the window. "I do love him."

"There's that," Sidney says, resigning us to our fate.

We know all about that emotion. After all, we've been in love before.

At least a half-dozen times apiece.

The snow is falling in thick white flakes, all the way from Penn Station to Fairwood, New Jersey. Which only causes us to spend the train ride counting reasons why we're glad we don't live in the burbs.

"No shoveling the car out," says Liv.

"Or scraping the icy windows," Nadine adds.

"No nothing," Sid says with a shudder as she studies the landscape, a wall of whirling white.

We're almost surprised to see Kate waving at us from beside a gray SUV as we step onto the snowy platform. It's as if we didn't believe we'd find her here, despite her eager invitation two weeks ago.

"I can't believe Steven let you drive on a day like today," Liv says.

"I'm pregnant, not handicapped!" Kate says, hugging us each in turn. "Besides, do you think Steven could have stopped me from coming to get you?"

We smile, climbing into the truck with barely contained relief. Yes, Kate is here. And Kate is still…Kate.

Sort of. We've never seen Kate drive a car. And in her blue down parka and white knit cap, she looks positively suburban.

Not that suburban is without its charms.

"Look at the size of that Home Depot," Sidney says as we glide past a mall.

"And a Target, too!" Nadine cries.

"You see? Lots of reasons to visit," Kate says, smiling, as if she has discovered a secret kingdom.

We even believe it, until we turn into the development where Kate lives.

Rows and rows of town houses, all in the same neutral beige shades, all with the same front porches, the same cheerful shutters bracketing barren, snow-tipped flower boxes.

It looks like a retirement community.

Stop the car, we want to shout. We're too young for this!

But we don't. We're old enough to know when to keep our mouths shut.

Besides, things look much better once we're inside.

Either that or we're distracted by the sight of Kate, who we discover, once she takes off her parka, is rounder than we remember.

"You really are having a baby," Nadine says, one hand tipped in dark polish going to the gentle slope of Kate's belly.

"I certainly feel like it," Kate replies, rolling her eyes, which we notice seem tired. Even her skin, usually flawless, looks ruddy.

"Is everything okay?" Sidney asks. "I mean, with your health?"

"Yes, yes," Kate says, dismissing our concerns. "Come let me give you a tour."

After we leave our coats dripping on a coat tree in the foyer, Kate leads us down a long hallway, into a spacious kitchen streaked by sunlight, where we murmur politely over the amount of counter space. We move on to a living room cozy with books we know Kate has never read and, God help us, ducks? Wooden ones, swimming about the mantel, the coffee table, the bookcase. "Steven collects them," Kate says, as if this explains everything.

We don't get it but we nod anyway, moving past a midnight-blue bedroom we can't picture Kate sleeping in, and finally, the nursery, which, ironically, is the first room where we find evidence of Kate.

Or something resembling Kate. Though nothing in the nursery is anything we'd ever seen before, the room rings out with her influence. We think of her trip to India when we see the colorful elephants marching across the papered borders of the room, remember her gift for drawing at the sight of the mural by the door. Even the hand-painted dressing table screams Kate (though in truth, we aren't sure why).

Then Kate sits down in the rocking chair, and as she studies her handiwork we realize how very much she looks like her mother right now. And how much she would hate to hear it. "Things are going to be different when I have kids," she used to say and now we wonder why we never heard her words before. Or if she'll be able to keep her promise.

The snow has stopped falling by the time we find ourselves lounging in the living room, our stomachs full from gorging on the feast Kate prepared for us.

"I'm never eating again," Nadine says, one hand going to her stomach. We know this is probably true. Nadine usually forfeits food in the name of flatter abs, but none of us can resist Kate's cooking.

"I'm really glad you guys came out," Kate says, her slender legs crossed on the ottoman before her, one hand resting comfortably on her rounded belly.

We smile at her, glad to be here, too. In fact, we almost don't want to leave. Maybe it's the thick snow piled up against the window or maybe it's the sight of Kate, smiling as if she has discovered some secret we have yet to learn.

Do we even know how these things really happen?

The front door bursts open and we nearly cry out in alarm. Who could be coming in like this, unannounced?

Steven, we remember, when he steps into the foyer, his smile broad at the sight of us.

We almost forgot about him.

"Hey," Kate says, smiling up at him. "The girls came to visit."

Girls? we think, suddenly feeling less like girls than we ever did, our stomachs leaden with food, our thoughts heavy with the realization that the day has nearly come to an end.

Still, we flutter about like girls, each of us greeting Steven in turn, all the while studying him with suspicion.

He looks smaller than we remember him, though we've only met him a few times. But his eyes are a pretty blue, crinkling at the corners when he smiles.

We suppose that we could live with him. If we had to.

That thought nearly does us in.

Is this the compromise we have to make in order to marry? A house valued for its mediocrity. A man, encumbered. We study him as he slips out of his coat, see the pride in his stubborn jaw, and imagine all the reasons his wife left him.

Then we see the way he looks at Kate, watch as he puts his arms around her, wonder at the way her face softens, and suddenly we are sure that some girls do find true love.

Even girls like us.

Meg Cabot was born in Bloomington, Indiana. Armed with a fine arts degree from Indiana University, she moved to New York City to pursue an illustration career, but when that failed to materialize, got a job as the assistant manager of an undergraduate dormitory at New York University instead, writing novels on the weekends (and whenever her boss wasn't looking). Meg has since quit that job and gone on to publish over thirty novels for younger readers as well as adults, including *The Princess Diaries* series, *Boy Meets Girl, The Boy Next Door,* and *Every Boy's Got One.* She now divides her time between New York City and Key West with her husband and their one-eyed cat, Henrietta.

Be sure to check out Meg's Web sites, www.megcabot.com and www.megcabotbookclub.com.

Reunion
Meg Cabot

To: All
Sent: April 25, 2005 11:45AM
Fr: Scooter Potts <Scooter@bloomvillemotors.com>
Re: Bloomville High School Class of '95 Reunion

Bloomville High School Class of 1995 10-Year Reunion
Hey, fellow Panthers! Guess what time it is? That's right:
Our ten-year high-school reunion! Can you believe it's
been ten years since we graduated?
Though I still see some of you regularly (remember, there's
a 10% discount for BHS grads here at Bloomville Motors),
it will be great to catch up with those of you who left Indiana for such far-flung places as New York City (Jo Bu-

chanon's mom says that Jo's band, the Raving Lunatics, got a real positive review in the *Village Voice* for their first-ever gig at King Tut's Wa Wa Hut)!

So put in that vacation request today, and start planning on an exciting weekend of fun connecting with your fellow classmates!

Friday Night, July 15 at 8:00 p.m.

Casual gathering at TGIF's on Main Street

Saturday Morning/Afternoon, July 16, from 11:00 a.m. until 2:00 p.m.

Join classmates for a family picnic on the BHS football field.

—A tour of the newly renovated school (we have a pool now, Panthers!) will be available for all who wish to take part.

—Feel free to bring friends and family.

—Activities will be planned for the children.

Saturday Night, July 16, from 7:00 until 11:00 p.m.

Reunion dinner, dancing and fun in the BHS gymnasium

Catered by Kroger Deli Department

Please plan on the fee to be $25-30 per person.

Looking forward to seeing you all—and don't forget, if you have automotive needs, Bloomville Motors will beat any price, anywhere!

Go Panthers!

Fred "Scooter" Potts

Your Class President

Owner/Operator

Bloomville Motors

Servicing Greater Duane County

We put the *Serv* in Service!

To: Jo Buchanon <JBuchanon@ravinglunatics.com>
Sent: April 25, 2005 11:49 AM

Fr:　Mary Hutchins <Mary@bloomvillehealthfoods.com>
Re:　Bloomville High School Class of '95 Reunion
Oh my God. Did you see it?

To:　Mary Hutchins <Mary@bloomvillehealthfoods.com>
Sent: April 25, 2005 11:55 AM
Fr:　Jo Buchanon <JBuchanon@ravinglunatics.com>
Re:　Bloomville High School Class of '95 Reunion
Oh, yeah. I saw it. I'm going to KILL my mother. She gave
him my e-mail address. AND she told him about the gig.
I thought I was through with these people. Now they're
STALKING me. Through cyberspace, anyway.
You're not going, are you?

To:　Jo Buchanon <JBuchanon@ravinglunatics.com>
Sent: April 25, 2005 12:10 PM
Fr:　Mary Hutchins <Mary@bloomvillehealthfoods.com>
Re:　Bloomville High School Class of '95 Reunion
Are you kidding? Do you see who they've got catering it?
I guess it never occurred to Scooter to ask a fellow alumnus
to cater our reunion. Instead he had to ask the deli department of a national grocery chain. I realize no one in our class
ever cared how many trans fats they consumed in a single
meal. But you would think they'd have thought of hiring a
locally owned business before seeking out the services of
a bloated national conglomerate that is strangling the small-
business person and ruining small-town life as we knew it.
Of course I'm not going.
I mean, you're not going. Right?

To:　Mary Hutchins <Mary@bloomvillehealthfoods.com>
Sent: April 25, 2005 12:27 PM

Fr: Jo Buchanon <JBuchanon@ravinglunatics.com>
Re: Bloomville High School Class of '95 Reunion
Oh, right. You mean because I was so popular in high school, and there are so many people from there that I miss? Seriously, Mary, the only person I still even SPEAK to from those days is you.
And what kind of grown man STILL calls himself Scooter?

To: Jo Buchanon <JBuchanon@ravinglunatics.com>
Sent: April 25, 2005 12:45 PM
Fr: Mary Hutchins <Mary@bloomvillehealthfoods.com>
Re: Bloomville High School Class of '95 Reunion
At least you didn't have to sit behind him in chem, like I did. I have seen enough of that butt crack to last me a lifetime. Why can't football players find jeans that fit? WHY?

To: All
Sent: April 25, 2005 1:01 PM
Fr: Terry Hicks <Thicks@aol.com>
Re: Bloomville High School Class of '95 Reunion
Thanks, Scooter, and everyone, for getting this organized. I can't believe it has been ten years! So much has happened since we all last saw one another—it will be so much fun to see everyone again. We'll be heading over from Carmel with the kids—can't wait!
Terry (Summers) Hicks

To: Jo Buchanon <JBuchanon@ravinglunatics.com>
Sent: April 25, 2005 1:07 PM
Fr: Mary Hutchins <Mary@bloomvillehealthfoods.com>
Re: Bloomville High School Class of '95 Reunion
What, are we going to start a string of "reply all" messages

from the whole class until reunion time? Is everyone else really thrilled about this? I, for one, am not thrilled about seeing Terry Summers Hicks again, with her rich, handsome husband and perfect little kids.

And did you see how she managed to slip in the part about living in Carmel? She thinks she's so great, in her Mcmansion with her McMercedes and Mcmink coat.

I'm going to be Mcsick.

To: Mary Hutchins <Mary@bloomvillehealthfoods.com>
Sent: April 25, 2005 1:17 PM
Fr: Jo Buchanon <JBuchanon@ravinglunatics.com>
Re: Bloomville High School Class of '95 Reunion
Remember the time she snapped the back of Jill Davis's bra and you "accidentally" spilled your wheatgrass juice all over her cheerleading uniform? God. That was so great. Oh wait—
OH MY GOD!!!!! LOOK WHAT I JUST GOT:

<To: Jo Buchanon <JBuchanon@ravinglunatics.com>
<Sent: April 25, 2005 1:15 PM
<Fr: Mike Saunders <MikeS@bloomvillegazette.com>
<Re: Bloomville High School Class of '95 Reunion
<Hi Jo,
<I don't know if you'll remember me, but we went to high school together. We didn't
<have any classes together, but I was a big fan of yours (I used to write for the school
<paper, so I had to cover all the band's concerts. Your solo keyboard rendition of
<Cream's "Sunshine of Your Love" at the Spring Jam totally rocked).

<I don't usually write to girls I hardly know, but I got the e-mail about the class reunion,
<and saw your address. Hope you don't mind. Congrats on the New York gig. Glad to
<know you're still pursuing a music career.
<Mike Saunders

WHO IS MIKE SAUNDERS????

To: Jo Buchanon <JBuchanon@ravinglunatics.com>
Sent: April 25, 2005 1:29 PM
Fr: Mary Hutchins <Mary@bloomvillehealthfoods.com>
Re: Bloomville High School Class of '95 Reunion
I don't know!
I'm going downstairs to get my yearbook now…back in a sec.
Okay, back, here it is…. Oh. OH. MY. GOD.

To: Mary Hutchins <Mary@bloomvillehealthfoods.com>
Sent: April 25, 2005 1:32 PM
Fr: Jo Buchanon <JBuchanon@ravinglunatics.com>
Re: Bloomville High School Class of '95 Reunion
WHAT??????

To: Jo Buchanon <JBuchanon@ravinglunatics.com>
Sent: April 25, 2005 1:39 PM
Fr: Mary Hutchins <Mary@bloomvillehealthfoods.com>
Re: Bloomville High School Class of '95 Reunion
Nothing. He's just got kind of crazy eyes.

To: Mary Hutchins <Mary@bloomvillehealthfoods.com>
Sent: April 25, 2005 1:42 PM

Fr: Jo Buchanon <JBuchanon@ravinglunatics.com>
Re: Bloomville High School Class of '95 Reunion
Crazy Eyes! Crazy Eyes Saunders is stalking me!!!!!

To: Jo Buchanon <JBuchanon@ravinglunatics.com>
Sent: April 25, 2005 1:48 PM
Fr: Mary Hutchins <Mary@bloomvillehealthfoods.com>
Re: Bloomville High School Class of '95 Reunion
Shut up, he's not stalking you. He just wrote to say hi.
And look, I remember him now. He used to do that
thing with his eyes on purpose, whenever anyone
would try to take a picture of him. There are shots in
here of him looking normal. He was on the yearbook
committee. And the school paper. He was just goofing
around.

To: Mary Hutchins <Mary@bloomvillehealthfoods.com>
Sent: April 25, 2005 1:52 PM
Fr: Jo Buchanon <JBuchanon@ravinglunatics.com>
Re: Bloomville High School Class of '95 Reunion
A nerd! A nerd is stalking me!!!!!

To: Jo Buchanon <JBuchanon@ravinglunatics.com>
Sent: April 25, 2005 2:00 PM
Fr: Mary Hutchins <Mary@bloomvillehealthfoods.com>
Re: Bloomville High School Class of '95 Reunion
Would you stop? I told you, I remember him now. He was
a nice guy! And he's now the features editor for the *Bloom-
ville Gazette*. He did a really nice write-up of the store
when I opened it.
You know, you could do a lot worse. And have. Consider-
ing some of your exes.

* * *

To: Mary Hutchins <Mary@bloomvillehealthfoods.com>
Sent: April 25, 2005 2:07 PM
Fr: Jo Buchanon <JBuchanon@ravinglunatics.com>
Re: Bloomville High School Class of '95 Reunion
Oh, right, Mary. Because it wouldn't be too much of a
cliché if I came back for my tenth reunion, met up with
some random guy I don't even remember, and ended up
marrying him and moving back to the small town I left behind a decade ago. Excuse me, this isn't a Reese Wither-
spoon movie. It's real life.
And besides, if he liked me so much back then, why didn't
he ask me out?

To: Jo Buchanon <JBuchanon@ravinglunatics.com>
Sent: April 25, 2005 2:22 PM
Fr: Mary Hutchins <Mary@bloomvillehealthfoods.com>
Re: Bloomville High School Class of '95 Reunion
Hmm, I can't imagine why he never asked you out. Possi-
bly because you were going out with Trent all through
high school? How could ANY GUY have asked you out?
Without getting a knife pulled on him, I mean.
How is Trent, anyway? Is he still in jail?

To: Mary Hutchins <Mary@bloomvillehealthfoods.com>
Sent: April 25, 2005 2:27 PM
Fr: Jo Buchanon <JBuchanon@ravinglunatics.com>
Re: Bloomville High School Class of '95 Reunion
Why do you always have to bring up Trent? You know he
never acted that way around ME. How was I supposed to
know what he was up to every night, after he dropped me
off? I mean, I had a ten o'clock curfew…he had NONE.

★ ★ ★

To: Jo Buchanon <JBuchanon@ravinglunatics.com>
Sent: April 25, 2005 2:34 PM
Fr: Mary Hutchins <Mary@bloomvillehealthfoods.com>
Re: Bloomville High School Class of '95 Reunion
Right. How were you to know your boyfriend was spending his nights stealing cars then stripping them and selling the parts back to the dealer?
And your track record certainly improved once you dumped him, considering all the stellar boyfriends you've had since. I just checked with my friend Cindy over at the *Gazette*. Mike's still single. And hetero.

To: Mary Hutchins <Mary@bloomvillehealthfoods.com>
Sent: April 25, 2005 2:27 PM
Fr: Jo Buchanon <JBuchanon@ravinglunatics.com>
Re: Bloomville High School Class of '95 Reunion
Oh my God, you know there are no straight, single men left in New York City. YOU'RE the one in straight-guy central, out there in the Midwest. But who have YOU gone out with since high school?
Anyway, I can't chat anymore, I have to go audition new drummers for the band. The last one quit to go to law school. Apparently he doesn't care that he's betraying his rock 'n' roll roots by going to work for the Man.

To: Jo Buchanon <JBuchanon@ravinglunatics.com>
Sent: April 25, 2005 2:42 PM
Fr: Mary Hutchins <Mary@bloomvillehealthfoods.com>
Re: Bloomville High School Class of '95 Reunion
Fine. Be that way. I'll find something to keep myself occupied until you get back. I'm going to write to Scooter Potts and give him a piece of my mind.

★ ★ ★

To: Scooter Potts <Scooter@bloomvillemotors.com>
Sent: April 25, 2005 3:15 PM
Fr: Mary Hutchins <Mary@bloomvillehealthfoods.com>
Re: Bloomville High School Class of '95 Reunion
Dear Scooter,

Hi. You probably don't remember me, but I used to sit behind you in chemistry in twelfth grade. I now own Bloomville Health Foods on Main Street. I'm sure you've seen it,
as it is located next door to TGIF's, an establishment I see
you enter nearly every day during their happy hour.

I am writing to ask that you reconsider using the Kroger
Deli Department as your caterer for the reunion din-
ner/dance. Not only is Kroger completely oblivious to the
amount of nitrates/chemicals used to preserve their meats,
but many of their foods are genetically engineered and
laden with dangerous trans fats—whereas at Bloomville
Health Foods I see to it we only stock free-range, antibi-
otic-free meats, as well as pesticide-free and locally grown
fruits, vegetables and dairy products. Don't you think our
class deserves the best? With Bloomville Health Foods,
they'll get it.

Please let me know.

Mary Hutchins
Owner/Manager
Bloomville Health Foods

If you don't know where it came from, why would you put
it in your mouth?

To: Mary Hutchins <Mary@bloomvillehealthfoods.com>
Sent: April 25, 2005 3:29 PM
Fr: Scooter Potts <Scooter@bloomvillemotors.com>

Re: Bloomville High School Class of '95 Reunion

Dear Mary,

Of course I remember you! Boy, did you ever help me with the periodic table—that song you made up, the one to help us remember all the elements? I still catch myself singing it to myself to this very day.

It's really great to hear from you. I had no idea you owned Bloomville Health Foods. How come you never come over for happy hour at TGIF's? It's right across the street!

Anyway, I'd love to hear any ideas you might have for catering the reunion. Why don't you meet me over at TG's tonight, say around six?

Can't wait to catch up!

Fred "Scooter" Potts

Owner/Operator

Bloomville Motors

Servicing Greater Duane County

We put the *Serv* in Service!

To: Scooter Potts <Scooter@bloomvillemotors.com>

Sent: April 25, 2005 3:35 PM

Fr: Mary Hutchins <Mary@bloomvillehealthfoods.com>

Re: Bloomville High School Class of '95 Reunion

I have a better idea. Why don't YOU meet ME at my shop, and I'll give you a sampling of the kind of food I think we should serve at the dinner/dance? We do have a café in the store, you know. And, though this might come as a surprise to you, we do serve things other than alfalfa sprouts. Of course, we don't serve beer. Do you think you can go one evening without a requisite "brewski"?

Mary Hutchins

Owner/Manager

Bloomville Health Foods
If you don't know where it came from, why would you put
it in your mouth?

To: Mary Hutchins <Mary@bloomvillehealthfoods.com>
Sent: April 25, 2005 3:40 PM
Fr: Scooter Potts <Scooter@bloomvillemotors.com>
Re: Bloomville High School Class of '95 Reunion
To tell you the truth, I only do the happy-hour thing to keep
my face out there—there's a lot of competition in the car-
dealer business these days! So my "brewskis" are of the
nonalcoholic variety—but don't tell anyone! It's a secret between me and the TG's bartender. Guy's got an image to
maintain, you know. Especially a former small-town high-
school football player.
See you at your place at six.
Fred

To: Mary Hutchins <Mary@bloomvillehealthfoods.com>
Sent: April 25, 2005 7:27 PM
Fr: Jo Buchanon <JBuchanon@ravinglunatics.com>
Re: Bloomville High School Class of '95 Reunion
Okay, so I wrote him back. Here's what I said:
<To: Mike Saunders <MikeS@bloomvillegazette.com>
<Sent: April 25, 2005 7:15 PM
<Fr: Jo Buchanon <JBuchanon@ravinglunatics.com>
<Re: Bloomville High School Class of '95 Reunion
<Dear Mike,
<Hi. The truth is, I don't remember you at all. We obviously
traveled in very different
<circles in high school. I did play "Sunshine of Your Love"
in a concert once, but I think

<you are otherwise getting me confused with someone else. It's totally fine, I just
<wanted to let you know. I won't be at the reunion because I don't really go in for those
<kind of things, or care to "relive" that time in my life, which wasn't, you know, all that
<great, although I'm sure it was to people like Scooter Potts and Terry Summers. But I
<hope you have a nice time and a nice life.
<Jo

That sounded okay, right? I mean, I didn't want to be TOO mean. But I didn't want him to think, you know, that I'm interested.
Drummer auditions were a bust. There apparently isn't a single soul in this town who can drum AND hold a normal conversation. I don't know what we're going to do.
Sigh.

To: Mary Hutchins <Mary@bloomvillehealthfoods.com>
Sent: April 25, 2005 8:56 PM
Fr: Jo Buchanon <JBuchanon@ravinglunatics.com>
Re: Bloomville High School Class of '95 Reunion
Um, where ARE you?

To: Mary Hutchins <Mary@bloomvillehealthfoods.com>
Sent: April 25, 2005 9:43 PM
Fr: Jo Buchanon <JBuchanon@ravinglunatics.com>
Re: Bloomville High School Class of '95 Reunion
Seriously, are you blowing me off or something?

To: Mary Hutchins <Mary@bloomvillehealthfoods.com>
Sent: April 25, 2005 10:23 PM

Fr: Jo Buchanon <JBuchanon@ravinglunatics.com>
Re: Bloomville High School Class of '95 Reunion
OH MY GOD!!!! OH MY GOD!!!! LOOK WHAT HE WROTE BACK:
<To: Jo Buchanon <JBuchanon@ravinglunatics.com>
<Sent: April 25, 2005 10:11 PM
<Fr: Mike Saunders <MikeS@bloomvillegazette.com>
<Re: Bloomville High School Class of '95 Reunion
<Hey, Jo. That's okay about not remembering me. I wouldn't actually expect you to,
<since you're right, we DID travel in pretty different social circles. I was always
<studying. But it seemed like whenever I looked up, there you'd be, doing something
<zany with that friend of yours, Mary, like protesting the lack of fresh greens in the caf.
<Seeing your name just brought back some old memories so I thought I would send an
<e-mail.
<Like you, I won't be attending the reunion. I agree, I'm not sure I want to relive those
<days either—they were fine for people like Terry Summers and Scooter Potts, but for the
<rest of us? Well, *sucked* is not a strong enough word. I actually won't be living in
<Bloomville much longer, thankfully. I'm moving out to your neck of the woods next
<week. I've landed a job at the *New York Journal.*
<Anyway, thanks for writing back, and good luck with the band. Did I mention I've
<taken up the drums? Maybe someday we'll bump into each other at *CBGB*'s!

<Take care.
<Mike
HE'S MOVING HERE!!!!
AND HE PLAYS THE DRUMS!!!!!!!!!!!!
And is it my imagination but does he sound kind of....
...Cute???????????????????

To: Mary Hutchins <Mary@bloomvillehealthfoods.com>
Sent: April 25, 2005 11:47 PM
Fr: Jo Buchanon <JBuchanon@ravinglunatics.com>
Re: Bloomville High School Class of '95 Reunion
WHERE ARE YOU???? I NEED YOU!!!! I need you to tell
me not to write back to Crazy Eyes Saunders and invite him
to dinner when he gets here next week. Because you know
what will happen: I will fall madly in love with him, and then
we'll get married, and then we'll have a baby, and then the
Raving Lunatics will fall apart because we'll always have to
be carpooling the kids to soccer practice.
I CAN'T BE THAT GIRL!!!!!!!!!!!!
WHERE DID YOU GO???? You're ALWAYS home by now.
E me as soon as you get this or I'm calling my mother and
making her go over there to check on you.

To: Jo Buchanon <JBuchanon@ravinglunatics.com>
Sent: April 26, 2005 10:34 AM
Fr: Mary Hutchins <Mary@bloomvillehealthfoods.com>
Re: Bloomville High School Class of '95 Reunion
I'm so sorry, I didn't mean to leave you in the lurch there.
Something sort of...unexpected came up last night, and I
had to deal with it.
I agree, Mike really does sound kind of cute. Are you going
to write back?

★ ★ ★

To: Mary Hutchins <Mary@bloomvillehealthfoods.com>
Sent: April 25, 2005 10:36 AM
Fr: Jo Buchanon <JBuchanon@ravinglunatics.com>
Re: Bloomville High School Class of '95 Reunion
Okay, what is the deal with you? Where were you last
night? What do you mean, "something sort of...unex-
pected came up"? Why won't you tell me where you were?
God, I HATE this stupid reunion thing! It's making everyone INSANE. I'm about to e-mail Crazy Eyes Saunders
back and ask him if he wants to meet me for dim sum next
week, and now you're acting all weird. Stupid Scooter and
his stupid REUNION!!!

To: Jo Buchanon <JBuchanon@ravinglunatics.com>
Sent: April 26, 2005 10:39 AM
Fr: Mary Hutchins <Mary@bloomvillehealthfoods.com>
Re: Bloomville High School Class of '95 Reunion
Well, the reunion's not really Fred's fault. I mean, he's
more interested in moving on from high school than any
of us. He's nothing like he was back then. Or how we
thought he was. Or how *I* thought he was. Really, he's
changed.
But since he was class president, it's not like he has a
choice. He HAS to put this reunion together.

To: Mary Hutchins <Mary@bloomvillehealthfoods.com>
Sent: April 25, 2005 10:36 AM
Fr: Jo Buchanon <JBuchanon@ravinglunatics.com>
Re: Bloomville High School Class of '95 Reunion
Wait—why are you calling Scooter Fred? Why are you *de-
fending* him? Did you e-mail him? Did you two meet up
or something?

OH MY GOD.
YOU SPENT THE NIGHT WITH SCOOTER POTTS!!!!!!!!!!!!!!

To: Jo Buchanon <JBuchanon@ravinglunatics.com>
Sent: April 26, 2005 10:40 AM
Fr: Mary Hutchins <Mary@bloomvillehealthfoods.com>
Re: Bloomville High School Class of '95 Reunion
I can't help it. I really like him. Really, REALLY like him.

To: Mary Hutchins <Mary@bloomvillehealthfoods.com>
Sent: April 25, 2005 10:36 AM
Fr: Jo Buchanon <JBuchanon@ravinglunatics.com>
Re: Bloomville High School Class of '95 Reunion
So you're going. You're GOING to the reunion. With Scooter. Aren't you? ADMIT IT.

To: Jo Buchanon <JBuchanon@ravinglunatics.com>
Sent: April 26, 2005 10:39 AM
Fr: Mary Hutchins <Mary@bloomvillehealthfoods.com>
Re: Bloomville High School Class of '95 Reunion
Yes.
So sue me! He's changed! I really like him. Really, really like him.
You hate me now, don't you?

To: Mary Hutchins <Mary@bloomvillehealthfoods.com>
Sent: April 25, 2005 10:42 AM
Fr: Jo Buchanon <JBuchanon@ravinglunatics.com>
Re: Bloomville High School Class of '95 Reunion
YES, I HATE YOU!!! Now I'm going to be the only person at this reunion without a date!!!!!
That's it. I'm e-ing Crazy Eyes right now.

I'll let you know what he says.

Hey, what are you going to WEAR???? To the dance, I mean?

To: All
Sent: May 15, 2005 11:15 AM
Fr: Scooter Potts <Scooter@bloomvillemotors.com>
Re: Bloomville High School Class of '95 Reunion

BLOOMVILLE
HIGH SCHOOL

BHS Class of 1995
10-Year Class Reunion
Please save the weekend of July 15 and 16
Friday night: Informal gathering at Bloomville Health Food Café at 8:00 p.m.
Saturday morning: Picnic and tour at BHS at 11:00 a.m.
Saturday night: Dinner and dancing at BHS at 7:00 p.m.
Catering by our own Mary Hutchins, Owner/Manager of Bloomville Health Foods.
Entertainment courtesy of the Raving Lunatics, featuring our own Jo Buchanon and Mike Saunders!
More details to follow at a later date.
If you know of anyone from our class who is not receiving e-mail updates regarding the reunion, please have them contact:
Fred "Scooter" Potts or
Mary Hutchins

Remember, there's a 10% discount for BHS grads at Bloomville Motors and Bloomville Health Foods!
—We put the *Serv* in Service!
—If you don't know where it came from, why would you put it in your mouth?

Emily Giffin graduated from Wake Forest University and the University of Virginia School of Law. After practicing law in New York City for several years, she moved to London and began writing full time. She now lives in Atlanta with her husband and twin sons. Emily is the author of the *New York Times* bestselling novels *Something Borrowed* and *Something Blue*. Her third novel, *Baby Proof*, has just been published. Please visit her at www.emilygiffin.com.

A Thing of Beauty
Emily Giffin

My manicurist, Betty, who doubles as a numerologist, has just informed me that I need to make some changes in my life. "Three changes, to be exact," she says as she massages lavender oil into my cuticles. She glances up at the low stucco ceiling of her salon as if to ponder further. "And you should make these changes within six days."

Normally, I don't put much stock in Betty's chatter. I am a pragmatic person, a Senser and Thinker on the Myers-Briggs scale. But I am long overdue for some upheaval in my life. Either that, or I should fill the prescription for Prozac that has been tucked into my date planner for months. I've always believed that drugs should be a last resort, so I take Betty's advice and opt for a rapid-fire trifecta: in the next six days, I cut off my long hair, resign from a job I loathe and break up with Peter, my boyfriend of nearly four years. In that order. Afterward, I consider that the haircut should have followed the breakup because Peter likes my hair short. It seems to add needless insult to injury. Still, I'm pretty sure he will get over me quickly.

I call my best friend, Kate, and inform her I have some news that is too big to share over the phone. We meet at Prohibition, our favorite bar on the Upper West Side. "What do you think?" I ask, pointing to my new pixie cut.

"I think you look fabulous!" she says, grinning. "Congratulations on leaving the nineties—and your 'Rachel-*Friends'* cut behind. It was about time."

"Thanks," I say, ignoring the backhandedness of her compliment. "Doesn't it make me look artsy?"

"You're an actuary dating an actuary," Kate says as the bartender pours our Chardonnay. "Nothing can make you look artsy."

"Not anymore I'm not," I say, beaming. I can hardly contain myself. I can't remember the last time I shocked Kate. Or anyone else for that matter.

"Nina," she says with a worried glance. "What do you mean by 'not anymore'?"

I announce that in addition to my Jean Louis David hair special, I also quit my job and dumped Peter. Normally I eschew the term *dump,* but it adds a nice dramatic flourish in this instance. Kate is a defense attorney, trained never to look startled, but there she is, mouth agape for several seconds before calling my actions rash and imprudent—two things I have never been accused of being. I smile, wearing the adjectives as a badge of honor.

"How foolish," Kate says, shaking her head and taking a sip of wine. "What in the world came over you?"

"Betty told me I needed to make three changes. So…job, Peter, hair," I say, ticking the items off on my fingers.

Kate rolls her eyes and takes a larger gulp of wine. "I can't believe you quit a high-paying job and ended a four-year relationship because of that wack job."

I shrug, run my fingers through my spiky hair and tell her that I feel liberated.

"Being single and unemployed is not the same thing as being liberated," Kate snaps back.

"I hated my job almost as much as I hated dating Peter," I say.

It's an overstatement—at least the part about Peter—but I'm on a roll.

"You should have held out for the ring," Kate says, admiring her own recently acquired diamond. "Peter was right on the brink of proposing. He just asked me again what kind you liked best."

I shoot Kate a dubious look. She knows full well that it has been nearly a year since I clipped the photo of a cushion-cut diamond ring from *Town & Country* and gave it to her to give to him, along with my ring size. Plenty of time to find a jeweler in the Diamond District and come up with a somewhat original proposal idea. Hell, he even had enough time to concoct one worthy of a Vows feature story in the *New York Times*.

"You never even gave him an ultimatum. Some of the worthiest bachelors need an ultimatum," Kate says, obviously thinking of her own fiancé and the end-of-the-year deadline she had issued only a few months ago. "It's almost like a ritual. Part of a modern-day mating dance."

"I don't believe in ultimatums."

"Ultimatums aren't part of a belief system," Kate says. "It's like saying, 'I don't believe in compromise. Or…I don't believe in sticking up for myself.'"

I disagree with Kate's premise but have learned not to argue with her. She can debate circles around me. Instead, I just say, "Peter didn't want to marry me. And deep down, I didn't want to marry him."

"I hope you know what you're doing," Kate says. She then adds, "You're thirty-four. You don't have to be an actuary to know that your odds of finding someone in your childbearing years are rapidly decreasing.... It's not the time to look for Prince Charming. Just Prince Charming *Enough*. And Peter could be really charming when he wanted to be."

I would have held the comments about my age against her, but I know she has my best interests at heart. She only wants us both to get married, have babies and move to the same neighborhood in Westchester. Now I have gone and ruined her plans that began years ago when Kate met Peter and his friend David at a wine-tasting course. After targeting the taller, more outgoing of the pals for herself, she insisted on setting me up with the other. "You and Peter are a match made in heaven," she kept saying, after her first successful date with David. "You're both petite Jewish actuaries."

Describing a man as petite would be a death knell for most girls, but I kept an open mind and went on the blind date, discovering that even when I had my heels on, Peter cleared me by a good inch. He was also well mannered, somewhat funny and articulate. So we kept dating. Kate, who by this time was spending every night with David, began her chatter of our suburban future. I told her not to get ahead of herself. "The jury is still out on this one," I said.

But as the weeks passed, I had to admit that Peter and I were compatible. We both enjoyed reading autobiographies, watching *The NewsHour with Jim Lehrer* and doing crossword puzzles. We both preferred the mountains to the beach, cats to dogs, and tea to coffee. We even liked our thermostat at the same temperature: sixty-nine in the winter, seventy-two in the summer. The most significant thing we shared, however, was the depth of our feelings for one other. We liked each other *a lot*—the word *love* even surfaced on occasion—but we weren't crazy about each other. There were no passionate embraces, longing gazes or sappy love letters. We could go more than a couple of days without talking, and neither of us seemed to feel much of a void. Which in the end was the real reason I never issued an ultimatum. I was afraid that Peter just might follow through, and that I might get caught up in the moment and say yes. I didn't like to think of what would come next, of how I might feel walking down the aisle on my wedding day. And every day after that.

I tell Kate some of this now, but I can tell she's too upset to really listen. Instead, she finishes her wine and orders another glass. Then she calls David on her cell and asks him in a loud voice if he's heard the tragic news.

The next morning, I return to Betty's salon under the ruse of a chipped nail. In truth, I want to ask her what to do next. I pose the question, and she pauses before telling me to "seek beauty."

"What do you think I'm doing here in a nail salon?" I say, smiling.

She ignores my quip and says again, "Seek beauty."

Later that day I buy a newspaper and check the want ads. I think of Betty's advice and find two jobs that fit the bill—a receptionist position at the Elite modeling agency and an opening at Milly's Floral Designs. As a five-foot-two, slightly pear-shaped ex-actuary, I decide that the job at Elite might not be the best for my self-esteem. So I go apply for the flower job. Milly and I hit it off, and I am hired on the spot.

When I give Kate the report over brunch at our neighborhood diner, she shakes her head and mumbles something about all of the tests I passed to become an actuary. "It's such a waste," she says, slathering her toast with grape jelly. Then she reminds me of the ferns in my kitchen that I underwatered, and how I had replaced them with artificial ones.

"Actually I *over*watered those ferns," I say. "And, anyway, if I could pass those tests, surely I can learn about flowers."

"But why flowers?" she asks, exasperation creeping into her voice.

I strike a noble pose and say, "Flowers are at the heart of every human drama. Births, funerals and every milestone in between. I want to hear the stories, and I want to create arrangements worthy of the people who share them."

Kate desperately doesn't want to admit it, but I can tell she's impressed by my reason. I have even impressed myself.

I start my new job the following Monday, and right away I love it. Milly's Floral Designs is located in the heart of Murray Hill, one of my favorite neighborhoods in the city due to its lack of tourist attractions or major shopping appeal. It feels quiet, more like Brooklyn than Manhattan. Milly is an older woman with a young spirit. She wears brightly colored tunics and speaks in a singsongy voice. Everything about her is sunny. Her only other employee is an overtly gay Mexican named Hector who boasts of how he swam across the Rio Grande to come to America. He tells me he got caught and sent back to Mexico the first two times but made it on the third. I tell him I am impressed, and he says he has a lot more stories where that one came from.

When we aren't busy, Milly, Hector and I play gin, listen to the radio and sit around and chat. Often we talk about relationships and love. Milly has been married to Dennis, a retired fireman, for thirty-six years. They never had children, only basset hounds, but she says her life has always felt complete. Hector, too, is in a long-term relationship with a man named Chuck, the head chef at an Italian restaurant in Tribeca. He and Chuck are planning to marry in Kauai this winter. I tell him that Chuck does not sound like a gay man's name and he laughs. Milly and Hector both think I'm funny, even when I'm not trying to be. I realize that nobody laughed much at my last job, and certainly not at my jokes. When I think of my old sterile cube and my stiff ex-colleagues, I feel giddy with my good fortune. I catch myself humming as I keep the books, sweep the back workroom and run to answer the phone.

In addition to my office duties, Milly and Hector teach me about a whole new world of flowers—a world of color, form and texture. I learn their tools and techniques—how to coax open poppies, hydrate the hollow stems of amaryllis and strip the thorns from roses. One day, when I create a fan-shaped arrangement of apricot calla lilies and golden holly berries, Milly calls me a natural.

The thing that I enjoy most about my job, though, is our customers. I am in charge of taking the flower orders and transcribing the notes that will accompany them. I discover that virtually no one can refrain from giving me significant background about their order. "My friend had a baby girl today!" one caller gushes. "She's my very best friend in the world—and she tried for years to get pregnant—so I want something really special. What do you suggest?" Or "I just met the girl of my dreams. She's amazing. Would two dozen roses scare you off?" Or "My daughter finally passed the bar. Three tries it took her—just like John Kennedy Jr. Only your grandest arrangement will suffice for this miracle!" I take my time with every customer, savoring the stories as I consult with Milly and Hector to select the perfect flowers for every occasion.

Then there is Byron Skydell. He is our sole regular customer who resists what seems to be human nature by never offering an explanation or any detail. He also comes into the shop rather than placing his orders by phone. My guess is that he works nearby, somewhere in Midtown. He wears handsome navy suits, carries an old-school leather briefcase and has a mysterious, dignified air. Milly and Hector tell me that he has come in about once a week for the past two years, ordering flowers for his wife, Ellen. He always takes his time looking around before making a decision and then writes his own notes. He is left-handed, and as he writes, my gaze always falls on his slim, gold wedding band.

One day when Byron comes into the shop, he places an order for pink begonias. I busy myself with a stack of paper near the cash register, but out of the corner of my eye, I watch him remove an elegant silver pen from his jacket pocket, write a note on his own monogrammed stationery and carefully tuck the flap in on the envelope.

He hands it to me and says, "The usual address, please."

I nod, feeling oddly nervous. "Thank you, Mr. Skydell."

"Thank *you*," Byron says, giving me a shy smile. His voice is a rich baritone, reminding me of Tom Brokaw. As he turns to leave, I admire the way his chestnut-brown hair curls at the nape of his neck. I glance down at the envelope and cannot control my impulse to read the card. His handwriting is distinguished yet romantic, like one of the signatures on the Declaration of Independence. He has written one sentence: *You looked so lovely in pink last night that I thought you might enjoy these.*

My heart beats double time. To think that a man such as this really exists! I wonder if perhaps Byron has a brother, preferably an identical twin. I can't help comparing him to Peter who only sent me flowers once—red roses and baby's breath along with a computer-printed card that read: *Happy Valentine's Day. Love, Peter.* At the time, I felt grateful, almost moved. I proudly displayed the vase, conspicuously shaking the packet of powdered flower food into the water. Now, in comparison to Byron's begonias, Peter's predictable red roses seem as lackluster as our relationship was.

When I next see Betty for a manicure, I confess to having peeked at Byron's card.

"Do you have a crush?" she asks me.

"No," I say a bit too emphatically. "It's just that Byron gives me faith that someone is out there. Someone who will love me the way he loves his wife."

Betty beams and tells me that she thinks I will find such a man very soon.

"When?" I ask her.

"Soon," she says, filing my pinkie nail into her trademark squared oval. "And I'm feeling a strong nine vibe—so that likely means September will bring him to you."

Later I tell Kate of Betty's prediction. Kate misses the point and demands to know how I'm affording manicures on my new salary. I remind her that I saved plenty of money in my former life. "Peter and I seldom went out. Remember?" I say, thinking of all our listless nights on the couch.

She frowns and says, "Speaking of Peter, I saw him yesterday. He and David went to look at tuxedos for our wedding, and we all had lunch afterward. He said to tell you hello."

"Well. Give him my best," I say, meaning it. Then I silently make a wish for Peter to meet his Ellen. To feel inspired to send her flowers on days other than Valentine's. To feel moved by something as small as the color pink.

The summer passes quickly as I fall into a new rhythm— one that feels pleasant and honest and real. I am alone but have never felt less lonely or more hopeful. All the while, my crush on Byron evolves into a small obsession. I think of him every night as I crawl into bed, imagining him with Ellen, bringing her a cup of herbal tea or smoothing her dark hair away from her ivory skin. I am holding out for something that special.

Then, one sweltering day in late August, a troubling thing happens that upsets the delicate balance emerging in my life. Hector is delivering a funeral arrangement to a church in his neighborhood when he decides to swing by his apartment to surprise Chuck who has the day off. Apparently, Chuck's personal trainer also has the day off because Hector discovers the two in bed together. Hector is beside himself with grief, but his anguish quickly gives way to a deep bitterness. He says he no longer believes in true love, and nothing Milly and I say can persuade him otherwise.

I sense a shift in our orders around this same time. Specifically, I notice a marked increase in apology arrangements—flowers sent to wives, along with cards reading: *I'm so sorry* or *Please forgive me.* The male callers clear their throats and sheepishly admit that they are in the "doghouse." Hector assumes the worst—that they, too, were caught red-handed.

"Dirty cheaters," he growls as he snips stems with a vengeance.

I struggle to find a more benign explanation. "Maybe they just forgot to take out the trash," I say. But I can't help picturing leggy mistresses wearing crimson lipstick and too much Poison perfume.

"The heat makes people do crazy things," Milly says. "They'll come to their senses."

Hector grumbles as he continues to flip through the order book, pointing out an influx of our regular, married customers sending flowers to women other than their wives. The cards read: *Thanks for last night* and *Thinking of you.* These orders are harder to defend so I don't even try. Instead, I remind Hector of Byron.

Hector looks at me for a long time and then says, "Byron probably cheats on Ellen, too. He's just smart enough to use another florist for his ho."

When I meet Kate for sushi later that night, I tell her of our unfaithful clientele. She sighs and says, "That's the thing about Peter. He would *never* have cheated on you."

I tell her that I aspire to more than the lack of infidelity in my relationship, but as I dip my tuna roll in soy sauce, I wonder if perhaps a faithful, steady man *is* a benchmark worth striving for. Maybe Byron is too rare a creature to bank on. For the first time, I picture Peter with another woman, and my stomach hurts just a little.

The next day I ask Milly how she knew Dennis was "the One."

"There was no particular thing," she says as she trims the stems of red geraniums.

"But there were fireworks, right?" I ask.

She thinks for a moment and then says no, there were never fireworks with Dennis. Just a quiet, mutual respect for one another. I must look disappointed because she says not everyone needs the earth to shift to be happy. She calls it a misguided conception of today's youth.

Hector nods vigorously. "I had sparks with Chuck. Look where that got me."

I find myself thinking of the quiet, mutual respect I had with Peter. My worry deepens. Even Betty's prediction, which she has steadfastly maintained all summer, doesn't console me.

Byron returns to the shop a short time after that. He smiles at me and then says hello.

"Hello," I say, feeling a shiver of excitement. "What can I get you today, Mr. Skydell?"

He glances around the store and then points to a white marble bowl on the shelf behind me. "I'd like that bowl filled with lilac delphiniums, purple cornflowers and starlight roses. Those are the silvery lavender ones, right?"

"Yes," I say, feeling myself blush. I remember that Milly once told me that the color purple is enigmatic—intense and reserved all at once. She also said that it symbolizes the first flicker of love. "That's a fine choice.... I'll make sure that your arrangement is beautiful, Mr. Skydell."

"I'm sure you will... And it's Byron," he says.

"Byron," I repeat nervously.

"And what is your name?" he asks, looking at me expectantly.

"Nina...Nina Lipman," I say.

He leans in a bit and says, "Well. You have yourself a nice day, Nina Lipman."

Our eyes lock for a long second. Then he turns to leave.

I feel guilt and pleasure knot in my chest. After the front door chimes have stilled, Hector shouts from the back room, "He's a *married* man, ya know!"

"I *know* that. I wasn't flirting with him," I yell back, although I'm not so sure that is true. My face is hot, and I have just filed his order in the wrong folder.

That night when I return home, I'm startled by the sight of a white bowl perched on my doorman's stand filled with lilac delphiniums, purple cornflowers and luminous starlight roses. It is my arrangement, the one I spent over two hours creating.

"For you, Nina," my doorman says, pointing toward them. "A nice gentleman dropped them off for you. And I must say, those roses smell deee-licious!"

I bite my lip and rip open the card, silently reading Byron's words: *Please have dinner with me.* I picture his sapphire eyes and my heart gallops. But the thrill quickly gives way to a rush of shame and then loss. The ideal of Byron is gone, and so is my hope of finding someone like him. Even worse, I feel a profound sadness for Ellen. She is married to someone much more deadly than a beer-guzzling, ball-scratching ne'er-do-well. Byron is lulling her into a false sense of happiness. I will not succumb to his charm, but someday, Byron will find a way to break Ellen's heart.

That night I have several glasses of wine and fall asleep on my couch. I dream that Byron and I are walking through a field of lavender when he suddenly drops to one knee and says he has something very important to ask me. As he removes a ring from his pocket, his face morphs into Peter's. I awaken in tears, feeling compelled to either call Peter or confront Byron. I decide on the latter, embarrassed that I have memorized his address. If Ellen answers the door, I will simply give her the flowers, say they are from her husband.

In the morning, I shower, dress in a simple black suit and find my way to the Skydells' town house on West Seventy-fourth. My hands are clammy as I ring the doorbell. As I wait, I can feel myself losing courage, hoping that Byron has already left for the day. I ring the bell again, and this time I hear brisk footsteps. An attractive, gray-haired woman opens the door and smiles at me.

"Is Ellen home?" I ask as I spot a black-and-white photo of a much younger Byron on the hall table. My stomach lurches.

"I'm Ellen," she says.

"Oh. Hi…uh…how do you know Byron?" I stammer, thinking that surely the woman standing before me is too old to be his wife.

"I'm his mother… And who are you?" she asks. Her expression is placid and curious.

"I…I work at the flower shop," I say.

"Nina," she says.

It is a statement, not a question, but I still nod in response. Then I think of Byron's wedding band and ask, "Who is his wife then?"

Ellen's smile fades. "She and my grandson died in a car accident three years ago."

"Oh…I'm so sorry," I murmur. "I didn't know."

"Byron is very private," she says.

"Oh," I say. "I mean…yes, he seems that way."

She pauses and then says, "You folks at Milly's have helped him so much. At first I thought he was sending me flowers for my sake. And they did help fill a void for me… But I also think the flowers have helped him heal. Life can be bleak, but we must continue to look for beauty…" Her voice trails off.

"Yes. Milly's flowers *are* beautiful," I say quietly, glancing down at the bowl full of flowers I am foolishly holding against one hip.

"I'm not just talking about the flowers," Ellen says.

I give her a quizzical look, and she reaches out, squeezing my free hand.

I realize I am on the verge of tears, so I look down and say, "So Byron's not here then?"

She shakes her head. "No, but would you like to come in? I just made some coffee."

"No, thank you," I say. "I…I really should go."

I wish Ellen a good day and escape back to the street. My head is spinning as I wonder what she will tell Byron, whether I should come clean with my assumption. I find my cell phone in my purse and consider calling Kate to arrange an after-work drink—or Betty to schedule a manicure. But for once, I realize I don't need any advice or predictions. I am sure of what to do and what I hope will happen next.

It is a brisk September day, and I decide to walk to work rather than take the subway. The blocks pass in a blur as I make my way across the park, down Fifth Avenue and over to the flower shop. I think about love and loss. I think about friendship and passion and all the hues in between. I think of Kate and David. Hector and Chuck. Milly and Dennis. Of how different people need different things to be happy. I think of my own breakup with Peter, and how no matter what happens from here, I know I have done the right thing. I think of Byron—his rich voice, loopy handwriting, shy smile. Mostly, though, I just walk, taking my time and occasionally lowering my face to smell my roses.

Carole Matthews is the international bestselling author of nine outstandingly successful romantic comedies. Her unique sense of humor has won her legions of fans and critical acclaim all over the world.

In the U.S. her books include *The Scent of Scandal, Bare Necessity, The Sweetest Taboo, With or Without You, More to Life Than This* and the upcoming *Welcome to the Real World. For Better, For Worse* was selected by Kelly Ripa on the television show *LIVE with Regis and Kelly* as one of her "Reading with Ripa" book club picks, sending it straight onto the *USA TODAY* bestseller list. In the UK her books are all *Sunday Times* bestsellers. *A Minor Indiscretion* is in development in Hollywood, and her books are published in eighteen different countries.

Carole has also presented on television and is a regular radio guest. When she's not writing novels, she manages to find time to trek in the Himalayas, skate in Central Park, take tea in China and snooze in her garden shed in her native England.

To find out more about Carole and her books, go to www.carolematthews.com.

Light Up My Life
Carole Matthews

Widows are supposed to be older ladies, enduring stoically their loss—sudden or otherwise—hanging on to precious memories while living out the rest of their own lives in resigned contentment. I'm too young to be a widow. I've barely reached half my allotted years on this planet and yet my love has already been snatched away from me.

Cell phones have a lot to answer for. They could be giving us a slow form of cancer for all we know, frying our brains as we chatter inconsequentially about this, that and, if you phone certain premium lines, the other. People order their groceries on them in their cars when they should be concentrating on the road and kill husbands on motorbikes who were minding their own business and were obeying the speed limit.

I don't have a cell phone these days. There's no one I want to call. No one to tell when I'm on my way home or that I'm stuck in another interminable meeting about budgets.

No one who misses me if I arrive home a few minutes, a few hours, a few days late.

"You'll be fine, Deanne," all of my friends said. Without, of course, the necessary knowledge to draw on. Some of them hadn't even found anyone they wanted to marry. How on earth could they know what this felt like? "You're young. A couple of years and you'll be back to your old self." They hugged me, clapped me on the back and held out more tissues.

"Chris would want you to carry on." And he would have. I just never seemed to find the right tools for doing that. Yes, I did try counseling. The poor woman was more screwed up than me. My blood seemed to change to ice that bright summer day when my life flipped upside down, and has never yet thawed out.

When the recognized time for grieving had come and gone—according to my friends—and I still wasn't my old self, the phone rang less often. In some ways, I can't blame them, I started to forget to return the few calls I received. I dodged invitations where I would be required to face other people's happiness alone. You can't imagine how many dinner parties I went to where there were three couples and me. Or, even worse, the ones where some other misfit had been dredged out of a swamp to make up the numbers and I had to endure hours of tedious conversation about some academic institution or another. My friends assume, because I am a librarian, that I like my men to be beard-wearing intellectuals. They are wrong. I now have an aversion to both tweed and corduroy jackets simply because of this.

When my husband slewed down the black tarmac road, crushed by the weight of some gas-guzzling monster, somehow my body ended up broken with his. Neither of us recovered from that crash. I now live in splendid isolation. And it's not a nice suburb just outside London.

I keep to myself—which is, I realize, how everyone describes serial killers. "Oh, he was a quiet person. Kept to himself," the neighbors say when the serial killer, a blanket over his head, is eventually led away by bemused-looking policemen. I wonder if that's how my neighbors view me. Living in London, I never have the necessity to speak to them. I'm only surprised we don't have more serial killers. Mr. Patel has run my corner shop since I moved here ten years ago. He gabbles constantly on his cell phone in Urdu while he serves people, never looking up as he slaps change on the counter. I used to wonder why it was too much trouble for him to look up and smile or say thank you. Now I'm glad for his disinterest in his customers, in anything but his own relatives' lives. I can buy all that I require to exist without ever having to engage in a conversation.

In recent years, I've become a great librarian—retreating into my books. I read nothing with pink covers or happy endings. My chosen stories feature loss, deprivation and hardship. On the few occasions I'm required to engage with the public, my expertise is faultless, if painfully extracted. I also read about heroic endeavors undertaken alone. Yachtsmen sailing the Atlantic single-handed, solo climbers, lone Arctic explorers. I don't go on holiday to fun places either. No Ibiza for me. My preference has turned from sun-drenched resorts with white sand beaches packed with laughing families and too much pink flesh on display to the more desolate regions of the globe. That's why I'm sitting in the panorama lounge at the very top of a Norwegian ferry letting the bleak winter scenery of the Arctic Circle slide slowly by my window.

This is a working boat, carrying post and other essential supplies to the tiny fishing villages nestled into the coast. They also let hardy tourists come along for the ride, but not many brave the subzero temperatures at this time of year. The lounge is vast, built to hold five hundred eager passengers in the long summer months of the midnight sun. Now there are three of us. I have staked claim to one corner, hogging a garish striped sofa, swathed in my cozy alpaca wrap. My book is open on my lap, but I'm gazing at the snow-capped mountains as we pass by. The other couple are British, too. They're probably in their sixties, married for some time I should think by their body language. They bicker over breakfast, even though they're on holiday, and don't hold hands. She walks two steps in front of him. He is dispatched regularly to buy coffee and hot chocolate topped with whipped cream from the brightly lit café on the next deck, while she click, click, clicks away at her knitting. It looks like a little jacket for a baby. Perhaps a grandchild. Do parents put their kids in homemade clothes anymore? Everything has to have a designer label these days, doesn't it? I push aside the fact that no one will be knitting for our future children. I wonder if Chris and I would have, eventually, grown bored with each other and I can't imagine it. For me, he will always be frozen in time. Young, laughing, carefree. We were at the stage where we still slept entwined around each other, a tangle of legs and arms, unsure where one body stopped and the other started. He will never be an old man.

The panorama lounge looks as if it was last decorated in the 1970s. Or perhaps this is considered the height of chic in Norway. There is a lift at one end and the doors open. A tall, broad man steps out. My mother would call him a strapping young chap. His wide shoulders are laden with camera bags, and a camera with a huge lens is slung casually across his body. He must have boarded the boat at our last stop as I haven't seen him before. A young woman staggers out behind him, similarly loaded down.

"Hey, hey," he greets the elderly couple in what I assume is Norwegian.

"Hello," they say in return.

And he lifts a hand in a friendly wave and continues on toward me, girlfriend in tow.

"Hey, hey," he says again.

"Hello." I smile my world-weary version of a smile.

"Ah." He halts his progress. "You're British."

"Yes."

"Welcome to our country." His English is impeccable, though strongly accented. My knowledge of Norwegian extends to saying thank you, and I'm once again embarrassed by the British reticence to speak any language other than our own when abroad.

"Thank you. *Takk skal du ha.*"

"This is my assistant, Anya."

I nod to her and she does the same. Her eyes are red-rimmed, as is her nose, and the next thing she does is sneeze.

"We are here to photograph the beautiful aurora borealis," he tells me. Another reason for my choice of holiday destination. I have long held a dream to see the strange phenomenon of the northern lights that grace the winter skies.

The photographer continues, "But Anya has developed the fly."

"The flu," I correct without thinking.

"I'm sorry," he says. "The flu."

On cue, Anya sneezes violently again and fishes a handkerchief from one of the many pockets on her utility jacket.

"I think I will get her into bed before too long," he informs me with a solemn look.

"Good." I suppress a smile. A genuine one. "It would seem wise."

He holds out his hand and shakes mine formally. The skin is tough, slightly roughened. Not the hands of an office worker. "I'm Harrold."

I want to tell him that Harrold is an old person's name. Not a name normally associated with a young hulk of Scandinavian beefcake. Chris is a young person's name and I wonder if the name we go by determines how long we will spend on this planet. Harrold has a shock of white-blond hair that is standing in tufts all over the place and weathertanned features. He looks younger than me. But then I have more frown lines and dark shadows than a person of my tender years should.

"I'm Deanne."

"I will maybe see you later," he says and they both continue on their way.

My attention returns to the scenery. The water is inkblack with a crusting of slushy ice floe, exactly like the stuff you scrape out of the icebox when you're defrosting the freezer. Except on a larger scale. The occasional seal slips momentarily out of the water to glance nervously around. They're not the sort of seals I've seen before—performing ones that will happily clap their flippers or spin a ball on their nose for the promise of a fish. These are hardy oceangoing mammals existing on the edge of survival in a stark and hostile environment. They look dangerous and vulnerable at the same time and I feel privileged to catch even a fleeting glimpse of them. At this time of year, the sun—like a surly teenager—doesn't rise until noon and sinks again barely an hour later. Soon there will be no sun at all and I rather like the idea of living in perpetual darkness. But then, I think, I am anyway.

The elderly couple are on their third hot chocolate of the day, and I find that I can resist the lure of the rich scent no longer and scamper down to buy myself a cup. It seems like a long time since I had the urge to indulge myself. I no longer have any appetite and I never sleep well these days. Even now, I lie with a long bolster pillow against my body for comfort, but it fools no one—least of all me. But when I grasp the cup of hot chocolate in my hands, the aroma is almost overwhelming. I feel weak and faint with desire. The peak of cream is like velvet on my greedy tongue and I drink the chocolate so quickly that I scorch my throat. And I taste it. Every last morsel of it.

Flushed with warmth, I decide to venture outside to watch the sunset. This is not something to be undertaken lightly. Going back to my cabin, I start the process of getting dressed to face the elements. I have one single bed and a couch that folds into another bed should I have been fortunate enough to have required it. My clothes are laid out on the couch and I work from the top down. Inside the boat it is hot and I strip off my light sweatshirt, replacing it with a thermal vest, long-sleeved top, sweater, velour jogging top, Puffa jacket. On the bottom, thermal leggings, jeans, two pairs of socks—one thin, one thick—hiking boots. Glove liners and leather gloves. It is, with windchill taken into account, hovering below minus 19 degrees outside. Not forgetting my woolly hat, I then head out to the rear deck at a stately waddle, hardly able to move for my layers of protective clothing.

As soon as I dare to leave the sanctuary of the boat, the

wind whips at my face and ice particles scour my hot cheeks. The deck is slick with ice and snow and standing up is no easy feat. I slither my way to the stern, hoping to find some sheltered spot to huddle in, clinging to the handrail to help me get some grip. My head is bowed down in determination and it's only when I reach my destination that I realize Harrold is also standing there. He's put a tarpaulin sheet on top of the snow, has piled all his camera bags on top of that and is snapping away at the sky. I go to turn away to find a solitary spot, but he's heard my approach and shouts out to me. "Deanne," he says. "Come and help me, please."

"No, I…" I what? I can hardly feign another pressing engagement. Sighing, I gingerly make my way over to him.

"Anya is asleep. Please help me with my cameras."

He takes pictures of the sunset, which is spectacular, checking the results on his digital display. The white of the mountains melts to the colors of crushed strawberries, blueberries and lemonade. Gulls caw in the fading light. The rhythmic thrum of the engines proves a soporific background noise.

"This lens, please…" Harrold points at his bag and I duly oblige while he struggles with frozen fingers to unscrew the present incumbent. "I live in Trondheim," he says as we exchange equipment. This is the halfway point of my trip. "Where are you going?"

"Down to Bergen."

"It is a beautiful city," he tells me. "But so is Trondheim. I would like to show it to you."

I don't say anything. Now that we're supposed to be Europeans every other nation seems to think we have dropped our British reserve. I say it's still alive and well.

Harrold clicks away some more and then points at another

lens holder. I do my duty again. The sun sinks lower on the horizon and the sea becomes purple.

"This is very beautiful." I feel like crying.

"Come," he says kindly. "You cannot stay out in this cold for long. I have enough photographs for now. You will freeze to death."

My breath catches on his final word and I see his eyes lock on mine, so I turn and start to slither my way back to safety.

Dinner is served at 7:00 p.m. prompt—unless there is any disagreement from the waves. Last night there was an alarming swell, which made me notice that all the chairs were held down by springs and that the tablecloths are made of sticky material so that nothing slides about on them. Tonight, the ocean is a millpond. The restaurant is quiet. Apart from the elderly British couple, there are a few Norwegian day passengers and me. Harrold sweeps into the dining room, ducking at the door. "I am here to get soup for Anya. Then I will be back," he announces to us all. The elderly couple smile across at me. I feel my cheeks color and wonder why.

I help myself to soup, remembering what it felt like to have someone bring soup to me when I was feeling unwell, and get a pang of unbidden jealousy toward Anya. Moments later, Harrold sweeps back in, collects another bowl of soup and squeezes his huge frame into the chair opposite me. "You do not wish to dine alone?" he asks as he runs his hands through his mad hair.

But I feel it's too late to object. I can hardly say no, can I? It wouldn't be polite.

"My friend has a temperature." He spreads his hands in a

rueful gesture. "Tonight there will be no aurora for her. Conditions are good. The sky is very clear and no full moon. I need more pairs of hands. Will you help me again?"

"I...er..."

"It is so wonderful," he continues without pause. "You will enjoy it."

"Have you seen the aurora before?"

"Many times." He shrugs. "But it always fills me full of awe. I was a fireman in Trondheim for many years. In the summer, I gave up my job to be a full-time photographer and make a record of my country. I am publishing, I think you would say, a book for the coffee table."

"Yes." I smile. "That's what we would say."

"Life is very short," he tells me as if I don't know. "I want to do different things with my time. To travel. To take photographs everywhere I go."

"That's very admirable."

"What do you do?"

"I'm a librarian." My book is on my knee. I'd planned to read it over dinner. It's an incredibly dull book and I wish I'd brought a bit of Bridget Jones with me instead.

"I like to read," Harrold tells me. "Trashy American thrillers and books about mountains."

"I like those, too."

"What about your husband?" He glances down at my wedding ring and I follow his gaze. "What does he do?"

"I lost my husband." I hate that term. It sounds as if I misplaced him. As if he dropped out of my pocket and slipped down the back of the sofa. Or as if I've put him in a drawer and can't remember which one. I didn't lose Chris. He was torn from me. Rent asunder. Too soon. Too cruelly and too soon.

"Recently?"

"No," I say, acknowledging for the first time that some considerable time has passed since Chris and I were last a couple. "No. Some years ago."

"I am very sorry. You are too young for that to happen."

I continue to spoon my soup into my mouth and notice that my hand isn't shaking as it usually does in these situations. "Yes," I say, then issue my stock phrase even though I don't believe it. "But life must go on."

And there's a spark inside me. Like that little explosion when you first light a gas fire, I feel something flicker inside me.

I have drunk three glasses of wine, which is more than I normally knock back in a week or more. Since Chris died, I've steadfastly avoided alcohol as a means of release. And I never drink on a school night. I don't want to be a raddled old alcoholic on top of everything else. Now I'm feeling mellow and my knees are a bit wobbly as if the booze has rushed around my system to make up for lost time. I giggle as Harrold leads me out onto the rear deck. The night is so dark that it's hard to make out where the sea ends and the land begins and where that blends into the sky. All around is consuming blackness. The temperature certainly hasn't risen since I came out here earlier today and the air feels as if it's freezing in my lungs.

"Here," Harrold says. "We'll set up next to the engine outlet."

The smell of marine fuel is strong, but there is a steady stream of warm air coming from the vents. My fingertips and my feet are numb already. I clap my hands together against the cold and enjoy the soft breeze on my face.

"We will be able to stay out for a longer time." Harrold meticulously assembles his camera on a tripod, which he places precisely in the snow. "Now we wait."

And we wait for a long time. While we do, he tells me about his life in Norway and I talk some more about Chris and my own life—such as it is—at home. It might well be the excess of wine, but the permanent pain around my heart is easing. This is the longest conversation I've had in ages and it isn't exhausting me as it normally does.

"Please," he says. "Let me take a photograph of you."

"Well, no…"

"Stand over there," Harrold instructs.

I inch across the deck and stand where I was told.

"Look happy," he says.

I force my lips apart.

Harrold frowns at me. "I will have to help." He bends down and, before I realize what he's doing, he throws a snowball at me. The soft snow showers all over me.

"Bloody hell," I splutter and then bend down to scoop up a handful and lob it straight back.

Being brought up in Norway clearly turns you into an expert snowballer and I'm no match for my opponent. In minutes I'm completely out of puff and panting like a knackered old horse and, of course, covered in snow. And I'm laughing. I'm laughing so much my sides hurt. There could even be a guffaw trying to get out. Harrold returns to his camera and snaps away. "Don't move. Don't move. You look beautiful just like that," he tells me. "As if you are trapped inside a snow globe."

I totter back across the deck toward him. "I will get you back," I promise. "You wait. I just need more practice."

Harrold turns to me and then his eyes are drawn away. "Deanne," he says breathlessly. "Look."

There is a ghostly green tinge like a spider's web moving across the sky in front of us.

"Oh my word."

It snakes and vibrates to silent music. Harrold clicks away and I try to pull my attention from the mesmerizing spectacle to see if he needs help. But he seems not to need me, so I focus on the sky once more. The colors shift and swirl, changing to red, yellow, purple.

"This is stunning," I gasp. This is the extraordinary uniqueness of life. Nature at its most exuberant, unleashed for our pleasure. The elements are putting on this light show just for us. For Harrold and for me. I lose track of time, all senses cease. I don't know if my hands are warm or cold. I can no longer hear or feel anything except the rush of blood in my ears and the fabulous, excited beat of my heart.

I want this life. I want it so much. Life is for living and I've done so little of that. There is a whole wonderful world out there simply sitting and waiting for me to rejoin it. I'm vaguely aware that the steady clicking of Harrold's camera has stopped and then I feel his strong arm grasp my shoulders. "Is this not magnificent?"

"It is," I breathe and hot tears course down my frozen cheeks. But they're tears of joy, not grief.

Harrold turns to kiss me and his lips are soft and warm. I press my body against his, experiencing emotions and sensations that I thought were lost to me forever. I smile up at Harrold and a shaky laugh breaks from my throat. There are recognized phenomena in life that can heal what is broken— the power of meditation, the miracle of swimming with dol-

phins, the kiss of a new lover. I don't know that the spectacle of the aurora borealis painting the sky with its Techni-
color beauty is one of them. But I rather think it should be.

Lolly Winston is the author of the novel *Good Grief* (Warner Books, 2004), which was a *New York Times* bestseller, #1 Booksense pick, and has been optioned by Universal Studios. Her second novel, *Happiness Sold Separately,* will be published in August 2006.

Only Some People
Lolly Winston

There once was a man and a woman—Mr. and Mrs. B we'll call them—who fought like jackals.

Mr. B fantasized about leaving Mrs. B as soon as he figured out where he wanted to go. Wherever it was, there would be a lake and he'd sit in a chaise longue and smoke cigars with a transistor radio tuned to *his* station and there'd be a sunset without any carping (yes, his cigars *do* stink), and maybe fireflies. Each time Mr. B imagined leaving Mrs. B, he added a detail to the fantasy. First came the image of the lake (as smooth and gray as slate), and then the fireflies (a boyhood fondness he'd had), and he figured eventually he'd work his way up to an actual spot on the map, and off he'd go, leaving Mrs. B to stew alone.

Mrs. B fantasized about Mr. B dropping dead. Nothing painful, just a little aneurysm as he lay on the couch watching *World's Scariest Police Chases* on TV while *she* did all the chores. As an escaped convict drove a stolen car screeching backward down a freeway ramp, Mr. B would suddenly hack and gasp and then fall silent, his sausagey fingers letting go of the remote control.

They'd been married twenty-two years, Mr. and Mrs. B. They had gone to the same high school but didn't really notice each other until a few years after graduation, when they wound up working at the same company that sold air conditioners. Mr. B installed units and Mrs. B answered phones.

"Cooley's Co-o-o-lers," the future Mrs. B sang into the phone. The future Mr. B took note of her long fingers circling the receiver and the way her necklace dipped into the creamy crevice between her breasts.

They went on a date to the town golf course and drank cans of Colt 45 without eating supper, and Mrs. B got pregnant behind a spray of bamboo near the seventh hole. They were married in Mrs. B's parents' backyard, Mrs. B's heels sinking slowly into the soaked summer grass so that it looked as though she might tip over backward. At the reception, Mr. B danced with Mrs. B's cousin and Mrs. B swore she saw him caress the woman's leg. That night, they made love with an angry intensity. Afterward, Mrs. B decided her husband had too many hairs and bumps and moles on his back, and Mr. B compared his bride's breath to cheese.

During the next twenty-two years of their marriage, they relished bickering the way some people relish a fevered Ping-Pong match. They were always fleeing each other — slamming doors, stomping out of rooms, screeching out of the driveway in their cars. Still, they always wound up back in the living room together, Mr. B on the couch, Mrs. B in the armchair, her long pointed feet on the ottoman, the flickering blue light from the TV making them glow slightly. And maybe Mrs. B would get them both a glass of beer and maybe Mr. B would ask Mrs. B what she wanted to watch. And Mrs. B would say it seemed hot tonight, did Mr. B think it seemed hot? And he'd nod and she'd fan herself with the *TV Guide.* And Mr. B would think that maybe he wouldn't take off for the lake place yet and Mrs. B would think that maybe she wouldn't want anything to happen to Mr. B just now.

We catch up with Mr. and Mrs. B in the kitchen one morning, as though tuning into a ball game at halftime. Mrs. B is a few points ahead. She *told* Mr. B not to pour boiling tea into a glass pitcher of ice. The pitcher would crack and break and there'd be a big mess. She'd been right. What *is* it about the Y chromosome?

Mr. B stoops to sweep up the shards of glass with a dustpan and broom. He is like a manatee—big and slow. He's pear-shaped, with a wide, flat bottom and a belly that hangs over his belt, his belly button an eye peering through the knit fabric of his shirt. He huffs a little as he works, his broad, rounded back turned to Mrs. B, his vertebrae outlined like knobs. The glass gets caught in the broom, and the tea, sticky with sugar, runs in a long trickle under the refrigerator.

All this seems to bring cheer to Mrs. B. She sits at the kitchen table, pretending to read the Living section, but peering around Ann Landers to watch her husband. Her pointed nose is red on the end from her allergies. Her teeth are small and her smile exposes mostly gums, although she doesn't smile often.

While Mr. B doesn't know anyone better than his wife, he is still surprised by her joy in being proven right, even when she's right about something awful. In fact, she seems to *prefer* to be right about something awful. An *I-told-you-so* thought bubble permanently floats above her head, vindication as sweet to her as a winning lottery ticket.

There was a man in their neighborhood who always mowed his lawn barefoot, a cap tilted low over his eyes, a beer waiting for him on his front porch, a sliver of grass pinched between his lips. Mr. B noted the air of happiness around the man as he worked. While everyone else in the neighborhood had gardeners, this young fellow, an engineer of some sort, seemed to enjoy doing the lawn himself. Mrs. B remarked that the man was a fool to use a lawn mower without wearing shoes. One day he would lop off a toe! And so he did. Mr. and Mrs. B didn't witness the event, but they heard about it from their gossipy neighbor, Stella. Mr. B's toes curled with empathy inside his loafers as he winced and listened to the story of the man's wife driving the man to the emergency room with the toe on ice. Sadly, the toe could not be sewn back on, and the man had to undergo physical therapy to learn to walk without wobbling. As they stood in their driveway and listened to the end of the story, Mrs. B clucked with knowing disapproval, crossing her arms over her chest.

Later that same night, while watching *Antiques Roadshow,* Mrs. B started to carp about the toe and the man's stupidity. Mr. B, who'd had too many beers, said that Mrs. B should drive over to the hospital and see if she could claim the toe. Wear it on a string around her neck as a badge of honor.

"That's ridiculous," Mrs. B said.

"*You're* ridiculous," Mr. B said.

"*You* are," Mrs. B said. "Who *cares* about Hepplewhite?" she added, waving a hand at the TV.

Now, as Mr. B finishes cleaning up the iced tea, it occurs to him that he and his wife are fortunate not to have anything significant to argue about. Child rearing, financial planning—it's all gone off without a hitch. They bought Cooley's Coolers when Mr. Cooley retired, and business has been steady ever since. Recession-proof. Their daughter, Minnie B, will graduate from college this weekend. Mr. B is very proud of Minnie—a pride that seems to embarrass his daughter. Unlike Mr. and Mrs. B, *everyone* graduates from college these days, Minnie always points out.

Mrs. B makes a great display of getting out the sponge mop and mopping the kitchen floor. The tea and glass are gone, but there's a sticky residue. Mr. B sits down and watches Mrs. B. She's as thin as a flamingo, with long sinewy legs that appear to bend backward at the knees.

Mrs. B hasn't bought Minnie a graduation gift yet because she's not sure what her daughter would approve of. Oh, she thinks she's something, that Minnie, majoring in political philosophy, whatever *that* is. And she's a vegetarian. Won't even wear leather shoes.

Finally, the floor is clean. On to the next squabble: The Bs are divided on their plans for getting to the college tomorrow. They debate what time to leave, which bridge to take and where to stop for lunch.

Meanwhile, cut to the college, Evergreen, up in Washington State, where Minnie B is dreading the arrival of her parents. She's confessing this to the school shrink.

"They're poison people," she tells the shrink, reaching for a Kleenex. The man nods soporifically and stares at Minnie. This is all he ever does. She's gone to him every week for four years and she feels like maybe it's time he gave *her* a little information. But their time is up.

"We'll have to continue next time," he says, looking ruefully at the clock. As if it were all the *clock's* fault.

Once back in her dorm showering, Minnie fantasizes about the parents she *wishes* were coming to her graduation: Their names are Elizabeth and David. They are tall and tan and tip their heads back when they laugh, and they carry World Wildlife Fund canvas bags, and they've saved enough money from running their little law firm that wins class-action suits against big companies like Dow to send Minnie to Italy for the summer.

While rinsing cherry-bark conditioner from her hair, Minnie also imagines that her senior project on acid rain has won the prestigious $1500 Remington Award. Yes, *she* is the one climbing the steps to the stage to accept the award—not prissy Leslie Sims who wrote that unctuous paper on refugees from Whereverthehellstan—and Elizabeth and David are in the audience beaming.

But it is Mr. B and Mrs. B who are on the road to the college now, and Mr. B has gotten his pudgy paw stuck in a can of Pringles potato chips. He shakes the can, trying to free himself. Mrs. B yanks it away, scraping his skin. Mr. B is *supposed* to be watching his cholesterol.

Mr. and Mrs. B both recently quit smoking, which has made them especially ornery and pushed Mr. B to constant snacking. Mr. B wears a patch. Mrs. B prides herself in not needing one. Patches are so expensive. Well, it must be nice to be perfect, Mr. B always tells her. He licks the salt and grease on his wrist and looks ahead at the road: Two hundred and thirty-seven miles to go. Mrs. B heaves a sigh through her lips, blowing her fading yellow bangs off her forehead, and changes the radio station from Dixieland jazz, which Mr. B was enjoying, to a call-in show about cooking.

"Uh, salmonella!" Mrs. B clucks in response to some tip.

Mr. B watches bugs splatter across the windshield. Two hundred and thirty-six miles to go.

Mrs. B is telling Mr. B that they should look for one of those salad-bar places for lunch when Mr. B suddenly begins swatting at his chest, as if trying to stamp out a fire there. He gasps a bit, then coughs, the veins in his neck two blue cords.

"What on earth?" Mrs. B says.

Mr. B's eyes bulge. He lets go of the steering wheel and the car swerves across three empty lanes, off the road, and up onto the median strip. As they bump along, highway daisies and shrubbery crackle and snap beneath them.

"What the hell!" Mrs. B shrieks, laying a hand across the dashboard. The car thumps to a stop. Mr. B holds his head in his hands. One tear creeps down his cheek.

"I think I'm having a *heart attack*."

Mrs. B climbs out of the car. "I'm driving." She opens Mr. B's door, helps him out and around to the passenger's side, shovels him onto the seat, then gets behind the wheel.

They screech back onto the highway then Mrs. B pulls over at the first call box to phone the highway patrol. She asks them to bring an ambulance. She *told* Mr. B they should get a cell phone. Surely they're the last people on earth not to own one. But Mr. B couldn't ever make up his mind about what plan to choose. Now look at the mess they're in.

They wait in the car by the side of the road.

"*This* will be an expensive cab ride," Mrs. B tells Mr. B, tossing the can of potato chips into the back seat and rolling down the window. Maybe if Mr. B gets some fresh air he'll snap out of it.

Mr. B has no comeback. He is dying. The only part of his body that moves are his eyelashes, as he blinks at Mrs. B. He is sure that he is dying and will never see his daughter graduate from college. He swallows. A cow crests a hill beside the freeway and stares down at Mr. and Mrs. B as it munches on grass.

Mrs. B does not remember how to do CPR. She knows you're not supposed to do it unless the person is unconscious. Maybe Mr. B remembers how. Should she ask him now, while he's still conscious? No, she doesn't want to get him all worked up. Should she take his pulse? What good would that do? Oh! What a nuisance this man is.

At the hospital, Mrs. B sits in the emergency room waiting area flipping through a magazine about movie stars' mansions. One star has an indoor basketball court and a fountain in the front hall. Who needs all that? Well, this certainly isn't a heart attack. Heart*burn* is more like it. What a baby. Probably all that junk food. Mrs. B has her own health problems—allergies and asthma—and you don't see *her* driving off the freeway. Mr. B should have heeded their family doctor's advice long ago to walk twenty minutes a day and eat low-fat foods. Mrs. B had bought him low-cal cottage cheese, but he let it grow a mossy layer as he feasted on pork rinds and Eskimo Pies. Another star's kitchen gleams with hanging copper pots. Who wants to wash all those? Besides, can't you catch something from copper? Legionnaires' Disease or Alzheimer's? Mrs. B could have nudged Mr. B a little more, could have gone walking with him. But she hated the image of the two of them strutting around the neighborhood like those other couples, holding hands and wearing those silly nylon jogging suits that look like circus tents.

A doctor emerges from two swinging doors and sits beside Mrs. B. He tells her that her husband has had a significant heart attack and lost thirty percent of his heart muscle. It's a good thing they came to the hospital as soon as they did. Mr. B will be admitted to cardiac intensive care. He'll be hooked up to a monitor and observed twenty-four hours a day. Does Mrs. B have any questions?

Mrs. B watches the doctor's stethoscope swing back and forth across his chest. She doesn't even know what town they're in. She catches her tiny reflection in the stainless steel.

Significant.

"But we're on our way to our daughter's college graduation," she tells the doctor.

"Well, you'll be stuck here for at least a few days." He looks young—not much older than Minnie—and smells sweet, like soap. *Great.* Mrs. B does not want to be stuck hanging around this hospital. What about Minnie's graduation?

The doctor explains that Mr. and Mrs. B must meet with the patient-education coordinator, who will tell them how to adjust Mr. B's diet and exercise. He'll need to go to cardiac rehab once they get home.

"See, I *know*," she tells the doctor, leaning forward. "But he won't listen to me."

The doctor nods understandingly. Mr. B will certainly have to listen to her now.

There is an incessant ticking inside Mrs. B's head, like a faucet dripping. She wishes she could reach in and scratch her brain. She pokes a finger in her ear and jiggles it.

The doctor smiles, cocks his head.

The movie star magazine slides out of Mrs. B's lap and smacks the floor, startling her. She jumps and grabs the doctor's arm, then lets go, embarrassed. She wants to ask him if Mr. B is going to be okay. But she can't think of a medical term for "okay."

Finally the doctor says, "I'll have the social worker come and meet with you. She's very helpful."

Mrs. B has to wait an hour before she can see Mr. B. First they want to get him stabilized and up to the cardiac unit.

She calls Minnie and tells her that they won't be able to make it to the graduation tomorrow.

"Your father's sick with food poisoning," she says, wrestling to straighten the gnarled metal cord on the pay phone. "Or maybe it's a heart attack."

"What do you mean *maybe* it's a heart attack?"

"Okay, well. It *is* a heart attack. But he's going to be fine. Take your friends out to dinner on us. Use your Discover card."

"*Mom.* No one takes that card. What's wrong with Dad?" There's panic in Minnie's voice now. "Is he okay?"

"He's fine," Mrs. B says. "I have to run. We'll be up there in a few days!" She uses the same singsong cheer she uses to answer the phones at Cooley's Coolers. Mr. B has said for years that they could hire a receptionist and Mrs. B could work on the books or stay home more often if she liked. But Mrs. B likes answering the phones—a task that requires her to be cheerful, donning a personality that she wishes were her own. It's like trying on an outfit she could never quite fit into or pull off.

"You're always nice to *strangers,* Mom," Minnie told her once.

★ ★ ★

At the gift shop, Mrs. B buys a pack of Juicy Fruit. She stands in the parking lot outside the emergency room watching ambulances drive in. She methodically unwraps, chews then spits out five sticks of gum, wadding them up into a tissue. Finally, she breaks down and bums a cigarette from a nervous, pacing man.

She wonders if she will sleep here at the hospital or alone at a motel. A quiet night's sleep without Mr. B snoring would be nice. Maybe she'll get some rest if he's not there thrashing like an injured water buffalo. Still, they haven't spent a night apart since they were married. Sometimes she sleeps in the guest room or Mr. B sleeps on the couch. But they are always under the same roof.

She will not tell Mr. B about this cigarette. They've made a pact that if either one smokes they have to give the other person two dollars. So far, Mrs. B is ahead, having collected twelve dollars from Mr. B. Ha! She should have been charging him for onion rings, too. She drops the cigarette and stamps it out. She should send this hospital bill to Arby's.

Fifteen more minutes until Mrs. B can go upstairs.

What if she has to leave the hospital without her husband? There is a hot pain in the bottom of her stomach, as though the cigarette is stuck there and still burning. Someone taps her on the shoulder. When she turns to look no one's there. Oh, for Chrissake! The doctor said only thirty percent. Is that so terrible? His words and demeanor were so vague. It was like trying to figure out the difference between a "partly cloudy" and "mostly sunny" forecast. Well, she can't *wait* to get upstairs and tell Mr. B about the rules in the nutrition booklet. She squeezes the booklet into a tube. She's been right all along about cheese!

A police cruiser brings a prisoner into the hospital. He's in an orange jumpsuit with his legs in shackles and his hands cuffed behind his back. His head is bowed and his feet shuffle along. Tattoos run up his arms like vines.

Mrs. B's eyes sting and the burning sensation in her stomach has worked its way up into the back of her throat. She closes her eyes and listens to the scratch and mumble of the police radio.

How do you get to a place where being right is your only pleasure? It is a feeling that has held Mrs. B on the verge of tears for some time now. She never cries, though. She doesn't see anything *wrong* with crying, but it seems silly to cry about something you can't put your finger on. Hormones, maybe, she's told herself in the past few months. And that nuisance, Mr. B, who refuses to listen to her. "A heart attack waiting to happen!" she always tells him as he reaches past the Egg Beaters for the mayonnaise. And now she's right. Again. So what? Mrs. B is afraid she's going to vomit. The feeling passes when an orderly approaches to tell her that she can go upstairs now and see her husband.

"Yttrium *is* a word." Mrs. B leans over the hospital bed, admitting this to Mr. B. The metal rail on the bed gives off a tiny electrical shock. "It's some kind of chemical compound or something. I should have given you those points in Scrabble last week." Instead, Mrs. B hid the dictionary under the bathroom sink so they couldn't look up the word.

"You were right. You would have won the game." Mrs. B feels compelled to make a confession, to offer Mr. B an apology, yet she's not quite ready to yield anything she might regret saying later.

Mr. B is sedated and uncomfortable, so he can't comment

on this confession, which has been given with the enthusiasm that might accompany a birthday present. He barely remembers their Scrabble game. His eyes hurt, so he closes them.

Mrs. B waits. She's not sure what for.

The hospital-room window is ajar. Mrs. B hears car doors slamming in the parking lot below and people making their way across the asphalt.

Mr. B seems to be sleeping, so Mrs. B sits in the chair beside the bed and flips through the brochure outlining healthy foods. There's an illustration of a papaya. It's shaped like the uterus in the filmstrip they show you in junior high. All the little seeds inside look like eggs. She wonders if she and Mr. B would have continued dating if she hadn't gotten pregnant.

Mr. B's hand fumbles under the covers then emerges, creeping across the sheet like a small animal. He blinks and his brown irises appear, cloudy, then watery, then cloudy. Mrs. B can see that he is frightened. She stands up. She doesn't know that he wants to speak but is too exhausted.

Mrs. B takes Mr. B's hand. It's dry and cold and speckled with two age spots she's never noticed before. Two irregular freckles that seem worrisome. His skin is chapped. Maybe later she'll go back to the gift shop for some aloe lotion. She lowers the metal rail on the bed and scoots up beside her husband. She lies on top of the covers, rolling onto her side and draping an arm over his girth. He smells medicinal, like alcohol and his plastic hospital bracelet. If the nurse comes in, she will probably yell at Mrs. B. You probably aren't supposed to lie down with the patients. Oh, screw it. She can feel the pulse in Mr. B's neck and his chest expanding as he breathes. While he has always been the heavier one, the one whose mass creates a gulch in their bed at home, Mrs. B is now afraid she's crushing her husband.

★ ★ ★

Four hours north of the hospital, Minnie B graduates without the Embarrassing Parents. She's worried about her father. But maybe this is the wake-up call that will force him to change his lifestyle. Minnie will go home for a few weeks after graduation and fix him bulgur salad, veggie stir-fries and wheatgrass smoothies. Get him to exercise. Maybe her parents will even stop fighting for once. They've been turning into one of those old couples you see at diners, who eat in silence, a wall of exasperation between them. Obviously they can't stand each other but you know they probably couldn't stand being apart either.

As Minnie and her roommate, Gwen, crawl into their beds after a night of graduation parties, Minnie tells Gwen how her parents never should have gotten married. They weren't meant for each other. It was all an accident. *She* was an accident. They hadn't even gone to college. They should have at least gone to community college, then gotten married.

"Only some people are happy," Gwen mumbles, drifting off to sleep.

"The room's spinning," Minnie says. She's had too much beer and champagne. Pink champagne that didn't even have a cork! Birds start to chirp and the blue light of morning is a spike in her head. She will feel better tomorrow, she tells herself. Maybe not tomorrow. Maybe the day after.

Mr. B reaches up and pats Mrs. B clumsily on the head. When he gets out of this dang hospital, he will go to that lake. No more procrastinating. He'll find a lake on the map and take Mrs. B with him. He might have to tape her mouth shut so she won't tell him how to drive the whole trip, but they will go together. Maybe they'll even sell their house and move to a cottage on the lake. Swim out to a raft every morning and lie on their backs in the sun. No more cigars or butter or cigarettes or Pringles. Just fish. Fish caught fresh from the lake.

Mr. B closes his eyes and drifts off, some medication in his IV carrying him away. As he falls into a deep canyon of sleep, Mrs. B sails behind him like a parachute.

Robyn Harding lives in Vancouver, B.C., with her husband and two children. After a seven-year career in the advertising industry, she published her first novel, *The Journal of Mortifying Moments,* in 2004. *Journal* has been published in North America, Italy, Holland, the UK, Australia, New Zealand, South Africa, Korea and Russia. Robyn's next book, *The Secret Desires of a Soccer Mom* (no, it is not an autobiography), will be published in August 2006. To learn more about her current and future books, or just to say hello, visit www.robynharding.com.

The Virgin Sherry
Robyn Harding

By no means am I the oldest virgin alive. There are eighty-year-old nuns out there who have never had sex. In fact, they've probably never even gone near a penis. And, of course, there are lesbians—although, I suspect that many of them *have* gone near a penis and just decided they didn't like it. But I am neither a nun nor a lesbian, and yet, I'm still a virgin at twenty-four. It's not eighty, but you have to admit, for a virgin, it's pretty old.

It would be one thing if my virginity was intentional. Then I could be proud of making it this far. I'd give speeches at high schools, and be a special guest on talk shows dealing with teen pregnancy. "Don't do it!" I'd expound. "On your wedding night, you'll be so happy you waited!" But alas, my virginity is purely accidental.

I'm not even sure how this happened. It's not like I'm covered in enormous warts; I don't have a weird deformity where my knees are fused together; and I'm not in an iron lung. In fact, I'm quite attractive, quite normal, quite *horny*... There has been ample opportunity. A few close calls even. But somehow, I have yet to go all the way. The fact that I am twenty-four and still call it "going all the way," is evidence enough that I need to get laid.

In some bygone era I may have been gifted to an emperor or king, but in this day and age, being a virgin is no longer a major selling feature. You need only watch an episode of *The Bachelor* to figure that out. Every series has one: some cute, bubbly blonde who is saving herself for her wedding night. Invariably, she confesses her purity to the guy and is subsequently dumped at the next rose ceremony. It freaks men out! They think you're religious, or frigid, or dying to get married. They get performance anxiety because they know you'll remember this one time forever. There's no denying it: It's a liability. I've got to find someone to go all the way with—tonight!

At this moment, I'm in the back of a cab with my girlfriend Jody, zooming across the Burrard Street Bridge to downtown Vancouver. It's our friend Naomi's twenty-fifth birthday and we're meeting her at a trendy nightclub to celebrate. My companion chatters excitedly as I stare out the window at the sailboats below, my thoughts firmly entrenched in my virginal predicament.

"I wonder if Naomi invited that Ben guy she's been seeing?" Jody is saying. "It could be a bit overwhelming for him, meeting all of her friends at once. But on the other hand..."

The lights of Granville Island are just beginning to twinkle as dusk slowly descends on the city. The sky is a promising pink as the sun lazily sinks into the Pacific. It is a beautiful evening, almost magical, really. I couldn't have picked a better night to become a *real* woman.

"Hey, Sherry! Hellooooooo? Sherry?"

Jody has noticed my distraction. I snap my head away from the window, momentarily terrified that she can read my thoughts. Instinctively, I clutch my small, black purse to my chest. Inside are no less than six condoms, hidden in a zippered pouch at the back of the bag. "What?" There is a hint of panic in my tone.

"What's up with you?" Jody asks.

"Nothing!" I cry. "I was just enjoying the view."

"Yeah…beautiful…" she says disinterestedly. "So, do you think she'll invite him?"

"Who? What?"

"You didn't hear a word I said!" she shrieks. "What's going on?"

I can feel heat creeping into my face. Jody knows me well, well enough to know when I am hiding something. Although…that's not entirely true. I've been hiding something from Jody for the past six years. I feel horrible to think that this woman, probably the closest friend I have in the world, thinks I have an active and rewarding sex life.

Exhibit A: The First Attempt

Jody and I grew up together in Quesnel, a pulp-mill town about halfway between the southern U.S. border with Washington State, and the northern one with Alaska. In Quesnel, virginity was not cool—at least it didn't seem to be from my perspective. The cool girls had sex in grade eight. They wore black eyeliner, tawny foundation and jean jackets. They smoked cigarettes and had coffee and French fries for lunch.

Their older boyfriends picked them up from school in noisy Trans Ams or low-rider trucks, taking them off somewhere to "do it" with them. They were just so mature, so worldly, so...grown-up.

My clique was not in league with those girls, but neither were we social outcasts. We were the nice girls—not easy, but not prudes, either. Jody lost her virginity when she was a respectable seventeen. Our other close friends, Paula and Nancy, were sixteen and sixteen and two-thirds, respectively. I was eighteen when I told the lie. I didn't feel that bad about it at the time. At that moment, I felt sure it was only a matter of hours before I consummated my relationship with my boyfriend, Todd, and absolved myself of any guilt. But it didn't work out that way, and now, six years later, my deception still haunts me.

On that fateful night, we were having a sleepover at Nancy's house. Her mom had gone away for the weekend with her new boyfriend, leaving us alone. We were old enough to be on our own. In a couple of weeks Jody and I would move to Vancouver to attend UBC (Nancy was going to study broadcasting at Ryerson in Toronto and Paula was going to work in her dad's Greek restaurant for a year to save up enough money to travel to Australia.) The night was a celebration of sorts, a farewell. Like many young women ending one chapter of their lives and about to embark on the next, we got drunk and talked about sex.

"Randy and I had such an awesome time last night," Paula giggled. She was our resident *sexpert* given that she and her boyfriend of four years did it approximately twice a day. "We were in his car and I did this thing to him with my tongue...like I kind of flicked it around the head of his—"

"Oh!" I interrupted. "My kiwi cooler's empty. Anyone need another?"

"Sure," Jody said. Paula shook her head no.

"I'm good." Nancy waved me away, turning back to Paula. "So…you flicked your tongue how?"

Alone in the kitchen, I stuck my head inside the fridge. The chill air did little to cool the heat of my face, or slow the racing of my panicked heart. I was humiliated by my physiological response to a frank discussion about oral sex. Instead of running from the room, I should have been picking up pointers! Tonight was the night after all. Todd and I were going to go all the way. It would be my goodbye present to him.

In a way, it was also a gift to myself. I did not plan to move to the city some small-town virgin! My grandmother had given me ample warning: The city was full of wolves just waiting to prey on an innocent like me. If I didn't have sex in the next thirteen days, I would be at their mercy. No, I would not arrive in Vancouver some defenseless fawn. I would be a sexually knowledgeable, tongue-flicking she-wolf! I had to pull myself together.

I wouldn't call what I had back then a *phobia,* per se. It was more of an apprehension, an…uneasiness. I was going to have to face up to it sometime, I knew that. It appeared that time had come. By now, you've probably guessed it— the source of my anxiety. It was the, uh…male member, the penis, or the…*cock* as Paula so casually called it. None of my friends seemed to share my reservations. They talked about these strange, serpentine appendages as if they were no more intimidating than a zucchini. They'd each had multiple hands-on (even lips-on) encounters with them. Their experience broke down as follows:

Jody—3 penises encountered

Nancy—4 1/2 penises encountered (The 1/2 was more of a *sighting*. The first time, she'd been too afraid to actually touch it.)

Paula—1 penis, but many, many encounters

I had none! Nothing! Zip! Okay…that wasn't entirely true. Since I'd begun dating Todd four months ago, I had become quite familiar with his zucchini—sometimes uncomfortably so. It was always digging into my hip when we made out on the couch in his parents' basement, or poking me in the back of the thigh when I threw my legs across his lap while we watched a movie. A face-to-face meeting with it was inevitable, but up until now, whenever I heard the menacing crunch of zipper-teeth releasing, I suddenly remembered that I'd promised my mom I'd call her at ten.

I'd considered a support group. Surely I wasn't the only female out there who grew up with two younger sisters, an extremely modest father and a pronounced unfamiliarity with these alien life-forms? It would be like treating a fear of flying. They would ease us into it, probably starting us off touching a cucumber, eventually moving on to a dildo, and finally a real penis, but while wearing rubber gloves. I scoured the Yellow Pages. Quesnel offered no such counseling services. I would have to overcome this fear on my own.

And on that night, I vowed to do it. Nancy's house was full of empty bedrooms just made for teenage conjugal visits. Tonight, when things got hot and heavy, I would not excuse myself to phone home. I would face it head-on! I would be friendly to it, affectionate even, like it was nothing more sinister than a harmless garter snake. Who knew? If I had a few more of these kiwi coolers, I might even try Paula's patented tongue-flicking move. From the sounds drifting in from the living room, it had driven her boyfriend, Randy, wild.

Rejoining my friends, I handed Jody her cooler and sat cross-legged on the floor amongst them. Nancy was saying, "When I was going out with Wesley, he loved it when I was on top. But Gord prefers it doggie style."

"Yeah, Steve liked that, too," Jody said rather wistfully, referring to her ex-boyfriend.

Suddenly, Paula was looking at me. "What about Todd, Sherry? What's his favorite position?"

"Oh…well…" I took a big swig of kiwi cooler, stalling for time. I couldn't lie to my girlfriends on this momentous occasion, could I? Never again would we find ourselves together, marking the end of childhood and the beginning of our adult lives. Despite the fact that I had been alluding to a very satisfying sex life since shortly after Todd and I started dating, it would be better to be honest.

"You have done it with him, right?" Jody confronted me.

"Like, duh? Yeah, of course I have!" I blurted. Oops.

"So?" Paula persisted. "What's his favorite position?"

"Well…" I said, raising my eyebrows up and down suggestively. "He likes it any way he can get it!"

My friends laughed. They believed me. It wasn't because I was terribly convincing, it was because of Todd. While I was not one of the *cool* girls, Todd was definitely a cool guy— a bad boy, even. He was twenty-one years old, lean and lanky with a mop of sandy hair and smooth, tanned skin. His lazy smile and hooded eyes made him look perpetually stoned (I would eventually realize that he actually *was* perpetually stoned). Few people would have believed that Todd would be dating a virgin—well, not for long anyway.

Todd usually went out with the *cool* girls, those eyeliner-wearing, French fry-eating females who could give expert blow jobs by ninth grade and popped birth control pills in homeroom. We were an unlikely couple. I got good grades and was eager to head off to university. Todd had dropped out in grade eleven and worked at the pulp mill. But since that day he'd pulled up in front of the Dairy Queen in his noisy black 4x4 and stared at me with those dark, sexy eyes, I was putty in his hands. What he saw in me, I'm not sure— a challenge? A corrupting-the-good-girl fantasy? Whatever it was, I felt lucky to have his attentions.

I really liked Todd. We didn't have many deep, meaningful conversations (he was the strong, silent type) but he was always nice to me, and surprisingly patient. And he was so sexy! Every time he looked into my eyes and smiled that slow, dangerous smile, I felt my groin heat up. I was incredibly attracted to him. Unfortunately, this didn't make his… *cock* any less intimidating.

But that was all about to end: the nerves, the anxiety, the lies… In fact, thanks to five—or was it six?—kiwi coolers, I was actually looking forward to it! By tomorrow, I would be an entirely new person: a sexually experienced she-wolf, on friendly terms with the male member.

It was all planned. The guys would arrive around ten o'clock. The "guys" consisted of: Randy (Paula's boyfriend); Gord (a guy Nancy had been dating for a few weeks); Gord's friend Brent or Trent or something, who Nancy thought Jody might like; and, of course, Todd.

Randy, Gord and Trent/Brent arrived together at 10:02. They brought a case of beer and joined us in the living room. I knew Todd would come by himself. He didn't really hang out with high-school guys. At 10:20, just when I was beginning to feel like a seventh wheel, I heard the sound of his 4x4 pulling up out front.

I ran down the hallway to meet him at the door. The minute I laid eyes on him in his faded jeans and black AC/DC T-shirt, I wanted him. I was ready. I was confident. I was drunk enough to be uninhibited and extra sexy! Grabbing his belt loops, I pulled him toward me and kissed him passionately.

When I finally released him, he said, "Heyyyyy…" in a Fonzie sort of way. "Awesome."

"Come with me," I whispered, taking him by the hand and leading him to the basement and the nearest vacant bedroom. Once inside, I pushed him roughly onto the single bed, the springs squeaking under his weight. Then I pounced. We had made out many, many times before, but this was different. *I* was different. Straddling Todd, I moaned; I said things like "You make me so hot" and "I want you so much"; I tossed my hair in a frenzy of passion. It was very *Red Shoe Diaries* (I had watched an episode late at night on cable when I was babysitting my neighbors' kids). When Todd's AC/DC T-shirt had been removed and I feared he might burst through the denim of his jeans, I knew we had reached the pivotal moment. I moved south.

A sense of serene acceptance had come over me. Maybe it was the numbing effects of the alcohol, maybe it was manifest destiny, but I felt no fear. Todd's excited moans encouraged me as I reached for him, tentatively at first, and then more firmly. I could do this, I could definitely do this. I was going to let the snake out of its cage.

That's when it happened. My hand was gripping the metal tag of his zipper when my mouth suddenly began to water. I paused as a wave of dizziness swept over me. It would pass. It had to pass! This was *the* night. But no, it was not going away. The kiwi coolers had revolted! My stomach churned violently and I knew I had no choice but to flee.

"What the hell…?" Todd sat up as I burst from the room. Oh God. Oh God. Where was the bathroom? There were so many closed doors. Frantically, I chose one and stepped inside just as a torrent of sickly sweet, green liquid gushed from within me. It took only a few seconds to realize my mistake, but by then there was nothing I could do.

Two weeks after I puked in Nancy's mom's sauna, I left Quesnel. Todd was not there to see me off. To his credit, he did try to phone me a couple of times after *the night that never was,* but I avoided his calls. It had been a disaster of epic proportions, permanently damaging to my psyche. Thank God I was moving. I could make a fresh start. And surely I would find a nice guy in Vancouver to do the honors?

I didn't. Six years later, I am still keeping my virginity a secret from Jody—and everyone else for that matter. As the cab leaves the bridge, heading for the Granville Street club where Naomi will celebrate her birthday, I deflect my friend's interrogation. "Nothing's going on!" I say, forcing a laugh. "I'm just stressed out about work. I'll be fine once I have a drink."

God, I've got to get some action tonight. The dark cloud of virginity looming over my head is beginning to cause antisocial behavior!

As Jody resumes her diatribe, I smile and nod along. But my thoughts return, unbidden, to the path that led me here tonight, to my present mission.

Of course, there were others after Todd, boyfriends who helped me overcome my penis-phobia and maintain the illusion of a full-on sex life. But somehow, for some unexplained reason, these relationships were never fully consummated. God knows I tried, but fate seemed to be against me.

Exhibit B: If At First You Don't Succeed…

I thought for sure Thomas and I would do the deed. He was an engineering student with shoulder-length, wavy hair and piercing green eyes. We'd only dated for a few weeks but I was convinced he was the perfect choice for my first time: funny, sexy, and he smelled terrific. We nearly made it. Lying there, entwined on the tiny bed in my UBC dorm room, I felt certain I was poised on the brink of womanhood. That's when Thomas suddenly had an attack of conscience. "I can't do this," he said, crawling off me. Next thing I knew, he had buried his face in his hands and was weeping uncontrollably, muttering something about a girlfriend back home in Nova Scotia.

Exhibit C: Try Try Again

Then there was Stewart. Not quite as ideal a candidate as Thomas, but by this time I was twenty-two and quite a bit less picky. He still lived with his parents and worked at Blockbuster, but I had been impressed by his in-depth knowledge of festival movies. He was also good-looking and seemed to have excellent hygiene. I thought Stewart would do nicely…. That is, until he took his clothes off and I saw it. A thong! He was wearing a thong! And it was red! I couldn't go through with it. As much as I needed to get laid, I couldn't have my first time with a guy in a red thong. The therapy it would take to erase that image would cost thousands!

Exhibit D: And Again

My most recent failure was Ron. I'd met him just after Christmas, and he'd seemed so promising. He had a good job, an incredible body, and he owned his own condo. But when he took me to that condo and coaxed me (albeit very easily) into his bedroom, I was met with quite a shock. Adorning the walls were a number of framed photographs featuring Ron. There he was in a black Speedo, tanned a deep mahogany, his skin glistening with oil, flexing his enormous pecs. There he was again, arm raised at a perpendicular angle to highlight his bulging bicep, left leg bent to maximize his massive hamstring. "I was a competitive bodybuilder for three years," Ron explained as I stared at the photo featuring his frighteningly large lats.

I wasn't quite sure why it bothered me. So he was proud of his body—that was a good thing, right? *My first time was with a competitive bodybuilder,* I would one day tell my children. Well…maybe not, but still! It was no reason not to go through with it. But when we started making out, I found that I couldn't keep my eyes from darting from one pose to the next. Even worse, it seemed neither could Ron! We hadn't gone very far when I began to feel rather…irrelevant, almost like he didn't care if I was there at all. I couldn't go all the way with someone that narcissistic. I mean, if I had, would it even count?

Exhibit E: Tonight's the Night…

But tonight will be different. Tonight, I am going to find a man and I am *finally* going to have sex. I don't care if he has wavy hair, an in-depth knowledge of movies or his own condo. At this late stage, the criteria I look for in a sex partner has dwindled. Now, he need only meet a small but stringent set of requirements:

1. STD free (obviously)
2. Clean and nice-smelling
3. Reasonably attractive (at least not repulsive)
4. Nice, but not someone I could fall in love with

The last one is essential. I don't want to fall in love with the first guy I have sex with. It would be just my luck that we'd end up getting married. Ten years and a cou-ple of kids later I'd be full of regret, pining away for all the lovers I'd missed out on. No, I did not plan on be-coming obsessed with having intercourse twice in my lifetime.

The cab pulls up in front of the club and I lean across the front seat to pay. "I'll get the cab home," Jody says.

"Sure," I reply, though I am quite positive I won't be rid-ing home with her. Instead, I will be in the back seat of a taxi, necking ferociously with the lucky guy.

We find the birthday girl at a booth in the back, sur-rounded by balloons and well-wishers.

"Oh my God!" Naomi squeals, excited to see us.

After a big happy-birthday hug, I greet the other guests. I know most of them, except for the really cute guy sitting next to Naomi's brother.

"Vince," he says, standing up to shake my hand. Our eyes lock for just a moment too long.

That reminds me—I should add another item to my list of requirements.

5. Must not be a member of my social circle

I don't want him to casually mention to a mutual friend: "Yeah, I slept with Sherry a couple of weeks ago. I couldn't believe she was still a virgin." To which the mutual friend would reply, "That lying…virgin!"

"So… How do you know Naomi?" Vince asks.

"We met at university. You?"

"I'm a friend of Robert's," he says, referring to Naomi's brother. "We play hockey together."

"Oh," I say, nodding and smiling. While Vince is cute and friendly, I don't really have time to make idle chitchat with a guy I'm not going to have sex with. "Excuse me," I say. "I'm going to go grab a drink."

At the crowded bar I order a Corona and peer around the darkened club for tonight's sex partner. The bartender is a possibility, but he won't get off until two and I'm not sure I can wait that long. Drink in hand, I return to my group of friends, leaning against a patch of wall Jody has claimed. Just as Jody heads off to do a tequila shooter, I spot him.

He is tall, broad-shouldered and giving me *the eye*. He has that just-showered look, which makes him a strong candidate, given my affinity for good hygiene. Taking a sip of my Corona, I give him my best come-hither look. It works. He is moving toward me. Oh God. I am suddenly so nervous. Am I ready for this? I take a large swig of beer. What am I talking about? I've been ready for six years! I've got a purse full of condoms! Suddenly, a petite Asian girl in a tiny halter top sashays by. She catches my potential conquest's eye, and he veers off in her direction.

But something is wrong. I actually feel...*relieved*. What's going on? I should be disappointed! Chagrined! He could have been the one! What is my problem? Do I want to carry this burden around with me forever? Do I want to be thirty-two and still trying to find someone to have sex with me? Forty-six? Seventy-eight? At some point, this is going to get really difficult!

"Hey..." It's that cute Vince guy.

"Hi," I say, smiling brightly.

"Mind if I share your wall?"

We chat amiably. Since he has been disqualified as tonight's conquest (see #5 and maybe even #4) I feel at ease. Vince is like a safe haven—an attractive and funny safe haven, but definitely off-limits. I'll just talk to him for a little while until

I scope out another prospect. I mean, I don't want to seem too *predatory.* Through our lively conversation I learn that he is the marketing manager for one of the local ski hills, which fits perfectly with his outdoorsy, healthy good looks. Since I work in PR, we find we have several mutual colleagues. He's embarrassed to admit that his favorite movie is *Old School.* I tell him, "That's okay. Mine's *Zoolander.*" Last year, he broke his wrist snowboarding and now it aches when it's going to rain. He thinks I have the best laugh he's ever heard.

Suddenly, the lights go on. "Oh my God," I moan. "I can't believe it's already 2:00 a.m."

Jody appears at my side. "Let's go."

But I can't go! I was on a mission. I was finally going to relieve myself of the burden of my virginity! And I failed! Now it will haunt me forever, distracting me at work, scaring off potential suitors and forcing me to live a lie. I can't believe I squandered the whole night talking to a guy who I'm not going to have sex with. Stupid, stupid, stupid! I could almost cry.

"So…" Vince says tentatively. "It was really great talking to you. Do you think I could give you a call sometime?"

I reach into my purse full of condoms and dig for a pen. I write my number on a cocktail napkin and hand it to him. Taking a moment, I look up at the tall, attractive man with the warm brown eyes. And then, impulsively, I lean in and kiss him. "That would be great," I say flirtatiously.

Following my friend out of the club, I feel a small smile spread across my lips. Suddenly, I don't really care if I *am* the oldest virgin alive.

Sarah Mlynowski is the international bestselling author of *Milkrun, Fishbowl, As Seen On TV* and *Monkey Business*. She also wrote the teen novels *Bras & Broomsticks* and *Frogs & French Kisses,* cowrote the chick-lit how-to book *See Jane Write,* and co-edited the *USA TODAY* bestselling collection *Girls' Night In*. Originally from Montreal, she now lives and writes in New York City. Check out her latest chick-lit novel, *Me vs. Me,* available August 2006, and say hello at www.sarahmlynowski.com.

A Little Bit Broken
Sarah Mlynowski

I plant a sloppy kiss between Pete's neck and shoulder. "It'll be fine," I murmur. "You'll find another job."

Duke, his—our—mini schnauzer, nuzzles Pete's left foot.

Pete ignores him but says to me, "I know." He never snubs Duke. Losing his job on Friday was clearly still upsetting him.

"Come on, Pee-Pee," I say, and lean back onto my side of the couch.

The first time I heard his mother call for Precious, I thought she was referring to her Chihuahua. But no. Pete was Precious. Aka Precious Pete. Aka Pee-Pee when I was trying to be funny/endearing. "You're allowed to be upset about this, hon. Let's talk about it." Feeling wifely, I reach into the red plastic popcorn bowl, take a handful of kernels and feed him one.

"I'm not upset about it," he says, chomping. "It's not like I didn't know it was coming."

Ever since the small robotics company he worked for was

sold to a conglomerate, the clock was ticking until the original employees were given their thanks but no thanks.

"Right, but something is bothering you, so what is it?" We've been married six months, living together for a year, dating for a year before that. I am not fresh off the boat.

"I…" He pauses, closes his eyes then opens them again. He runs a hand through his short red hair. "Nothing."

I scoop up Duke, rest him on my stomach and stretch out my legs so that my sockless feet are resting on Pete's knees. "So something is the matter, but it's not work."

"Kind of."

"Now we're getting somewhere!" I sing, punching his thigh. "Hmm, okay, did your mom do anything especially infuriating?" That wouldn't be too surprising. She calls every night at seven-thirty. During dinner. Wanting to know what I'm cooking for Precious. Long Island is so not far enough away from Manhattan.

"No."

Uh-oh. "Did I do something?" I run through a mental list of Things I Occasionally Do That Annoy Him: let Duke sleep on our bed when he's out of town and I'm lonely; not call back his mother; not turn off the computer at night, which apparently allows viruses to breed on the hard drive.

Whoops. I committed all three sins this weekend while he was away at Corey's bachelor party. He always knows, too.

"Definitely not," he says, shaking his head.

So then what? "I know *something's* wrong. You might as well spill it."

He takes a deep breath. "You're not going to like it."

All right already. "Just tell me."

Blink, blink. "I…things got a little unsanitary at Corey's party."

I'm not quite sure what this means, but it doesn't sound ideal. Duke moans, apparently in agreement, then buries his nose in my armpit.

"Unsanitary, how?" I ask.

Pete's eyes dart nervously from my questioning glare to the window and then back to me. "There were strippers."

"No kidding." That's it? I reach for a handful of popcorn. I knew there would be strippers. I have nothing against stripping. I did Strip Aerobics at the gym once. The women have to make a living, right? Heart of gold, paying for school and all that. I mean, I wouldn't be thrilled if Pete was a strip club *regular,* but once or twice a year for a bachelor party won't kill him. Or me. I pull Duke back to my stomach with my free hand then scratch behind his ears. "I assumed there would be strippers at a strip club."

"Well…they weren't at the strip club. They came to the hotel suite."

My fingers feel hot. I stop scratching for fear of setting Duke on fire. "They? How many is they?"

Pete turns bright pink. Oh the troubles of being a redhead. "Four," he says slowly.

Now my wrists have caught fire. "Four strippers. You guys ordered four strippers to one hotel suite." Ordered as though they are a pizza. Four strippers, please! And don't forget the pasties!

"Yes."

"And you found this unsanitary." I am clenching both my hands. Unfortunately one of them is filled with popcorn.

"Yes."

My arms are burning up. My elbows, my shoulders. "Did you *do* something unsanitary?"

"Yes."

My neck, my face, my brain. "Did you sleep with a stripper?" I ask rather coolly, considering the now-scorching temperature of my throat and tongue.

He shakes his head while blinking rapidly. "No, I swear, I didn't. But I—I definitely crossed the line."

"What does that mean?"

The phone rings. And rings again. And rings a third time. Duke barks.

"Don't you dare answer that," I hiss. It's his mother. It's always his mother.

"I screwed up." He is looking at me, still blinking. His eyes are red and…teary? "There was touching involved."

"Touching? Of you?" I throw the popcorn from my now-damp hand at his lap.

"Yes."

Two kernels have engraved themselves into my palm. I concentrate on removing them while I ask, "By a stripper?"

"Yes."

"With her hands?"

"Yes."

"Just with her hands?"

He hesitates. "No."

The logistics of what took place finally dawn on me. No.

"Jessie, I am so, so sorry."

Duke barks again.

I on the other hand am speechless. How did this happen? I am clueless. What am I supposed to do? I am cold then hot, then cold then hot then sliced in half.

Break plates?

Break plates. Yes, that is what women in this situation do. I spot the box of white china from our wedding registry in the corner of our living room. It's under the leafy houseplant that Pete always waters because I never remember to. The dishes haven't been unpacked because we have nowhere to put them. We thought the whole china thing was a big crock, and couldn't pick a pattern, they all seemed so ugly, but then Pete blindfolded me in the store and spun me around and when I opened my eyes I was pointing to this set, so we took it.

Now I slice the tape with my thumbnail and throw open the flaps. I lift the top package, unwrap the white tissue paper and find a coffee saucer. I was hoping for at least a dinner plate, but this will do.

I throw it to the ground.

It teeters, and chips, but doesn't break. I pick it up off the floor, angle it and hurl it down a second time, using more arm muscle.

Pete winces as it shatters.

Mazel-tov to me! I am a woman who breaks plates! Well, coffee saucers.

I am reaching for the next dish when it occurs to me that I might have to return these plates if I divorce him. Won't I? We've only been married six months. It seems vaguely unfair for the guests not to get their money back. Can I fix the broken ones? I'm almost positive we don't have any glue and I doubt Scotch tape will put them back together. Worst-case scenario—I will have to subway up and down the city returning dishes in garbage bags. "Broken, just like their marriage," the dyed-blond yentas will say.

A car alarm goes off outside on Broadway. I cross my arms into a knot against my chest and prepare to scream. "We've been married six months, and you're already cheating on me!"

"I am so sorry," he whimpers. "I hate myself."

"You should! I hate you, too. Really. I can't stand you. I think you're repulsive. Have you no self-control? Did you not think about me at all?"

"It all happened quickly. One second they were stripping, and the next second she was…it was only for a few seconds, I swear. And then I stopped it."

"How many seconds is a few? Ten? Twenty? Sixty?" One Mississippi? Sixty Mississippis?

"Not a lot. Like twenty. Twenty-five tops."

One Mississippi.

Two Mississippi.

I count twenty-five silent Mississippis as I begin pacing the living room, managing to cross the room three and a half times during these so-called few seconds. "There is a line! One a married man isn't supposed to cross!"

"I know, I know. I didn't realize it until I crossed it."

"And what? Did everyone else see? Cheer you on?"

"No, no, I'm pretty sure no one else saw."

"How could no one else have seen? What were they doing? Watching HBO?"

"They were…occupied."

"Oh, right, I forgot there were three additional whores." I say the word like my mother would say, like *who-ers*. Suddenly all the politically correct good feelings I had toward strippers/working girls/whatever evaporates into my steamy skin. Making money for school, my ass. Heart of *plutonium*.

Two minutes and I'm already blaming the woman.

Oh, God, my mother. My mother, who threw my father out after she found his secretary's red lipstick on his collar. My mother, the painter, who was as insulted by the cliché as she was by the transgression. My mother who said Pete was a good choice—for a first husband. I can't tell my mother about this embarrassment. "I can't even look at you," I say. "You make me sick." I storm into our bedroom and slam the door. Take that!

"I make myself sick," he declares from the other side of the wall.

"I hope you don't think you're sleeping in here tonight!"

"I'll do whatever you want me to do. I love you. And I hate myself for having done this. I'm a moron. It will never happen again, I swear. Where should I sleep?"

"You shouldn't sleep! You should stay up all night repenting what you've done!" I press the lock on the door to make my point. "Sleep on the couch."

"Okay. I'm sorry."

"You ruined everything. What we had was perfect. I hope you appreciate the magnitude of your actions."

I back away from the door and climb into bed, fully dressed. I reach under my shirt, unclasp my bra and throw it to the floor. I take out my contacts and leave them to shrivel up on my night table.

Then I realize that the stupid lights are still on, so I have to get up again and turn them off.

When I'm back in bed, I squint at the alarm clock and see that it's only nine-thirty.

Pete is moving around the living room.

Duke scratches at the door, and as much as I want to let him in, I don't want to see Pete, so I don't. Even though Duke's official doggie bed is behind the couch, he usually winds up sleeping on the rug at the foot of our bed. Or in the bed if Pete is out of town. Duke moans, and I hear Pete tiptoe into the kitchen to find the dog a treat.

Chomp, chomp, chomp.

One Mississippi, two...

I think about all the details I collected tonight and realize the one I missed: What kind of man did I marry?

My knees shake. My head pounds. My eyes burn. I close the latter to make it all go away. Ah, denial. The first stage of grief.

I wake up at five-thirty. Then remember. Stab through the heart. What am I going to do? I creak open the door and peer into the living room. Pete is asleep on the couch, the purple throw blanket (from our wedding registry, *'natch*) covering his head.

I am the type of woman whose husband cheats on her at a bachelor party.

I am the type of woman who makes her husband sleep on the couch.

I am the type of woman who…kicks her husband out?

Three car horns honk in succession. I don't know how he's managing to sleep until I see the pack of earplugs on the glass coffee table.

I shower, get dressed all in black to reflect my mood, and then try to make a quick exit. But when I pass the living room, he's sitting up and giving me his wet and wide-eyed hopeful look, the one Duke imitates when he spots the leash.

"Can we talk?" Pete asks, pleading.

"There's nothing to talk about," I say, and pick up my purse.

"Of course there is. I'm so sorry. Jessie, I—"

I hold up my hand to stop him. "You should go to a doctor. In case you have syphilis." I slam the door behind me.

Delete. Delete. Delete.

What can his e-mails possibly say to undo any of this?

Becca, the pregnant and gossipy secretary, buzzes to tell me I have a delivery. The moron sent me flowers, I know it. Pathetic. As if I want his sniveling daisies. He knows I hate flowers. Wasting energy cutting the stems, finding a vase, filling the vase with water. When they're only going to die in two days, anyway. I graciously rise from my cube to accept my delivery.

It's a package of forms from the head office of my consulting company.

Jerk. He could have *at least* sent flowers. Perhaps even jewelry. No, that's too pathetic. I would never wear a bribe ring. Even if it was a diamond.

Although I could use new earrings.

No, no, no! One Mississippi, two Mississippi, three Mississippi.

I plop back onto my chair and swivel. The client I'm consulting at the moment makes boxes. I've been helping them come up with corporate strategies to (groan) box out the competition, but my stint here is almost done. Two more weeks and I'll be on the beach until the head office finds somewhere to staff me. Pete and I were planning on sneaking away for some sun and sex during my break.

One Mississippi, two Mississippi, three Mississippi.

Yesterday's dinner creeps up and I bolt to the bathroom and puke in the handicapped stall. Nausea should be one of those grief stages. Denial, nausea, anger, bargaining, depression, acceptance?

And what does acceptance mean in this situation? Accept him back? Accept that I wasted two and a half years of my life?

When I step out from the stall, Becca is applying lipstick. "I know what that means," she says, rubbing her belly. "You can tell me, I won't say a word."

Oh God. Hardly. And since I just finished my period last Friday, and we haven't had sex since, it's pretty much impossible. As I wash my hands, I coax myself into smiling. In the mirror, I can see that my lips have confused smiling with what they do when I'm twisting off a bottle cap with my teeth.

I hurry back to my cube to stare at my screen. It could be worse. I could be pregnant. I've been planning on going off the Pill soon. To start trying. Lately, whenever I pass BabyGap, Pete pretends he gets a *ping!* in his stomach and we go inside and try on baby bonnets. Pete looks best in the baby blue farm animal chambray hat. He prefers me in the floral bucket safari bonnet. Eventually a salesperson glares at us and we depart for ice cream. Then we debate the order of our three children (boy, girl, girl; girl boy, boy; boy, boy, girl?). They would all have his height, his thick red hair, his big smile, my blue eyes and my olive skin. He likes to tease me that they'd all be short like me and freckled and hairy like him.

How can the father of my theoretical babies be a cheating bastard? That's not what I signed up for. What am I going to do with him?

From: Jessica@Wzzmail.com
Sent: Wednesday, June 07, 2006 3:50 PM
To: Pete Blumenthal
Subject: You
I think you should stay somewhere else tonight.

When I return to our apartment, I smell Duke's discontent. He has peed all over the rug.

"Bad dog," I scold. "Bad, bad dog." Bad husband. Bad, bad husband.

I cry, wash my face, then take Duke out for a walk, ignoring the ringing phone.

Pete calls ten times, leavings ten messages. Instead of phoning him back, I watch all the sad movies I own on DVD. *Ghost, Terms of Endearment, Titanic.*

Leonardo would have never done something so…unsanitary to Kate Winslet. Although what do I know? Since there was gambling and booze on the boat, there were probably wenches.

The phone rings during the closing scene when Kate is about to throw the diamond into the ocean.

I miss him, I think, and almost pick up. But the call display says it's Sandra Blumenthal, Pete's mother.

I can just imagine the conversation. *You're having pizza… again? I thought you were watching your weight, Jessica. Precious always loved the meat loaf I used to make him.*

I stop the movie. I need to get out. I take Duke, stop at a bodega to buy a pack of Camel Lights and go to the dog park. Then I light up. As soon as I inhale I cough terribly, mostly because I don't smoke. I tried it when I was thirteen because my girlfriends told me to. This is the first time I've ever bought my own pack. I chose Camels because their ads make me giddy. Sunglasses on a camel, ha! I call Ann from my cell. "Pete cheated on me," I blurt out before she bothers with pleasantries.

Her gasp terrifies me. Since Ann is a hairstylist in Soho, she has heard pretty much everything. Shocking her isn't a small feat. "Shit," she says. "Meet us at Sweet and Vicious."

By the time I finish my cigarette, drop Duke at home and find a cab, Ann and Megan are comfortably seated at our booth, drinks already on the table.

I rehash the story.

"What an ass-wipe," Ann says, shaking her pixie cut. "Next."

I almost swallow my tongue at her choice of expression. *Next* is our code for move on. *Next* is what she told me after I waited by the phone for two weeks for Jake, aka Bald Guy, to actualize his "I'll call you later." *Next* is what we said when The Actor told Ann she should cut down on the blue cheese and join a gym. *Next* is what we said when Megan caught The Smooth Talker peeing in her shower.

But *next* about a husband is uncharted territory.

"You deserve better," Ann states. "Cut him loose." She makes like a scissors with her middle and index fingers.

The room sways and I sip my martini to steady myself. "Is it possible it was a mistake?" It could have been a mistake, I tell myself. I can live with one mistake. Hello, bargaining stage. If he never does it again, he can come home.

"If he's making that kind of mistake after six months, what will he be up to after ten years?" Ann asks. "Keeping a second family in Connecticut?"

Oh, right.

Megan gives Ann a dirty look and reaches over to squeeze my hand. The tips of her nails are painted a perfect white, and they remind me of my box of mostly intact wedding china. I don't know how she keeps them so clean when she's running after six-year-olds all day at school. "It could have been a mistake," she says. "People make mistakes." Megan's current boyfriend, Nicholas, is a workaholic investment banker, and Megan is skilled at apologizing for why he's always standing her up.

"I don't." Not those kind of mistakes.

"You've never stuck around long enough to make them," Megan says softly.

"Excuse me?"

"You broke it off with Zach when he got transferred—"

"I'm not good with long-distance relationships!"

"And you bailed on Graham because of a so-called lack of passion—"

"I wasn't going to stay with someone I wasn't attracted to!"

"But you barely even gave it a try! Relationships take work."

"I got married, didn't I?" I turn to Ann. "Do you believe this?"

"No, I don't," she says, slamming her fist on the table. "This is not Jessie's fault. Stop making her feel guilty. She should be pissed. She can't forgive him. People don't change. If he did it once, he'll do it again."

"You don't know that!" Megan snaps. "They have a solid relationship. She shouldn't throw it all away because of one screwup. He was in a bad place. He got *fired* that day, for Christ's sake. Pete is a great guy."

Ann waves her away. "A great guy doesn't cheat."

Megan sighs. "He didn't really cheat. Only a little bit. And doesn't he get points for telling her?"

"Not enough to make up for the points he lost," I say.

"Relationships are about compromise, okay?" she says, her voice fever pitched. "My parents have been married for forty years. And they're happy. They work at it every day."

"So your dad does the nasty with strippers?" I trace my finger around the rim of my glass, and around again. I wish it was last week and my life was still intact.

"Jessie," she says in her teacher voice. "No one knows what *really* goes on behind closed doors except the husband and wife."

Ann snaps her fingers. "I know what will make you feel better. You'll come with Megan and me to the Hamptons next weekend."

Ann and Megan have a twice-a-month house share in Sag Harbor.

Megan nods. "Excellent idea."

"It's the hot lawyer's weekend, too," Ann adds. "He'll make you forget you've ever been married."

"Ann, please. She needs our company, not some random guy's. Nicholas is hoping to come up, too, if he can get away from the crazy deal they have him on—"

"Thanks, ladies, but I can't, it's Corey's wed…" My words evaporate in midsentence, and I get angry all over again. "Sounds like a plan."

He calls me in the middle of the night. I pick up.

"I was worried about you. Can I come home? I miss you."

"No."

"Please? I'm sorry."

"No."

"But…you hate sleeping alone."

"I hate you more. Don't come home tomorrow, either." Back to anger again.

Duke nuzzles my chin. I hang up and unplug the phone.

On Thursday, I continue ignoring Pete's phone calls and e-mails. What am I going to do? Kick him out for good? Try to get over it? What's the right choice?

On the way home, I realize that our mailbox has probably overflowed, since Pete's the one who takes care of collecting our letters.

Bills, bills, bills. Plus request packages for Pete from the

ACLU, from NY Harvest and from something called The Wall of Peace. Pete is on every nonprofit list in the world. Once a week, he sits down at the kitchen table, reads through all the solicitations and decides where to donate. He is often swayed by free, thoughtful gifts such as printed return-address stickers. "They get an A for effort," he says as he writes them a check.

I order pizza and watch a *Law & Order* marathon. I feel bloated and dirty and I cry every time the late Briscoe has to tell someone that their loved one has died. I think I'm depressed. Stage four already? Wahoo.

The phone rings at seven-thirty sharp. The caller display says unknown name and I foolishly pick up.

"Hello?"

"Jessica? Is that you?"

Holy crap, Pete's mother has learned to block her number. If Pete was that smart he might have gotten me on the phone.

If Pete was that smart, he wouldn't have cheated on me.

"Yes, Sandra, it's me. How are you?"

"I'm fine. How are you? Busy, I assume, since you haven't had time to call back your poor mother-in-law."

I so don't feel like dealing with this now. "Yes, work is busy."

"You modern women. Trying to do it all." Sweet Sandra is still bitter that I didn't take her son's name.

"That's us," I say.

"We just finished my lamb chops. What are you having for dinner?"

Sigh. "Pizza."

"Oh, really? Again?"

"Yup." How does her husband stand her? How how how?

"Well, I'm glad you're all right, dear. If I'm not interrupting, can I speak to Precious?"

"Pete isn't here."

"Oh, poor boy, is he working late again?"

A balloon of anger begins to expand between my lungs. "No. He's at a friend's."

"So late? Why?"

"Because."

"Because why?"

"It's personal," I squeak through my highly constricted chest.

She clucks her tongue. "I'm only his mother."

The balloon explodes. "He got a blow job from a stripper at Corey's bachelor party, so I kicked him out."

Silence. Finally.

"If you don't mind," I say, suddenly cheerful. "I'd like to finish my dinner now."

I pretend to work, but my anger returns and increases exponentially. Am I going to wait around until he's screwing his secretary? Until I'm star sixty-nining the hang-ups? Until I'm saddled with stretch marks and a household of screaming kids and he tells me he's not fulfilled?

Divorce, I key into Google. There are 14,400,000 hits, and I feel a wave of mild anxiety, which leads to full-blown panic.

Is that what I have to do? Will I need a lawyer? My mother had a lawyer. My father had a lawyer. Not that Pete and I have anything to divide since we own nothing but the dishes from our wedding registry.

Of course, he'd get Duke. He loves that dog. Megan didn't want to set us up because of the beloved dog.

"You don't understand. He lives for that dog. He broke up with his last girlfriend because she thought he smelled funny."

"Pete or the dog?"

She groaned. "The dog."

I agreed that dogs were smelly. But I had met Pete at a friend's birthday and thought he was cute. "Come on, fix us up. I've always wanted to date a redhead. They're just so cute. We can't let a little thing like an animal get in the way."

"That's the point. Pete doesn't see Duke as just a pet. He's his everything. His family."

With my two parents, one ex-stepparent, two stepparents, two siblings, three half siblings and four stepsiblings, I considered myself stocked up on family members. But still. Cute boy trumped smelly dog.

Pete brought Duke on our first date. He also brought cupcakes and red wine, and we sat on the grass in the park. Pete took off his sweatshirt, and then his sandals, and stretched out his toes. I liked that his arms were built, though pale and freckled. Later, Pete showed me how to throw a football.

"Come on, Dukey, let's show her how it's done."

When we were resting, Duke inched his way onto my lap. Pete complimented the dog on his good taste. And I fell in love with them both.

When I get home, the workweek finally over, Pete is in the lobby of our building, scratching behind Duke's ears. The air feels too thin.

"I came to walk him," he explains. "And to talk to you."

"I have nothing to say." I push past him to the stairs but he follows me up the five flights.

"Aren't we worth talking about?" he asks at the third floor.

"I thought we were. You apparently don't think we're worth more than…I don't know, what do *who-res* charge these days? A hundred bucks? Fifty for just touching?"

"I made a mistake. A horrible mistake. But ending this… ending us…that would be a bigger mistake."

My hands tremble as I reach into my purse for the key. "Don't blame me for your screwup."

"I love you," he claims, and makes a grab for my hand.

I shake him off. "You have a stupid way of showing it." As I turn the lock, my arms feel like bags of sand. Eyelids like glue. It suddenly occurs to me how exhausted I am. As if I haven't slept in weeks. I don't have the energy to get through this. I want him to go away so I can lie down, pull the covers over my head and drown.

Duke scurries into the apartment and I look up at Pete, feeling raw and empty. "I want you to move out."

He whips his head away from me, like my words are a blast of winter air and he needs to shield his face.

"I don't love you anymore," I say, mostly to hurt him, but also because I'm hoping saying so will make it true. I slam the door.

Acceptance.

Next.

I spend the weekend in a haze. I e-mail Pete that I'd like him out by next weekend. It's my apartment after all. He's not even on the lease. We were saving up, putting away a little bit each month, hoping that maybe we'd be able to buy something in the city. In about fifteen to twenty years. Pete liked to collect our spare quarters in the bag of change he kept near the spice rack, which he called our Ziploc Future.

I offer to keep Duke until he's settled. I almost offer to

get him free boxes from work, but I decide he should have to suffer and beg at the wine store down the street.

I go to a work function on Tuesday night, and drink too much on an empty stomach. Back home, I spend the night puking in the bathroom. At least the seat hasn't been left up. Stupid Pete. Just before passing out, I recall the time last year when I actually fell into the toilet.

I wake up at seven the next morning, the lines of the purple bath mat that we bought on our first "We're Living Together!" shopping spree stamped into my cheek and forehead. I shower, get dressed. Go. I get off the subway because I think I'm going to be sick again, but I dry heave into the garbage.

"Excuse me," says a homeless man. "Can you spare a thousand dollars? I could really use some liposuction." I almost laugh, so I give him a five. An A for effort.

You're going to miss him, I think. Of course I'm going to miss him. But that's hardly the point.

I return to the platform and wait for the subway. One Mississippi, two Mississippi...

It's Saturday. I am in the Hamptons, sitting on an old beach towel, pretending to chat with Megan, Ann and the two tanning Manhattanite men who are also up at the beach house this weekend.

One of them, a lawyer who's at least six foot three, has been trying to get my attention all day, and at first I pretended I was asleep so I wouldn't have to deal with him. But now I am sitting up and smiling and smiling and smiling as though my husband isn't currently packing his belongings and then going to a wedding without me, as though the ring that I wore every day, the ring that I was constantly terrified of accidentally leaving behind at a public restroom, the ring that had belonged to his grandmother, is still on my finger, and not back in its blue velvet box, next to Duke's toys, all soon to be taken away by my soon-to-be ex-husband.

While Corey is somewhere else getting married, I am at a bar becoming a dancing machine. I am sweating, I am shaking my head. I am even doing the YMCA. I haven't danced like this since the hora at my own wedding.

Tall Guy is cute. And tall. Very tall. A giant. Potential rebound guy? He moves closer to me, placing his hand on the small of my back.

His slimy hand. Oversize, sweaty, bony, wrong hand.

I excuse myself to the bathroom, sit on the closed toilet seat and cry.

My cell phone rings, and I pick up, hoping it's Pete.

"You're going to get over him," Ann says. I open the stall and she's leaning by the sink.

"I know," I say. But I don't know if I want to.

Back in the city, a moving van is double-parked in front of my building. On the third floor, I collide with Pete, who is holding a large lamp I didn't even realize we had.

"Hi," he says, his face dripping with sweat. "I only have one more box."

"All right," I say, attempting to swallow the razor-sharp lump in my throat. He's leaving. Pete is actually moving out. This is it. I continue climbing up to the apartment. My one-box-from-Pete-less apartment.

Duke leaps at me when I go inside. I see the one box Pete's talking about. And then I see the dog toys, the food, the bowl. All things Duke.

I stand frozen until I hear and feel Pete behind me. "Last one, Jessie," he says.

"What about Duke?" I ask, not turning around. "You forgot his stuff."

"Well…I just thought…after what I did…I know you hate sleeping alone." His voice cracks. Duke runs over to him and barks. "Be good, Dukey," he whispers.

He's giving me his dog? His everything?

I hear the slop-slop of Duke licking Pete's face. The cars honking outside. The blood pulsing in my ears.

Am I willing to listen to him? To try? Can a relationship be Scotch-taped back together? Do people make mistakes?

What comes after grief?

I say, "I think we should talk."

I turn around, and see that he is crouched down and looking up at me, first with surprise and then wide-eyed and hopeful.

He nods, slowly, and then stands up, closing the door behind us.

Elizabeth Buchan read for a double degree in English and history at the University of Kent at Canterbury. She began her career as a blurb writer for Penguin Books and later became a fiction editor at Random House. After a couple of years, she decided that she should do what she wished to do: write. Since then, she has written nine novels: *Daughters of the Storm, Light of the Moon, Consider the Lily, Against Her Nature* (which reworked Thackeray's *Vanity Fair* set against a backdrop of the Lloyd's disasters during the 1980s), *Secrets of the Heart, Revenge of the Middle-Aged Woman* (a *New York Times* bestseller that has sold all over the world and was made into a television film for CBS starring Christine Lahti), *The Good Wife Strikes Back* and *Everything She Thought She Wanted*. Her latest novel, *Wives Behaving Badly*, is a sequel to *Revenge of the Middle-Aged Woman*.

She reviews for the *Sunday Times* and the *Daily Mail*. Her short stories have appeared in various magazines, including *Good Housekeeping*, and have been broadcast on BBC Radio 4.

Find out more about Elizabeth and her books at www.elizabethbuchan.com.

Kindness
Elizabeth Buchan

At Rome airport, Sable Farrer climbed into a coach labeled "Euro Culture 'n' Fun Ltd." She was dressed in her customary muted way—a matching knitted caramel-colored sweater and skirt that could have been elegant but on Sable looked dull and lumpy. Already, the outfit felt far too hot.

As usual, she kept her head down. This was, in part, due to her terror of being noticed but, as she had grown older, in part a deepening desire not to look at things too closely. The world did not, in her view, bear too much examination. Nevertheless, she knew perfectly well that several pairs of inquisitive, speculative eyes would be sizing her up.

She manhandled her hand luggage to the back of the coach and slipped into an empty double seat. "I wish more than anything I was not in this bus," she thought. "I wish I was not in Rome." Above all, Sable wished she was not scheduled to endure a week in the company of strangers.

Yet, in a moment of uncharacteristic impulse, and on a depressing winter's day in the office where she worked as a billing clerk for a utility firm, this was precisely what she had chosen to do and, furthermore, *paid* for. Why? Outside had been rain-lashed, her stomach had been a little bilious and she had discovered the pamphlet advertising the trip in her in-tray. She remembered its thin, glossy texture as she held it between her fingers. *We promise you marvelous things,* it seemed to say.

The coach jerked forward and Sable clutched at her tote bag, which toppled over. A woman in the opposite seat reached over to help and said, "I had no idea it would be so much warmer than home. It's only April, after all."

Sable waited for the woman's gaze to fixate on the lower part of her face, which she knew from thirty-five years of experience would take approximately ten seconds. (She could see *What happened to her?* slide like news tape across the mind of any observers.) Sable almost never satisfied their curiosity. It was nobody's business but her own as to what had turned her mouth from the pretty, childish pink bow it once had been, into the twisted thing that marred her adult face. Equally, since she had no family, not even a cousin, there was no one who could supply chatty asides such as, "Of course, Mary was heartbroken by what happened" or "It was just one of those things" or any other nuggets of information to anyone who was interested. As far as most people were concerned, Sable was a blank sheet. Puzzling, but definitely blank. That was the way she preferred it and, occasionally, when someone proved too curious, too invasive with their questions, she could be quite ferocious in her rejection. A psychologist might have concluded that Sable was allowing a trick of fate to cut her off from full participation in reciprocal relationships. Sable would have replied, "It's none of your business. No one has the right to know what goes on inside me."

The woman opposite looked taken aback at the lack of response and Sable made an effort. "Yes, it is surprising" (which was not the case for they were in Italy). She pitched her tone to suggest she was willing to be polite but had no interest in continuing the conversation. It was a neutral tone, as neutral as Sable had schooled herself to appear. Rebuffed, the woman settled back into her seat and concentrated on the view.

It was early evening. The traffic clotted the roads and progress was inch by inch. "To your right is an example of *Cypressa sempervirens,* the Italian cypress…" droned the tour guide who had introduced himself as Paddy, "the man on whom you must rely." In the becalmed coach, Sable stared hard at a slender, green exclamation mark of a tree that had been planted on a roundabout. Didn't *sempervirens* mean "to live forever"? This did not strike her as a welcome proposition.

In the foyer of the Merry Bacchus Hotel, a bald modern building so ugly Sable felt like crying out in protest, Paddy issued them with instructions, including the exhortation to appear at seven-thirty sharp for dinner. As she hoped, no one spoke to Sable as she hauled her luggage up to the tenth floor and into a room from which all individuality had been carefully—and successfully—planned out by the architect. She swept back the curtains from the plate-glass window, sat down on her bed and watched the traffic roar up the Via Aurelia, which snaked past on the way into Rome's center. With a bit of luck, she could contrive not to speak to anyone much for the entire trip. After that, she would return

home to the flat on the housing estate and the office in the
utilities firm, and drop back into her routine and out of
sight.

The following morning, Sable ate breakfast with her eyes
fixed on the sugar bowl on the table. She must have counted
the packets in it at least ten times. Her silence and hunched
shoulders did not go unnoticed and when the group assem-
bled (many of them breathing out the fumes of strange coffee overlarded with toothpaste) for the morning's outing,
Paddy drew her aside and asked, "Is everything in order?"
Sable now riveted her gaze on Paddy's feet, which were
shod in suede lace-ups, the kind she considered that only
cads wore. "Everything's fine," she replied. "Quite fine."
Paddy was too harassed to take it further. He had done his
duty and moved swiftly on to question a fit-looking couple
dressed in matching green shorts and polo T-shirts.

Very quickly, it became apparent that Euro Culture 'n' Fun
was a tour company that believed in quantity as opposed to
quality. To this end, it floated the sights of Rome as fast as
possible past its clients, so neatly captive in the coach. The
itinerary was rapid and furious. "To your right," Paddy
crooned through the microphone, "is the Palatine Hill, home
of the Roman emperors." He threw in the additional sop.
"Up ahead is the Coliseum."

"Can you tell us about the gladiators?" A man three rows
ahead was curious. "Do you know any details?"

"Yup, that's where the gladiators fought," said Paddy.

This, clearly, was to be the sum total of information he
was going to grant the group and, with a blare of its horn,
the coach accelerated and as to what the Coliseum was, or
had been, was left to private conjecture.

In this manner, Rome slid past in a blur…Pantheon, Piazza Navona, St. Peter's, the Tiber—color, shape, smells melting into one another, nothing distinct, nothing sharp—much as Sable, on her bad days, hoped that her own life would pass—in fact, was passing. *Soon I'll be thirty-six, then forty, then forty-five…and it will all be over.* In this respect, the holiday suited her very well.

"Day three," declared Paddy on day three, "is our villa day, ladies and gentlemen. We take a break from the city in order to enjoy the delights of the country around the capital." He herded them into the coach and they were driven up into the hills at Tivoli. Formerly an ancient playground for wealthy Romans, the town scrambled up the slope, offering a cool, summer retreat from the baking plain and relief from the stew and swelter of the streets. Later, in the sixteenth century, it provided a playground for the rich (and no doubt) spoiled cardinal who had built the Villa d'Este and laid out its fabled garden.

Still, the cardinal had possessed great taste, concluded Sable, intrigued despite herself by the beautiful sight lines of the garden, which was constructed on several levels, and by the ingeniousness of the fountains. And she wondered more than a little about a man of God who had been so enamored of the good things of the world that he had devoted such energy to them. Surely the cardinal should have been concentrating on the next?

Perhaps it was fatigue, perhaps it was the rebellion of the overshepherded, but the group displayed a tendency to fragment and to wander in different directions. "Over *here,*" cried Paddy more than once. "Over here." Under her unsuitable jersey jumper and skirt, Sable felt the sweat force its way from her armpits down her body. It was so warm, hot even, and the smell of jasmine mingling with dust and new growth, so very invasive. Its sweetness, its suggestion of heat and languor, were unsettling. Sable's nerve endings were quivering with feelings and yearnings with which she was unfamiliar, and for which she had no explanation.

She made her way to one of the larger fountains and sat down on the marble lip that surrounded the pool and willed herself to think of nothing very much. It was cool here and, if she remained quite still, she could imagine herself merging into the background of green box and oleander. Merging so completely until she, too, turned into a shade from the past, like those men and women who used to walk up and down these paths in their rich, colorful garments talking and laughing, plotting and planning. If that happened, if Sable faded into nothing, became merely a memory, then everything would be over: all the grief and boredom and disappointment of being what she was. *Why am I thinking like this?* But she knew why. If Sable was truthful, if she dug right down into the dark of her subconscious and looked properly at the mysteries that lurked there, she would find anger. *I am angry that I have not been bolder and braver about myself.*

Sometimes, in her better moments, she planned to make changes. Of course she did. "One day," she promised herself, "I will take myself by the scruff of the neck, give myself a good shake. Instead of looking at a glass and perceiving it as half-empty, I will declare it half-full."

That would be a sensible, positive attitude to life.

Then (ran her fantasies), a new Sable would emerge: a bright, confident woman who would say things such as: My mouth? I *never* think about it.

"I'd say, Dora, that she's had plastic surgery…" said a voice, and continued with a triumphant inflection, *"which went wrong.*" It was a rich voice, full of humor and dark velvety tones. If one had to describe it as metaphor, this voice was a fruitcake stuffed with cherries and raisins.

Sable stiffened.

"Rubbish, Margaret. She doesn't look the type. Still, you can never tell." This second voice lilted: it ran like a stream, lighthearted and almost girlish.

"Haven't you seen the ads in the magazines? You can have your bottom rebuilt if you wish. If you are prepared to pay enough."

"My bottom?" reflected Dora of the lilting voice. "They'd have a job."

"Girls nowadays don't know if they're supposed to be mothers or that Jo-Lo person. I pity them. Very confusing. Paddy says you can't get a word out of her."

"Plastic surgery." Dora sounded both amused and perplexed. "I wonder what she asked for? Lips like my settee?"

"It didn't matter what she asked for, it's what she got that's the problem."

Sable turned her head in order to identify the speakers. But she already had a suspicion. And yes, it was the two women who always bagged the front seats in the coach. They wore brightly colored cotton shirts and trousers in which they seemed completely comfortable and straw hats. They had capacious handbags and guidebooks they read out loud to each other. On the return to the Merry Bacchus the previous evening, they had led the coach party in a group sing-along—"Summer Holiday." They had sung the words with gusto and swayed from side to side, and Dora had seized the microphone in order to whip up a response from the rest. "Come on," she admonished, looking straight at Sable on her back seat. "Everyone join in."

It went without saying that this Dora and her friend, Margaret, were talking about her. Or rather, the mouth— Sable had reached the stage when she could not think of it as "her" mouth, for it had a life of its own. This discreet, separate existence to which Sable played host was an insoluble conundrum, for wherever and whenever she strove to make herself as inconspicuous as possible, she found herself continually thrust into the spotlight of speculation.

This is what Sable imagined.

No, not imagined. At work, or on a station platform, queuing for tickets at the cinema, she knew the disaster of her face always triggered speculation. But why was the urge so strong in people for explanations? For her part, she had no interest as to why Mrs. Whatson next door was seen frequently stuffing empty whiskey bottles into the refuse bin. Or in the rumor that her boss, Damien, was probably having an affair with his assistant. It was no one's business but theirs, and Sable respected the boundaries. Grief and love were private. Feelings were private, and not to be shared. Everyone was alone. Everyone was an island. And that was that.

But she knew, she well knew, that she *was* an object of pity, conjecture, malice even. On those better-moment days, she wondered if she might be—just—developing a sense of humor about the subject. But on the cold, despairing days, she shook with rage and humiliation at the way these chatterers and speculators helped themselves to her story without her permission *and got it wrong.*

The two women moved in the direction of where Sable was perched. Their shirts were loose and bright, and so *appropriate* in the sunlight, their cheeks and arms were sheened with sweat, their feet sensibly shod. They were making no concessions toward beauty or fashion and they wore smiles of complete enjoyment.

Margaret transferred her capacious bag from one shoulder to the other, and plumped down on the rim of the fountain. Dora followed suit, and they sat closely together, with the intimacy of friends who knew each other through and through, and Sable heard: "You'd better ask her, Dora, then we can sort it out. *Was it plastic surgery?*"

Sable looked down at her reflection in the water. Somehow (a trick of the refraction?) the scar was not so obvious and a watery portrait of a woman with large and rather beautiful eyes stared back at her. *A bold, bright confident person?*

All around, the warmth was insistent and the sweet scents of spring and growth beguiled.

She opened her mouth and from it issued words that had been rarely uttered. "If you must know," she said, "it was my mother."

The two women whipped round and Sable had the satisfaction of witnessing the color storm into their cheeks.

"Yes," she continued. "My mother was a failed actress but she liked to keep her hand in. She was demonstrating to my father just what Lady Macbeth should have done with the knife and, unfortunately, I was in the way. It must have been a vicious swipe but I was too young to judge."

"Oh," said Dora.

Margaret was quite silent. Red, but silent.

"She died not long after," added Sable.

Dora's hand flew to her own mouth. "What a terrible story."

"It's funny," said Sable, "how wrong you can get things."

More silence.

"I didn't ask for it," said Sable, who was experiencing an extraordinary sensation. Inside her, a tap was gushing forth, rather like the fountain behind her, and she wondered how on earth she was going to stop it. "And for your information, I have had two operations to put it right, but it won't *go* right, and I am stuck with it." She plucked at her skirt. "People think they can talk about it as if they owned my problem. But they don't."

It was Margaret who collected herself first. "No, they don't," she said. "And even if they did, they have other things to think about."

"*You* were talking about me."

"We were." Margaret placed a hand on Sable's knee. She was plump and determined but, on more detailed inspection, a kind-looking woman. "But only because you've let your mouth spoil your looks."

And Sable heard herself exclaim. "*What* looks?"

She felt the weight of the other woman's good intentions and flinched. That she hated more than anything: kindliness bestowed as a duty—as a form of moral obligation.

But Margaret appeared bent on an instant crusade: to put Sable right. "You've got it wrong, love," she said. "Now that I can assess you properly, I can hardly see anything noticeable. Anyway, you should look up. Then we can see your eyes."

She took Sable by the arm and made her turn around to face the fountain, which was composed of several marble figures—a god, a couple of nymphs, a flying dolphin—over which the water arced and flowed.

Attended by a few loyal stragglers, Paddy came into view. "This fountain here has been extensively restored…." He paused, gesticulated irritably in the direction of the three women, and then moved on. "Now, if you would look to your right…"

"*Do* look up, love," insisted Margaret in a voice dripping with plums and satiny warmth. Sable considered flight. She considered flinging herself into the fountain. But actually what Sable did was to raise her eyes. "Go on," said Margaret. "See that little nymph."

As Paddy had pointed out, the cracks and repairs to the figures were obvious. They were particularly marked on the face of the smaller nymph who crouched at the feet of the god bearing a triton. Whereas her larger sister was untouched and glowed with a frozen, somewhat cruel, beauty, this one's nose had crumbled, and a chunk had fallen out of her chin. Her face was half shielded from the onlookers and yet, thought Sable, and yet the expression on the marble features was of a quiet, and secret, humor. *Too bad,* that expression said. *I don't mind. I have what I have. I know what I know.*

Sable stood between Dora and Margaret, feeling their stocky bodies press against hers. A living, breathing solidarity.

"Isn't she pretty?" said Margaret. "Much prettier than the other one."

Dora captured Sable's hand and patted it. "Why don't you join us?" she said. "We're going to have an ice cream at the cafe."

Sable felt the sun beat down on her neck, smelled the sharp spicy smell of the box, heard the plash of the water. She shaded her eyes and gazed down the avenue at the solid outlines of the box hedge, the softer tracings of the olive trees and, behind them, the villa, and they registered so vividly and clearly that it was as if they had sprung into focus for the first time.

"We are not the only ones who were wrong," added Dora. "Don't you think?"

And then something happened. Sable felt her mouth stretch in a novel fashion. The muscles in her lips were tight and unwilling and unpracticed but, eventually, they yielded. "Perhaps you're right," she agreed, and the smile she directed at Dora and Margaret held the beginnings of an unfamiliar joy.

Lynn Messina lives in New York and works in magazines. Her books include *Fashionistas, Tallulahland* and *Mim Warner's Lost Her Cool*.

Troublemaker
Lynn Messina

When Jamie Levin closes her eyes she sees herself on the grand staircase of the St. Charles hotel, swathed in yards of elegant white silk, with long satin gloves and a diamond tiara. Her skin is like porcelain in the moonlight, creamy and smooth, and her eyes, her gorgeous golden eyes, are reflective pools of light. The image is startlingly clear although somewhat inaccurate (her eyes are actually an impenetrable mud brown and her skin is frequently blotchy, but such is the transformative power of the ballroom at the St. Charles), and it's always there—a sweeping fresco painted on the rear wall of her mind. Sometimes she doesn't even have to close her eyes to see it.

Like now, as she ecstatically holds her hand out to Bryan. She's watching him slide the winking diamond solitaire onto the fourth finger of her left hand, watching him lean in to kiss her, but she's really seeing the beautiful ballroom—the miles of calla lilies, the glittering chandeliers, the marble balustrade along which she trails her hand lightly as she floats down the staircase, which was brought to the St. Charles from a castle on the Rhine in three parts (if you stand on the fourteenth and twenty-seventh steps and look down you can see the seams).

Even though the moment is perfect, even though it's exactly what she's always wanted—Manhattan skyline, setting sun, Dom Perignon, one dozen red roses—Jamie's mind can't help racing ahead to the next moment and the next: calling her mom, telling Beth, picking a date, floating down the staircase.

While Bryan pours a second round of bubbly, Jamie, already feeling like the luckiest woman in the world, sizes up her ring. At a single glance she can tell everything: color, clarity, cut, carat (white, flawless, ideal and two, respectively). Jamie is good at this—so good she's made a career of sizing up things and deciding how to proceed. Her company, Troublemakers, Inc. ("Where creative solutions are just the beginning"), takes the familiar endeavor of creative problem solving to its logical conclusion: creative problem making. She and her crack team of specialists come into a company, observe the operation and spot tiny fissures that will become giant crevices if left untreated. She's like an auditor for the IRS looking over the books, only her actions are preemptive, not reactive.

She had Bryan sized up the second they met—cute, as it were, in treatment room B at Allure Day Spa, where they had been assigned to the same chamber for a massage. While he was pulling the edges of his robe ever more tightly together, she was imagining how they'd tell the story of their cute meeting to their friends: the way she'd pause tantalizingly before mentioning the concealing terry cloth. What she'd liked right away, other than his embarrassed blush and the quick apology he offered even though she was clearly the one intruding, was his build. Bryan was thick and solid like a Russian peasant, and although there were no fields to till, she liked a man who could wield a plowshare in a crunch.

They'd been dating for three years before she gave him an ultimatum. It wasn't simply that she wanted the house in the suburbs and the gaggle of children (although she did, of course, have neighborhood and names all picked out), it was the fact of the indecision itself. The rest of your life seemed like a simple thing to her—either you wanted to spend it with a certain person or you didn't—and his hemming and hawing made her question the strength of his character. But after four months (just enough time, she realizes now, for him to feel like it was his own idea) he'd risen to the occasion with a gorgeous flawless diamond and a pristine sunset against the majestic New York skyline. The happiness she feels is so solid, she can't imagine anything destroying it.

But less than twenty-four hours later Jamie is in the ballroom at the St. Charles having her heart broken.

"I'm sorry. It's been all over the news," says the events coordinator, Abbey Frankel, with a sympathetic smile. She's been fielding women like this all week—prospective brides who don't know that the St. Charles is booked between now and kingdom come, an event scheduled for the first Monday in September, when a series of C4 charges would implode the building in order to make way for a shiny new sports facility.

"But I don't understand," Jamie says, suddenly lightheaded. She struggles to calm herself with several deep breaths. Her lungs expand dutifully but the air doesn't travel to her head. She sits down on step fourteen, right over the small fissure. "How can this happen?"

Abbey shrugs. "Progress. You know how it is."

Yes, Jamie does indeed know how it is. She'd been dealing with co-op boards and health club managers long enough to realize that progress is just code for back-room politics, for payoffs and paybacks and outsize egos being appeased by elaborate gestures that someone else pays for.

She takes another deep breath, rests her head against the balustrade and closes her eyes. The image is still there—impervious to reality, just as it's always been.

Jamie knows she has to do something. Talk to a historical society. Get an injunction. Chain herself to the front door. Organize a demonstration with thousands and thousands of angry brides in white dresses protesting down Fifth Avenue with posters and chants—a wedding march.

"I can take your name," Abbey offers.

Jamie opens her eyes. "Excuse me?"

"In the unlikely event of a couple canceling, I can take your name and give you a call," she explains. "As I said, it's highly unlikely but we've done it in the past."

It's only a sliver of hope, but Jamie grabs on to it with both hands. "Yes. Please."

"Very good. If you'll just come with me."

Her office is plush, with deep-pile carpeting, wood paneling and two oversize armchairs before a large oak desk. Jamie sits down and sinks into the thick cushion. Abbey opens a drawer, takes out her calendar and reaches for her glasses. They're not around her neck.

"I seem to have misplaced my glasses," she says, standing up. "Will you excuse me for a moment?"

Jamie nods absently, sighs pathetically and leans her head against the soft leather. Three generations of Levin women have stood on that staircase with their bridegrooms, three generations of strong-willed, determined matriarchs who could size up a situation in seconds; she would be the first in ninety-seven years to not.

The thought is too terrible to contemplate, and Jamie, realizing there is only one thing to do when left alone in a plush room with a broken heart and a black leather calendar filled with unworthy brides, grabs a scrap of paper, opens the book and starts writing down names.

Jamie begins with June because she's always wanted a June wedding, not simply for the customary blessings late spring bestows like blooming flowers, gentle breezes, golden sunlight and a soft color palette (though the thought of blushing-pink bridesmaids dresses does inspire a certain amount of fairy-princess giddiness), but also for the heart-pounding optimism it makes her feel. Anything is possible in June.

Through a series of Google searches and anonymous phone calls, she tracks the first bride, Meghan Carter, to a bar on the Bowery, where she's hosting a fund-raiser to benefit an organization that places stray dogs with loving owners. For a half hour, Jamie listens as Meghan presents cute abandoned puppy after cute abandoned puppy for adoption. She leaves when the impulse to take one home—a three-month-old golden Lab named Schmootzy who looks just like her childhood dog—becomes almost overwhelming.

She finds the next candidate in a Bronx elementary-school classroom teaching twenty-seven fifth-graders how to solve simple algebraic equations. She's not hovering in the hallway for five minutes before Miss Wheeling helps poor little insecure Charlie Meyers realize that he can figure out the value of X all on his own. She walks away in disgust.

By the time Jamie enters the Chelsea Barnes & Noble for the book reading of contestant number four, Samantha Berkis, she's thoroughly discouraged by the generous nature of her fellow New Yorkers (she doesn't even bother seeking out number three, a nurse at Sloan-Kettering). But the title of the book gives her the first glimmer of hope in weeks—*Wondercouple: Tales from the Perfect Relationship.* The sign next to the podium indicating that all who stay for the reading agree to their image being used in a documentary about the author gives her the second.

The event is well attended, and Jamie snags a copy of the book before finding a seat in the middle of the last row. A few minutes later, the manager takes the podium to welcome the crowd and to run through a list of upcoming events. He's halfway into the month when Samantha Berkis decides she's waited long enough for her introduction.

"Thank you, Mr. Warner," she says, gently but emphatically pushing him to the side with her shoulder, which is as thin and bony as the rest of her.

Jamie tries to imagine her standing on the landing of the St. Charles staircase swathed in elegant white silk but only sees a flapping duck with a tiara perched on a tuft of feathers. She leans forward in her seat.

"I'm so delighted to be here to discuss my book, *Wondercouple: Tales from the Perfect Relationship.* Before I begin, I'd like to hand out some tools that will help us all to be wonderful." Samantha holds out a bag of plastic rings. "Mr. Warner, would you be so kind?" Before he can respond, she drops the bag in his hand and moves on. She picks up a satiny red cape in her left hand and waves it. "This is for the relationship superhero among you. Does anyone feel like a relationship superhero tonight?" The audience is silent. "That's all right. I'll wear it first. But as soon as one of you feels relationship superhero-y, please speak up."

She ties the cape around her neck as she continues with her presentation. "No doubt you are wondering what the rings are for. It's very simple. Being a Wondercouple means recognizing the force of your combined power. The two of you are a team, and the ring is a subtle, ever-present reminder that you must always work together. When you go somewhere, say, to a dinner party, remind yourselves that you're a team. State your goals. How do you do this? It's easy. Is everyone wearing their ring? Good. Turn to the person next to you and touch rings. Now repeat after me—Wondercouple powers activate. Form of the perfect party guest. Shape of sparkling conversation."

Several members of the audience, somewhat embarrassed but also intrigued, comply with a low rumble. Samantha cheers their effort, then singles out a woman in the second row who has remained silent.

"No need to be shy," she says. "Wondercoupledom is not for the faint of heart. Now, go on, repeat after me. Wondercouple powers activate. Form of a mortgage holder. Shape of a fiscally responsible budget."

The woman blushes and stammers while Samantha nods approvingly before moving on to the next recalcitrant audience member. Suddenly the book reading feels like a second-year tort-reform seminar with a tenured law professor.

Now this, Jamie thinks happily as she slips on the ring, is a proper nemesis. Jamie knows that the best way to end a relationship is to let nature take its course. As the adage promises, familiarity will breed contempt as passion dulls into a polite form of indifference and small pet peeves snowball into insurmountable grievances. Affections erode, tempers fray and the inevitable dividing of the book collection follows, with a heated argument over who gets possession of the *Complete Works of Shakespeare,* which neither person actually wants.

But Jamie doesn't have time for the second law of thermodynamics. The Berkis-Taylor wedding is 203 days away.

Instead, she treats the Berkis-Taylor problem as she would any other Troublemakers assignment, giving the project a name (in this case, Operation: Wed Unlock), observing her subjects closely, putting together a PowerPoint presentation and reporting her findings to her staff during a meeting for input and feedback.

"An affair," says Beth, maid of honor and business partner, as soon as Jamie shows the last slide. "It has to be an affair."

Carl nods abruptly. He's been at Troublemakers for as long as Beth and has just as finely honed a sense of possibility. "It kills me to say it, but I agree. If we had unlimited access— if we, you know, could rent the apartment across from theirs and watch twenty-four hours a day—we'd obviously find tons of material to exploit. If nothing else, there have to be some in-law issues. But we don't have that kind of access so I have to agree."

Jamie listens to their recommendation with a sinking heart, even though it's exactly what she expects to hear. It's inevitable, of course. In the absence of real data, a torrid little back-alley affair is the only logical conclusion. But it doesn't sit well with her. She knows there's no totally honorable way to break up a couple to get their wedding date, but she can't help wishing for something a little less sleazy, a little more front office.

Jamie is still trying to overcome her scruples when she meets Bryan for dinner at a trendy little bistro that just opened on the Lower East Side. They have to wait an hour for a table, something Bryan finds ridiculous in a city full of trendy little bistros, and by the time they sit down, he's in a bad mood. Jamie longs to tell him about the St. Charles and the sports stadium and Samantha Berkis, but she holds her tongue—and not simply because he's now annoyed. Bryan is a Good Guy. He plays stickball with his best friend's five-year-old son, always offers to help a buddy with a move, even up five flights, and never fails to pick up the first round. He is, she knows, her better half. His generous nature balances out her sometimes stingy one. It's another reason she loves him.

But he wouldn't understand breaking up a couple to get their wedding date, even if she explained the ninety-seven years of tradition at stake and her lifelong dreams. He'd accept the situation with that soul-deep fatalism, shrug unconcernedly and suggest they get married somewhere else, perhaps the Friar Tuck catering hall in Passaic, New Jersey, where his nephew David had his bar mitzvah two years ago.

Remembering the soggy cream puffs, the least of Friar Tuck's offenses, Jamie says nothing and orders a salade niçoise with seared tuna. Sometimes she feels sad that she can't share everything with Bryan, but she knows that's how relationships are. Her mother has kept many things from her father, mostly credit card bills and salon appointments, and they've been happily married for thirty-one years. ("The human bond," Mom always says, "can take only so much honesty.")

Thinking of her mother, Jamie swallows her reservations. Three generations of Levin women have overcome worse to stand on the grand staircase of the St. Charles. Potato famines, Great Depressions, recreational drugs—a little flirting is nothing in comparison.

Besides, she reminds herself the next day as she slides onto a stool at the trendy East Village dive where Samantha Berkis's fiancé works, it's not her fault if he takes the bait. Society sets up the crime and the criminal commits it.

It's early on a Wednesday night, and the bar is empty except for a couple playing pool in the back and a middle-aged guy in a booth near the men's room. The place is dark and smells of beer and faint cigar smoke. While Jamie waits for service, she fiddles with a bowl of peanuts.

She doesn't have to wait long.

"Hey, what can I get you?" Jeremy Taylor asks.

Samantha Berkis's fiancé is tall and thin, with dark blue eyes, short red hair and freckles across the bridge of his nose. He has nicely defined biceps and a lithe build, but she cannot imagine him tilling anything other than a window box.

"I'll have a beer. Whatever you have on tap."

He nods and grabs a glass. "How's Heineken?"

"Good, thanks. Slow night," she says, knowing it's a line. If it weren't in service of a nobler goal, she'd be embarrassed by it.

He shrugs. "This place doesn't get going until after eleven. By 2:00 a.m., it's shoulder to shoulder."

"I've never been here before. What's the crowd like?"

He shrugs again. "The usual. Some hipsters. Some artists. Some drunks."

"Which are you?"

He laughs and puts her drink on the bar.

"You know," she says, wrapping her hands around the cold glass, "have we met? I feel like I've seen you before."

It's another line, a more obvious one, and he grins, amused. "Yeah?"

His tone makes her blush but it's dark so he can't see it. "Yeah. Oh, wait a second. I know. You're Jeremy Taylor."

He stops wiping down the bar and looks at her.

Before he can say anything, she continues. "This is amazing. I've seen everything you've ever done." It sounds like a lie but it's the God's honest truth: In the last forty-eight hours, she's watched all four of his films, including a short on Central Park he made during his senior year at NYU. She bought a worn-out copy from jeremytaylorrocks.com. "Don't worry. I won't pester you with a million questions."

"Please," he says, relaxing, "feel free. It's a slow night."

Jamie rests her elbows on the bar, takes a sip of beer and asks him about the Huaorani of Ecuador. All his films center around his experiences with endangered indigenous peoples, even the undergrad short, which was about homeless men in the Rambles.

Jeremy is flattered by the attention. He gives long, thoughtful answers and encourages more questions. She stays on the stool talking to him for several hours, nursing three pints of Heineken, and only leaves when the hipsters, artists and drunks start elbowing her in the back.

But she returns the next night and the next and the next. When she runs out of things to ask about his previous work, she switches to his current project, the Ulaan Baatar of Mongolia. For two hours they talk about funding possibilities and grants. For ninety minutes they discuss clearances and logistics of filming in the Gobi Desert. For an entire night they chat about Troublemakers and the underdeveloped field of creating problems to solve them.

A rapport is established.

Two weeks later, Jamie knows it's time to take the plan to the next level. Bryan has started to complain about how little he sees her, and she wonders if he's getting suspicious. He's called Beth twice asking where Jamie was.

But now that she's met Jeremy, she's even more reluctant to proceed and has to remind herself with increasing regularity about society and criminals. During her weakest moments, she opens *Wondercouple* to a random page and reads. The offensive absurdity of Samantha Berkis's advice ("Build a Hall of Justice in your heart and take refuge there") makes her feel like she's doing a good deed by breaking them up.

She starts calling their apartment when she knows he's got a shift. If Samantha answers, she asks to speak to him in a breathy voice. After a few times, she hangs up as soon as Samantha picks up the phone. She sends herself roses from a local florist and uses his name and number so they have to call him when the address turns out to be wrong. She has Carl call from the W Hotel about a reservation. She has Beth call from Le Petite Coquette about silk underwear.

"Okay," she says, handing a Canon EOS Rebel to her maid of honor. "This is the final phase. All we need is one good shot that we can send her."

Beth takes the camera. "Gotcha, boss."

They're in the Troublemakers office going over the plan one more time. "Remember, you sit in the third booth from the back. I've tested out all of them and this one has the clearest sight line to the bar. I'll be on the second stool from the corner. That's the front corner, not the back corner."

Beth nods as the phone starts ringing. Jamie picks up. It's Bryan inviting her to dinner at a Soho hot spot. "You know, that new place you've been dying to try. I had a meeting on

Grand, so I'm in the neighborhood. I could be there in two minutes."

"Oh, that sounds lovely but I can't," she says. "I've got a thing tonight."

Bryan is silent for a moment. "But you've had a thing every night for almost three weeks," he says plaintively. "I feel like I've hardly seen you since the engagement."

"I know. But it's work. I can't do anything about it."

"Are you sure?"

"That I can't do anything about it? Well, the client is calling the shots."

"No, that it's work. You're not freaking out about the wedding, are you?"

Jamie laughs at the idea. "Of course not."

"All right," he says reluctantly.

"I'll call you later," she promises. "Maybe the thing will wind up early enough and I can stop by."

She hangs up the phone and looks up to find Beth staring at her consideringly.

"He sounds suspicious," her friend says. "Another few days and he's going to start following you around."

"I know. So let's get this over with."

Beth puts the camera in her shoulder bag, grabs her coat and follows Jamie to the elevator. On West Broadway, they flag down a cab and ride in silence to the bar. Once there, they separate. Jamie waits outside while Beth goes in. She counts to twenty, then thirty. Her stomach feels queasy, but she thinks of potato famines and Wondercouple powers activating and gorgeous marble balustrades. Nerves somewhat settled, she opens the door and goes in.

Jeremy is behind the bar pulling a Guinness but he smiles the second he sees her.

"Hey, I didn't know you were coming," he says. "This is great. There's someone here I'd love for you to meet."

She tries to return his greeting with an easy smile, but her effort is stiff. Everything about her at the moment is stiff. When she turns her head to make sure Beth is in the right booth (she is and with the camera discreetly placed on her lap), the movement is jerky.

As she gets closer and closer to Jeremy, Jamie's heart pounds harder and harder. Get it over with. Get it over with, she tells herself during the interminable walk to the bar. Do it now. When he leans in for a harmless hello peck on the cheek, turn your head at the very last moment. Kiss him long and deep for the camera. Then pull away, stutter an apology, run out of the bar and never come back.

The never-coming-back part makes her sad though, as does the thought of him seeing the photograph. She likes Jeremy. He tells interesting stories and makes her laugh.

But she loves the grand staircase.

The second her lips touch his, her heart stops its furious beating. Her lungs expand and her muscles relax and she finds herself wondering what she was so worried about. She closes her eyes. She leans forward. She wraps her arms around his neck.

Suddenly he pulls away. Suddenly he's stammering an apology ("Oh, God, Sam…I'm not…I didn't…") and Beth's calling out a warning ("Jamie, behind you") and Bryan is yelling at the top of his lungs ("I fucking *knew* it!") and all she can do is hold on to the bar and stare: at Jeremy's pale face, at Samantha's understanding eyes, at Bryan's clenched fists.

The pounding in her chest starts again, as does a new pounding in her head. She tries to straighten. Her knees are too weak, and she stumbles against the bar stool. She reaches out a hand to Bryan, but he doesn't take it. He doesn't come over to her or smile forgivingly. Nor does Samantha slap Jeremy on the face, take off her ring and storm out of the bar.

But that's what Jamie sees when she closes her eyes.

When we asked Nicki Earls to contribute a story to *Girls' Night Out,* she seemed strangely reluctant. "Talk to my agent," she said. "I do everything through her. I'm very, very girls' night in." Eventually she relented, but she never quite moved out of the shadows, or removed her pashmina, and she spoke in a deep voice that she claimed was badly affected by a virus. When we asked if she was in any way connected to Nick Earls, author of the novels *Perfect Skin, Two To Go, 48 Shades of Brown* and *After Summer,* co-editor of the latest Australian edition of *Girls' Night Out*—and chair of War Child Australia—she replied rather brusquely that she'd never heard of him, and preferred cats. She finished by saying she had far better things to do with her time than visit www.nickearls.com, and called the site's very existence "an act of gross self-indulgence."

Ladies' Night At the Underwood Pet Hospital
Nicki Earls

Perhaps boredom runs in the family. My mother was bored and decided that might be fixed if she dragged my father to a five-star Thai spa where she could take classes that would teach her how to carve a carrot into something that looked like a rose. I was bored and decided I had to meet the guy next door.

My parents were gone for a month, so I had agreed to move into their place to look after their high-maintenance sleek black cat Arabella and to try to keep at least a few of their plants alive. I gave no guarantees about the plants, so my mother gave detailed written instructions.

"It's not that I don't trust you, Sally," she said, "but I've grown used to some of these plants."

She had the instructions printed out and in a plastic sleeve before I had even told her there were no guarantees. "I'm twenty-eight," I wanted to tell her. "I'm twenty-eight and promoted from weather presenter to newsreader for the summer, so stop treating me like I'm ten and just accept I have no affinity with plants." She gave me the sheet of Arabella instructions then, which annoyed me since I'm great with cats, and started talking me through her appliances.

And then she told me about the guy next door. He was house-sitting for his parents too. They had left on Boxing Day to gray-nomad their way all around Australia, and he had moved in to look after their place while he was writing up his Ph.D. thesis in marine biology. So I thought of the last scientist I knew, and he dressed like the eighties, walked like a thunderbird and had wing-nut ears—not that there's anything wrong with that—and I didn't hold out much hope for the neighbor.

Not that neighbors are about hope, and not that I'm shallow when it comes to thunderbirds who have ears like satellite dishes built onto the sides of their head, but… But my luck hadn't been great lately. I had been single since the last series of *I'm a Celebrity Get Me Out of Here* was shot at the Gold Coast, and my line-producer boyfriend had decided to "console" one of the cast's evicted busty East-Ender slapper non-celebs by taking her for long lingering hand-holding-type walks on the beach.

He took about two days to go from "Aussie mystery man" in the UK tabloids to "line producer Dan Chappell" in the *Sunday Mail*—same grainy photo, next to one of the two of us at a theater opening night with the caption "Dan and Sally in happier times."

I later read that it started in the spa at the Palazzo Versace, when she tried to teach him something about some English game called "bobbing for apples."

"Honestly," my mother said when she called me about it. "That's a children's game involving actual apples. They've spoiled it for everyone now."

Among all the conversations you hope never to have with your mother, top of the list would have to be the one about the ways used to describe the blow job a slapper gave your boyfriend in a spa.

But I had put that behind me, handled it with dignity and the support of the station publicist, and moved on. Moved on, as it turned out, to cohosting the news for summer. "This will be a year to focus on your career," my horoscope said, and I was sure it was right.

Then I saw the Ph.D. guy, and wished I had paid more attention to my mother's briefing. But I'm sure she completely omitted to tell me that he was no thunderbird, that he jogged early in the morning and then peeled his singlet off in the front yard, that he sat on the back veranda late at night with his guitar playing Paul Kelly songs.

And she certainly didn't tell me that he did that to the silent accompaniment of me sitting watching TV, singing along in my head and sending him a telepathic message that went, "Watch my news…watch my news…"

Arabella the cat had ceased to fascinate me with her extreme neediness, most of my friends were out of town for the holidays and the Ph.D. guy drifted around the edges of my world without even knowing it, looking better and better as the days went by.

I wanted to meet him. I wanted to meet him, but in one of those natural unhurried ways that kept everyone's dignity intact. Nothing too overtly staged, nothing embarrass-

ing, nothing that could end up in "Q Confidential" in the
Courier-Mail if it all went wrong. But I wanted one of those
natural unhurried ways to come along right now.

I was completely charming on the news. I'm sure I read
each intro in a way that told him that he was welcome at
my door, but I saw him less, if anything. He was putting in
far too many hours on that Ph.D. for my liking. What was
I supposed to do? Coincidentally take up morning jogging,
straight after the *Sunday Mail* had done a piece on my regular Tae Bo workouts? Find my primary-school recorder in
my parents' spare room and start playing "Annie's Song" on
their back veranda late at night?

"I'm on TV," I kept thinking. "You're supposed to want
me. I get mail, you know. From people who want me." Okay,
the word *people* should actually read "creepy old man who
writes only in limericks" but, at a technical level, it *is* mail.

Two weeks had passed. It was far too late to go over and
knock on his door out of simple uncluttered neighborliness.
No, I needed a plan. And freeloading, annoying Arabella gave
it to me. The next night, when I wasn't back at the station
doing updates, I picked Arabella up from the rug, and moved
with the silence of a commando out the back door, down
the steps and across the garden. The Ph.D. guy, meanwhile,
was singing "To Her Door." He was taunting me, surely.

I held Arabella up to the top of the fence, but she grabbed
at it with her front paws and started to kick. I pushed, she
hissed. I pushed, she tumbled over the fence and into the garden next door. I snuck back inside, I checked in the hall mirror that all was as it should be—I was going for the
"newsreader-relaxing-at-home" look, which takes a good half
hour more than it actually takes to be a newsreader relaxing
at home—and I picked up my keys and went out the door.

I walked to the neighbors', mentally practicing my "I think our cat might have jumped over the fence" line until it clearly said, "I'm into Paul Kelly, too, and you need to invite me in for a drink right now." I was most of the way up their front steps when it all went wrong. Wrong with the mad barking of a dog, the yowling and hissing of a cat, the thump of a guitar hitting the veranda and feet running down the back steps. Arabella howled, the dog howled, the Ph.D. guy shouted, "Get back, get off her."

I ran down the steps and around the side of the house. There were monsterias and ferns, and one of my Birkenstocks—which should have sent just the right signal—caught on a hose and sent me tumbling into the tan bark. I yanked them both off and stumbled around into the yard, where the Ph.D. guy was holding a small dog in his arms and Arabella was lying on the grass. He turned when he heard me and his shirtfront was dark with blood (or, as it turned out, urine, since the dog had been caught rather badly by surprise).

"I think our cat might have jumped over the fence," I said rather alluringly, since it was too well rehearsed not to be the first thing that came to mind. A piece of tan bark fell out of my hair.

"Are you insane?" he said, which was not a good start. "You pushed it. I saw you."

"No, no," I said, and then, "No," again, because of course I had pushed it, but he wasn't supposed to see.

"You pushed it with both hands."

"I was trying to stop it."

"It was trying to stop you."

"Oh my God, Arabella," I said with something of a wail, as if I'd just noticed her. "What's this dog done to you? I told you not to come next door."

Why had my mother never told me there was a dog? Why wasn't that printed out and slipped into a goddamn plastic sleeve somewhere?

I kneeled down and Arabella looked up at me, her eyes full of fear and dog saliva. I picked her up and she went limp. She panted and oozed blood messily onto my arm from a head wound.

"I'm Sally," I said. "I'm minding my parents' place next door while they're away."

"Right," he said. "Right. I'm doing something similar. I've got to get Charlotte to a vet, I think. She's been pretty badly cut up." He turned and walked to the back steps. "It's the second of January. It's ten o'clock at night on the second of January. What's going to be open?"

"We can find somewhere," I said. "I'm sure we can."

Okay, so it wasn't the plan, but we were back on some kind of track. We were working together now. Arabella yowled weakly as I walked toward the Ph.D. guy and Charlotte.

"Um, Brendan," he said. "I'm Brendan." Then he walked up the steps and led the way into the house.

We called Charlotte's vet and got an answering machine with an emergency number that turned out to be the after-hours pet hospital at Underwood.

"Where's that?" Brendan said, and I told him: "It's a long way. Distant southside. I'll drive."

And he said, "Oh," and looked hesitant. I'm sure he was trying to remember the moment when we'd agreed to go together.

I went home with Arabella and found her cage and put her into it with her favorite blanket. It took me much longer to find my Paul Kelly CDs, and then to choose one, but by the time I backed the car out "Under the Sun" was playing at a respectful volume. Arabella's cage was behind my seat, and Brendan got in the front with Charlotte wrapped in a towel. She growled, Arabella yowled. It was a bad, bad idea taking the two of them there in the same car, but there was no way we were changing the plan now.

"So, you're a marine biologist?" I said as we drove along Coronation Drive and he said, "Yes. I think there's blood soaking through the towel." He maneuvered Charlotte and looked underneath her. "Yes, it's blood."

I turned the music up, he continued to fail to notice it.

He turned it down and said, "What the hell were you doing pushing the cat over the fence?"

"I love this album," I said. "I love it. I think it's one of his best."

He stared at me, and then looked back at Charlotte.

"Are you navigating?" I said. "This could all go to shit if you don't get the navigation right."

"As opposed to already, you mean."

Charlotte panted, Arabella yowled, Brendan had a point but I couldn't concede it.

"So, you're a marine biologist?" I said, and he said, "Yes, still."

He wasn't liking me quite enough so far.

"You're not from Brisbane though?"

"No." He looked at the blood on his hand, made comforting noises down toward Charlotte. "I've been working on Heron Island, but my family's from Port Macquarie. My parents moved here a few years ago." He turned the map light on and worked out where we were on the freeway. "It'll be the exit just before *Ikea,* I think."

He navigated us flawlessly to the pet hospital and we pulled up outside the door in the near-empty car park. The waiting room was large and bright and lino-floored, and we rang the bell at the desk. For the first time, I got a good look at Charlotte, a well-cared-for spaniel with blood oozing through her white-and-ginger hair. She was blinking, panting, distressed. I had no idea the neighbors had a dog. I'm sure I wouldn't have pushed Arabella over the fence if I had. Why couldn't I just have gone to the door and introduced myself?

The vet came out from a back room and introduced himself as Alasdair. He was pale and ginger-haired and thirty-ish, and he spoke with a thick Glaswegian accent.

"I'm Sally," I said, and I shook his hand.

And he said, "Of course you are, Sally, it's you who tells me what the weather's like at the beach on my days off. And you're doing the news now, too, I've noticed. Very nice."

"You know each other?" Brendan said, just not getting it, and Alasdair gave a laugh and said, "No, I'm just a viewer. A fan."

Then he blushed and took us through to an examination room. Arabella hissed and scratched him when he took her out of her cage. Charlotte barked in response.

"I could put you in separate rooms," he said, "but I can tell they're going to fight me whether I do that or not. I think they'll turn out to be okay, but they're going to need sedation for me to take a proper look at them."

So we sat in the waiting room, Brendan and I, and we watched midnight pass on the wall clock and we tried to read ancient copies of *National Geographic*.

"Suddenly," he said, "I notice the smell of dog urine." He picked some dried blood off his wrist and looked down at his shirt. "I really hadn't expected that I'd be seeing midnight under bright fluoro lighting with dog piss down my front."

"Sorry."

"It was just an observation." He picked off some more blood. "Admit you did it. Admit you pushed the cat over."

"I pushed the cat over."

"Ha," he said, finally the winner.

"I pushed the cat over because I thought it would be nice to meet you. I didn't know you had a dog. I thought I'd just come to the door and say…"

"'I think our cat might have jumped over the fence…' I think you did say it." He looked at me, and then looked back at the heartworm poster on the wall. "You wanted to meet me?" He smirked.

The door to the back area opened again.

"Come through," Alasdair said. "It hasn't exactly been the ideal night out for these two young ladies, but they'll both be okay."

We followed him into a room that was much bigger than I'd expected, with bandaged animals in cages all along one side and three operating tables. Arabella and Charlotte were on two of them, partly shaved and wide-eyed and dopey.

"It's the sedation," Alasdair said. "It makes them a bit dissociated, but they should be all right to go home and sleep it off."

Guilt hit me again as I looked at them, slumped and stitched up. I patted Arabella, who looked up at me with huge unseeing pupils and then dropped her head onto the table again with a clunk. Brendan was down on his knees patting Charlotte and getting the same kind of response.

"Hey, Charlie," he was saying quietly. "It'll all be okay."

Alasdair introduced me to the three vet nurses, who each shook my hand. He introduced me to some of the other animals in cages and told me what had brought them in. He went across the room to fetch a specimen jar that contained an air-rifle pellet he had removed from under the chin of a large ginger cat. They handed me a drowsy Arabella so that they could take a photo for their notice board.

"How lucky is it that you're not the one with the urine and blood all over your shirt?" Brendan said, and he made them take a shot of the two of us, each holding a wounded pet. "Now, let's have a big TV smile," he said to me.

He wrote down his e-mail address so that they could send it to him. Alasdair told me he thought the air-rifle pellet would make a good animal-cruelty story for the news. Or the large number of dogs injured running away from New Year's Eve fireworks—that'd make a good story, too. I said I'd put it to the news director.

We went back out the front to pay, and I handed my credit card over to one of the nurses and said, "It can all go on that."

Five hundred dollars later, we were on our way out with our drugged-out pets and our bottles of antibiotics.

There was peace in the car on the way home. Arabella moved around in her cage but kept slumping to the floor, while Charlotte looked out at the streetlights with big eyes and no comprehension.

"I've been wanting to meet you for the past few weeks," Brendan said. "I've been e-mailing my parents—who will love the picture, by the way, once I can assure them that Charlotte's actually okay—and fortunately *your* proud parents talk about you all the time, apparently. So, it was easy to find out quite a bit about you." He started humming Paul Kelly's "To Her Door," and then laughed. "You make me feel very subtle." He patted Charlotte's head and smoothed out one of her ears along her towel. "We might have to watch these two, don't you think? How about we set up some bowls of water and a couple of trays of pet litter and open some wine? I've just found my parents' cellar, and they've been keeping some of those elderly reds far too long, I'm sure."

Emma McLaughlin and Nicola Kraus live and write in New York City. They are the authors of two internationally bestselling novels, *The Nanny Diaries* and *Citizen Girl*. They are currently working on their third.

Cinderella Gets a Brazilian
Emma McLaughlin & Nicola Kraus

Without fail, the Big Night Out only seems to present it-self when you have insane deadlines, have not eaten, drunk anything uncaffeinated, showered, exhaled, or even peed in minimally forty-eight hours. When you are living on fumes until you can collapse, coat still on and remote in hand, with a big *whumph,* in your long-neglected apartment. When you have been getting from minute to pressure-filled minute by fantasizing about flannel pajamas and Chinese takeout, not about shivering atop three-inch heels by a drafty window in a jam-packed bar. When there is not so much as an ounce of small talk to be had from your little, tuckered-out self.

When you are just plain shot to shit.

As your boss screams for you and the copy machine si-multaneously implodes, it is, of course, at this exact moment that your perkiest friend, whose perfectly relaxing job has got her "positively bored to sobs," calls to remind you about so-and-so's midweek cocktails. While a billowing cloud of errant toner transforms you into a chimney sweep, Perky wants to know if you're wearing your hair up, if you want to "duck out" early and get matching pedicures, if you are as b-o-r-e-d as she is. And you are overcome in a lightning flash of pure, murderous rage. You want to reach through the phone and drag Perky all the way through the wire, morph her into your sweaty, toner-stained, hunched-over-the-broken-copy-machine self and scream, "WHAT?!"

Instead, tears welling, you attempt to extricate yourself gracefully. "I have to go to the bathroom. I'm thirsty. My feet hurt. My contacts are rolling back into my brain."

But Perky knows exactly how to get you, knows it is merely a matter of five little words, knows not to waste time dillydallying when she is armed with a spinning gyroscope; "_____ said he'd stop by," she mentions casually.

BLANK!!!!

As in long-hot-romantic-Labor-Day-weekend-at-Perky's-summer-share Blank? As in, "I'll-call-you-before-your-tan-fades" Blank? As in has-not-been-at-a-single-party-since and may-have-joined-the-witness-protection-program Blank?!

And you are back. You are in. Fuck the copy machine. Fuck the deadline. Fuck even being employed. You have a mission! NASA has called in your number! The wagons must be circled. Pronto.

Having put you wholly under her power, she proceeds to play dumb. "Yeah, I heard he was stopping by around some dinner thing."

"Around? What does 'around' mean?! Before?! After?!" You grip the phone, hover over the copier, ready to spring, awaiting the specifics.

"I don't know! *Coooommme ooonnn,* let's sneak out for margaritas! I'm *dying* for a drink, my day has been *soooo* tediously *b-o-r-i*—"

But you are flying out onto the street, your purse still open, a battle plan forming in your head as you elbow your way through tourists and Salvation Army Santas. You look at your watch and try to calculate how to get the biggest grooming bang from your minimal-time buck. Because, let's face it, you could be crossing paths with him in less than two hours. Less than two hours to stand before him and look so fucking great that all of New York will be stopped in their fucking tracks.

You get yourself to a nail salon and are momentarily paralyzed in front of their price list by the cosmic implications of which services to select. Option A: The He's Just Going to See Me for Five Minutes and Regret His Entire Existence Package—above the neckline, below the ankle (manicure, pedicure and upper-lip wax). Or Option B: The He's So Overcome By My Smooth Upper Lip That We Have Mad Passionate Almost and I Leave Him at the Height of It All Regretting His Entire Existence Package (manicure, pedicure, wax everything). Virgin. Whore. Virgin. Whore. "Wax me! Wax me NOW!"

Your entire body is chafing and violated, screaming against your winter woolen wear, you still haven't eaten, had a glass of water or peed since, like, two days ago. Only sixty minutes to go and there is still dirty hair to contend with, makeup and the matter of wardrobe. Think, think, think. What to wear to make someone regret his entire existence in the dead of December?

Halfway across Fifth Avenue you take a full moment to look up at the cold evening sky and scowl angrily, like Moses, at a God who has waited to present you with this opportunity in entirely the wrong season. You waste a good ten minutes on a crowded subway car lost in a nostalgic haze over your summer wardrobe: sexy little sundresses, bare tank tops, strappy sandals. All of which positively scream, *"Trying!"* in the dead of December.

"Fuck." You startle the businessman hogging the seat beneath you, the *Financial Times* spread to its full width between his relaxed thighs, his stubby legs outstretched. You hate him because it's a pretty safe bet that he has not just waxed his entire body—nor does he have a five-minute window in an eight-hour evening to make someone regret his entire existence. Fucking seated asshole.

Then you are home. You bounce through the apartment on one foot while pulling off your boots. You reach your closet. Hateful, winter woolen, frumpy closet that it is. You stare each other down. Humph.

"By the time I return from my shower I fully expect you to have found at least one borderline-fabulous suggestion."

It shrugs.

You are naked in the bathroom, telling your skin to just get over it already, everybody gets waxed, and it needs to stop having a pity party and begging you for aloe. You are not doing aloe tonight. Better yet—how about lemon shower gel, astringent and a brief salt scrub?! It's an S&M fest with you and your skin while you both wrestle in the bathroom to become a supermodel.

You pant back to your closet with half an hour on the clock, hair wrapped tightly in a towel. You take a deep tantric breath, say a quick prayer to the long-neglected laundry gods, open your lingerie drawer and let out a sigh of relief as you spot The Bra. The one that practically comes with its own boobs. Then you just need the angora sweater with the deep V that shows the cleavage, which goes perfectly with the red pants. A choir of angels clears its throat—but the red pants are at the cleaners—#%&!!—which leads to the leather skirt, which means the boots, which need to be polished and THERE IS NO FUCKING TIME FOR THAT. So back to the sweater—you consider for a nanosecond forgoing clothes from the waist down because that would definitely accomplish the mission. And then, as the last garments fly over your head and onto the coverlet, you remember the black evening pants you got in the Christmas sales last year. And you dig, sweating, on all fours through the back of your dark, dusty, hateful closet until you find them, flattened in their shopping bag between the hamper and the wall.

And then you are in the shower again and your skin just CANNOT BELIEVE that you won't even leave it alone for just one single minute!

Less than sixteen minutes to go, in which ensues a cloud of perfume, a WWF match with your stockings, a makeup job timed for speed and an attempt to blow-dry your hair by the open oven door to shave off valuable minutes.

And it all comes to a screeching halt on the street below, which has suddenly emptied of its holiday traffic and is traversed by a lone deliveryman peddling slowly on his bicycle against the snow. You contemplate throwing his burritos to the sidewalk and leaping in his basket. But he cycles on, oblivious to your desperation. You run in your three-inch heels to the nearest avenue, hopping up and down in oncoming traffic for an empty taxi. Or a clean pickup truck.

A sweet, merciful cab finally pulls up and a guy in a

camel-hair coat opens the back door. "Hey, you goin' up-town?" he asks.

You hop right in, despite the fact that he could be a well-dressed serial killer, because risking death while in pursuit of getting-someone-to-regret-his-entire-existence is noble.

"You looked pretty desperate out there…" He heh-hehs, taking advantage of a sharp turn to sidle closer and engage in a bit of holiday cheer. "Man, red's your color," or the more strategic, "I bet your boyfriend loves you in red," or, forgoing the niceties, a classic yet elegant, "Blow me, red girl."

"Well, um—" you reach "—since I'm a cop I have to wear blue for work and I'm really an autumn, but mostly I'm just a cop. With a gun. A cop with a gun."

Then he presses even closer and you are beyond grateful to be let out within even a mile of your destination. You hobble like a madwoman through snow-lined streets, any sensation in your feet slowly ebbing as throbbing gives way to tingling gives way to numbness, and, quite possibly, frost-bite.

Miraculously, at exactly eight o'clock, you reach the over-crowded apartment. Heart pounding from adrenaline and four flights of stairs, you breathlessly seek out Perky, who you find in the kitchen, rooting through the host's cabinets in search of fat-free hot chocolate. You lock her in your trac-tor beams for The Shakedown.

"Yick! You are so totally sweaty…"

"Am I [wheeze] late? Is he [wheeze] here?" Deep breath, take her firmly by her shoulders, "TELL ME."

She confesses and tells you you're a "weirdo."

You win! You have not missed him! He's ON HIS WAY. The choir of angels belts it out for all they're worth.

Now it's just a matter of waiting, an hour, or two, or six.

You get a drink and strategically maneuver toward the nuts. Every time the buzzer rings you gulp. Every time the crowd parts you smile. You make hours of agonizing chitchat with guests who have had way too much to drink and are way, way too rested.

Disgustingly rested.

Your focus wavers as anecdotes about golf club member- ships and restaurant openings blur. Of course, in your cur- rent state, even an actual Beatles reunion concert by the carrot sticks could not hold your attention. Every twenty minutes your adrenaline lags so dangerously low that it hurts to speak, to smile. You take the cheese into the bathroom. Shaky and nauseous with exhaustion, you still haven't had any water, eaten a vegetable or closed your eyes.

"*You* got a promotion? Sorry, that, uh, didn't come out how I meant it." You are not making friends. An invitation to the July Fourth barbecue is looking more and more like a long shot.

And then it's one fifteen. Perky went home. Promotion went home. Barbecue went home. It's down to you and the host. In her pajamas. You have helped clean up to the point of reorganizing her spice rack. She is looking at you oddly as she leaves to brush her teeth. You now must hit on her or there will be no other way to explain your behavior.

You gather your coat where she has left it, not so subtly, by the front door, and let yourself out. Defeated.

You were prepared for every alternative—he could have arrived with a model, a gay lover or a tonsure and you'd have handled it with aplomb, but *this?!* This anticlimactic noth- ing? Inconceivable!

What kind of a person says he's going to go to a party and then just *doesn't show up?!*

You stand immobilized in the stairwell.

People buy drinks and food based on a number and one can't just say that one's going to attend a party and then just not show up!

You gingerly traverse the icy steps of the brownstone, pausing momentarily to consider a new option.

He doesn't exist!

Which would be so like him just to apparate randomly on the earth one weekend a year to brush people's hair off their faces, massage suntan lotion on their backs, whisper unsolicited promises about the future, and then just not call any of them before their tans fade!

"MY TAN HAS FADED!!!"

Dejected, you hail a taxi and head back to your apartment, which looks like an eighties hair band used it as a dressing room. You pull your mangled, frozen feet gingerly out of your salt-stained shoes, peel off your clothes and stand under the hot shower, letting the makeup and styling cream swirl down the drain with your exalted expectations.

You pull on your favorite pajamas: worn sweatpants, bunny T-shirt and your dad's old wool socks. Too wound up for bed you sit down on the floor and slump back against the base of the couch, all adrenaline spent.

And then you are hungry. Oh, man, hungry like a teenage boy in spring training. You want eggplant parmigiana, a loaf of bread, pie and a glass of whole milk. Maybe a ribeye steak. You crawl to the fridge. Seltzer, a yogurt and one furry bagel.

You grab your keys and head down to the deli. You order a roast-beef sandwich and open a bag of potato chips while you're waiting. You're peering into the ice-cream case, your mouth full, when a familiar voice behind you requests a pack of Marlboros. This is when you're supposed to look up, softly lit by the brightly colored frozen dairy, glowing in your natural state of beauty, and be struck by how pointless it was to pour yourself into a socially supported dominatrix outfit. By what a bigger person you are. By the revelation that this scruffy, sexy smoker from your past is just another human being with whom you are fully at peace.

But the moment you catch his eye it's that same jolt through your spine of months past. And he smiles lopsidedly in that way he does, as if he has just remembered the idea of you and likes it. He gives you a "Hey" and then reaches over to tuck your hair behind your ear. And you are ready to throw down with him right then and there in front of the deli guy. Ready to sacrifice any amount of sleep, hydration, comfort, financial solvency, for one more fucking kiss. And then, as he is asking for your number—the one that "accidentally got washed" in his jeans pocket by some idiotic roommate—his gaze flickers behind you and you follow it. Straight to the flash of long blond hair leaning impatiently from a cab window outside.

And you give him your number without flinching.

Taking it directly from the Heimlich maneuver hot line on the poster behind him.

With a "Cool," he is gone. And maybe someday, if his roommate stays away from his wash, he will call for you and find out exactly how to make someone throw up. WHICH IS PRETTY GODDAMN CLOSE TO MAD PASSIONATE ALMOST! And even closer to making him regret HIS ENTIRE EXISTENCE! Damn close! And you'll take it! You are running a victory lap around the bagel bin, past the produce, grabbing your roast beef on the way out the door.

And you couldn't have planned it better if you tried.

You are Perseus gloriously gripping the head of Medusa. You are Alexis with Crystal knocked out cold at your feet. You are exhausted.

Laura Caldwell, who lives in Chicago with her husband, left a career as a trial attorney to become a novelist. She is the author of *Burning the Map*, *A Clean Slate*, *The Year of Living Famously*, *The Night I Got Lucky* and two novels of suspense, *Look Closely* and *The Rome Affair*. She is a contributing editor at *Lake Magazine* and an adjunct professor of law at Loyola University Chicago School of Law. Please visit her at www.lauracaldwell.com.

What I Found
Laura Caldwell

"That bra makes you look aggressive." This was one of the last things my mother said to me. She was in the hospice, a place that tried so hard to be cozy and comfortable—with chenille throws and crocheted plant holders—that the decor sometimes broke my heart.

On that day, about thirty-eight hours before she died, I had visited alone. Dale had been diligently coming with me, but I feared that the whole tragic-illness-of-parent thing might be taxing our relationship. We'd only been together nine months after all, and at twenty-seven, he was a few years younger than me. He had a fun-filled life of bands that didn't start playing until 1:00 a.m. and friends who "crashed" on his couch for a day or ten. Then there was his time with me, which included hospice visits, late-night crying jags, fashion consultations about which black dress to wear to the funeral, decisions about which pine condo would be my mother's final real estate.

Plus, my mom had made a comment one recent night when I kissed her goodbye.

"It would be nice to see my daughter," she said.

She'd been sick, both mentally and physically, for a long time, and she was heavily medicated, but when she said that, I assumed she meant she wanted to see me, by myself, just the two of us. Now, I wonder.

I went back the next night. Her light gray hair, worn in a shorn cap since her treatment, had been washed and combed by the staff. She was dressed in her favorite marigold bathrobe, although it pooled around her. She was tired, as usual, and cranky, as always, yet she'd found her sense of humor. God knows how she did it, but despite the leukemia that was carrying her surefooted toward her death, my mother had days of clarity when she saw things with the cool eye of a stand-up comedienne.

As I came in, an orderly delivered her dinner tray. The woman had fluffy gray hair, rolled on either side of her face and pulled back in a ponytail. My mother thanked her, watched her retreating back and said, "Hair by George Washington, circa 1796."

I laughed and stripped off my parka. Underneath, I wore a cotton-candy pink turtleneck I'd bought during a recent lunch break. It was silk and cost entirely too much, but I felt the color might cheer up my mother. And myself.

I hung my parka on the coat tree and tidied the books on her nightstand—a Picasso biography and a diary of Anaïs Nin. I felt Mom staring at me. When I turned, I caught her eyeing my breasts the way she used to when they were first growing and I still allowed her to join me in clothing-store dressing rooms.

"Suzanne," she said, "and I mean this in a good way." She stopped and coughed. "That bra makes you look aggressive."

"What?" I said, annoyed. I looked down at my chest. I had to admit she made a good, if strange, argument. My breasts looked hard, rounded and with a determinedly upward thrust.

She squinted. "You should wear that to a job interview."

When you fade from the world, you're granted a hall pass of sorts. You are suddenly and utterly relieved of all the crap, clutter and chaos that crowded your home, all that *stuff* you couldn't get around to dealing with. Instead, your sad-sack children or your best buddies will have to clean and organize and debate about whether to save the little silver salt and pepper shakers, whether to throw away that worn, green cashmere sweater.

Since this buck-passing, courtesy of the Grim Reaper, is a universal truth, it was not surprising that after she died, I found myself sorting through the dense mess of my mother's house.

What was surprising was what I found.

My mother lived the last decade of her too-brief life—only fifty-seven years—in a cottage on Lake Michigan. It had brown wood shingles, which weathered to gray every few winters, alongside white-trimmed windows and a high, curved roof fashioned like an upside-down U. Two Adirondack chairs sat on the back deck, peeking over the immense lake, waiting for someone with a glass of wine and a reflective mind to slip into one of them. My mother was a poet and an artist, someone very much aware of perception and beauty. But no one had ever looked in her goddamned closets.

"Jesus, Suz, what are we going to do with all this stuff?" asked Dale. He stood, holding open a closet door. His face, with its rounded features and green eyes, had taken on some of the despair I knew from my own appearance.

I stepped next to him and let out a long breath at the sight of clothes crammed tightly on hangers, hatboxes stacked one on top of another, shoes and books and photo albums, all packed onto a few shelves.

"I'll take care of it," I said quickly. I couldn't push him too hard. I wasn't sure if he would run. And yet, I craved Dale more than I ever had before. There was something so appealing, sexy even, about the fact that he was here, the fact that he'd consulted with the funeral director about seating and the way he loaded all the flowers into his Jeep afterward. These actions smacked of a partnership. Or at least the potential.

I looked back in the closet, and felt stricken. It must have showed.

"I'm sorry," Dale said.

"Don't worry about it."

"No, seriously, I'm sorry."

I knew he felt helpless. It was the way all my friends felt. No one had been able to take away her problems. No one could erase her death or my continual sleepless nights.

"You've done so much," I said. "It's fine."

"It's not. I'll do it. Hell, I'll sort out her underwear drawer if you want me to."

I looked at him and laughed. "Will you sweep out the garage?" It was still a lot to ask. My mother's garage appeared as if it hadn't been cleaned since the Nixon administration. But it only contained never-used tools and buckets of salt for a snowy driveway. It wasn't intimate the way the closet was. It didn't have the scent of her.

"Of course."

"I'm glad you're here," I said.

For a moment, Dale put his hands in my hair. "Love you."

"I love you." I still tingled when I said it. I wondered if it were possible for such a feeling to last forever.

His boot steps were heavy in my mother's hallway. The garage door creaked open, then shut with a thud. I was alone in my mother's closet.

Her Irish-wool sweaters, perfect for Michigan winters, went into the charity bag. Ditto my mom's shoes—dainty satin heels, rarely worn, and lace-up leather boots. The magazines, mostly *Paris Review* and *The New Yorker,* I threw away. The books I would keep myself. But what to do with all the paper, all the personal documentation? Her transcripts from Sarah Lawrence, where she got her English degree. Christmas cards from her parents, long dead now. As I sifted through these things, I felt the sharp fact that my mother and I had been each other's only family. Slim volumes of her poetry existed—some were even studied occasionally at her alma mater—but I would have to be custodian of all things personal. There was no one else to take such things, no one else to become the historian, the rememberer of Natalie Ames.

And who would be there to watch over me? Who would needle me about my career? Or my lack of one? Natalie Ames thought her daughter was destined for greatness. When I took violin lessons for five painful years in grade school, she imagined future duets with Isaac Stern. When I dabbled with photography during high school, she saw another Annie Leibovitz. And when I announced that my college major would be psychology, she envisioned the walnut-paneled office and the bookshelves bursting with tomes I would author. I had disappointed her with my job as a jury consultant. She didn't like that I spent much of my time in a courtroom, dissecting the words, blinks, nods and expressions of potential jurors. She didn't realize I'd learned this talent from living with her—knowing a bad day by the way she scurried around the kitchen instead of sitting with me at the breakfast table, knowing it was time to call Dr. Huber when she sighed and tapped her fingers against her chest.

I sifted through hatboxes of cards and notes and scraps of poems written on gas-station receipts. I was into the fourth box when I found the letter. I noticed it first because it was written on thick parchment paper, and also because my mom's handwriting appeared in neat, well-scripted rows, when she usually wrote like a shrimp-boat captain caught in high seas. Like many writers, my mother was a scribbler. But on this heavy, ivory paper, she had written legibly, making her words appear formal and forced.

Dear Booker, the first line read, and I felt a quickening of the blood in my wrists. Phillip Booker Joyce was my father.

I checked the date written in perfect penmanship at the top. *November 13, 1974.* The date of my first birthday. But more importantly, ten full months after my father supposedly died in a car accident on an icy country road.

Dear Booker,

I'm writing to tell you that one year ago, I gave birth to our child, a beautiful, apple-cheeked delight, who I've named Suzanne. I felt you had to know, even though I can't allow you to see her.

I know I'm troubled, Booker. I know better than you, of course. And because that's true, I know I can raise this baby. I won't harm her. I wouldn't have harmed anybody. You didn't believe that, nor apparently did the courts. But no matter what the doctors say about my "mental fragility," I have always been aware of the limits of my mind. I know that part of me will die every day without Anna, but I am reborn, too, now that I have Suzanne.

Despite everything, I hope you're living a content life,

Natalie

"This is like a soap opera," Dale said, holding the letter. A dust mask pushed back his black hair; his hands were ensconced in the white gardening gloves he'd been wearing to bag the contents of the garage. "You've always thought your dad died two months after you were born?"

"Right."

"You really think your mom would make up the story of your father's death?"

"Why would she have been writing to him if he wasn't alive?"

"Who's Anna?"

"No idea."

"So this letter is a copy?" he asked. "Or did she never send it?"

"It seems like it was never sent."

He took his eyes away from the letter and studied my face. "Are you pissed off?"

I shook my head. I knew I should be. I knew anger, resentment, confusion and regret probably lay in wait around my next corner. But now all I felt was a slice of excitement.

My life and my mother's, as far as I knew, had been relatively simple. Yes, she had financial problems, like those visited upon many writers, and yes, she had the flares of severe depression that would soon immobilize her unless she was treated by Dr. Huber, the well-known psychiatrist at the university. But I'd gotten used to all that. It was part of us, of her. I pushed away the thought that it would ever get better, a skill that aided me as I treaded water at a job that didn't fulfill me.

This letter, though, ushered in brand-new elements. If my father hadn't died when I was two months old, then he might still be alive. I might still have a dad. Hell, he might live two miles away for all I knew.

Dale read the letter again. He flipped it over and back, studying it. "What should we do?"

"Well," I said, thrilled at his use of the word *we,* "we have to find him."

In the Jeep, Dale couldn't stop talking. "God, I wish I'd brought my damn laptop, but as long as the library has public computers, we'll be fine." We'd already packed away my mother's computer, and although Dale was a programmer, someone rarely without his laptop, he'd left it at home when we'd gone to clean the house. "This time is for you," he'd said. "And your mom."

"I know at least ten places we can search," he continued now. "We'll be able to find him."

"If we do, do you think we can get a phone number?" I asked.

"Yeah, usually."

"I could call my father." I said this with awe.

"Absolutely."

"I might talk to him tonight."

"Definitely." Dale's voice was excited. He kept talking about the different searches he'd do, the different Web sites. I tried to follow every word of his chatter and let each distinct syllable make fingerprint impressions on my brain, blotting out the question that was growing and starting to steam—*How could she?*

The library was a modern, slanted structure of steel and glass, which hulked over the town's quaint clapboard houses.

Inside were a row of computers, and Dale took a seat in front of number five. I slid into a wheeled chair and moved behind him. His large hands were surprisingly delicate on the keyboard, like they respected the machine.

"Cards, please." This from a large woman with a tennis-shoe charm on her necklace.

Dale and I looked around the library. There was one other person on the six computers. It was a Thursday at two in the afternoon.

"Library policy," the woman said. I could tell she felt official and industrious. I had to stop myself from commenting on the tennis-shoe charm.

"We'll pay a fee," I said. I lifted my purse off the floor.

She held up a hand and averted her eyes, as if I were trying to bribe her. "I'm not supposed to allow this."

"Please," I said. "We're researching something important."

"Can't do it," the woman said. She shook her head and pursed her mouth in a fake-sad kind of way.

"My mother died three days ago," I said. "And, well, it's kind of ironic, but I just found out that the father she told me was dead might still be alive." My voice got louder, and tears burst like hot beads from my eyes. "We're trying to find him, okay? I'm about to find my dad, who I've never even met. Can you give us a break? *Please?*"

The woman looked at me, blinking. "Oh…well. One hour." She turned and left.

Dale sat silently for a moment. He was good at that. "You okay?"

I wiped my eyes. "I'm fine. Sorry. I don't know where that came from."

"Hey, it'll happen." Another moment of quiet. How amazing it was that he was here, that he was doing this for me. "Ready?" he said.

I rubbed his forearm. "Yeah."

"Breathe."

I did.

He turned back to the computer.

We found a number of Phillip Joyces on the Web, but none of them could have been my father. Too old, too young, too Chinese.

"Try his full name," I said. I wrote it on the back of one of my business cards and held it out for Dale to see—*Phillip Thadius Booker Joyce.* An East Coast name, my mother had once said. (Her exact words, I believe, were, "A waspy, East Coast name with a twist." This said with a wry bend of her mouth.) A wonderful name, I'd always thought, a name for a man who would have been a devoted father, were it not for that car accident.

As Dale got back to work, I watched the clock. I watched his lovely hands click, click, click—working away at the keyboard for me, trying to find my father. My father! I liked the concept of Dale being the one to track him down. It was a story we could tell at our wedding.

I thought then of that saying—*When life closes one door, another opens*—which I'd always ridiculed before, lumping it in with the similarly grating story about footprints in the sand. But it was true. The door to my father was about to swing. And then there was Dale, wide open.

After fifteen torturously long minutes, Dale said, "I think I've got it."

I scooted my chair closer, and hugged him around his back. "Really?" It seemed strange that this moment was happening at a public library in a little town in Michigan.

"Yeah, yeah."

I turned my head and put my cheek against his back. "Tell me."

I felt Dale's heart beating fast under the silky cotton of his T-shirt. I felt the muscles moving underneath. Then he went still.

"Maybe you should read this," he said.

I peered around him.

There on the screen was an obituary for Phillip Thadius Booker Joyce. It was only a year old. Proof that the icy country lane I'd heard about had not, in fact, spilled my father's car into a ravine two months after my birth. Or if such an accident had occurred, it hadn't killed Booker Joyce, a small man with longish, blond hair and a large grin (for this was how I'd always thought of him from the photos I'd seen). Instead, my father died of a "coronary event" when he was fifty-nine. He had short, gray hair later in life, according to the accompanying picture, and he'd been a prominent city planner in Connecticut.

I stopped reading after those first few sentences. I sat back and covered my hand with my mouth, then took it away.

"There you have it," I said, trying, inanely, for some jocularity. Instead, my voice sounded as bitter as the taste creeping into my mouth. I felt the stirrings of rage and regret in equal parts.

Dale was silent again, watching me. He leaned forward and kissed my forehead. "Should we read the rest?"

"Can we print it out first?" I couldn't stand the thought of the clinical letters on the brightly lit screen. My face felt hot, my breath coarse. Another death in the family, and I couldn't even confront the woman who'd killed him the first time.

The printer next to the computer whirred into life. From the corner of my eye, I saw the librarian with the tennis-shoe charm exaggeratedly checking her watch. I desperately hoped she would challenge us, maybe ask us to move along. I was ready to pick a fight. I was ready to scream. A voice in my head chanted, *Both gone. Both gone.*

A white sheet of paper was birthed from the printer, then another, but neither Dale nor I looked at them. I could feel him watching me. I hoped for more of his silence.

Instead, he said, "Hey, it's all right."

"How is it all right?" My voice came out quick and loud.

"Look at me."

I pursed my mouth to stop from shouting at him. Finally, I turned my head and stared into his green eyes.

He nodded. He squeezed my hand. "Suzanne, it is all right."

I thought of all he'd done for me, for my mom, over the last few months. I saw him with armloads of funeral flowers and bags of garbage from the garage. I felt his arms that had been around me every single night since this all started.

"It is all right," he said one more time.

This time I believed him.

Dale turned and lifted the white sheet from the printer tray. He read it, then offered it to me. "Congratulations."

"What?"

He held the obituary in his hand and pointed to the last line. *Mr. Joyce is survived by his wife, Paige, and his daughter, Anna, from his first wife, the poet Natalie Ames.*

"His daughter, Anna?" I said.

"Congratulations," Dale said. "You have a sister."

I looked at those eyes, and I smiled. I had a lot more than that.

Imogen Edwards-Jones is an award-winning journalist and broadcaster. She has written four critically acclaimed novels, including *Tuscany for Beginners*. She is the author of the travelogue *The Taming of Eagles: Exploring the New Russia,* as well as two bestselling exposés, *Hotel Babylon* and *Air Babylon*. She has edited two of the War Child anthologies, including *Ladies Night* in the UK and Australia, and is currently working on a BBC Television series of *Hotel Babylon*. She is an honorary Cossack and speaks fluent Russian.

A Blast from the Past
Imogen Edwards-Jones

Claire takes the train to London to get away from her husband. It's eight months since they got married and, quite frankly, things have become a little dull. After all the excitement of the wedding, with the dress, the presents, the party and all that lovely attention, married life is turning into something of a letdown. Living in the countryside, away from all her friends, the great big happy ending isn't quite as great or as big or as happy as she'd expected.

No one had warned her that the first year of marriage was not a bed of elegantly sprinkled rose petals. In fact, none of her friends had ever really actually discussed marriage beyond the altar very much at all. Viewed as an end in itself, something to aspire to, along with a flat stomach, size-six jeans and a Balenciaga handbag; marriage was just another one of those things to tick off on a lifetime-achievement board.

In fact, the only marriage that Claire had witnessed up close and personal was that of her parents. Three decades of quiet compromise and disappointment; it ended in the most banal and passionless of solutions—an amicable divorce—when Claire was twenty-five years old. And as Claire sits in her country cottage in the middle of nowhere, she can't help but think that this is exactly where she is headed. All she really has to look forward to is thirty years of domestic drudgery, peppered with occasional bouts of polite sex with her less-than-dynamic husband, Howard.

So last Thursday when she saw Jefferson's name, hidden in there amongst a group e-mail sent by an old friend, it was like a lifesaving bolt from the blue. And Claire grabbed it with both hands.

You see, Jefferson represents everything that Howard is not. Jefferson was her ex-boyfriend from years back and he was glamorous, he was intelligent, he was drop-dead handsome, he was American, good in bed, wild, hedonistic, tanned, toned and totally reminded her of her youth. Not that Claire is at all old, mind you. She is thirty-two. But let's just say that in the recent past, catalogs have become much more interesting, and cropped tops from Top Shop are increasingly out of bounds.

It took her all of ten seconds to reply. Her tone was flirtatious, racy and, for a recently married woman, it was rather forward.

Jeff, darling! It's been a long, long time. Still as sexy as ever? Still playing the guitar? Still traveling the world? Still got that little tattoo? Still single? Wld love to hear from you. Love, Claire.

She held her breath for a second before she sent it. What if Jefferson didn't reply? What if he didn't remember who she was? What was she thinking? She smiled. Of course he would. Jeff was one of the great loves of her life. Were it not for circumstances beyond both of their control, they'd be together right now. He was one of those significant lovers that Claire tended to talk about when she was sharing with girlfriends, drunk, at two in the morning. The mere idea of him put a spring in her stride. She pressed Send and sat back in her chair.

That night when Howard came home from the coalface of estate agenting, he found his wife was unusually chatty. She'd had a bath, washed her hair and put some makeup on. She was altogether different from the tracksuit-wearing, monosyllabic woman he normally returned to. She'd even done some cooking. Not the sort of Nigella cooking that he craved and that she'd produced in the early days of their relationship, but she had cut open a few sauce bags and jazzed up chicken breast in his honor, and he was pleased.

Well, Claire had become a little difficult of late. She had changed from the carefree soignée girl about town that he'd married into this rather tetchy, grumpy withdrawn woman who could barely be bothered to speak to him when he came home. Howard had been so worried about the change in her, he'd spoken to his mother about it from work. He always spoke to his mother when he was concerned about things. She always gave such great advice. His mother had originally suggested that Claire might be pregnant, and when he said that there was no chance of that, his mother suggested that he give her a wide berth. "The first year of marriage is difficult," she warned. "There are lots of teething problems. Particularly for a girl who had a career and a life in London before moving to the country. Give her some space and she'll find her feet."

So Howard had been giving Claire space. Plenty of space. So much space, in fact, that they hadn't had sex in six weeks. As a result, Claire was under the impression that her husband no longer fancied her, and Howard thought that he was being a caring, sharing new man.

However, that night, after their chicken supper, Howard thought that perhaps Claire might have had enough space and suggested that they get an early night. But Claire politely refused, saying she had a few e-mails to send.

Sitting in the darkness, her husband asleep next door, Claire hoped against hope that her ex-lover had replied. She stared at the screen as the computer dialed up: a message from her sister, spam selling her Viagra, an invitation from her old boss. And then, there it was—Jefferson Allen's reply.

Hey there sexy!!!!!!!—long time no hear—definitely still single, still playing the guitar, still got the tats, am coming over 2 ur neck of the woods nxt wk, poss record contract, u still there? U still got great tits? JA.

Claire could hardly contain herself. Jefferson's response was so quick, so funny and so flirtatious. He'd always been such a laugh. He'd always been so entertaining. And he was coming over next week. Claire leaned forward on the desk and smiled. She ran her hands through her blond hair and looked down at her own cleavage. She did still have rather nice breasts. Round and pert and rather underwired—she'd always been quite proud of them. She was pleased that he remembered them, too. But then he would, wouldn't he?

They were meant to be together. So he would remember every inch of her, as she remembered every inch of him. His dark hair. His blue eyes. The way his lips curled when he smiled. His smooth back. His long, strong legs. She'd lost count of the number of times she'd lain in bed at night and imagined it all, poised above her, on the point of penetration. She curled a strand of blond hair around her finger and bit the end of her nail. And he was still single.

J—can't believe u r coming over here nxt wk. Of course I'm still in town. Where else wld I be? Let's meet up? C. ps tits still great.

It took another flurry of flirty e-mails for Claire and Jefferson to finalize the rendezvous. It was hard for Claire to keep the arrangements from her husband. She had to get up early to make sure he didn't check their shared e-mail before she'd the chance to delete the messages. And she had to go to bed late to ensure the same. Howard thought that her behavior and sudden computer interest was a little erratic, but nothing dramatically out of the ordinary. However, the tension in the house was something else. Claire's temper was even shorter than usual. She seemed to be sighing out loud a lot. And she was overly critical of everything he did. The way he brushed his teeth seemed to annoy her. The way he blew his nose. The way he ate. The way he laughed. The way his socks never quite made it into the laundry basket. In short, all his little old habits that she used to find endearing now apparently got right up her nose. So when she suggested she wanted to see a girlfriend in London, and that she planned to spend the night, Howard was only too pleased for her to go.

★ ★ ★

Sitting on the train, looking out of the window, Claire's heart is racing. Her hands are clammy, her top lip is moist and her desire is mounting with each mile traveled. She hasn't felt this excited since her wedding day. There is only an hour to go before she sees Jefferson again. Will he be the same? Will he still fancy her? It's taken ten years for their great love to be reunited. All she has to do is keep herself together for a little while longer.

She exhales through her mouth, trying to relieve some of the tension, and looks at her reflection in the glass. Perhaps she should lengthen her bra straps? She's pulled them so short and pushed her breasts up so high, she can practically lick her own cleavage. She tweaks the collar of her white silk shirt and undoes another button. Now is not the time to be subtle, she thinks. Jeff has got to realize immediately what he has missed out on. She takes out her handbag and starts to rattle around inside for her compact. Her mobile rings.

"Hello?" she answers.

"Hi. It's…me."

"Who?" she asks.

"Me? Howard? Your husband?" he says.

"Oh, Howard," she stutters. "Sorry. I was miles away."

"You sound it," he replies. "Um, I was just calling to wish you a great evening. I hope you have a wonderful time and I can't wait to hear all about it. Oh, and send my love to Sue."

"Right," says Claire, fighting the hot wave of guilt that suddenly engulfs her. "Will do."

"Love you," says Howard.

"Um, thanks," is all Claire can manage in reply.

She hangs up, just as the train pulls into Marylebone Station. The fuss, confusion and rush for a taxi, fortunately, prevent her from dwelling on her lies and duplicity all that much. And by the time she is in the back of the cab, on her way to Duke's Hotel, the anticipation and the adrenaline more than take over. Pulling up outside the hotel, Claire checks her appearance one last time. The tight black pencil skirt, the sheer black stockings and high black shoes, teamed with the white silk shirt, all go to make up the slim sexy secretary look that she is after. She smooths down her hair, adds some extra lip gloss and, finally, removes her wedding ring, popping the gold band and diamond-solitaire engagement ring into her handbag.

She is the requisite ten minutes late as she walks into the quiet, paneled bar. It smells of tradition and old cigars. She searches the leather-padded armchairs. There's a fat bald bloke in the corner. Is that him? She looks confused. There's a couple talking. A man in a suit. A woman on her own, staring expectantly at the door. Where is he?

"Claire!" comes a familiar voice with a Boston brogue. She turns around to find Jefferson sitting in the corner. Her heart stops, her mouth goes dry, her heart is racing…. He is… Oh? A little shorter than she remembers. Dressed in jeans, with a blue jacket and a white T-shirt, he's thicker set, older, with more lines, less hair and round horn-rimmed specs.

"Jeff!" she exclaims, stepping backward as she takes it all in. "You look…exactly the same," she lies.

"So do you," he lies right back.

"How great to see you." She leans in and kisses him. Even his skin smells different.

"God, it's great to see you, too." He grins. His bright white heavily orthodontized teeth haven't changed at all. "So how have you been? Still working hard?"

"Absolutely," she lies again, perching down next to him. "I've had such a busy day in the office."

"Well, you need a drink," he says. "Waiter!" He clicks his fingers. Claire blushes slightly. A charming white-jacketed waiter approaches. "A martini for the lady," says Jeff. "And another one for me."

Jeff and Claire sit there, eating peanuts, drinking their incredibly strong cocktails, searching for topics of conversation. Claire shifts uncomfortably, Jeff laughs too loudly, as a ten-year gap yawns before them. He tells her about his music career, omitting the fact that it is still going nowhere. She fills him in on her stunning rise through her legal firm, not mentioning that she gave it all up to get married and move to the country.

They order another drink. Claire cracks open her first packet of cigarettes in six years. She keeps staring down at her left hand; her wedding-ring finger looks rudely naked and vulnerable. She drinks some more vodka. They resort to talking about old times. Claire leans forward, pushing her breasts together. Her lips are wet with booze.

"God," she drawls, "do you remember when we made love in that little hotel in Paris and you covered me with bits of chocolate?"

"No?" laughs Jeff, leaning in. "Did I really?"

"Yeah," says Claire. "You licked them off, crumb by crumb."

"Really?" says Jeff, smiling away. "I don't remember that at all!"

"How about when we were on holiday in Spain?" suggests Claire.

"Oh," he replies. "That was great."

"And we drank all that sangria…"

"Oh yeah," he nods.

"And we made love on the beach…"

"Yeah," he nods.

"And we swam naked until dawn…"

"Did we?" He grins. "God…you've got a great memory." He laughs.

"I have," smiles Claire. "So many great memories."

"We've got plenty of those," says Jeff. He leans over and starts to run his hand up and down Claire's leg. The feeling is electrifying. She can hardly move, breathe or concentrate. "You do look really great, you know, Claire," he mumbles, looking directly into her eyes. "Just like I expected…"

Claire's stomach lurches as all the old familiar feelings come flooding back. She and Jefferson were always made for each other.

"Why did you never ask me to marry you?" she says suddenly. "Why did you never ask me to run away with you? Back to the States?"

"What?" he says. His face falls with confusion. He snaps back into his chair, withdrawing his hand. "Ask you to marry me? Why would I do that?"

"Because we're soul mates."

"We had a fling."

"Because you love me."

"It was just sex."

"Sorry?" says Claire. The color drains from her cheeks as she begins to feel sick.

"Yeah," he says. "Sex," he repeats. "That's what I always loved about you. We had great sex but with no commitment. Don't tell me you didn't get that?"

"Well…" Claire struggles. She looks around in her handbag for another cigarette.

"That's one of the things that I loved most about you," continues Jeff. He rubs his hands together, warming to his theme. "You were so strong, so independent, clever and sexy, and we did it like rabbits all over Europe. Happy days," he smiles. "You were one of the best flings I ever had."

"Fling," repeats Claire.

"Yeah," he nods. "I have no idea where you get this marriage thing from. It was the last thing on my mind." He starts to laugh. "You're not marriage material, Claire. You're far too filthy." He grins and gives her thigh a squeeze. "What are you thinking?"

"You're right," says Claire, getting out of her chair and draining her glass. "What am I thinking? Listen," she says. "It was nice to see you. Rekindle an old fling, that sort of thing, but I'm afraid I've got to go."

"What?" says Jeff, sounding a bit surprised. "I thought we might… You know…for old time's sake."

"Well, you thought wrong," says Claire. "I'm afraid I have a train to catch and a husband to see."

"You do?"

"I do."

"Someone married you?"

"Someone did."

"Well, he's a brave fellow."

"I know," smiles Claire. "It's just a shame it's taken me this long to realize it."

Claire calls Howard a few times from the train but there is no reply at the house. She wishes she'd listened more this morning when he was saying goodbye, because then at least she might have an idea where he might be. She calls again from the cab but still there is no response. His mobile is switched off. Maybe he is working late? If only she could remember.

Letting herself back into the cottage, Claire suddenly shivers. The air is remarkably cold. Turning on the lights, she looks around the sitting room and it all looks a bit bare. Have they been robbed? There are bits and pieces missing. Empty shelves, missing objects. She runs upstairs to check on the computer. It is still there, purring away in the darkness. She turns on the light, the window is open and there are reams and reams of curling paper blowing in the wind. As she walks across the room to close the window, she looks down at the paper on the floor. "Of course I'm single!" she reads. "My tits are still great!" "I can't wait to see you." "It'll be just like old times." "Remember the night of chocolate chips?" The sentences swirl around her feet. Claire cups her cheeks in horror and slowly sinks to the floor. The full extent of her undoing slowly dawns on her. She had never totally deleted the e-mails. Tears of self-pity crawl down her face. She looks up at the desk and there, stuck to the screen is a note, written in neat controlled script and it says: "You're a liar and a cheat. I want a divorce."

In 1995 Chris Manby met a New York psychic who told her she would write seven novels. She has just published her ninth, which means she probably won't marry that millionaire either! Raised in Gloucestershire, England, Chris now lives in London. Her hobbies include Pilates and finding creative excuses for avoiding it.

Chris Manby's novels: *Flatmates, Second Prize, Deep Heat, Lizzie Jordan's Secret Life, Running Away From Richard, Getting Personal, Seven Sunny Days, Girl Meets Ape* and *Ready Or Not.*

Saving Amsterdam
Chris Manby

There are some advantages to being single, Lisa told herself. She didn't have to pretend to play badly at *Goldeneye* on the Nintendo 64 in case she beat him and sent him into a strop. She didn't have to smell his socks or iron his shirts and get shouted at when she left the slightest crease somewhere that would never be seen. She didn't have to put up with his tedious friends, or babysit the younger members of his family while he went ahead and had fun in the name of work. In short, she didn't have to do anything she didn't want to anymore.

And she knew that she should have been happy by now. I mean, she told herself, it had been six months since he did the deed—ending their relationship and an entire life mapped out in Hallmark-card moments with just a few simple words.

"I don't think I love you anymore."

Lisa stared at him as if she'd misheard. Any second now, she told herself, he's going to break into a big smile and take me into his arms and hug me. Perhaps, that particularly mad bone inside her cried, he's playing a last cruel joke before he asks you to marry him. But he didn't break into a smile. And he didn't ask her to marry him. He really did want to finish their relationship and he wanted her out of their shared flat as quickly as humanly possible. He'd help her pack, he said, seeing as he was such a kind and thoughtful bloke. Would she like him to drive her back to stay with her parents?

The shit. She didn't see it coming. Not at all. She had believed him when he said that his unassailable miserableness was something to do with extra pressure at the office. Only that afternoon she had spent a fortune stocking up the fridge with his favorite foods so that they wouldn't have to leave the house all weekend if he didn't want to. She only wanted to make his life easier. He repaid her kind efforts with twenty-four hours' notice to quit. Later her best friend christened him the Bastard Ex.

Six months on, she was, as her friends had predicted, getting through whole weeks without crying. Of course she was. And sometimes she would catch herself laughing in a strangely unfamiliar carefree way as though he had never been in her life and scraped the surface of her heart into mince with his carelessness. Sometimes she was the old Lisa. The Lisa who would have been sick with hilarity at the idea that she would ever iron a man's shirts and claim to enjoy doing it. The Lisa who would have had little time for a girl who could no longer walk down certain streets in London because, even if she wasn't likely to bump into the man who had left her brokenhearted, she was sure to see something that would remind her of him.

That was the worst part of being alone. Toward the end, he hadn't been so much in her life that he left such a gaping hole when he finally went anyway. But there were certain things that would always be inextricably linked to the best times with him. Certain things that would take her back to the happy times at the beginning of their relationship when he still opened car doors for her and helped her to put on her coat. Things that would make it seem impossible that he had spent their last few months together sitting in front of the TV like a vivisectionist's monkey with half its brain cut out while she lugged the shopping home from the supermarket on foot.

On a good day Lisa was well versed in the reasons why she was better off without him. But in the words of the song, there was always something there to remind her of the halcyon days when that hadn't been the case. Stupid things.

Red wine, for example. The bouquet of a fine Merlot reminded her of his first fumbling attempts to seduce her. Chicken korma reminded her of evenings in his flat watching *Friends* and really wanting Rachel and Ross to be happy together, because didn't everyone deserve to be as happy as Lisa and her loved one were back then?

Well, that was then. Now Lisa had moved on to vodka tonics, become a vegetarian and stopped watching *Friends*. That wasn't too much of an inconvenience. The real pain was the constriction she felt around her heart when the tube sailed past Sloane Square. She hadn't walked down the King's Road since the night he said he no longer loved her. It was as though she might see the ghosts of them peering in through the window of a jeweler's shop. He was always looking at watches—though he was still unable to get anywhere on time if it mattered to Lisa. She had harbored a wild fantasy that one day he might spend a couple of minutes measuring up the diamonds for her left hand instead of the latest Breitling.

So, the King's Road was out of bounds, too. At least until her mashed-up heart was a little less scabby. Perhaps in ten years' time she might once again brave the hallowed halls of Peter Jones. But as for Amsterdam...Amsterdam, she would never be able to go back to. Because, if there was a defining moment in their relationship it was a weekend spent in Amsterdam four winters earlier. Bright but cold. Frost crystals glittered the pavements. The trees along the canals wore little white lights in their bold bare branches. She thought she had met her soul mate. They were *in love.*

When she closed her eyes, Lisa could almost feel the icy tip of his nose as he kissed her on a dainty bridge somewhere near Dam Square. She remembered feeding him French fries and mayonnaise in a tiny café under the disapproving eye of some old matron; she remembered laughing with him at the dull brown pictures from Van Gogh's potato period in the Van Gogh museum; talking for each other in pidgin Dutch; learning the words for bedroom and whipped cream... He had loved her then, hadn't he? Looking back, with the sound of their last argument ringing in her ears, it was difficult to tell. Before the end, she had suggested that they go to Amsterdam to celebrate their anniversary. Now she knew she could never go back.

Shame her boss didn't quite understand the new world map of the recently brokenhearted.

Schiphol Airport, Amsterdam. Just twenty minutes to go before Lisa was due to make a presentation to her company's new Dutch clients. Lisa yanked the blue Samsonite trolley case off the luggage carousel and in doing so nearly managed to pull her arm from its socket. She thought she'd traveled a lot lighter than that. With one eye on her watch, as if constantly checking the time might stop it from passing so quickly, she hurtled through the arrivals lounge. A small gang of men leaned against the barrier to separate new arrivals from overeager loved ones. Lisa scanned the drivers' hand-scrawled boards for her own name and, locating it with bionic long-distance vision, hurled her bag over the barrier toward her own driver before following the bag with a pretty spectacular vault.

They made it to the bleak out-of-town offices of the H & P Advertising Agency with two minutes to go. Lisa clipped her way into the building on executive heels, praying that she looked efficient and enthusiastic rather than plain (or should that be plane) manic. Her plan had been to arrive a whole two hours earlier. Where but at Heathrow could a girl find fog to ground a scheduled flight at the beginning of June, for God's sake?

A round-faced assistant showed Lisa straight to the conference room. She tossed her jacket on the back of a chair, grinned her biggest grin and opened her case to get out her notes. But she couldn't find them. Instead she found three pairs of stars-and-stripes boxer shorts.

Back at her hotel—The American (that irony was not lost on her)—Lisa finally let go the tears that made her feel as though her eyes must be bulging cartoon style throughout the rest of the abortive meeting. She said what she could without the notes and her carefully drawn storyboards, but she couldn't remember the deal-clinching figures. She had her laptop in her hand luggage but the battery in that had run down and no one could find her the right kind of adapter to use with Dutch plug sockets.

"Don't worry. Anyone could pick up the wrong case," said the super-cool MD, but Lisa knew that kind of mistake had never happened to him, nor was it ever likely to.

"Imagine how the bloke who did get your case will feel when he pulls out *your* knickers at some high-level meeting," said Jane when Lisa called the London office to check for messages and voice mail.

That was no comfort either. Lisa had packed the grungiest pants imaginable. So grungy that the thought almost made her ready to resign her own case to history forever. Even if he had handed it in, how would she be able to face claiming such disgraceful luggage?

"What else was in your case?" Jane asked in a further attempt to make light of the disaster. "Vibrator!"

"Worse," said Lisa. "How about a self-help guide to finding your ideal man?"

"Sheesh," said Jane. "You're never going to be able to get that bag back."

It was hot in the hotel room. Lisa leaned her forehead against the cool glass of the window and looked out into the square below. It was still light at seven o'clock. A beautiful summer night. Tourists milled about in search of somewhere to spend the evening. Café proprietors drew attention to their menus. Hot-and-bothered culture lovers were tempted from their museum tours by the prospect of a long cool beer.

Lisa had a sudden unwelcome flashback to the French fries and mayonnaise. Her bedroom window was almost opposite the café where the BE had licked her fingers clean and whispered promises for the night ahead. As if on cue, a young couple chose a seat in full view of Lisa's depressing hotel room and snuggled close. Lisa suddenly felt very sorry for the middle-aged woman who had once been subjected to a similar display and drew her curtains on the scene.

She had three more nights of this. A room with a view of the place where she had once been so happy. Miserable memories and not even a pair of clean knickers to do her wallowing in. She had phoned the airline but no one had handed in her case. The receptionist at the hotel promised to let her know if it turned up there instead. In the meantime, Lisa didn't have anything to wear but her best boardroom suit. It had been crumpled by the plane journey, sweated in on her race to the first meeting and, even as she inspected part of the hem that was starting to come down, she somehow managed to spill half a cup of coffee on her skirt.

She ripped the skirt off immediately but within seconds the scalding heat had colored her legs lobster red. Lisa cried again as she tried to rinse the stain out in the adequate bathroom basin. Pale blue linen. Dark brown coffee. She rinsed without a hope.

Lisa sat on the edge of the bath and squeezed her eyes tightly shut. Maybe she would wake up. Maybe she would open her eyes and find herself back in her own little bedroom, ready to start the day with an entirely unmistakable bag. But when she did open her eyes, the stranger's case was still in the corner of the room and the stain on her skirt was starting to dry in the shape of the British Isles.

Lisa ran her fingers over the Samsonite impostor.

What if the owner of this case had a pair of jeans or

something in exactly her size? She could put on clothes from this case and go shopping. It wasn't quite right.

Lisa opened the case and took a better look. The three pairs of stars-and-stripes boxer shorts were exactly where they had been when she opened the case in the H & P office. Gingerly taking each pair by the waistband, she made a neat little pile on the bed and began to investigate further. She guessed by the careful folding that the stuff in this case was clean, at least. She pulled out a T-shirt, a bright souvenir from a Thai beach full-moon party. So the owner of this case had traveled or he knew a man who had. Ralph Lauren Polo socks. Not too impoverished either, by the look of things. Lisa admired his smart leather toiletries case. Took a deep whiff of his aftershave. Jean Paul Gaultier for Men. Nice. Different. Her ex had never liked it.

Beneath the wash bag—bingo. Lisa nodded with approval when she pulled out a pair of battered 501s. Whoever owned this case must have a pretty neat backside. And long legs. Tall. Slim. Beautifully scented. He could be her ideal man.

But there was no point getting quite so attached to someone she would never meet. For all the identifying evidence in his Samsonite, the idiot hadn't taken the time to fill out his name and address on the luggage tag. Lisa resolved to leave the bag with the airline staff when she went to catch her flight home and zipped it shut again. Minus the jeans.

Combined with her neat black court shoes and her smart suit jacket, the look was a bit Farrah Fawcett Majors, but at least Lisa was fully clothed once more. By the time she got to the lobby, she had convinced herself that she almost looked stylish in a very retro way.

She waited behind a man with spiked blond hair at the

desk to hand her keys in. The concierge was taking her time with him. Lisa had been appraising his neat bottom for a couple of minutes before she realized that she was idly gazing at the backside she had been fantasizing about as she rifled through the poor man's case.

At the same time, the concierge noticed that Lisa was standing behind the stranger, and with incredibly unwelcome efficiency, announced: "Well, this is Miss Glover, right here."

Lisa was pulling an expression that wouldn't have looked out of place on a halibut when the stranger turned to her with a milk-steaming smile.

"I think I got your case," he said.

"I think so," said Lisa.

"Are those my jeans?" he asked.

Right then, Lisa knew there was no God. What benign celestial being would have allowed her worst knickers and her well-thumbed copy of *How to Attract True Love Into Your Life Through Meditation and Positive Affirmations* to fall into such divine-looking hands. And then to be caught wearing his trousers?

The stranger was still grinning at her.

"Mark Law," he introduced himself. "And I do believe I'm wearing your knickers."

After that, it would have been rude not to agree to go for a drink with him. Feeling only slightly less self-conscious in her own clothes, Lisa joined him downstairs in the hotel bar. Scanning the room for him, she was surprised to feel a long-forgotten shiver of expectation when she caught sight of his face. He smiled at her as though he had chosen her to be his companion, not as though she was a random nutter who had somehow picked up his bag. When he told her she looked much better in her own clothes, she colored to match her pink jumper.

"Pink suits you," he told her.

She went two shades short of cerise.

They ordered martinis and talked about work. He was American. In Europe to drum up funds for his new Internet ventures. She told him about the disastrous meeting at H & P. He told her about the receptionist's face when he arrived at his own hotel and opened his case to reveal a pile of women's clothes when searching for his letter of reservation.

"Is this your first time in Amsterdam?" he asked.

Lisa had been laughing at his impression of the shocked matron at the hotel. Now she felt the cloud passing across her face. "No," she said quietly. "This isn't my first time."

"Then you can show me around," he said.

And before she could explain that there were too many places in the town that she really didn't want to have to go back to, Mark had spread his map out on the table.

"I'm leaving for Switzerland tomorrow morning so I've got to get the best bits done tonight. Are you into art?" he asked her. "Some of the museums are open late. We should see the *Night Watch,*" he announced.

Lisa started to pull a face. "You know, that picture is..."

"One of the great works of the seventeenth century."

Lisa shrugged. That was true. It was one of her favorites. But it was also one of the great works of art she had seen with the BE. She remembered all too vividly standing in front of the painting with his arm slung round her shoulders in the way that she loved. He had kissed her in front of that picture. In fact, she didn't think there was a single significant work of art in Amsterdam that he hadn't kissed her in front of.

"You don't mind seeing it again?" Mark asked. "If we hurry we'll catch the museum before it closes, then we can go and get something to eat. If you want to."

He fixed her with a grin that told her he wasn't often refused.

Fifteen minutes later, they stood before the famous painting. They stood close together, whispering in the reverential quiet of the gallery. Mark drew Lisa's attention to the little girl stepping through the soldiers.

She was suddenly aware of his hand on the small of her back.

"Rembrandt had such an eye for light and shadow," she said, turning toward him to whisper in his ear. But her lips didn't meet with Mark's ear. They met with his own smiling mouth and brushed against his lips ever so lightly. Lisa pulled backward and stumbled, which only had the effect of making Mark take her farther into his arms.

"Do you think we look as though we've known each other for a long time," he asked her as he held her close.

Lisa didn't know what to say. Or where to look. His face was so close to hers that she could no longer focus on his individual features.

"I think we look like we're lovers," he told her.

She felt her most important organs melt.

Van Gogh didn't stand a chance. The museum tour was over. Back in her hotel room, Lisa fumbled for a light switch.

"Leave the light on," Mark breathed hotly. "I mean I've already seen your knickers."

Sex with her ex had become perfunctory. Always starting and finishing in exactly the same way. It worked perfectly, she had told herself. But there had been no surprises for a very long time.

Now, with Mark, Lisa felt a prickle creep up the back of her neck like ghostly fingers. She felt the hot seeping sensation as blood colored her breasts blush-pink with arousal. She felt the inside of her thighs become hypersensitive to his touch. His fingertips seemed so hot on her legs that she expected to see burn marks wherever he laid them upon her. And meanwhile his tongue was in her mouth. His thigh was between hers, easing them apart. She wondered if she was getting giddy through lack of oxygen or the rising heat between their bodies. He took her hand and placed it on his penis. Carefully he wrapped her fingers around the shaft and encouraged her to stroke the hard length of him.

She came before he did. She tightened her thighs round his waist, squeezing hard as he too reached a climax. She felt at once frightened and triumphant as she watched him come. The unfamiliar expression of a new lover... A new lover. She could hardly bear to think.

With his body still pinning hers to the soft white sheets, Lisa began to cry. The tears ran across her cheeks and down the side of her neck and onto his hand, still tangled in her soft brown hair.

Mark eased himself up on to his elbows and looked down at the tear tracks glittering on her face.

"Did we do something we shouldn't have done?" he asked.

She wasn't sure. She wanted to say no to reassure him and herself. At the same time she wanted to nod yes and burst into disappointed tears. Lisa turned the bedside lamp off in an attempt to hide.

"Do you wanna talk about it?"

This time she did nod. In the dark, she felt she could tell him almost everything. If he couldn't clearly see her lips moving, perhaps he wouldn't connect her so inextricably with the story she was about to tell. Perhaps it didn't matter anyway if he thought she was sad or a quitter. They would probably never see each other again.

"The last time I came to this city," she began, "I was with someone I really loved."

And out it spilled. And Mark listened. Never interrupting. He just stroked her hair and listened as she told him about the plans she had made for her and her beloved. The shock of the ending. The numbness that had been with her since. The red wine she could no longer drink, the curry she'd had to abandon, the television she couldn't watch, the music to which she could no longer listen.

"You've got to make new memories," he told her when she finished. "That's the only way to save the things you love for yourself."

"I know that now," she told him. "And I feel like you've helped me to save Amsterdam."

"I'll make it my mission to help you save the world," he said.

Lisa knew that he would be gone when she woke up. Mark's onward flight to Switzerland left Schiphol at 8:00 a.m. It was three minutes past now. Was he still taxiing down the runway? Hearing a plane pass high overhead Lisa pushed her hair back from her eyes and gazed up at the blank ceiling of her hotel room. There was still a faint scent of his aftershave about the pillows. When she put her hand to her chin, it felt sore where his stubble had rubbed at her pale skin as they kissed.

Idiotic, she told herself. Six months of careful, heart-stealing celibacy blown on a mad night with a stranger. But there wasn't time to think about it now. Lisa had another meeting at nine-thirty.

She opened her case. On top of her own clothes was a pair of crumpled stars-and-stripes boxer shorts and a note on hotel paper.

Lisa expected a "thanks for everything" at most. A sweet gesture but no contact number. Instead, she found not only a number but another hotel address.

"Your mission," he had written, "should you choose to accept it. Next weekend, save Paris."

Born in 1977, Kristin Gore is an Emmy-nominated comedy writer. She graduated from Harvard, where she was an editor of the *Harvard Lampoon,* and has written for several television shows, including *Saturday Night Live* and *Futurama.* Her first novel, *Sammy's Hill,* was published in September 2004 and became a *New York Times* bestseller. Kristin is currently working on several projects, including the screen adaptation of *Sammy's Hill* for Columbia Pictures, and another book.

Stray
Kristin Gore

I've never been on a plane I didn't assume was going to crash. Even on the smoothest flights, I still manage at least one moment of sheer, liver-gripping terror—one moment of complete certainty of imminent doom. I have yet to be in an actual plane crash, though I generally average a couple flights a day. I'm a flight attendant, or stewardess, if you prefer, which I do. Few join me in this preference. Most people consider it a politically incorrect term. I consider it a spiritually satisfying one. The Bible instructs us to be good stewards of the earth in a passage that's particularly popular with environmental groups. The Bible talks a lot about mankind, and makes it clear that my gender came from a rib, so when it talks about stewards, I can't help but think it's addressing men. And if I were a man, I'd be a steward of the earth. And probably gay. As things stand, I'm a stewardess. A stewardess with a fear of flying.

I realize I'm a throwback, but I'm a sucker for the "ess"

suffix in general. To me, Meryl Streep is not a phenomenal actor, she's a stunningly talented actress. Similarly, Audrey Niffenegger is an engaging authoress. And the fact that I stole a pack of Big League Chew Bubble Gum from the Rite-Aid when I was eleven didn't make me a burglar, but a burglaress. I suppose I'm still a burglaress, though I'm no longer practicing.

I'm non-practicing when it comes to a lot of things, actually. I'm a non-practicing exerciser, a non-practicing inventor, a non-practicing genius. When I was younger, I was a non-practicing child prodigy. The brilliance of the "non-practicing" adjective impressed me from the moment I first came across it. It allowed one to declare oneself something and then never have to actually back it up, since that would be against one's beliefs. I *am* this, but I choose not to demonstrate it, so you'll just have to take my word for it. Genius. Like me. Non-practicing.

One might think a non-practicing genius like myself would find another job that didn't panic me several times a day, but I don't feel qualified for anything else. I got into stewardessing because of a fascination with the tiny liquor bottles available on planes and in hotel minibars. These perfect little vessels never fail to soothe me. I stare at them and feel happy that not everything is forced to grow up. I decided early on that I wanted to be near them.

The hotel industry was slow to respond to my overtures, but the airline snatched me and my largely fictional résumé right up. I soon realized I was a naturally talented stewardess and felt less guilty that I may have been hired thanks to false claims of extensive hot-air-balloon work. I am disturbingly good at fake-smiling when I feel like crap, which is the single most important skill a stewardess can possess. That, and the self-restraint not to ram the knees of obnoxious passengers with the beverage cart. So far I've made the cart assaults seem like lawsuit-proof accidents. Micro-turbulence is a trusty alibi.

One of the perks of being a professional stewardess for a major airline is that I get to fly for free whenever I want. I appreciate this benefit, though I've never taken advantage of it. I won't step foot on a plane unless contractually obligated to do so. No, flying is much, much too risky, which is why I'm presently driving the eighteen hours back to my hometown. I know the statistics about driving being more dangerous than flying, but I don't believe them. I think they're perpetuated by the airlines attempting to drum up more business, just like I suspect the movie *Attack of the Killer Tomatoes* might have been funded by the Pickle Lobby.

I've asked if I can cash in all the free flights I'm not taking for some other kind of perk, like use of the stair car during holiday house-decorating season or free massages at the Shiatsu Stall in terminal A, but my requests have thus far been denied. I plan to continue pestering HR, because those massages are worth fighting for.

I could certainly use one of them now. I sense the familiar stiffness in my neck settling in for a long stay as I pilot my banged-up Dodge Neon down the back roads I prefer to the highway. A learner's-permit driver sideswiped my car months ago, leaving me with a handicapped passenger door that can only be opened from the outside and a persistent case of whiplash.

I try to self-administer a quick neck rub and am suddenly reminded of a ghost story I heard when I was younger, back in the non-practicing-prodigy days. It was about a woman who always wore a ribbon around her neck. Her husband repeatedly asked her why but she refused to tell him. Finally, when she was a very old lady, she told him to go ahead and untie the ribbon. He did, and her head fell off. This story haunted me when I was little, and to this day, I'm very wary of women wearing chokers.

I glance over at the passenger seat to check on Grant. Or rather, to check on Grant's ashes, which are resting in a slightly mangled plastic Elmo doll that used to be one of his favorite chew toys. It's made of some sort of canine teeth-cleaning material that he'd really flipped for. He'd loved holding it down with one paw and leveraging his lean torso into an optimal chewing position, turning his tail into a thumping metronome. If they made human dental products that exciting no one would ever have cavities. Grant had been a large, happy, loyal dog and I never imagined he would be insubstantial enough to fit inside one of his little toys. He didn't even fill it all the way up.

I blink a few times and wonder what my aunt and uncle are doing. Most likely, my uncle is setting up one of his elaborate Domino's exhibits in the room that used to be my bedroom, before he and my aunt garage-sold all my childhood possessions to make more space for themselves. And when I say Domino's, I'm not referring to the small plastic rectangles people arrange to cascade in spotted waterfalls. I'm talking about the pizza boxes. My uncle eats a small Domino's pizza every day and then glues the empty boxes together to construct various sculptures.

He started doing this soon after I came to live with them. I've heard that the Domino's corporate owners give tons of money to anti-choice groups and I've suspected my uncle's sculptures are more political than he's let on, but I've never had the energy to investigate.

My aunt, I feel sure, is asleep. That's what she does when she isn't taking pills. She hasn't always been like this. Just for the last twenty years. I sigh and remember the phone call that led to an earlier eighteen-hour drive to pick Grant up in the first place.

"We're going to put him down. He's old and it's for the best."

"Is he sick?"

"No. But we're sick of taking care of him."

I'd gotten in the car a half hour later. Grant had lived three more years under my care before dying on his own terms.

Were there some meaningful place to scatter Grant's ashes that didn't involve a trip home, I gladly would have pounced on it the way he used to pounce on the mail the instant it slid through the slot. Wrestling it away from him before he managed to shred anything important was always an adrenaline-pumping project. But for better or for worse, there was only one place where Grant could rest in peace—the ravine behind my aunt and uncle's place.

Grant and I had escaped to the ravine every day of our lives together in that house, no matter the weather. It was our refuge—our land of magic and intrigue. Anyone observing would have seen a sad little kid and a dog not fitting in together, but we saw ourselves as world-weary adventurers ever determined to plot one more mission. Grant was the copilot, my Chewbacca. I, obviously, was Han Solo. We were devastatingly significant, whether or not anyone else realized it at the time. Often the fate of the universe rested in our hands.

The summer I turned nine, my aunt and uncle toyed with the idea of clearing out the ravine and putting down Astroturf. When I heard about this scheme, I screamed for sev-

enteen minutes and thirteen seconds. I knew the exact du-
ration because I used my mom's old watch I'd started wearing to measure it. After minute fourteen, my aunt and uncle
just left the house. That's how they tended to deal with difficult things. But they never brought up Astroturf again.

Sometimes I feel like screaming for extended periods of
time on plane flights. Not in response to obnoxious passengers—I handle them with cart rams and practiced ignoring—but in reaction to repetition. Instead of telling people
the same useless lines about their seat buckles and flotation
devices, I often feel like screaming. Or actually like high-
pitched shrieking, à la Yoko Ono, but I never go through
with it. I mentally add non-practicing artist to my résumé.

The only part of the standard stewardess recitation that I
attach any sort of significance to is the part about the emergency exits, because I think one of the instructions is phil-
osophically profound. I infuse my voice with subtle but
palpable reverence whenever I utter the line "Bear in mind
that the nearest exit may be behind you." How true. To me,
the words are poetic and wise. And tragic, because in real
life I can't go back to those exits.

Approximately every third flight, I fantasize about jumping out of the plane. My neighbor told me when I was
younger that falling through clouds makes a person go blind.
I'd been suspicious of this claim but never had the chance
to prove it wrong. Doing so is one motivation for jumping,
but the stronger one is the shock value. No one would ever
expect it. People would be so surprised. I therefore find the
prospect almost overwhelmingly tempting. If opening the
door midflight and leaping out wouldn't endanger the lives
of my fellow passengers, I might consider it. But I know that
it would and therefore can't in good conscience seriously

fantasize about it. Maybe jumping off a building would be a better bet, if I could ensure that no passersby would be landed on. The building would need to be tall enough for clouds.

I don't consider myself suicidal, just fundamentally bored. But maybe that's occasionally the same thing.

And when I think about jumping, I think about my aunt and uncle. My guardians. I suspect they'd be surprised, and sad, and probably annoyed to have to deal with the aftermath. Would they even deal with it? Or might they just leave it to someone else?

I sneeze violently and wonder whether I'm allergic to Grant's ashes. Or to his absence. I've never had any problems with live dogs, but dead ones are a previously untested allergen. In general, they shouldn't be too difficult to avoid.

My aunt and uncle had never liked the idea of Grant. They warned me that I didn't know how hard it could be to take care of another living thing and did everything to dissuade me from adopting him, short of forbidding it. They told me I'd regret it, that I'd grow to resent him, that I'd be driven crazy by the demands of his simply existing. I listened to them, knowing they were really talking about me, and reminded them that my parents had promised me a puppy before their accident. They sighed and shut up.

As I think about these people who never chose to have me, it begins to rain regularly, then unreasonably. I have to pull over because I can't see anything except my windshield wipers drowning. I'm annoyed, but also pleased that nature is still capable of such sabotage. I'm happy we haven't completely won, and I feel like this sentiment elevates me to the ranks of enlightened stewardesses.

When the river of rain finally slows and I can discern actual individual drops again, I hear barking. I look quickly at the Elmo urn, but Grant remains in ashes, which shouldn't surprise me but does. The barking is close and ostensibly part of the land of the living. I stretch myself up to look farther over the steering wheel and see a three-legged dog engaged in a fierce face-off with my car's right tire. My money's on the tire. The dog must be a stray since I know from previous drives that there's no one and nothing around for miles. I purposely drive this stretch of back road *because* it's lonely and abandoned—I don't feel like either of us has to put on any airs.

But just as I've begun to empathize with the loner life this three-legged dog must lead, I spot a disheveled man limping out of the woods toward my car. He whistles to the dog as he stares at me through the windshield. He's completely soaked.

I stare back at him. He jerks a hitchhiker thumb but doesn't smile or soften his expression in any way. I feel like he's double-dog daring me to be crazy enough to pick him up. I consider the options. He could either kill me or make the drive much more interesting. Or both. On the other hand, I could just drive away and stay alive and bored. I roll down the window.

"Where you headed?"

"End of the rainbow."

"Is that off Route 9?"

He glares at me a moment before nudging his dog toward the passenger door. I open the glove compartment and carefully place the Elmo urn full of Grant inside. The man opens the door and climbs in, getting the seat wet and muddy. His dog takes care of the floor.

"What's your name?" I ask. I should at least know his name.

"Tall," he answers.

He's not really that tall, but I notice he has enormous feet. Maybe he'd been born with them and his parents had made assumptions. I wonder if they're still alive, worrying about him. I put the car in gear and ease back onto the bumpy road.

"And that guy?" I nod to the dog.

"L. Like the letter."

L is pretty cute, in a mangy and wild sort of way. For the first time, I notice a bedraggled ribbon tied around his neck. It might have been red or blue once, but it looks as though it's been the color of damp, dirty fur for a long while. I wonder where this pair has been.

"How'd he lose his leg?" I ask.

"Accident," Tall answers. "Wrong place at the wrong time."

"Mmm. People say timing is everything."

"What people?"

His tone is unmistakably challenging. And paranoid? I wonder if he battles imaginary enemies. I wonder if the metal flashlight in the pocket of my door could be an effective weapon.

"Um…I don't know. My mom. My mom always said timing is everything."

I glance sideways at him to see how he takes this. His forehead appears deep in thought though his eyes look dull and dead.

"What's your dad say?"

"I don't know. He agreed, I guess."

Tall breathes in and out in loud, irregular gasps, before sneezing raucously. I feel the spray on my arm and grow nauseous. When Tall speaks again, he speaks slowly in a low voice, drawing out each word.

"Do you love your parents? Would you die for them?"

I continue steering with my right hand and close my left one around the flashlight, testing its weight. I'm left-handed, like my father.

"My parents passed away when I was young," I reply, trying to keep my voice even. "My aunt and uncle raised me. As much as they bothered to, at least," I can't help but add.

"What's that mean? What'd they do to you?"

He's confrontational again. It's getting dark and the rain is still battering the windshield. I wish it would stop so I could just see a little better. Maybe the back roads weren't such a fantastic plan.

"They didn't do anything to me. They didn't want to deal with me."

Tall bursts into gravelly laughter. I hold my breath, waiting to hear what's so funny. I wonder if it's the gleeful thought of my imminent strangling.

"Maybe *you* were bad timing."

Lightning flashes overhead and I mentally review what to do if it strikes the car. We can survive it, as long as we don't touch anything metal. Grant's chain collar is metal. I've been wearing it as a necklace, since it felt better to put it against my skin than away in some box. The flashlight in my hand is metal, too. I fake-smile at Tall.

"Maybe I was."

He seems mollified. He slides his neck around in a reptilian stretch.

"Got anything to drink?"

I do. I have a backpack full of tiny liquor. I don't drink, but I'm always encouraging others to partake so I can have the empties. I like filling the little bottles up with things I think are better for them. Tall is having none of it.

"I meant water."

He sounds angry and offended. I don't have any water, which I tell him. Buying water depresses me. It should be free and available, like air and love.

"We'll have to stop then. L is dehydrated."

Tall says this defiantly with a smack of his gums, like he's challenging me to argue with a toothless maniac. L doesn't look particularly dehydrated. He's curled up beneath the glove compartment, snoring the stuffy snores of flat-faced dogs.

"I'll find someplace when we make it back to the highway."

I sneak another sideways glance and am alarmed to see that Tall's face has twisted into a menacing sneer. Behind him, the side of the road drops off abruptly into a steep, rocky ravine.

"Stop now," he hisses abruptly. "You don't have a choice, YOU'RE GOING TO STOP NOW."

He's reaching into his coat for something. A knife or a rope. I am instantly hot with the panic that comes with sheer, liver-gripping terror. I think about Grant in the glove compartment and wish he were in the passenger seat instead. I open my mouth to finally start screaming.

Suddenly, I remember that the passenger door is broken and can only be opened from the outside. My panic flees. I feel calm, practically giddy. I break into a real smile as I curl my fingers tighter around the flashlight. It's all I can do to keep from giggling. I glance down at L and know I won't have to throw Grant's toys away after all. The ribbon's coming off though. I'll give him a nice chain collar instead.

I take a long, deep, free breath. As of right now, I'm a non-practicing victim. Tall is the one who's trapped, not me. Though he hasn't been told yet, his only exit is behind him.

As the adrenaline courses through me, I catch a split-second glimpse of his weapon: a soggy pack of cigarettes. The truth is, people have been killed for less.

British-born novelist Maggie Alderson spent eight glorious years living in Sydney, Australia, before returning to the UK in 2001. Moving to Australia was the inspiration for her bestselling first novel, *Pants on Fire,* and she has since published two more. *Mad About the Boy,* also based in Sydney, and *Handbags and Gladrags,* which is set at the designer fashion shows of New York, London, Milan and Paris, which she has been covering as a fashion writer for over fifteen years. Before becoming a full-time author, she was a magazine editor and newspaper columnist. Among other titles, she was editor-in-chief of British *ELLE* and has contributed articles to magazines including *Allure, Gourmet* and *Travel & Leisure.* She is married to a retired soccer player, has one daughter and lives on the south coast of England. She is published in the United States by Berkeley.

Are You Ready Boots?
Maggie Alderson

"Dang diddy dang diddy dang diddy dang…" I sang to myself as I zipped the boot up to my knee, the soft black leather stretching to hug my calf. I got up and looked at myself in the full-length mirror.

"Nancy Sinatra, eat your heart out," I said to my reflection. "These boots were made for me."

I couldn't believe my luck. Not only were those killer boots fifty percent off in the Barneys' shoe department sale, they were even my size. And they weren't just boots—they were actual Manolos. Here I was in New York City shopping just like Carrie Bradshaw. *Sex* was the word for it—and for these very high-heeled, very black, very pointy boots. Boots so high and black and pointy, indeed, that all I could do after admiring myself in the mirror was to turn round to my pal Spencer and growl. "Grrrrrrr," I said, copping a vamp pose with my boot leg forward, my teeth bared.

"Good Lord in the foothills, Miss Lulu," said Spencer in his hilarious southern accent—he had come to New York from Charleston when he was seventeen. "You are such a true minx in those boots, I swear I am quite afraid of you."

Now totally overexcited—Spencer always had that effect on me, not unassisted by the second bottle of Cristal he had insisted on ordering for us at lunch—I asked the nearest sales assistant for the other boot.

I zipped it on and set off stalking up and down the shoe department, working those heels like Ru Paul.

"These boots were made for strutting," I sang to Spencer.

"Yes, ma'am," he agreed. "So why don't you just strut right off and pay for them? It is nearly the cocktail hour and Spencer is one thirsty boy."

I was still admiring the boots—while the sensible side of my brain tried to reason with the champagne-fuddled one, which was insisting they were a bargain—when my other great New York pal, Betty, came shuffling over in a pair of red patent mules that were clearly three sizes too big for her. She looked like a little girl dressing up in mummy's clothes.

"What do you think of these?" she asked us. "They're only $95, down from $400."

"They'd be real nice on The Hulk," said Spencer.

"If only the size had gone down along with the price they'd be great on you," I added. "But look—check out these boots. Aren't they totally perfect?"

"Wow," said Betty, momentarily distracted from the tantalizing bargains on her own feet—she was famous in our crowd for never paying full price for anything; it was like a religion with her. "Those are so hot. They look great on you. How much are they?"

"Who cares?" I answered, strutting around a bit more.

"They make me feel like a Bond girl, I totally have to have them."

I finally came to a halt in front of a full-length mirror, where I was quite mesmerized by how good I thought the boots made me look. They seemed to lengthen and slenderize my legs. They made me look browner. They made me look richer. Kinder. More intelligent. I felt like I had won the shoe lottery.

"These are the boots I'm going to be wearing when I meet my husband," I proclaimed.

And they were. Kind of.

I didn't wear my kinky boots—as Spencer had dubbed them—for six months after I bought them. Even though they were real Manolos and truly beautiful and half price in the sale, I felt so sick and ashamed about how much I had spent on them—money I could ill afford after blowing two months' rent money on that four-day trip to New York—I couldn't bear to look at them, let alone wear them.

They were still in the Barneys carrier bag, which I had brought home in my suitcase as a style souvenir, stuffed under my bed.

And that's where they stayed until one dreary winter Sunday evening when Spencer was over in London for one of his hectic visits and called up to tell me I was coming out with him and six of his favorite boy pals that night to the launch of a new restaurant.

"But it's Sunday, Spencer," I whined at him. "We went out last night, we went to brunch today and an exhibition, we're having drinks again tomorrow. It's not like I haven't seen you and it's not like you have no one else to go with. You've got your usual posse of pooftas lined up, haven't you? Why do you need me?"

There was silence on the other end of the phone. A loud silence I knew all too well from the three years I had shared a flat with Spencer, before he had moved back to the States. He could say more just breathing than most people could put over with RADA coaching and a Hollywood script.

"Spencerrrrrr," I whined, stretching out on my sofa. "It's already past seven, it's a school night, it's drizzling, I'm knackered, my hair's dirty and I have nothing to wear. Nothing."

"I'll pick you up at eight, Missie Lulu," said Spencer firmly. He paused, then continued, "Why don't you wear those kinky boots you bought in Barneys that time? They made you look like a trailer-park Honor Blackman. I like that look on you."

As always with Spencer, who had a personality so charismatic he could have set up his own evangelical TV ministry, I did what I was told. I put the pointy boots on and, standing in front of my mirror wearing nothing but them and my undies, I had to say, they looked pretty damn good.

Inspired by their sex-kitten appeal I backcombed my filthy hair and tied it up into a Bardotesque high ponytail, with my fringe falling over one eye. Then I threw open my wardrobe and raked through the hangers for something good enough to wear with my special boots.

Almost immediately I found the perfect thing: a vintage Pucciesque (i.e., psychedelic bri-nylon from a charity shop) mini kaftan. I slipped it over my head and felt immediately compelled to dance the pony with myself. It was a great look, but I couldn't hack it. Apart from everything else, the restaurant was in Mayfair and the nylon mini was definitely not a West End look. So instead I played it safe with a classic black shift dress and some Jackie O–style ropes of pearls, with my kinky boots as a wicked statement at foot level. I pouted at my reflection one more time and ran downstairs.

It was the usual night out with Spencer and his merry men. Hilarious laughter, totally unnecessary nastiness about everyone else there and far too much to drink. I was on my way to the loo after about five glasses of champagne in half an hour when I first spotted Charlie. You couldn't miss him. He was seriously handsome with a great tan and floppy blond hair, and wearing a beautiful suit. He was standing alone in a corner of the restaurant and as I passed I could feel him checking me out.

When I came out of the ladies', he was still there, still incredibly handsome, still—incredibly—alone and still looking at me. And I could tell by that look that he definitely wasn't gay. He wasn't admiring my dress or my French manicure—he was admiring me. I felt a bit giddy.

I went back to the boys, but found it less easy to concentrate on their antics, even though Spencer had cranked himself up into his most evil mood and was now doing impersonations of people simultaneously as they walked by. It was hysterical, but my gaze kept returning to the mystery man in the corner. Still there. Still gorgeous. Still alone.

I'm sure it was the boots that made me do it, because I can't remember my brain actually forming the thought, but suddenly my feet were on their way over to where Mr. Cutie Dream Man was standing.

"Hi," I said when I got there. "You've been standing alone for ages. I've come to keep you company."

His broad smile revealed perfect white teeth as he held out his hand to me. His eyes were very pale blue.

"Great," he said. "I was hoping you would. I'm Charlie March-Edwards. How do you do?"

Well, I did very well, and from that moment on we did very well together. That first fated encounter led to a drink after the party—Spencer and the boys hardly even acknowledged my departure, as they had spotted a group of Argentinean polo players in the corner—and a chaste kiss as he dropped me home.

From that we moved on to a couple of dinner dates, a walk in the park, an exhibition, a movie and finally into a relationship. A boyfriend. I really had a boyfriend. A good-looking boyfriend with a really good job in the City. He even had a Porsche. He was the full 99 with a Flake, sprinkles and raspberry sauce. Amazing.

Even more amazing, Charlie seemed to understand how it all worked. He was very cuddly, always rang me when he said he would and after a few weeks of seeing a lot of each other he said the words every single woman most dreams of hearing.

"I want to be your boyfriend, Lulu, your proper boyfriend. Are you cool with that? Will you be my girlfriend? Will you come and meet my parents? I've told them all about you."

I smiled like a watermelon.

Needless to say, Spencer didn't approve.

"I don't know, Miss Lulu," he said when I rang to tell him about the weekend with Charlie's parents at their beautiful house in Berkshire.

I was furious and gave him a taste of his own silence routine, until he continued, "See, honey, I know all you girls think you want to marry stockbrokers and live in Chelsea and drive around in cars like trucks with two little towheaded kids in back, and I do grant that Charles is way over on the handsome side of pretty, but are you sure he isn't just an eensy-weensy bit straight for you? That's straight as in dull, darlin'. You know, boring?"

"You're just jealous," I said.

I couldn't believe Spencer wasn't happy I'd found the perfect man. He had always been trying to set me up with people before. I figured he just didn't like the fact that I had found Charlie all on my own.

But while I was furious with Spencer at the top level of my brain, I soon began to wonder if he hadn't planted a tiny seed of doubt at a lower level. I started to notice little things about Charlie that hadn't bothered me before.

For one thing, he told jokes. He didn't *crack* jokes like Spencer and I did—off-the-cuff, spur-of-the-moment one-liners. He repeated formulated jokes people had told him. And some of them were a little bit sexist and a little bit racist. I tried to dismiss it as one little fault in an otherwise perfect package, but then other things started to annoy me, too.

Like the skiing stories and the anecdotes about his so wild (so not) days at school. We'd both left school over ten years earlier, but Charlie was still talking about it. And then there were his friends, most of whom he had known since he was at that stupid snobby school, with their own repertoires of offensive jokes and unhilarious skiing and drinking stories.

So the doubts were there, but they were only small annoyances in an otherwise glorious scenario and Charlie didn't seem to have any such problems with me. He was truly a loving and affectionate man and his parents seemed to like me, too. So I wasn't really surprised when he asked me to marry him.

Okay, so it wasn't the most original proposal—he took me away for the weekend to our favorite country-house hotel and went down on one knee beneath the rose arbor, but it was still thrilling. And it was a huge diamond. I accepted.

We went back to our room, called his parents and mine with the good news, made love with the ardor appropriate to the occasion and then started to get dressed for dinner.

I'd had such a strong inkling that the big question was going to be popped that weekend I had packed the kinky boots and the shift dress and pearls I'd been wearing the night we met, as a bit of fun. I thought it would be rather witty to put them on and see if Charlie noticed.

He did.

"Oh no," he said, coming out of the bathroom with a towel around his firm brown waist. "You're wearing those awful boots. I hate those boots."

I was too stunned to speak. Charlie continued, "Please don't spoil this special night by wearing them, Lulu darling," he said. "They're so tarty. They nearly put me off you the night we met. I was so relieved when you never wore them again."

I looked at him and for the first time saw right through the dashing handsome exterior, to the bigoted bore inside. Spencer had been right. Charlie was a handsome ass.

As he opened the wardrobe to get out his cyclamen pink–lined Savile Row suit, his Paul Smith shirt and his Hermès tie, I folded my arms and looked down at my kinky boots. They were so great.

"Are you ready boots?" I said to them. "Start walking."

Alisa Valdes-Rodriguez is the *New York Times* best-selling author of the novels *The Dirty Girls Social Club* and *Playing with Boys.* Her next novel, *Make Him Look Good,* will be published in the spring of 2006. An award-winning print and broadcast journalist, Alisa was on staff at the *Boston Globe* and *Los Angeles Times,* and holds a master's in journalism from Columbia University. She lives in New Mexico.

The Corruption of Father Scott
Alisa Valdes-Rodriguez

Mandi sipped the cheap yellow airplane Chardonnay from the clear plastic cup, on her way to meet a priest in Chicago, and thought again about how much she loved her job. Production assistant to a big Hollywood TV producer. Cool! Seriously, what other job had assignments like this? *Travel the country in search of the hottest, hunkiest young Catholic priest. Make sure he's affable and eloquent. Liberal and labor oriented. This is just what the left needs to rev up its Christian base against the Republicans. Liquor him up if you have to—priests love wine, don't they? Then bring him to L.A. and make him a star, baby.*

Mandi had already been to Baton Rouge, where she'd heard rumor of a sexy young Creole priest. The guy wasn't handsome enough, and he was defensive and suspicious of television and women in general. His feet were small and his head was large and soft. *Troglodyte* is the word that had occurred to Mandi as she watched him scowl at her in his dingy, mothball-scented office. He was not bright enough, either, and Mandi, who was quick as a caffeinated greyhound, had little use for him.

She'd told her boss she was following some other leads around town, but basically she'd ended up spending her whole two days in New Orleans in her hotel room, raiding the minibar (could they *make* the vodkas any *smaller,* hello?) and watching movies on the pay-per-view, hoping her employer wouldn't find out—especially about the porn. Mandi wasn't a porn *addict* or anything like that. She would never admit to anyone that she even watched the stuff on occasion. It's just when you're on the road all alone, in a hotel room, and you've recently spent time with an evil, woman-hating priest with a large, soft head, you do things you might not ordinarily do, things you are curious about. What was she, a saint? A priest? None of the above. Mandi was nothing more than human.

At least that's the only justification Mandi had for the fact that, after an evening of stupid hotel porn, she'd stripped like a pro in front of the mirrored closet door to see how she measured up to the porn *stars.* It was the sort of thing that, if anyone found out about it, would make Mandi die of embarrassment. Mandi, who was thirty-five but worked out like a beast and had recently gotten herself breast implants and lipo on her inner thighs, was quite proud of her reflection. She turned herself on, which she found odd, scary and comforting all at once. She wondered, for a brief, drunk moment, if she might be wise to start moonlighting as a porn Goddess. She'd pay off her car in no time that way. Not even all that fancy a car, either. Just a Subaru.

Next, she'd gone to South Boston, where she had been told she'd find a hot Irish priest with brawny buns and abs of steel. The priest had been all that and a bag of (fish and?)

chips. She thought he looked like a sober Colin Farrell, but couldn't be sure she'd ever seen said actor sober. He had a spectacular package in the front of his dowdy black priest's pants, pants that reminded her of busboy pants for some reason. Pants aside, Mandi had been ready to sign him up, until, that is, she caught him making out with the male organist when she showed up unexpected one day with the faxed TV contract. And even though she didn't have a problem with the dudes-kissing-dudes thing, he'd withdrawn his interest in being a talk-show host on CAT-TV, the formerly conservative network that now figured the real money was in getting the country to lean left again, ever since the chairman of the company married a Chinese woman and moved to Beijing.

"I can't risk being outed," said the priest with a girlie swish of his busboy pants.

"I won't out you," Mandi promised him.

"I only went into this job because my parents made me," he said. Was that a lisp she heard? Did gay men have lisps all over the world? Even in Ireland? How weird. "They thought my lack of interest in girls meant I had a higher calling."

"A bigger calling," joked the organist, of quivering brow and brown teeth.

"You little devil," said the priest, blushing around his grin.

"Organ grinder," said the organist.

Luckily for her, Mandi, a Catholic girl from Los Angeles who now thought of herself as spiritual but not religious, had lost her religion when she went to Wellesley.

Mandi wound her way through Chicago in her rented blue Taurus, missing her Subaru mightily. She was certain they used recycled soda cups to construct Tauruses. The church was around here somewhere. She had it on good sources that a gorgeous priest from Glasgow had set up shop in this impoverished neighborhood. Women from the area had sent in e-mails to her boss's Web site, detailing their fantasies about Father Scott, his pale blue eyes and dark curly hair, his full, red lips and glossy white teeth. Most of all, they'd noted Father Scott's ability to flirt without seeming unpriestly.

He was said to be a dead ringer for Mexican telanovela superstar Eduardo Verastegui.

Mandi found the redbrick, pitch-roofed church with its assortment of broken stained white statues and patchy, mangy lawn. It leaned lopsided off the sort of chipped residential corner where you found this sort of church, in a neighborhood of cigarette butts, skinny pigeons and empty 40-ounce beer bottles.

Inside the church Mandi found the faithful few, on their knees in gray dresses and baggy stockings, praying as this type does in the middle of the day during the middle of the week. They were mostly older women who didn't seem to notice she was there for all the spirits that swarmed them with guilty ghost whispers. When she passed the older women in the aisle, they bumped her with elbows and hips, the way older Chinese women always seemed to do near cabbages and oyster sauce in downtown L.A.

One of the faithful was much younger and much more busty than the others. With fake blond hair and a great gash of cleavage bounding firmly above her hot-pink tube top, she sat in the front row, applying lipstick in a red that matched precisely the red of the blood on the wooden Jesus nailed to the wooden cross behind the altar. Here, thought Mandi, was a woman who might be able to help.

"Excuse me. Do you know where I might find Father Scott?" asked Mandi.

The woman with the fake blond hair stopped primping for a moment, and looked Mandi up and down with the slow deliberation of a confident panther. "Who are you?" she purred.

"A parishioner," lied Mandi.

The woman with the fake blond hair knew instantly that this was a lie, and laughed with her dark brown, nearly black, eyes. "I've never seen you," she said with a flip of the fake, shiny and straight blond hair. Her breasts did not move. Mandi realized they must have been very expensive to make, those breasts. Mandi wished she'd gone for the D implants instead of the conservative Cs. "And I attend every service."

Mandi sighed, and told the truth. "I'm here from L.A. to interview Father Scott about possibly hosting a talk show for CAT-TV."

The woman with the fake blond hair sat up sharply and smiled. Her bare belly was bronzed and flat. She reminded Mandi of a younger Pamela Anderson. "Did you get my e-mails?" the woman asked. "Is that why you're here?"

Mandi nodded, and the woman with the fake blond hair leaned toward her in a musky burst of dark perfume. "I've done my best," said the woman in a low, throaty whisper. She licked her rubbery, flexible red lips with a whitish tongue, wavy on the sides from dehydration, and trembled her top like an exotic dancer. "But Father Scott? I'm telling you, girl, he's made of stone. No man can say no to Darla." She ran her hands over her breasts. "To these." She spread her jeaned legs apart and grabbed what was between them with a tiny bite to her lower lip. "To this. No man. *Stone.*"

Mandi turned to see whether the old ladies were poised to attack them. Drown them in holy water, beat them with a chalice, something. Darla was talking openly in a church about trying to seduce a *priest*. Mandi cringed against the lightning she suspected would zap them through the ceiling at any moment. And then, in spite of herself, she had a brief fantasy of a threesome with Darla and a priest who looked like Eduardo Verastegui. Mandi had never kissed a woman's nipple, or not unless you counted nursing, which she didn't. She couldn't even remember that. She had never touched the moist space between another woman's legs, not unless you counted being born, and she didn't remember that either. There were so many taboos she told people she supported but which, in secret, she longed to break. Women. Priests. Married men. Married women. Married woman priests. Mandi suspected she was having some sort of midlife crisis, which might have been the reason her last boyfriend left her, saying she was "irrevocably immature and possibly pathologically puerile." He was a failed poet who blamed her for his failings but who had, last she checked, continued to fail in her absence as well.

Mandi did her best to look like a professional. "So, how do I find him?"

"Even *you* want me," said Darla with a wry grin.

"Do not," said Mandi.

"Do so," said Darla.

"Do not," said Mandi.

"Do so," said Darla.

"Do not *infinity,*" said Mandi.

"I don't live far from here," said Darla. "After thinking about Father Scott all morning, I'm bot and hothered." She smiled at her mangling of the language. "I could use some relief. You're very pretty. We could help each other out."

"No, thank you," said Mandi.

"It doesn't mean you're gay."

"No, thanks. Really. I'd just like to know where I can find Father Scott."

Darla shrugged, and pointed toward the back of the church. "Go back, and follow the scent of CK1 and bread dough, through the blue door on the left. He smells so good. He smells like sex. Yeasty."

"Yeasty?" Gross. Did Darla have an infection? Rephrase: Was Darla herself an infection?

Darla grinned. "You'll see. I hate him. I love him. That's his office, the bastard."

Mandi looked over her shoulder at the back of the church, and spotted the blue door. "Thanks," she said.

Darla opened her purse and produced a hot-pink business card, holding it with her French-tipped fingernails. Darla Natasha, Massage Therapist. "Here's my number if you change your mind. I'll be waiting."

"Uh, okay," said Mandi. She took the card without touching the other woman's flesh. She considered shaking Darla's hand, but worried that Darla might be the kind of woman who didn't wash her hands often enough, a woman who touched herself much too much in the yeasty parts.

The kind of woman Mandi feared she herself was becoming.

Father Scott did not look like a priest. That was the first thing Mandi noticed. He wasn't in priest pants. He did not wear priest shoes. He wasn't even wearing a white collar, or anything like it. Rather, he was wearing one of those shirts from Urban Outfitters with a pithy, juvenile slogan about one of the less glamorous of the fifty states, a slogan that, probably by design, made everyone in said slandered state write letters to the media about how offensive and oppressive the clothing chain was, thereby giving Urban Outfitters buckets full of free publicity.

Father Scott also wore cargo pants, slung low enough that his plaid boxers showed over the top, and sneakers. Unlaced sneakers, the big round elephant-paw kind that high-school kids wore. With his rumpled, pop-star hair and sparkly, cynical eyes, he looked like a college student, like a guy you'd maybe call "son" or "dude," but definitely not "Father."

"Hey, gorgeous, what's up?" he said as Mandi peeked her head in the door to his office. He had an adorable Scottish accent. He dropped the "r" in *gorgeous,* so it came out *go-juss.* A deep yet boyish voice. He leaned back in his swivel chair, feet on his desk, with a copy of the *Sports Illustrated* swimsuit issue in his hands. Mandi's jaw dropped. He had biceps as big around as paint cans, a jaw arranged by straight-edge. He was, in an overused word her failed poet ex would have frowned to hear, beautiful.

"Hello," said Mandi. She stared at the model in the bikini on the cover of the magazine, and wondered if priests were allowed such reading material. Didn't the nuns get jealous? Or were nuns all lesbians?

"We can *look,* mind you," said Father Scott with a smooth familiarity all out of proportion to the situation. "It's the bloody touching that's not allowed."

Wasn't "bloody" a curse word in Scotland?

"Like getting a lap dance," said Mandi, realizing only too late—as she generally did when she opened her mouth to speak to men in any form—that she'd said something wildly inappropriate, again.

"Exactly," said Father Scott. An impish grin spread across his slightly stubbly, chiseled face. "Not that I've ever had one. Though I have."

"I'm sorry," said Mandi, apologizing to a man for no reason, as was her habit. She held out her hand to shake his. "I'm Mandi Rollins, from CAT-TV. I sent you an e-mail a while back? About the talk show?"

"Right, Mandi, with the priest talk show. Welcome." Father Scott shook her hand and grinned. His hand felt pleasantly rough and big in her own, thick, and she wondered for a moment whether or not priests were allowed to touch themselves the way other mortals were. Did priests masturbate? Surely they did. But did they feel bad about it? She'd have to ask him. Once she got to know him better. She was always rushing things with men. Even priests, apparently. With that smile and those eyes, he seemed to be a priest you might feel comfortable asking such a thing.

"Do priests masturbate?" she blurted. She thought she was only thinking it, but then it popped out of her mouth like a bit of vomit after a night of drinking. Maybe she hadn't sobered up yet from last night's minibar binge after all. God. Er, Gosh.

"Yes," he said, as if she had asked about the weather, or the service on Sunday. "We're not saints," he added. "Well, most of us aren't. I'm not, anyway." He grinned. Then, gesturing to the black leather sofa along one wall, he said, "Please, have a seat."

"I'm sorry," she said.

"No need," he said. "Priests are normal human beings. Is there something you want to talk to me about, something personal?" He leaned forward in his seat and cocked his head to the side like a dog listening to a faraway train whistle.

"The show, of course," said Mandi, but she knew that probably wasn't what he meant.

"A personal something you want to talk about," he said. "That's what I meant."

"No, why?"

Father Scott smiled flirtatiously. At least Mandi took it that way. Did priests flirt? "Well," he said. "Usually, when someone brings something up out of the blue, something taboo like, say, masturbating, it might be because it's on their mind for their own reasons. I'm here to listen and help. That's part of my job description."

Mandi gulped and remembered the New Orleans hotel striptease. Father Scott got up, and came to sit next to her on the sofa. She felt the heat of his body, though they were nowhere near to touching.

"Go on," said Father Scott. "Get it off your chest."

"Get what off my chest?" asked Mandi.

"Women do it, too," said Father Scott, steady and even. "You needn't feel guilty for it."

"I think you're perfect for the show," said Mandi as she tried to ignore the heat growing between her legs.

"Yeah?" asked Father Scott.

"Oh, yeah," said Mandi.

Within weeks, Father Scott had found a replacement priest for his parish, an old and limping man who did not interest Darla in the least, and he'd been signed as the host of the new CAT-TV talk show *Straight Talk with Father Scott,* airing five days a week directly opposite Dr. Phil. Mandi, for her part, got a raise for having found him, and used most of the extra money to upgrade her Subaru to a Lexus.

Father Scott moved to Los Angeles, into a Studio City apartment Mandi helped him find. She even helped him unpack his boxes, and found it surprising that he had framed posters of race cars with girls on the hoods.

The first show featured women whose husbands had cheated on them with other men. Father Scott gave them almost the exact same advice Dr. Phil gave such women, with the added twist that Father Scott looked like Matthew McConaughey, whereas Dr. Phil looked like, well, Dr. Phil.

One morning, Mandi came into work after a long, restless night fantasizing about Father Scott, and her producer and boss told her that the ratings for the new show were "through the roof." What was more, *People* magazine wanted to include Father Scott in their Sexiest Man Alive issue, but Mandi's boss thought Mandi ought to talk to Father Scott about it first, to see what his feelings on the matter were.

Mandi knocked gently on Father Scott's dressing-room door, and gasped when he opened it in nothing but sweatpants. Father Scott had the abs of a prize fighter, and just a few wisps of hair on his chest. "Mandi," he said with that sideways grin. "What can I do you for?"

"I'll give you a hundred dollars," she said, only half joking. Father Scott got the joke instantly, and winked.

"Trust me," he said. "If the church weren't so anal about these old rules, I'd do it for free, gorgeous."

Father Scott moved to one side so Mandi could enter the dressing room. It smelled of freshly baked bread and sex. Father Scott picked up a set of dumbbells and started to do curls as she sat on the leather sofa. She told him about the Sexiest Man Alive thing, and he laughed.

"Are you cool with that?" asked Mandi, feeling weird for using "cool" with a priest, but feeling even weirder that he didn't seem priestly to her.

"Heck yeah," he said, staring at his reflection in the mirror. "I mean, just because I'm restricted in my behaviors by my vow to God doesn't mean everyone else has to be celibate, too. I should tell you, I've considered going Episcopal for many years now. I just did the Catholic thing because of my mother, and she passed away a year back, and I'm thinking it might be time to jump ship to the more rational religion."

Mandi gasped, gulped and stared at the muscles in his back. They rippled as he pumped the weights.

"You couldn't switch religions now," she said. "With the show and all."

"Oh, I know. I'll wait. But know it's on the radar."

Mandi wondered if she was on the radar, too, and suddenly wished the ratings would tank so that Father Scott could be Episcopal already and they could get it on. "Isn't it hard?" she asked. "Never, you know. You're like that forty-year-old-virgin movie, only without. I don't know. You know what I mean."

Father Scott grinned. "I wasn't always a priest," he said.

"You mean, you've been with women before?"

Father Scott set the weights down and mopped his brow with a white hand towel. "That's between me and God," he said with a wink. "Well, between me, God and a couple of chicks back in Glasgow."

"Really?" Were priests allowed to say "chicks" in a non-Easter, non-fluffy-yellow context?

"Don't look so shocked, Mandi. Those girls will tell you, I was pretty good at tying a cherry stem with just my tongue."

"Gotta go back to work," said Mandi, afraid she might have a seizure of some sort. Flushed and breathless with the thought that Father Scott was not a virgin, she scurried back to her office and made the call to *People* magazine. They set up a photo shoot for the following week, at the W Hotel in Westwood. When she went back to Father Scott's dressing room to tell him the news, he was dressed in his priest clothes for the day's show—about following your heart in life and trusting that God knows what's best for you.

"Cool beans!" exclaimed Father Scott, surprising Mandi yet again. "I guess that means I better get some new shades, right?"

By the time the piece in *People* came out, Mandi was fully in love with Father Scott, unable to think of anything but him. For his part, Father Scott had become a household name, and everywhere he went, people of various religious persuasions swarmed him for his autograph, or in some (generally female) cases, for a chance to touch him. He was a good listener, and a good thinker, and he had great wells of understanding, respect and forgiveness in him. People loved him for it, Mandi included. She had never met a man like Father Scott, and now that she had, no other man looked remotely appetizing.

The producers for the show decided that with his newfound popularity, it might be a great idea to take Father Scott on a "road trip" around the country, so that he could do "sinner-on-the-street" segments from Seattle to Miami. Father Scott was game. The producers decided Mandi ought to accompany him on the trip, to serve as his personal assistant. Mandi, loathing herself, packed lingerie, a jar of stemmed drink cherries and a book on the history of the Episcopal church in New England.

The first stop was San Jose, California. The travel department at the network had booked adjoining rooms for Mandi and Father Scott at the very posh, very swank Hotel Montgomery. They arrived on a Saturday night for a Sunday taping. Mandi apologized to Father Scott for the adjoining-room thing, but he said he didn't mind. "The door between us locks, anyway," he said. "In case you're worried I'll take advantage of you. Hey, wanna go down to the bar?"

Mandi and Father Scott went to the bar downstairs, an elegant, minimalist space with a distinctly Asian vibe, down to the rock gardens outside. A crowd of young, trendy, beautiful people mingled inside and out, and a few of them stopped by to tell Father Scott they loved the show. Mostly, people left Mandi and Father Scott alone, even though they whispered in recognition of the newest star of daytime talk TV. The Hotel Montgomery was way too cool for them to admit to watching TV, and the hotel much too Buddhist in sensibility for fawning admiration of a priest.

Father Scott ordered a blue martini, and Mandi stared. "Why must you always look so surprised when I do normal things?" asked Father Scott.

"I don't know," said Mandi.

"It's okay," said Father Scott, tipping his martini glass in her direction. "You're adorable when you look surprised. You make the cutest faces."

"I do?"

"Yeah. You have no idea you're doing them, either. That's the cute part. You want a drink?"

Mandi had not come downstairs wanting a drink, but the sight of Father Scott in his white linen shirt and his pale denim pants, and his flirty nature, made her need one. "A mojito, please," she told the bartender. "Extra rum."

They drank in relative silence. Two drinks each. And then, with the music blasting, and people all around them laughing, Mandi found herself in the familiar throb-blurting landscape of tipsy and stupid.

"Tell me about the girls in Glasgow," she said.

Father Scott grinned. "I'll need a couple more of these first," he said.

"Should you really be drinking in public?" asked Mandi.

"You prefer I do it in private?" he asked. "Isn't that a sign of alcoholism?"

"I don't want people to get the wrong idea about you," she said.

"Too late for that," said Father Scott.

"What do you mean?" asked Mandi.

"Never mind."

They ordered two more drinks apiece, and then Mandi asked her question again. Father Scott scooted his stool closer to hers, planted his elbows on the bar and talked. There were two girls, he said, his eyes on the wall behind the bar. Both back when he was in high school. The first was a passive girl who had been adopted and lacked confidence in every way. They'd dated a while, and had sex once.

"She was fishy and bloody boring," he said with a distant look in his eye. "It made me wonder, and I've always loved the Lord, that's the thing, but being with her made me wonder if I wasn't cut out for some other kind of life."

"A religious life?"

"Yeah. My uncles were priests, and it was something in the family. A noble, honorable profession."

"Without fishy girls."

"Essentially, yeah. Though that was never appealing to me, being without girls."

"Only without the bloody boring fishy kind," said Mandi, hoping she herself did not fall into that category.

"Right."

"But the second girl?"

Father Scott's eyes lit up, and he licked his lips. "Angela," he said.

"Sexy name."

"Sexy girl. Very bossy, but I like that in a woman in bed, you know?"

"Like? Present tense, Father?" She said this last word with sarcasm.

"Liked," said Father Scott. "I'm faithful to my vow. For now."

"Bossy how?"

He grinned. "Let's just say she didn't have a problem opening up for me, with all the lights on bright, and pointing to where I needed to go."

Mandi felt the space between her own legs grow damp. "Go?" she asked.

"I know how to find and push the little buttons, you might say," he said.

"Oh." Mandi guzzled the last of her mojito and ordered another.

"I miss it," he said. "Thus the Episcopal escape plan."

"It?"

"A woman's buttons. Pushing them. Or rubbing actually, in a little soft circle, like this." Father Scott took the tip of Mandi's finger and with his own, rubbed the skin in a delicate, exquisite little circle. Mandi felt her pulse surge.

"I think I better go to my room," she said.

"Me, too," said Father Scott.

"To my room?" asked Mandi, clapping her hand over her mouth after she'd spoken, aware of the gaffe.

"No, gorgeous," said Father Scott with a knowing smile. "You'll have to wait till the ratings drop and they cancel my show for that."

"I won't tell anyone," whined Mandi.

Father Scott smiled a priestly smile, said nothing and escorted Mandi to the elevator.

Upstairs in her room at the Hotel Montgomery, Mandi felt the room spin. She was drunk, and Father Scott, the sexiest and most unattainable man on earth, was right next door. Alone. With those biceps. *Man.* And he wanted her. She unlocked her side of the door, hoping in some weird way that he would unlock his and maybe wander in.

Then she called up a porno on the hotel pay-per-view. Why not? It wasn't like she had men lining up to get at her. She was too busy to go out, unless you counted babysitting a sexy priest, which was, now that she thought about it, perhaps the cruelest assignment on earth.

Too drunk to care, she left the volume up. She stripped in front of the mirror and took a bottle of chilled red wine from the minibar. "I might as well enjoy myself," she said out loud.

When the tapping came on the door adjoining her room with Father Scott's, Mandi was too drunk and too busy to hear it. By the time Father Scott unlocked his side and, concerned about the sounds of a woman in pain that he had heard muffled through the wall, came in, Mandi was intimately involved with her favorite battery-operated electronic device, and it wasn't her laptop—though it was somewhere in the lap area.

"Oh my God!" she screamed when she saw him standing there with a goofy smile on his face in the orange light the TV cast around the otherwise darkened room. He looked sunburned in that strange light.

"I thought you were hurt," he said. "The sound from your…movie. It was like screaming. Sorry."

"Not hurt," she said, diving to bury herself in the sheets of the bed. She pointed the remote to the TV and turned it off.

"Yeah, I can see that. I should have known. I'm so stupid."

"I'm so embarrassed," she said. "How long were you standing there?"

"Maybe a minute."

"A whole minute?

"I was paralyzed," he said. "It was…lovely."

"Oh my God," she said. "It's your fault, you know. You make me crazy. So it's your fault I'm so disgusting right now."

"You're not disgusting. Don't worry about it. Come out from there," he said. He didn't move.

"Out from where?"

"Under there."

"Why?"

"I want you to finish what you started." He was still smiling. He looked so comfortable with the whole thing, like she was cute.

"With you in the room, Father?"

"Yeah. If that's okay with you. But quit calling me Father. It's creepy."

"I couldn't do that," said Mandi. She had always fantasized about masturbating in front of a man. But she'd never actually *do* it. "I'm actually sort of not in the mood anymore, Father Scott."

Father Scott smiled at her. "Scott, if you please. Plain Scott. I understand. I'm sorry. I'll leave you alone."

"No, that's not what I meant."

"What did you mean?"

"I don't know. I'm drunk. And tired. And totally completely embarrassed."

"And cute."

"I don't know about that."

He came to the bed and sat next to her, smiled warmly. "Listen. I'm a conflicted guy, okay? I'm not honest with myself. I'm not leading a godly life because I'm not really feeling it. I mean, I'm always, like, why would God give men and women these feelings, these good, amazing feelings, if they weren't holy in their own right? I don't know…" His voice trailed off.

"What?" asked Mandi.

"It's not so much the church, which I love. The church is fantastic. So important. And it's not God or Jesus. It's me. It's that I think I made the wrong choice. I shouldn't be a Catholic priest. I'm not cut out for it. God knows it."

"Everyone knows it," said Mandi, snuggling down in the sheets.

"Yeah, probably," he said with a laugh. "What the heck kind of a priest is one of *People* magazine's sexiest men alive? I'm not cut out for it."

"No," she said as she touched the side of his face gently. "Probably not." Her heart jackhammered.

"I might have made it," he said, leaning into her caress with his eyes closed, savoring her touch.

"Made it?"

"Though my life, celibacy, the whole thing. But I met you."

"Me?"

He grabbed her hand and kissed it. "Yeah. The perfect girl."

"Me?"

Father Scott answered with a soft kiss to her lips, and a sweet finger-tap to her nose. "You."

Mandi found herself in the mood again, and said, "You're going to be excommunicated."

"We'll have to cancel the show," he said, and he kissed her again. "Because tomorrow I'd like to switch to Episcopal. And I'd like to date you."

"There will be scandal," said Mandi.

"There always is with Catholics," said Scott.

"No, Scott. I mean, like supermarket-tabloid scandal, like death-threat scandal."

"Jesus endured worse for following his heart," said Scott. He noticed she was shivering, and pulled the comforter up over her, tucked her in.

"Maybe you could still do the show?"

"Maybe we'll talk about it in the morning," he said with a smile and a kiss to her forehead.

"I want you," Mandi whined as Scott moved away from her and toward the door to his room.

"I know. I want you, too," he said. "More than you know. But I want to do this right, by God."

And with that, Mandi's future husband left the room and locked the door behind him.

Tilly Bagshawe went to Cambridge at the age of eighteen with her ten-month-old daughter in tow. At twenty-six, she was the youngest-ever partner in one of the world's most prestigious head-hunting firms. Now a freelance journalist, she is a regular contributor to *The Sunday Times, Daily Mail* and other major British publications. Tilly lives with her husband and two children in L.A. and London. Her first novel, *Adored,* was published in 2005. Her Web site is: www.TillyBagshawe.com.

Dog Lover
Tilly Bagshawe

The irony is that I've always thought of myself as a dog lover.

No, really. Even as a kid, I was crazy about them. Dogs, I mean. Particularly Chihuahuas, funnily enough. That's partly why I took the job in the first place. Well, that and the enormous salary, the guest house in Beverly Hills and the free use of the boss's Bentley Continental on weekends. But it was mostly the dog.

I can remember the advertisement now, word for word. I can even remember the taste of the big, delicious, gooey slab of carrot cake I was eating at the Coffee Bean as I read it (a cake that, by the way, I gave a good twenty percent of to the cute little bichon frise tethered to the table leg next to me. I hate to see dogs tethered, don't you? No? Well, I do. Because whatever anybody says, I have always, ALWAYS loved dogs. If you don't believe me, ask…well ask whoever you like. Because what happened was *totally* out of character for me, I assure you. Totally.)

Where was I? Oh, yes, the advertisement. "Housekeeper required," it said. "To provide domestic assistance for single lady in early sixties. $50,000 P/A, including guest-house accommodation and use of car. No kids. One dog. Only animal lovers need apply."

Well, I mean, it was written for me, wasn't it?

Written. For. Me.

I called up then and there, right from the coffee shop. It was a bit awkward if you must know, because the bichon frise had thrown up, poor little mite. Apparently she was allergic to sugar, but I mean, really, how was I supposed to know that? The guy who owned her was *extremely* rude to me as a matter of fact. I can give you a description of him if you like. No? Well, I *will* tell you that he was cursing and yelling so much I had trouble concentrating on the call. I ask you! Some people!

Anyhoo, long story short, I called and I got an interview for the very next morning.

What was that? Was that the first time I met Mrs. Andrews? Well, of course it was, silly! Never seen the woman in my life until that moment. Of course, now I wish I'd never seen her at all. Amazing how *wrong* you can be about someone on a first impression, isn't it? I mean, some people think that, just because I'm a little heavy, I have no self-control! How ridiculous is that? Let me tell you, just because someone battles with their weight is no reason to make assumptions about…hmm? Oh, yes, sorry. Mrs. Andrews.

Well, I met her at the house and she seemed a nice enough lady. A little quiet, perhaps. Soft spoken. Very well dressed. You know, genteel. Not all "Beverly-Hills-y' with one of those stretched-out surgery faces and too much makeup and jewelry. She asked me a bunch of questions. Just regular stuff, you know, my background, references, experience I'd had with dogs, that sort of thing. And then she had the maid bring him in.

Nebuchadnezzar.

On a red velvet pillow.

Wearing a crown.

You probably think I'm exaggerating, but I swear to you on my departed mother's grave, God rest her soul, that was exactly what happened. A *tiny* little Chihuahua, not much bigger than a jumbo avocado. On a pillow! With a crown!!

Of course I know what you're going to say: Why didn't I get out then and there? Go on. Say it. "Why didn't you get out then and there, Mrs. McIntyre?" I mean, if the writing was on the wall… But you know what I say to that, Detective? *Hindsight is 20/20!* That's what I say. *Hindsight is…* Oh, well, all right. There's no need to lose your temper. If you'd just let me finish without interrupting all the time… OH YES YOU ARE, YOUNG MAN!… I'd get to the point a mighty sight quicker.

So anyway, in comes Neb. (You'll understand I couldn't keep calling him Nebuchadnezzar, although Mrs. A insisted upon it whenever she was around. Poor woman. She loved him, but she was obsessed. *Obsessed!* I mean, I ask you. What kind of a name is that to saddle a dog with? Thank the Lord the woman never had children, that's what I say. Oh she did? A daughter? That's funny. She never mentioned her. Oh well, my mistake, Detective. I stand corrected!)

So at first I felt sorry for him. For the *dog.* Do try to keep up, Detective. Truly, I did, I actually pitied him. With that ridiculous crown squashing his little ears. Oh, and he had leg warmers on. Did I mention that already? Little pink leg warmers shot through with silver thread. He looked like a kid from *Fame*. Did you ever see that show? With Leroy, the dancer? He's dead now, you know, poor man. AIDS. Turned out to be one of those, you know, doo-dahs. Fairies. Anyway, Neb reminded me of Leroy. Except, obviously, he was a dog. And as far as I know he'd never taken a modern-dance class, although knowing what I know now, nothing would surprise me!

I think she picked the leg warmers up at Chateau Marmutt. Do you know that place? On Third? No? Well, I do. When I think of the hours, not to mention the *thousands* of dollars she had me spend in that store. Two words for you, Detective: *Emotional Torture*. Write that down, would you? I want it on record: What I suffered in that job was *abuse*. I swear to God, if I saw that place now, I think I'd have a panic attack. Little doggie sweaters and diamond collars and silver nail clippers and Lord knows what else they have in there. It's a crazy world we live in, Detective. A crazy, crazy world. Not everyone's as nice and normal as you and I.

So, needless to say, I took the job. If I hadn't I wouldn't be sitting here now, talking to you, now, would I? I took the job and the next morning I arrived and I'd barely finished unpacking in the guest house…have you seen Mrs. A's guest house by the way?

Guest house? Doll's house more like!

I should have sued her then and there for false advertising, but you know what I always say. That's right! *Hindsight is 20/20.* Now, I grant you, I may be a smidgen over my ideal weight—oh! Detective, here, have some more water! Did something go down the wrong way?—but honestly, Calista Flockhart McBeal would have had a tough time squeezing into that so-called queen–size bed. Queen of the dwarfs maybe! Queen Ant! Queen…oh, right. My statement.

So anyway, I'd barely finished unpacking when Mrs. A came over and handed me my "List of Duties."

Oh, look, you have it right there in your hand. How funny! Is that Exhibit A? Ha ha ha! Exhibit A, like on Court TV, geddit? What was that? It *is* Exhibit A? Oh. Dear. Well, take a look at it, would you, and you'll see my point.

3:00 a.m.: Check on Nebuchadnezzar. If his doggie blanket has slipped, re-cover him gently. Make sure room temperature is set to a constant sixty-eight degrees.
6:00 a.m.: Check Nebuchadnezzar again. If he stirs, see if he wants to go pee pee. I prefer him to use his tray, but if he wants to go outside, make sure he's wearing his cashmere wrap. The blue one.
8:00 a.m.: Breakfast. Please follow the menu cards provided. If Nebuchadnezzar is reluctant to eat, taste a few mouthfuls yourself first to reassure him. Make sure you do this on all fours or he may take fright.

It goes on for eight pages. Eight pages! Look. The last entry isn't until midnight.

12:00 midnight: Insert Chihuahua womb-sounds CD into player. This helps Nebuchadnezzar sleep soundly through the night.

Womb sounds? Can you imagine, Detective?
At first I thought it was a joke. I mean all these doggie

duties were on top of my regular work as a housekeeper, you understand. But Mrs. A looked deadly serious.

Hmm? No, no, I didn't say anything about it at the time. Well, she was my new employer, wasn't she? I wanted to make a good impression. And, like I say, at first I felt sorry for Neb. I thought perhaps if I stayed, I could help him, have him lead a more normal, carefree dog's life. Because, you know, I have always, ALWAYS loved dogs, whatever anybody might tell you. But of course, all that was before I got to know him. Before I found out firsthand what an evil, Machiavellian little *snake* he was.

And still is.

Oh, yes! You may look surprised, Detective. But he planned all this, you know.

Who? What do you mean *who?* Neb, of course.

Indeed I am serious! Don't you watch Court TV? Hmm. Well, perhaps you should. If you *did,* you'd know that the first question every good detective asks himself is: *Who stood to gain the most from the crime?*

Go on. Ask it. Ask that question!

See? Am I right or am I right? There you have it! You have your prime suspect right there.

Yes, I am aware that he's a dog. There's really no need to take that patronizing tone with me. I don't mean to be rude, Detective, but *wake up and smell the coffee,* would you? Don't you see? That's exactly what he *wants* you to think. Poor, cute little Chihuahua, wouldn't hurt a fly! Butter wouldn't melt, that's what you're thinking, isn't it?

Isn't it?

I suppose I can't blame you for being skeptical. He had me fooled at first too. So much so that I actually figured I could *help* him—ha! That's why I took Mrs. A's list with a pinch of salt. I suppose I thought that I'd be on my own with Neb for much of the day, and she wouldn't know the difference if I took him to Toy-Breeds-Yoga or out for a walk in the park. Plus, she wasn't hauling her bony ass out of bed at 3:00 a.m. every night to check on the dog, was she? So how would she know if I did? And yes, if truth be told, maybe I was also thinking about the money. Fifty thousand is a good salary after all. Okay, yes, and a little bit about the Bentley, too. Maybe. I wanted to drive it by the Coffee Bean at the weekend, you see, and put one over on that dreadful, abusive little man with the bichon frise.

Who's allergic to sugar now, asshole?!

But I digress. I'm not a vengeful person, Detective, as you know. Nobody can accuse me of that. No, no. Neb's welfare, at that time, was my main concern.

Anyhoo, long story short, for the first couple of months everything worked out just fine. I stuck to the parts of the list that seemed most important. I gave the dog the specially imported foie gras and the truffle oil, just as Mrs. A asked. I made *endless,* and I mean endless, trips to Chateau Marmutt for all his little accessories. I even brushed his teeth for him, morning and night, with the tiny silver brush she'd had specially made at Fred Leighton. And believe you me, Detective, that is *humiliating,* even for a dog lover like me: sticking your hand into its mouth and pulling out all the leftover pieces of pâté and whatnot? *Eeeugh!*

But what can I say? Neb was the woman's life, her reason for living, her *world.* And I tried to respect that, Detective, truly I did. Within reason.

No, any complaints the old lady had about me at that time were nothing to do with the dog. I'm sorry? Oh, well, it was nothing really. A silly misunderstanding. Those little things, foibles, what have you, that always come to the surface when one starts a new working relationship. What *exactly?* Well, if you must know, she complained—and I mean this is quite ridiculous, there was no basis for it whatsoever—but she complained that I talked too much. *Me!! Can you imagine,* Detective?

Well, yes, I suppose if you're going to be literal, she did say that once. That I was driving her to suicide. With my constant prattle, yes. But you know, it was said in a very *light-hearted* way. It's really not at all what you're implying…

Gosh, now you're *really* blowing this up out of all proportion. No, I'm not denying it as such. She *may,* in the heat of the moment, have threatened to sack me. And make me homeless, yes. But she wouldn't have *done* it, Detective. Don't you see? Mrs. A and I got on like a house on fire! Two peas in a pod we were! And we would have carried on that way, for years and years, I'm convinced, if it hadn't been for Neb stirring the pot with his evil, pink leg-warmered paws.

It all started going wrong when she brought in the pet psychologist. You see, I'd started to introduce a little discipline into Neb's life, and he didn't like it one bit. Not that I was cruel, you understand. Far from it. But when I saw him, just minutes after we'd got home from walkies, deliberately lower his little ass over my brand-new Victoria's Secret pink mohair slippers…Oh yes, he shat in them, Detective. Cool as a cucumber, looking right at me. It was quite deliberate I can assure you. Well when he did that, I told him "no!" in a firm voice and I smacked him on the butt. In fact, I wouldn't even say it was a smack. You can cross that out. CROSS IT OUT! It was a tap. It was nothing, really. But *boy* did he not like that! I saw a different side to him from then on, Detective, yes indeedy. And things went from bad to worse.

Whenever Mrs. A was around he would ham it up, moping and rolling his eyes, cowering whenever I came near him as if I was about to hit him. I mean *me,* Detective. Me, who has ALWAYS loved dogs. Especially Chihuahuas! Neb as good as told the old lady that I was abusing him! Well, no, obviously he couldn't speak. That would be ridiculous. He's a *dog.* But he didn't have to, did he? His eyes, his evil, scheming little eyes—they said it all.

Anyway, in the end Mrs. A hired Dr. Maxton, an animal shrink, to take a look at him. Dr. Doolittle I called him. You know why? Because he *did little!* Geddit? In fact, scratch that. He did *nothing.* Dr. Doonothing! Neb had him twisted around his little manicured paws since day one. He'd be right as rain, playing with his so-called friends down at Tumblepups (I say "so-called' because there was no loyalty there, Detective. None whatsoever. Neb didn't understand the meaning of the word *friendship.* Uh-uh. He was rotten, rotten to the core!) But then he'd come home, take one look at Dr. Doonothing, and start sulking and whining like someone forgot to give him his Prozac.

And the shrink fell for it! Not that I blame him entirely. Neb gave an Oscar-winning performance. Forget Leroy from *Fame.* He was Laurence Olivier! He was Marlon Brando! Before he got fat, obviously. Poor man. People are so quick to judge heavier citizens, Detective. In the old days it was blacks and Jews and doo dahs, but now it's the plus-sized that have become America's pariahs. Let's face it, that has a lot to do with me being here right now, doesn't it? If someone has to be blamed, it may as well be the fat woman, right? RIGHT?

Sorry. It's just sometimes, the *injustice* of it all… What? Yes. Yes, after that Mrs. A did let me go. Uh-huh, yes, on the doctor's recommendation, although of course legally she couldn't give that as the *only* reason.

The other reasons? Oh, I can't remember, Detective. Some trumped-up nonsense about me talking too much—I mean, *please*—and skimping on my agreed duties. Well, yes, if you're going to get literal about it, I did cut back on The List a little, but who wouldn't? And as for what she said about pilfering petty cash and taking the Bentley during the week without permission, well, that was outrageous. Totally groundless.

Sorry? The midweek episode at the Coffee Bean? Oh, you mean the assault charge? Yes, yes, yes, but that got dropped. It was all a silly misunderstanding, I can assure you. No, it was Neb who got me fired, Neb who turned her against me.

That was why I had to act.

Don't you see? I had no choice.

I got the arsenic off the Internet, believe it or not. Amazing thing, the Internet. Have you ever been on, Detective? Ever *surfed the Web?* See, I've got all the lingo! I can show you if you like. It's a wonder! You can buy just about anything you want there nowadays: fancy Christmas gifts, furniture, intimate feminine apparel, lethal poisons. But I was very careful. I only bought a small dose—enough to kill a household pet, they said—and a little bit extra, to make doubly sure I got the job done cleanly. I wouldn't have wanted to leave him suffering, you see, Detective. I'm not a cruel person. But I couldn't just let him think he'd gotten away with it, could I? When we start letting animals lord it over us, it's a slippery slope, isn't it? I had to take a stand.

But then…then…oh, Detective, it's all so *horrible!* And it's all Neb's fault. He could smell the poison somehow, I'm sure of it. And he stepped back and took his chance. He seized the moment.

How was I supposed to know she'd get down on her hands and knees and taste his food?

Or that she already had a weak heart?

And why, why in the name of Jesus, did she go and eat all of it?

Anyway, Detective, I think I've said enough. Like I said, I don't really want to say anything about this until my lawyer gets here. But you are *terribly* easy to talk to. I feel we really connected on some level. Don't you?

All I *will* say is that this whole idea that I was taking my revenge on poor dear Mrs. Andrews is absolute codswallop. It was Neb! It was all Neb! He's the one who should be in here calling his lawyer, not me.

You do realize that she left him everything, don't you? The house, the car, the art collection? Oh yes. Nebuchadnezzar cleaned up.

It all worked out exactly the way he planned it.

Lauren Henderson was born in London, England, where she worked as a journalist before moving to Tuscany and then to Manhattan. She has written seven books in her Sam Jones mystery series, which has been optioned for American TV, and three romantic comedies—*My Lurid Past, Don't Even Think About It* and *Exes Anonymous.* Her latest book is *Jane Austen's Guide to Dating,* which has been optioned as a feature film. Her books have been translated into over fifteen languages. Together with Stella Duffy, she has edited an anthology of women-behaving-badly crime stories, *Tart Noir;* their joint Web site is www.tartcity.com.

Last Waltz
Lauren Henderson

Mack and Kate are driving to the fair. It's a balmy August evening, a Bank Holiday, and the fair is an easy drive from Kate's flat. On an evening this perfect many other people have had the same idea, and the narrow streets are clogged with cars winding in lines up and down the hills of Hampstead, all their noses pointing in the same direction. Pedestrians wander between the crawling cars, observing little distinction between road and pavement. Mack, who's driving, would usually find this annoying in the extreme; but today's coincidence of weather and activity is rare enough to make both Mack and Kate feel instead that they are part of a privileged moment in time. Everyone they can see—the people in cars with the windows rolled down, playing loud music on their stereos—the people promenading in the streets, Bank Holiday-pink—are all a part of this community of rejoicing in the sunshine.

Dance music drifts in the air above the cars, reaching

them faintly in their hot blue metal bubble. Kate leans her head back on the car seat, feeling the heat wrap around her like a favorite blanket, and closes her eyes. From time to time she peeps at Mack, just to make sure that he's really there, and as good-looking as she remembers. And though she knows that she shouldn't, that it's bad luck and smug to do it, she can't help thinking that they look like a scene from an advert, a young, handsome couple in jeans and T-shirts, driving to the fair in a magic bubble of blue car, completely at their ease. She hugs the blanket round her at the thought. This is not an advert, they're real. This is real. I'm here. And this is more than enough to satisfy her completely; it's not that Kate is easily satisfied, or simple, but she has an enviable, uncomplicated simplicity in her desires. Being here with Mack is perfect, undiluted happiness, and that's all there is to it. Mack, too, glances over at Kate, her head tilted back in the seat, her mouth a little open, her short fair hair rumpling on the headrest. She looks so beautiful, he thinks, and she's here, she likes being with you, she likes sleeping with you. What have you done to deserve this?

They've been going out for a month, they met at a friend's party, exchanged phone numbers, went out to dinner, went to bed. Just like that, very quickly, very simply, a rare simplicity for which their respective friends envy them. But such a smooth, fast progression has its own problems, creating a need for them to balance what they know about each other, which seems like everything, with what they don't, which is nearly everything. They are so familiar with each other's bodies that it seems awkward to know where someone is most ticklish or how many moles they have on their back, but not the names of their siblings.

Kate watches Mack's hands resting on the wheel, ready to steer when the cars ahead of them move forward, and slowly follows his arms up to the white sleeves of his T-shirt. His forearms are tanned, sprinkled with fair hairs that the evening sunlight turns to gold, corded with lines of muscle. She loves male arms, the contrast of the sinewy muscle on the outside with its pale underbelly; she wants now to turn Mack's arms so that his palm is uppermost, and run her fingers along the white strip of skin that runs from the base of the palm of the elbow, where the veins can be seen, not pumped up but faint and blue. The skin will be surprisingly soft and vulnerable to the touch, a reminder of babyhood. She closes her eyes and imagines it. The car starts up again and she pictures Mack's hands moving on the wheel, graceful and assured.

His assurance was one of the main characteristics that first attracted her to him; he seemed to have an easiness about him, a relaxed quality in the way he moved and stood, a familiarity with the way his own body worked. She knew that she had to talk to him, and she could see that he felt the same but might not do anything about it. Shyness? Reserve? So she asked a friend of hers about him, to see whether he had a girlfriend or not.

No, he's a lone wolf, Jack said. Wow, he's really staring at you.

Is he? Kate said, knowing that he was; she could feel his gaze on the back of her head.

Definitely, Jack said.

What's he like, then? Kate asked.

Very nice, actually, despite all that Action Man stuff, Jack said, I've heard he's very sporty but he doesn't seem to be stupid.

You're so snobbish, Jack, Kate said, turning to look at Mack again.

But from Jack's Action Man description she had assumed, pessimistically, that despite Mack's air of calm he would turn out to be an aggressive squash player who could never relax, like a man in advertising she'd gone out with a while ago, or an amateur footballer who spends his evenings drinking with the team and disappears completely at weekends. She was wrong. Mack turned out to prefer the solitary, uncompetitive sports—windsurfing, parachuting, hang-gliding—when he could afford them. She asked him about them and he told her in a way that gave her some sense of what they were like. His shyness with her made his answers more than usually short and self-deprecating, and as she interpreted this correctly as shyness, it endeared him to her in a way that boasts about his bravery would never have done. She liked the fact that he seemed to have so little to prove.

She looks at him again, only half-opening her eyes in the hot sunlight of the car, and reaches over to run a finger slowly up his leg. His jeans are soft from many washings and she can feel the long lines of muscle through the material. A wave of lust sweeps over her. Mack's left hand comes off the wheel to cover hers, and the sight of his hand lying over her smaller one on his thigh triggers another surge of lust; this time it settles on her body and demands relief. When the car stops again she pulls down his head to hers and kisses him thoroughly. They come up out of breath and sticky with saliva and sweat. Mack dries her lips gently with his fingers, then pushes back her hair from her face, arranging each strand to lie along her head. She closes her eyes for a moment as his hands move through her hair. She finds Mack so sexy that she can't help but worry that his sexiness, his good looks, are all that interest her about him; or maybe, more flattering to her, that she is so over-whelmingly possessed by the way he looks that she doesn't have room to fit in anything else. Maybe she has created a mystique around him, the lone parachutist dropping confidently through the sky; maybe, despite the fact that it's her who asks more questions about him, she isn't looking at him as a person; maybe, as her last but one boyfriend said to her only half in joke, she just wants a sex robot who's totally reliable whenever she wants someone to sleep with or go to films with, someone who's handsome enough to raise her status proportionately when people see them out together. Maybe her questions are a way of concealing that from herself. She doesn't know. It's not the kind of thing she thinks about much; she's not analytic, she sees things simply.

"Do I treat you like a sex robot?" she asks Mack suddenly.

"Not enough," Mack says with a straight face, looking ahead at the road.

"Oh well, I was trying to be concerned about your Feelings," she says, giving the last word a capital letter, "but if you don't mind, I'll just go on abusing you."

"Anytime," Mack says, smiling. She laughs, and the moment of worry passes. She closes her eyes again.

Mack's nervous, too, but it's not because he thinks he's treating Kate like a sex robot. He's always so careful not to give that impression to anyone he gets involved with that he doesn't think it could sneak up on him while he was looking the other way. In any case, girls nowadays tell you very firmly if there's anything remotely resembling the demeanor of a sex robot owner in your behavior; they are alert to the

slightest nuance of attempted button-pressing. He'd know
if there was anything Kate took exception to.

No, it's not that. He's thinking about the fair. He knows
that, for Kate, this is an idyllic moment; he has gradually become aware how much she likes them to go out together as
a couple and watch people's heads turn at the sight of both
of them together, tall and fair and strikingly good-looking.
He has to admit that he likes it, too. It makes him feel he has
a place in the world, next to her, with her arm around his
waist, her hand twisted around the belt on his jeans.

He'd wanted that, this afternoon, when Kate suggested
they go to the fair. Despite his reservations, he had wanted
to go out with her, a couple, complete in themselves,
drawing envious stares for their unity. He'd wanted to feel
what she feels, that included sense of happiness that
would come from going together to the fair, a place that
is ideal for couples. And for a while, he had thought it
would be all right. He floated in a bubble of happiness
that surrounded him completely and allowed no lesser
emotion to reach him, quietly peaceful, as a cloud seems
to people on earth; as they pottered around the flat, getting ready, as he kissed the back of Kate's neck and
watched her put on her lipstick in the bathroom mirror,
as they got into the car and smiled at each other over the
noise of the engine starting up. Then he pulled the seat-
belt over himself and snapped the buckle home with a
little click and at once he was fourteen years old, back
on the Waltzer with Lucy Miller, locking the bar over
their seats into place, bursting with excitement at having
persuaded Lucy Miller, no less, to come on a ride with
him. Taking the sudden convulsion in his stomach, as he
slammed shut the safety bar over their laps, to be what

real love feels like. It was only when the car of the Waltzer started to move that he realized this was a warning of hubris instead. Greek tragedies happen in miniature all the time.

"Let's go to the fair!" Kate had said at last. It sounded like another suggestion of the kind she had been making for a while now, but she had the air of someone who has finally settled on the correct formula for the day. She was lying on the floor, a dog-eared listings magazine under her elbows, open at the children's section. A radio churned out loud, pleasantly depthless music by the meter. "I haven't been to one in years," she went on, "and today's the last day."

"It's the last day of that exhibition, too," Mack pointed out from the bathroom, where he was shaving. This took up a disproportionate amount of time whenever he was going out with someone, he had noticed. It was a mystery to him why women found the look of stubble so attractive but complained bitterly about the reality. Someone in America was probably on the verge of inventing a fake stubble rug for chin wear; you could whip it off when you got into the clinches.

"It's too hot for an exhibition, it must be 80 degrees." Kate raised her voice a little over the radio.

"You never wanted to go, really, did you? You keep putting it off." Talking to his reflection in the mirror, Mack realized that this was true also of himself; the exhibition was something he felt he ought to see rather than a genuinely desired object. He hadn't made this connection before. Perhaps he should talk to his reflection more often.

"There are things I'd rather do than go to an exhibition on a hot Bank Holiday when the museum's going to be packed with sweaty tourists," Kate said from just behind him, also speaking to his reflection. They contemplated this projection of himself for a few moments.

"If the museum's going to be crowded, then so's the fair," Mack said reasonably. "And sweaty tourists…"

"Don't you want to go?"

"Not very much."

"But you must like fairs! All those rides and things, you must love them—"

"Why?" Mack reached for the aftershave lotion.

"Oh, it's just like all that hang-gliding and stuff you do, diving through the skies—"

"It's not the same at all."

"I expect it doesn't seem very exciting to you—"

"No, it's not that. It's just different." Mack could hear himself sounding much more terse and dismissive than he meant to be, and he tried to get a grip on himself.

Kate ignored his curtness. "Well, I'd enjoy it. I love fairground rides."

"I like the Octopus, and the Dodgems—" Mack offered. He was about to add, "But that's about it," but Kate cut through him.

"Great," she said firmly, "we'll start on those." She slid her arms around his waist. "I want to go out somewhere with you," she said persuasively into his back, "be out with you…"

"We'd be out together at an exhibition."

"It's not the same…as going to a fair, it's a really nice thing to do together. It doesn't matter, an exhibition, in the same way, who you go with."

And Mack didn't say anything. Maybe it'll be all right, he thought. It's been a while, after all.

★ ★ ★

From the air, the Octopus must be mathematically satisfying to watch; the eight arms, each with a carriage on the end, swing back and forth around each other in an endless mating dance, almost touching but never doing so, weaving in and out as if performing a pavanne. A ritual of human contact, like the man and woman in the weather house who never come out at the same time. Stately, from a distance; less so up close, with the screams, the bright glaring painted colors, the open mouths and flying hair, the people thrown up against each other every time the carriage jolts over to one of the walls, stops for a poised second, then hurls itself off at another wall like a kamikaze who repeatedly fails to summon the nerve to destroy himself.

The Octopus is the one ride Mack will go on, because he knows from experience that when it gets up enough speed to make him feel that he won't be able to stand it if it goes any faster, it miraculously stabilizes at that precise, just-bearable rhythm, and he realizes suddenly that as long as he takes deep breaths and keeps calm, he'll be fine. He'll even, very gradually, enjoy it. He and Kate have their arms round each other and clutch on as it judders against each wall in turn, smashing first one and then the other into the edge of the seat. It's wide enough for at least three people, so they slide back and forth, screaming in fun. They could hold on to the bar and move much less, Mack thinks, but that wouldn't be the point, he can see. He sees, too, what Kate means about going to a fair as a couple; it induces intimacy more than anything else he can think of, not just the enforced physical intimacy. Even that, intense though it is, gradually becomes secondary to the mental bond that forms as you cling to each other and shout, half-screaming, half-smiling, into the face that is inches from yours. It's a trade-off; you share your naked fear and in return you get companionship. The Octopus is slowing to a halt, and Kate reaches over and kisses Mack thoroughly. It's overpoweringly exciting; she pulls away for a second, stares into his eyes, her own sparking hectically, and then they kiss again, with her as much on his lap as they can manage. The speakers are cranking out tinny music from all around them, the smells of candyfloss, popcorn, petrol, greasy leather hang in the air. They both think, independently, that this is perfection.

"I just don't, I just…" Mack's run out of words and gives up, standing there a little off the main gravelly thoroughfare in an alley made by two huge vans parked a few feet away from each other. Kate is facing him. The Ferris Wheel rotates over their heads through the deep blue of the late-evening sky. "I don't understand what the problem is!" She's said this twice already.

Mack shrugs helplessly. "I get scared, I just don't like them. I can't see the point—"

"It's just fun! Being scared is the fun!"

"Well, I don't like that kind of being scared."

"You don't mind jumping off a fucking great mountain with a pair of plastic wings strapped to your back when you could get blown into an electric power line! All I'm asking you to do is get in a fucking chair—carriage—whatever you call it—and go round in a circle! Much safer!"

She clearly thinks she's won the argument, and on her terms she has.

"That IS different," Mack says again, spacing his words. "That's me. That's me choosing to do it, taking the risks myself."

"But so's this! D'you mean you're scared of the cable snapping or something?"

"No, not at all. It's much more—it's deeper than that, it's the being completely—" he raises his hands, desperately trying to express himself—"helpless, I expect."

"But—oh, I don't understand. And you're obviously not going to help me," Kate says. Her initial, disbelieving reaction has hardened into a low-burning anger. She doesn't really think that Mack is taking this position to ruin her perfect evening out at the fair, but she feels as furious as if he were.

"Look," she says, changing tack, "the Ferris Wheel is perfectly safe. I'll be there next to you, you can hold on to me and scream as much as you want. It won't be half as bad as you think."

She goes up to him and puts her arms round his waist. Her voice softens, becoming genuinely tender. "Really, Mack, it'll be all right, I promise. I just can't believe that you won't be okay. We'll walk off it afterwards and we'll be laughing. Really. Trust me."

Mack wants very badly to put his arms around her too, to agree, to go with her. But he can't. His arms hang by his sides and, seeing the expression on his face, she pulls away from him, feeling rejected and untrustworthy.

He knows what he has done and tries hopelessly to heal the breach. "I did tell you," he points out, "in the bathroom. I said I didn't like those kind of rides—"

"No, you didn't."

"Well, I said I only liked the Octopus."

"You didn't say *only.*"

"Well, I'm saying it now! And I like the Dodgems."

"We have been on the Dodgems," Kate shouts, "about ten

bloody times! I've suggested we go on everything else in the whole bloody fair and all you'll go on is the Dodgems!"

They stare at each other for a moment, neatly frozen in opposition, before Kate turns and walks away. She goes over to the Ferris Wheel and stands in the queue for seats, careful not to look over at Mack at all. When she reaches the front of the queue, she pays the attendant with a slightly fixed expression on her face, to indicate that she has no interest in looking around to see if Mack's still there. A young man who's been standing behind her pushes forward to ask if he can sit with her, but she shakes her head and climbs into the next car, which is swinging slightly back and forth.

Mack watches her as the wheel cranks up into motion, and her car starts to rise up; she still has that posed, eyes-forward stare, like a bad actress trying to look as if she doesn't know that the cameras are on her. He wished he could have explained to her properly; he knows that everything he's said has come out wrong. Or shown her a picture of himself on the Waltzer with Lucy Miller, screaming in terror and panic, pleading with the operator to stop the ride; or afterwards, with his head between his legs, sick to his stomach, wanting to vomit but unable to bring anything up for a few gobs of spittle. Wanting to vomit because at least that would seem dramatic, a badge of suffering, rather than just branding him as a hysterical cry-baby. He couldn't explain then, as he can't now, how much being out of control frightens him; he doesn't quite understand that himself. He just knows that when he's making a parachute jump, he calculates the risks, works out the air speeds, is in charge of his own safety as much as possible. But climbing onto a fairground ride that seems, to everyone else, nothing by comparison is impossible for him, because he is at the mercy of the ride, out of his own control.

He doesn't think it would have helped, in fact, to have explained this to Kate; it wouldn't have made any difference to what is for her the single, salient fact, that she's on the Ferris wheel by herself when he could have come on it with her. He looks up again, and sees her chair descending in a forward arc. She's leaning out a little, her eyes and mouth wide in a huge, screaming smile, ecstatic with controlled terror. She screams with gusto; he knows that well enough by this time to tease her about it; but now her screams are for herself alone. He's on the ground, and can't hear them; he can only seen her lips move.

Kathleen DeMarco is the author of *Cranberry Queen* and *The Difference Between You and Me*. She lives with her husband and son in Manhattan.

Entranced
Kathleen DeMarco

"I can promise you that Encanto is going to be one of those restaurants where people don't go for just a week, or a month, or a year, *but for their life.*" Amelia grew excited as she spoke into the phone, as she always did when she praised people and companies she actually liked.

"Are you sure you want to go on record with that?" said Rita Nelson, fifth of the six critics she was calling today. "Don't you want to wait till it's open for at least a week?"

By the end of the conversation, Amelia had convinced Rita to attend Encanto's opening next month, as she had done on four previous calls. The easiest had been with handsome Jack Wyatt, the food writer for *Metropolitan Magazine,* who'd said that wherever she told him to go, he'd go.

"You're your own crystal ball," he'd said. "It's like you cast a spell and *voila!* Instant restaurant success."

"Oh, stop," she'd replied, before encouraging him to bring

Micheline, the gorgeous French dress designer he'd been with for the past year. She's a lucky girl, thought Amelia after Jack hurried off the phone to take another call. Lucky, thin and *just* a little bit bitchy.

She was anticipating her final pitch to be the hardest: Tommy Lentini, the critic for the *New York World,* the most eminent newspaper in America. But after she explained that it was another Eduardo Casas restaurant, Tommy replied in his gravelly voice, "I haven't been out to an opening in a while. I liked Eduardo's first place quite a lot though."

By the end of the call, with only a little prodding from Amelia, Tommy had promised he would be there, and as she hung up the phone she had that lovely, karmic feeling that she was doing exactly what she was meant to be doing. She was an agent for Mangia Media, the leading restaurant public relations firm in New York, and she was vibrant, independent, respected, assured. The fact that the critic for the *New York World* promised to go to her restaurant launch was a coup; everyone knew that prickly Tommy Lentini almost never agreed to go to openings.

Amelia picked up the phone to tell someone her good news. She wanted to call her boyfriend. But there was one problem. She didn't have a boyfriend. Which was basically the only thing wrong in her otherwise-perfect thirty-five-year-old life. Why was it that this one tiny imperfection had the power to spread into a full-blown crack?

It had never been her style, but lately, she felt as if she was conceding defeat to all those righteous lifestyle-purveyors and married friends and supposedly wise self-help-book authors who pushed romance as the number-one essential ingredient for a meaningful life. She was under constant assault—not just from friends and family but from the world at large. She couldn't walk down the street without seeing a free newspaper with the headline Never Be Lonely Again, or go by a bookstore display without the title *Learn How To Flirt* beckoning to her, as if this stupid book knew more about her than she did. Amelia felt like a human kiosk, with little notes stuck to her by well-meaning people. "Buy *Be a Vixen,* why don't you?" said her friend Jeanne. (Jab, jab.) "Take that 'Picking the Right Man for Once in Your Life' class," said her colleague Sam. (Poke, poke.) "Please tell me again what is wrong with Richard?" asked her mother. (Push, push.)

(That her mother wanted her to be with Richard, an ultraconservative political adviser with greasy hair and a penchant for trite aphorisms, was a sure sign that Amelia was in desperate condition.)

So when she heard Girard's message, she felt a thrill. Dr. Girard Fowler was the eminent nanotechnologist she'd met last week. Well, remet. Apparently they had gone to college together. "I can't believe I'm talking to the famous Amelia Petkevis," he said after they had been introduced. That he remembered her so clearly from their college days meant something valuable to Amelia, especially as she did not remember him at all. She was *memorable.* Memorable to a viable, attractive *nanotechnologist.* Whatever that was.

He'd seemed charming and interesting and (most importantly) interested, and she'd felt hopeful for the first time in a long while. As she dined at her favorite neighborhood restaurant, El Cielo, she told the chef, Eduardo, all about him. Eduardo was not only one of Amelia's best friends (and favorite clients), he was also the chef behind Encanto, the new restaurant that Amelia had been lobbying for that day.

"He said he liked Bruce Springsteen," she told him.

Eduardo, a man so energetic he seemed combustible, was not particularly impressed. "Not a stretch. Every guy likes Bruce Springsteen. What else?"

"He's tall," said Amelia.

"And—"

"He's tall. And smart. He went to Harvard and then Yale and then Stanford. Or Harvard and then Stanford and then Yale. He played the accordion."

"The accordion?"

"Yeah. Weird?"

"Invite him to dinner."

"I don't invite my mother to dinner," Amelia said. "The last time I cooked was in college. I gave my boyfriend salmonella."

"Here. Invite him here," Eduardo told her. "I'm sick of hearing about these guys long before I meet them."

"I don't talk about guys that much," snapped Amelia. "Hardly ever."

"Martin?"

"Well—"

"You had me thinking that Martin was a good guy."

"He was. Until he slept with that guy he met in the ATM line. Not that there is anything wrong with that."

"And the banker, the one with the skinny nose—"

"Yes, Rick, but—"

"You told me he was the first gentleman you had met."

"He was. He was a gentleman to me, and I expect when he gets out of prison, he'll still be one. You realize there are tons of hedge fund managers who deserve to be in jail more than he does?"

"You need an impartial observer. Right, Maurice?"

Eduardo motioned to his right-hand man (and Amelia's favorite waiter), Maurice.

Maurice, never a big talker, nodded. He adored Amelia as much as Eduardo did, and in fact, at night, would tell his wife all about Amelia and how her eyes lit up when she talked about her nephews, and her job, and whichever book she was currently reading. Maurice's wife once asked why she wasn't married. Maurice had shrugged. "American girls are crazy," he had said. "They make everything so hard."

"What's the holdup?" Eduardo asked Amelia. "Just call him back."

Amelia looked at her food. "I—"

"What?"

"I'll ruin it. Let's say he's a great guy. Let's say he's perfect. Undoubtedly I'll do something to ruin it. I don't know what it will be, but something will go wrong. I know it."

"Here? You insult me. I'll make a feast."

"No, not with you. With me."

"You give yourself too much credit. It's not always about you."

"Yes, it is. That crap that it isn't you, it's me, is the biggest line in the world. Of course it's me, if it wasn't, we would work out. But I'm okay. I'm fine with my life—it's just the world that's out to prove how unhappy I am."

Eduardo made the cuckoo sign next to his head. "Relax. Just see what he's about. Don't make snap judgments, that's all. You don't have to be scared."

"I'm not scared," Amelia responded quickly. "I'm just…" She looked at Eduardo. He waited. She grinned. "Scared."

"Maurice!" Eduardo yelled. "Bring the wine. For me, not for her. She's nuts."

Amelia promised Eduardo before she left the restaurant

that she would bring Girard to his restaurant later that week…that is, if he was still interested.

Amelia didn't know that after she left the restaurant, Eduardo had brought Maurice back into the kitchen with him to discuss Amelia and her love life.

"This isn't your business," cautioned Maurice.

"Of course it's my business—if not mine, whose? Who? She needs some help. A little guidance. Something to help with her taste in men, so to speak."

"Your magic mumbo jumbo—" Maurice sputtered.

"My unique cultural gift, you mean."

"What is it? Santera?"

"No, not Santera. I'm only a quarter Cuban. I call it *Eduardia.*"

"You're much crazier than Amelia."

"Just be quiet," Eduardo said. "And help me."

For the next fifteen minutes Eduardo and Maurice mixed together a potion of roasted chicken juices, red wine, wasabi sauce and special Latin American olive oil. Eduardo cooked it slowly over the hot stove, dropping some special herbs in it while it boiled. Then he looked over at Maurice.

"Cover your ears," he said.

Maurice grudgingly covered his ears with his hands while Eduardo murmured some Spanish and English words over the boiling potion, *spiritudiosamorcrazyAmericannoviostruelove-penguins.* He clapped his hands twice. Maurice uncovered his ears.

"Penguins?"

"Don't ask."

"Are you done?"

"Not yet. It has to be frozen until Amelia comes back into the restaurant. And then—you'll see. I'll put it over her food, she'll eat it and then—" Eduardo clapped his hands together "—magic! Just watch what happens when she touches her food."

"Amelia won't eat with her fingers," muttered Maurice.

"Just watch," gloated Eduardo. "And don't be so literal."

Dr. Girard Fowler rang the buzzer for Amelia's apartment building at exactly 7:25 p.m. He was twenty minutes early.

"It's me," he said through the intercom.

"Come in," Amelia replied.

"Sweet pea," he exclaimed when she opened the door for him. "For you." He held out one long stem of a blooming star lily. She took the flower and tried to not let the fact that he'd just called her "sweet pea" bother her.

"How beautiful. Thanks." Amelia took the flower and put it in a vase. "I'm almost ready. But didn't we say seven forty-five?" Amelia was silently assessing Girard as she spoke. He was dressed well, a button-down shirt tucked into well-fitting khaki pants and expensive leather shoes. His hair was thick but not styled, and his face was pleasant. He was tall, but because his shoulders were so narrow—barely jutting out beyond his head—he looked like a long plank of wood.

"The early bird gets the worm," he replied. "Are you objecting?" Girard sat down with a grunt on the couch and picked up *Us Weekly*.

"No, it's fine." Amelia decided he was cute.

"You know," said Girard, looking through the pages of the gossip magazine. "Even Nicole Kidman has a can on her."

Amelia was not sure she'd heard correctly. "Nicole Kidman is one of the most beautiful women in the world."

"Calm down, sweet pea." Girard smiled. "I'm just saying she has a can. I didn't say she wasn't beautiful." He looked at her. "You're the beautiful one," he said without a note of humor in his voice.

Amelia smiled, but it was forced. She focused on how she'd felt when he'd asked for her number, and how nice he'd been when she returned his call. SINGLE, SMART, HAND-SOME, STRAIGHT, SINGLE, SMART, HANDSOME, STRAIGHT, SINGLE clanged in her head. She turned toward him. "Ready? You're going to love this restaurant, I know it."

"I'm ready," Girard said, a smile spreading across his wide, bony face. "Let's go."

Eduardo and Maurice peered through a small window in the kitchen door as Girard and Amelia entered the restaurant.

"It's time!" Eduardo took the potion out of the freezer and placed the bowl into the microwave.

"You can microwave a magic potion?"

"What, have you read the potion rule book? Of course you can microwave it. How else will it be ready?"

Eduardo pressed the buttons on the microwave. In the meantime, he prepared two special appetizers. When the potion had defrosted, Eduardo poured it over one of the appetizers and grabbed the plates.

"I can do it," Maurice said.

"It's not your potion," Eduardo replied. "I'll do the honors, thank you very much."

Maurice got out of Eduardo's way as he walked forcefully out of the kitchen and toward Amelia and Girard's table.

"Hello," Eduardo said. "Some appetizers to get you started." He was sure to place the special appetizer in front of Amelia.

"Girard Fowler," said Girard, extending his hand.

"Eduardo Casas. Welcome."

"So my girl comes here all the time?" Girard asked.

"We wish she'd come here more. So listen. If it's okay with you, I'm just going to send out some things. You don't have to look at the menu."

"Sounds ideal," said Girard.

"I'll check in after the meal." Eduardo bowed a little, which made Amelia giggle, and then he strode back to the kitchen. Immediately after he stepped through the doors, however, he turned to peek through the window.

"What do you think of him?" asked Maurice.

"Too soon to tell," said Eduardo. "But we'll know what Amelia thinks of him soon enough."

Back at the table, Girard spoke quietly to Amelia. "I'm looking forward to the meal." He hesitated. "But I'm not used to buying anything I don't know the price of."

Amelia immediately saw Girard in a different light—a struggling scientist, someone very proud, a man unused to reckless spending. She admonished herself for being so judgmental; he was just someone who had to work hard his whole life, she decided. Of course money was an issue.

"He won't charge us."

"He won't?"

"No. We should just leave a tip."

"Of course." Girard nodded. "I'll just follow your lead. I'm just the follower." He smiled at her then as he reached over and put his hand near hers. Amelia decided she needed to be more daring. She covered his hand with hers. Girard looked at her, surprised. But then confidence crept through his features, and Amelia felt, as Girard clutched her hand, as if she were drowning. She yanked her hand away and began to devour the appetizer.

"Of course, there's nothing wrong with a little frugality, right, sweet pea?" Girard ate some of the appetizer. "What is this?"

"Eggplant?" Amelia guessed just as Maurice arrived, delivering two plates of mesclun salad to their table, accompanied by a dish of poached pears.

"He's pulling out all the stops for you," said Amelia, finishing her appetizer.

"You know, I really admire the Spanish people. They work so hard and send all their money back to Mexico, Puerto Rico—" Amelia saw Maurice raise his eyebrows as he walked away.

"Eduardo's grandparents were born here," Amelia interrupted, but Girard kept talking.

"Colombia, some pretty terrible places, I should know. I mean, I've done a lot of reading about these cultures and for someone like Eduardo to become a chef—"

"What are you saying, exactly?"

"Oh, don't get your pretty head out of whack, I'm just saying that this looks like a terrific salad. Don't you think?" He pricked at his salad with his fork and ate a large mouthful of leaves. "Delicious."

Amelia plunged her fork into a leaf. How dare he—

She stopped chewing. There was something wrong with her salad.

Girard had begun another conversation. "…radical feminist mythology, essentially, sparked by you-know-who. Hillary. Need I say more? A total fallacy to say that productivity increased when women entered the workforce—not that women haven't been useful, of course I'm not saying that, sweet pea—"

Amelia was barely listening. She was staring at the lettuce

on her plate. It was vibrant, fresh and green. She stabbed another leaf with her fork. And as soon as she did, the same thing happened.

The leaf wilted.

She removed the lettuce from the fork with her knife and watched as it sprung back to life.

"There's always room in every culture for women to leave their children but—"

"Would you excuse me for a minute?" Amelia asked.

"Something wrong?" Girard's face crumpled into an expression of annoyance.

"No. I just remembered. I need to tell Eduardo something. Business."

"Duty calls." Girard nodded. "Don't mind me if I keep eating."

Amelia ran into the kitchen. Eduardo and Maurice, who had been watching by the door, scurried back to the ovens.

"Eduardo! There's something wrong with my salad."

"Be more specific."

"More specific? Okay. It tasted like pond weeds. Slimy. Flaccid. On the plate it looked fine. On my fork, it wilted into something inedible. Is that specific enough for you?" The entire evening was a disaster. When she saw Eduardo and Maurice exchange glances, she grew even more angry. "What? What's going on?"

"Here. Try this." Eduardo picked up a salad resting on top of an aluminum sideboard. She grabbed a piece of lettuce with her fingers and ate it. It was perfectly fine.

"I'm not lying. The one you gave me wilted."

"I believe you," he said. He looked at her for a moment and then asked, "Are you enjoying your date?"

"What?"

"I'm just wondering. Lettuce is alive, you know. Plants can pick up on human emotions."

Amelia stared. "Please don't go New Age-y on me. Please. I just have never seen my food change its…its *form* before. Did you do something to it?"

"Amelia— I don't know about this guy. Maybe you shouldn't waste any more time."

"Excuse me?"

"Just that."

"No. No way, Eduardo. You're the one who told me no snap judgments. He's a scholar! A scientist! He went to Yale! And Harvard! And he's here!"

Eduardo just looked at her. She glared back at him. But then, her angry features grew glum, resigned. She shrunk against the kitchen wall.

"He's a jackass," she said quietly. "And probably a misogynist. He calls me 'sweet pea' and acts like we're in love when we barely know each other." She turned her head, looked at the white tiled wall. "I have the worst taste in men."

Eduardo and Maurice glanced at one another.

"Amelia—I did something to—"

Amelia shook her head. She felt weary. "I don't want to hear it. Whatever you did. I have to go and tell this pompous jerk—who I'm supposed to fall madly in love with because he's single and straight—that he's a pompous jerk. I don't care what you did. I've had enough for tonight. It's hard to have your expectations rise and crash in less than an hour."

"But—" Eduardo started.

"I'll call you tomorrow," said Amelia. She peeled herself off of the wall, lifted her chin and marched out of the kitchen. Eduardo and Maurice watched as she stood at the table and spoke to Girard. She sat down only after he stood up and walked out.

"I'm going to go talk to her," said Maurice.

"Leave her alone," said Eduardo. "You heard her."

A few nights later Amelia met up with five friends at a new restaurant in the Lower East Side. Amelia was late, and took the last seat available. It was next to a lawyer named Dan, who had gone to graduate school with her friend Jeanne. Dan was smiley and funny, and for a second, Amelia felt a flash of connection. But then she dug into her grilled salmon and almost gagged. She looked at the fish. On the plate, it was in perfect condition. On her fork, it had turned raw. She looked back at Dan, still smiley but now staring down the breasts of the woman across the table. Amelia put her fork down. She turned to the other side, where Jeanne sat.

"Do you like him?" Jeanne whispered.

"Who?" Amelia answered.

"Don't be funny. He's a lawyer!"

"Not gonna happen," Amelia said. "I'm sure he's a nice guy. Just not right for me."

"How do you know that?" Jeanne hissed. "You just met him."

Amelia thought of Girard and the wilting lettuce leaf. She recalled Eduardo telling her that lettuce is alive and the secretive looks Maurice and Eduardo exchanged. She remembered sharing a bottle of wine with Eduardo late one night and him telling her that he liked to experiment with potions. She had thought he was joking or drunk or tired, but now she wasn't sure. Okay, then, she thought. Eduardo is my guardian angel, my food angel, my find-a-good-man angel.

She smiled and then she leaned over so that her mouth was near Jeanne's ear. "He turned my food bad," Amelia whispered.

Jeanne turned to her, irritated. "What did you say?"

"Don't worry about it," said Amelia, knowing how ridiculous she sounded. "Just trust me like I trust my food."

"You've lost your mind."

"There are worse things," Amelia replied. "Much worse."

Over the next few weeks, Amelia used food as her divining rod. She went on more dates during this time than she had in the past two years. She felt as if she had been given a supreme and unerring gift. She never discussed it with Eduardo—just silently thanked him as she turned away another unsuitable partner. (She also, completely as a side benefit, lost four pounds.) When he asked her which of her gentleman callers she'd be bringing to his opening, she smiled.

She was going alone. She'd had an epiphany during the weeks of turbo dating—an epiphany in the form of a continuum. On one end of the continuum was Girard. And on the other was, well, usually Bruce Springsteen. Girard = the face of incompatibility, a life of carping, a life of settling. Bruce = the *idea* of someone, a man as yet unknown, with whom she could love and be loved. And with whom she could share a nice meal.

In the middle was Amelia by herself.

Until she could be with Bruce, or *a* Bruce, she'd be alone. And content.

"Amelia!" Eduardo welcomed her on the night of the opening. A tomato stain dripped down his pant leg and she could see that his shirt was on inside out. He looked a wreck. "Listen, I want to tell you something."

"There's no way people will not like this place," Amelia assured him.

"Not that," said Eduardo. "It's...well—remember that scientist—"

"Eduardo!" It was Maurice. "Come into the kitchen! You need to check the pork—"

"We'll talk later?" asked Eduardo. "People are starting to arrive."

"Everything's going to be fine," said Amelia.

"I wasn't talking about the restaurant," Eduardo answered.

"Go to the kitchen," Amelia told him. "I'm not going anywhere."

She looked around the room, satisfied. Guests had begun to fill up the intimate space; fun, sultry Celia Cruz music streamed through the air and people seemed animated, alive. When Amelia saw Tommy Lentini walk in and be seated at the best table in the room (just as Amelia had ordered Eduardo's staff), she figured her work was done and went to get a drink.

"Hey, Amelia! Come join me."

She turned to see Jack Wyatt, the *Metropolitan Magazine* reviewer, sitting by himself in the back of the dining room.

"Big success," Jack said as she walked over to him.

"Hate to say it, but I told you so," she answered. She saw Maurice heading toward them with appetizers of *papas rellenas* (potatoes stuffed with beef) and *tostones* (fried plaintains). Just at that moment, the music blared from the speakers; combined with the din created by the horde of guests, it was impossible to hear.

"I haven't—" Jack spoke loudly.

"I can't hear—" Amelia responded. Jack pointed to the food. Amelia nodded. They both tasted the appetizers at the same time.

"Eduardo's done it—" Jack yelled.

"This is fantastic—" Amelia called back. "So where's Micheline?"

Jack shook his head. She moved her chair closer to his.

"What did you say?" Jack asked.

"First I said this was fantastic," Amelia answered as she picked up another plaintain with her fork. It was an ideal golden color, singed slightly on the edges. And it was perfect.

It was perfect.

"What is it?" asked Jack.

"Nothing," Amelia said, and then, daringly, put the plaintain in her mouth. It was delicious. She stared at Jack.

"What?" he asked again, amused.

"Wait a second," Amelia answered. She put her fork through a stuffed potato. "Where's Micheline?"

"Oh," said Jack. "That's a long story."

"I've got time," she said. And then, because her instinct told her to eat before she heard his story, she put her fork in her mouth. She chewed, swallowing slowly. It was superb. When she looked up, she saw Eduardo watching her across the room. He winked.

"Not that interesting. Tall man, French. I didn't stand a chance." Amelia watched his face as it moved into a charming smile. "It happened a couple of months ago, so I'm okay with it." He stopped. "Well, almost okay with it. If she walked in here right now, I'd probably go from okay to bad. But…"

Amelia listened to Jack as she devoured her food. *He's sin-*

gle. Jack's single. My food is fine, better than fine. It is delectable, it is perfect, it is—

"Are you listening at all?" Jack interrupted. "You seem entranced by your food."

Amelia looked up at him. "Not anymore," she said, putting her fork down. "Not anymore." She scanned the room once again for Eduardo, but not seeing him, she sat back and gave her full attention to Jack (who, now that she was focusing, *did* look a little like Bruce Springsteen) and she relaxed.

Man with a Tan
Anna Maxted

When you meet the man you're going to marry, you just know. Apparently. I suppose it's like walking into Whistles and just knowing you want the pink spangly halter-neck top. You slink it on in the matchbox changing room and are instantly transformed into a sparkly, if curiously undernourished, sex goddess. It's only later in the cold light of your bedroom that you realize you look like a camp frankfurter brought to life in a mad experiment. Marriage can have a similar effect—though in this case your husband turns out to be the sausage.

Pardon me if that sounds harsh. I have nothing against buying spangly tops or tying the knot—either one ensures you oodles of attention and fuss, and if you look like a pig in a poke no one is going to mention it. Very nice. The reason I'm skeptical about the cupid's arrow theory is because, in my experience, love isn't as instant as a cup of Nescafé. It's a screamingly slow, foot-dragging process. I can only compare it to glaciers that move about one millimeter every thousand years.

When *I* met the man of my dreams I didn't notice him. I was too busy posing in a deadly new pair of needle-sharp stilettos. And when he brought himself to my attention—"Ah, excuse me, but you're treading on my toe"—I *certainly* didn't think in terms of marriage. It would have been such a killjoy thought! Like binning the candy floss and eating the stick. When the man of my dreams announced himself, my first thought was, "So that's why the carpet feels lumpy."

Maybe I'm cynical about happy-ever-after because I hail from a family as dysfunctional as *The Simpsons* without the exonerating factor of unusual charm. (My partner, whose middle name is charm, can't quite get over it and avoids his in-laws like other people avoid ink clouds in swimming pools.) Ah yes. My partner. Wasn't that who you were waiting for? I have my eldest sister, Gloria, to credit for bringing us together. Thanks to her I live in a big sunny house where I don't have to lift a finger. And I can buy as many pink spangly tops as Whistles will sell me.

It all began on the second day of summer, the sky a weak lazy blue for the occasion.

"You know," Gloria remarks to our dappy sister Denise while ogling a celebrity's over-pined home in *Hello!* magazine, "I used to think that money didn't matter. But I want my three holidays a year!" I suggest she could earn it herself, but she blanks me. "MC Magimix has his three holidays, all right," she drools. "Oooh, he's practically mahogany."

I make a face at Robert, and say, "What a shame, he'll clash with his pine. I'll be making my own millions, won't you?"

Robert says, "I'd rather be kept by a rich DJ personality,

thanks," and then Gloria tells us to shut it and get on with our work.

Robert and I giggle because Gloria—who doesn't know the meaning of the word *tacky*—fancies her chances with Magimix. Gloria, who has a high squeaky voice and a bony nose, is the worst aspect of being employed by our family business, which, I'll tell you now so you're not disillusioned later, is a contract cleaning firm. Dirty work and filthy pay. The one advantage is that I get to spend time with Robert— an old friend of mine employed by my mother and paid a pittance after he was sacked by Tesco. (He didn't change the doughnut oil in their bakery for a month and it went green.)

Gloria drops *Hello!* on the table, declares, "I'm off to Prada, I need a new business suit. Page if you need me," and sweeps from the room.

Denise snatches up the magazine, flicks to a page and stares at it. She has yolk on her Laura Ashley cardigan from breakfast, but hasn't noticed. She squints, and her face wrinkles up like an old peach.

"What *are* you doing?" I say, trying to keep the irritation out of my voice. At least pretend to be working!

"Checking for dust," she replies.

This bizarre response doesn't surprise me as Denise is away with the fairies and rarely makes sense. I glance at the clock. Twelve thousand miserable pounds per annum divided by 48 × 5 = fifty quid a week. I'm paid a tenner a day.

It's 3:00 p.m., so I say loudly, "Denise, I've got a meeting with our accountant, it'll probably take hours, so I'll go straight home. And Robert is accompanying me to take the minutes." I nod at Robert who smiles winningly and brandishes his notebook.

"Have a nice time," says Denise absently.

We take advantage of her mental blip (so far it's lasted thirty-one years) and head straight for the pub where we spend today's tenners.

Robert shows me a fancy way of lighting a match that really impresses girls. I can't do it but he twirls a curl of my hair around his finger and says, "You have other talents. You're a *sensational* liar."

Sadly, when I stagger into work the next day in the grip of a vicious hangover, my stepmother proves him wrong. I know the game's up when I see her pacing the purple carpet in Christian Lacroix.

"Where've you bin!" she shrieks.

"Sorry, Edith," I whisper. "The car wouldn't start."

She purses her mouth, and her bright red lipstick bleeds into her violent tan. She snaps, "Don't lie, you've bin drinkin', I can smell it!" I stand still to avoid being sick. Her voice is so shrill my brain might shatter.

"Where is everyone?" I whisper.

"Brent Cross Shoppin' Center," she replies in a smug tone.

"Why?" I say.

"Because!" bellows Edith. "Unlike you, yer sisters 'ave a brain in their 'eads!" That sounds right, one between two. "Yesterday, when you was off drinkin'," Edith adds, "Denise was proposishinin' clients!" I find this hard to believe, but suspect linguistic error rather than career change. "And MC Magimix's agent got back to us, and said that Crispian—that's 'is real name, Crispian Bartholomew—it jus' so happens 'e *is* lookin' for a top-flight cleaning service, so we're goin' for an interview and the girls are off buyin' new kit. 'E's seein' us at two."

The curse of *Hello!* strikes again.

Happily, Edith decides I look too much of a state to stand trial and delegates me to another, less crucial client.

"Gloria doesn't want to be upstaged," whispers Robert as I wave them off. How come *he* looks as fresh as a daisy that drank water and went to bed at 9:00 p.m.?

"Rob," I say, "you don't have to console me. I'm not so sad that I get off on scrubbing the toilets of minor celebrities, especially those with orange skin."

Robert jumps into the Range Rover behind Denise. As they roar off, he shouts, "Orangist!'"

I smile into the silence that follows their departure. If it weren't for Robert my life would be pure drudgery. His teasing presence and filthy sense of humor promote it to impure drudgery, and make it just about bearable. An hour until I'm expected at my next job—cleaning the town house of Hattie Hayter, barrister. Time enough for a nap under my desk. I tootle back inside. The next thing I know, I am rudely awoken by an ear-piercing blast. I stumble out from under my desk, fumbling for the phone.

"Hello?"

I am nearly deafened by Edith yelling, "Why int you at 'Attie 'Ayter's, you shoulda bin there ages ago!"

My brain is too fuddled to lie plausibly so I stammer, "Oh."

Edith growls under her breath then hisses, "Git yer arse over 'ere, 'e only wants us to clean 'is 'ole aas—"

I interrupt. "Pardon?" I squeak—I expect celebrities to be debauched but MC Magimix sounds disgusting!

Edith snaps, "Just git over 'ere! Robert's gardenin', Gloria's goin' over the rates with Crispian an' chattin' about 'is job an all, an Denise is in 'is bedroom, she's bin tryin' to

straighten' out 'is water bed for the last 'arf hour, an I int
doin' no aaswork, so that leaves you, so ring 'Attie 'Ayter's
an tell 'er you'll do 'er later, then git over 'ere!"

Never mind that I'm still over the limit, I scrawl down the
address, brush my hair, crawl into my green Datsun and
trundle off.

Hattie Hayter is understanding and when I offer to clean
at half-rate she says, "Don't be ridiculous."

Twenty minutes later, I crunch up the tree-lined driveway leading to Crispian's white house and park the Datsun
in a leafy corner. I expect a sign saying Magimix Towers and
gray stone lions guarding the porch and for the doorbell to
sing the initial notes of "Heartbreaker" when you press it,
but there are no signs, lions or singing. I ring an ordinary
buzzer and four seconds later the red door is flung open and
I look into the stunning green contact lenses of MC himself.

"Wotcha!" says Magimix, but before I can reply, Gloria appears and says, "There you are, did you remember your
apron? Now, Mr. Bartholomew—oh! *[simper]* Crispy, if you
insist! how kind!—Crispy has a soiree tonight and he needs
the house pristine, and if we do a satisfactory job, the account is ours. Come along now, Ella, don't stand there—
make use of those large capable hands. Hurry, time is
money!"

Money and money, it's all she ever thinks about. I scowl
at Gloria and smile at Crispian—"Crispy" indeed—who
steps aside to let me into the hallway.

"Ecstatic to meet you," he says, and winks.

Gloria stares after him like a fox after a hen. Then she says,
"Start from the top of the house and work your way down.

You've got three hours to do the best frigging job you've ever done in your life. I want him to be able to serve his soiree off the toilet seat."

I bite back the response, "I believe that's the norm in media circles," and plod upstairs. I peer out of a stained-glass window and see Robert pulling up weeds in a flower bed. I rap-rap and he looks up but can't see me. I fling open the window and sing, "Woo-ooo!" He grins and blows me a kiss through mud-stained fingers. I shut the window, still smiling, look up and scream.

"Oh, sorry," I gasp. "I didn't see you."

MC Magimix laughs and says, "Am I that terrifying?" He has an air of cool confidence and a voice as rich and creamy as a glass of Baileys.

I blush and say, "I was just saying hi to my colleague."

MC Magimix drawls, "Live dangerously, sweetheart." He looks close to a smile.

"Is that what you suggest?" I say.

He reveals white teeth and murmurs, "I suggest your sister's an ogre and you're destined for better things."

I can't resist a flirt and open my mouth to say, "Crispian, you are *so* right, but you needn't look so smug, because by employing us you are propagating my misery," but from downstairs Gloria's falsetto voice tinkles, "Ell-ar! I do hope you're not chatting!"

I wince, excuse myself, rush to the top floor and sweep it.

I give it some elbow and we get the Magimix account and Gloria is torn between elation and fury. She and Edith are thrilled because Crispy wants us to "clean his 'ole aas" three times a week, but she and Edith are not thrilled because Crispy specified that he wanted *me* to clean it because I was "a great scrubber." If that's a compliment I'm not thrilled either.

"If you've got designs on Crispy, think again," says Gloria as she clambers into the Range Rover.

Robert—who has sat in grim glowering silence since Crispy's "scrubber" remark—looks at me. "You *are* kidding," he says. "Ella?"

"Don't be daft," I reply. "I passed him on the stairs and he leered at me and said hello. I bet he tries it on with everyone, the postman included. Anyway, what was I meant to do, blank him?"

I drive on to Hattie Hayter's with Robert. He spends the entire journey scraping the dirt from under his fingernails. He has nice hands.

"Too hard for gloves, are you?" I tease, but all he says is "Ho ho," in an unamused way. When we arrive at Hattie's he stalks into her garden without a backward glance. I feel anxious without knowing why.

I shrug, let myself in and start gathering the army of coffee cups stationed about the house.

"Hello!" says Hattie as I swish on the hot tap and squirt a squiddle of Fairy Liquid into the kitchen sink.

"Hattie!" I say, jumping.

"So," she says, leaning against the door frame, "how was Radio Man? Ghastly?"

I shake my head. "Not bad actually," I say. "Not as orange as I thought."

Hattie draws up a chair. "Indeed!" she exclaims. "Do tell."

Not much *to* tell. But Hattie's interested so we chat as I work. I would say that high-flying Hattie sees my mundane life as a diversion, but she's sweeter than that. Every week, she demands installments. So every week I tell her about Crispy, who also likes to chat to me as I work, and Gloria, who is spending a fortune at Michaeljohn thrice weekly, and Robert, who can't stand Crispy, although Crispy is friendly and offers him tickets—offers all of us tickets—to his new clubnight ("MC Magimix plays deep and funky house"— admission £10, includes ONE FREE DRINK before midnight).

When Crispy offers, Robert says quickly, "Thanks, mate, but I'm away that week, I'm visiting my gran in Seattle."

Later in the car Gloria is triumphant and snatches away my ticket and says, "Don't think you're going, he only asked you to be polite," and I say narkily, "I wouldn't go if you paid me, I loathe funky house, I prefer Beethoven."

When I say this, Robert gives me a strange look. His long-lashed brown eyes seem bigger than ever. For a second he is five years old.

Then he says shyly, "We could go out tonight, Ella, if you like—you know, sex, drugs and an ice-cream-eating competition?"

He's been so offish that I seize on his invitation like a stray dog on a scrap of chicken, and he collects me on his secondhand moped and we go to Banners in Crouch End and drink vodka martinis and eat corn bread and ice cream and laugh and lean closer and closer. It's happened before but we've always pulled back.

Not tonight though. Suddenly we're kissing and half of me is thinking, "This is *Robert!*" and the other half is thinking "*This* is Robert?!" and then we ditch the moped and get a taxi and because I still live at home and we don't fancy sneaking past Gloria and Edith, we speed back to his Kilburn flat where we rip each other's clothes off in the hallway and it's all rather fairy tale.

Making love to Robert knocks me sideways, as do the beautiful things he says. It's wonderful but weird because I've known him for all this time and while I *saw* he was gorgeous and funny and clever, he was so familiar to me I never thought of him in that way. And if I did I quashed it. But this warm summer night changes everything. It's as if my heart is rewired in the heat of our passion. I am shyer and awestruck in his presence, it's like I'm born again and he feels the same.

He says he's always adored me but was scared to say, he's got peanuts but he'll get rich for me, he'll start his own business, we'll do it together and we'll live in a big sunny house—although he'd be happy with me in a damp hovel—and there'll be no more housework I won't lift a finger and he doesn't want to go to Seattle tomorrow but he can't disappoint his gran but he'll phone me every day.

So when he doesn't ring I am surprised to say the least.

I tell Hattie and she says, "Don't take any shit."

I think, surely, there's got to be a reason, but I don't have his gran's number, and I can't believe he hasn't rung and three days pass and then I think, see if I care, the bloody bastard, and that'll teach me to sleep with my friends. Life is hellish enough but Gloria and Edith make it worse as they both have their knickers in a twist about MC Magimix's clubnight and keep snapping at me like a pair of crocodiles. Edith is hoping that Frank Butcher will be there (she has no clue) and Gloria is planning to cop off with Crispy. Denise is excited because she's too dim to know any better.

I tell Hattie that I'm not going; I'll stay at home and watch

Denise's vast collection of *Brookside* videos to make killing myself a more attractive proposition.

Hattie says, "What nonsense!" and tells me I should get a grip and put on a frock and go to the club and dance to "I Will Survive" or whatever they play in clubs these days.

"I've got nothing to wear and can't afford anything new," I tell her.

Hattie says, "Wait" and disappears into a room and returns brandishing a skinny rib silver top and bootleg leather trousers. I gawp, and Hattie says, "*Not* mine, dear, my sister's. They'll fit you perfectly."

I am doing my makeup thinking spiteful anti-Robert thoughts, when the phone rings.

Gloria cries, "Ella, why didn't you return to the office after Hattie's! The accounts need to be sorted before tomorrow morning, you'll have to work late tonight."

"Oh," I say.

"I'll pay you overtime," she adds.

"Right," I say.

She says edgily, "You didn't have any plans?"

I tell her, "No." I put down the phone and consider doing the accounts. Truth is, they do need to be done before tomorrow. And I should have done them last week. Then I think, balls. My life is mush, I'm going to party!

There's a massive queue for the club but I march to the front and show my ticket and am ushered inside. I am a VIP and in a shallow nihilistic sort of way it feels *great*. It feels even greater when I totter to the bar to buy a drink and feel warm hands on my hips and spin round and see Crispy, his smile fluorescent in the strobe lights. He shouts over the bass,

"Gloria said you weren't coming." I shout back, "I'm supposed to be working, if she sees me I'm toast." Crispy takes my hand and snakes through the crush. Girls grab at his T-shirt and he unpicks them, leads me upstairs, opens a door and bows, and it's a room full of squashy red sofas and beautiful people.

"They won't find us here, sweetheart," says Crispy. "Might I fetch you a drink?"

I let Crispy "fetch" me a drink. He does have a remarkable tan, but it is *not* orange. And he has great teeth and exquisite manners.

"Don't you have to DJ?" I say.

"Not till midnight," he says. "Don't think you'll escape from me that easily."

I giggle and say, "Aren't you embarrassed to be seen out with your cleaning lady?"

Crispy says solemnly, "Not when she has the face of an angel." I think, how naff but consider Gloria and smile anyway.

And after that we talk about the music business. Crispy loves music but hates the business, it's so false and backbiting but he shouldn't complain, he's done well out of it, but anyway, that's a yawn, what about *me,* why the hell am I cleaning loos for a living when I could be a model, and I say "Well, *you* employ me!" and he says, "If I didn't I wouldn't get to see you," and I turn pink and Crispy says, "Sweetheart, do you really think I need my house cleaned three times a week?"

I'm flattered, I don't know what to say. And then he kisses me, which solves the problem.

It feels good and it feels bad and best of all it spites my aching heart.

We don't stop kissing until midnight strikes and Crispy yells, "Shit!"

He lifts my hand to his lips and kisses it and says, "I'll call you!" and I think "Yeah right," but I am all aflutter with alcohol and lust, and I am that dizzied up I take a cab straight to the office and sit there in leather trousers and silver top and do the accounts and fall into bed at 5:00 a.m., and when the alarm wakes me two hours later I rise like a zombie, wash my face and sleepwalk in to work.

Gloria is in a foul mood because Crispy arrived at the club at 9:50, disappeared at ten and reappeared at 12:02 but that was no sodding use because he was spinning discs and out of reach, but she can't take it out on me because when she snarls, "Where are the accounts?!' I reply, "On your desk," and there's no quibbling with that.

I think I'm safe but I sneak out to get a sandwich and when I return Gloria is sniffling and wiping her bony nose with a purple tissue and Denise is subdued and Edith grabs me by the wrist and yanks me into the corridor and hisses, "What the 'ell are you playin' at!"

I twist out of her grasp and say, "I beg your pardon!" and Edith says, "You knew 'e was spoken for! 'E was Gloria's route to easy street! Don' come the innocent with me, jus' tell me why Crispy 'as called this office three times in the last 'arf hour askin' to speak to *you!*" Hmm.

I tell my stepmother that last week while I was doing his bathroom Cripsy mentioned that he was looking for an Art Deco set of taps, and did I know anywhere. I said I did and I'd get back to him and that, of course, is why he's calling. I know Edith doesn't believe me and when I spin the same story to Gloria she shoots me the nastiest look I've ever seen apart from on a warthog with indigestion at London Zoo.

Then she says, "Give me the number of the tap shop and *I'll* get back to Crispy for you." I make up a number on the spot then excuse myself because I'm due at Hattie's. I want to call Crispy but I don't dare.

But in the end it doesn't matter because the next day Gloria and Edith go to Ascot and Denise goes to the dentist and I'm shuffling papers round the office and the phone rings and the receptionist is so excited she can hardly speak but I have a famous visitor and can she send him up?

I feel hot and I know it's not because of the summer sun. It's lust and defiance and I check in the mirror that my nose isn't shiny and scrabble around Denise's dusty desk where I find a mint and I crunch it up and Crispy walks through the door holding the biggest bunch of lilies you ever saw and I can tell they're from a swanky florist and he says, "Doesn't your sister *ever* pass on messages?" and drops the lilies on a chair.

He's wearing tight trousers and a tight T-shirt, which is not the sort of getup I go for on a man—Robert is a loose-fitted kind of bloke—but who cares about pale absent Robert when I have Crispy who is tanned and tantalizing, if tight-trousered. I feel briefly evil because four days ago Robert and I were forever and he so seemed to mean it. I believed him because I *know* Robert and he doesn't lie, and although Hattie might say, "If you and Robert were meant to be it would have happened sooner," I think that some people *grow* to love one another and I don't think that sort of love is inferior to snap-bang love but then Robert isn't here and Crispy is.

Our office has lax security, by which I mean no cameras, so when Crispy bends me over a desk I don't worry about being caught, although the prude in me thinks that this isn't the most romantic position for a first bonk—I think of Robert wanting to gaze into my eyes but I banish the thought—although I do wonder because Crispy is so charming, I would have expected the missionary but the slut in me thinks just give it to me, baby, oh yes, that feels good and it keeps feeling good until Robert walks in and walks right out again and I wriggle out from under Crispy and run after Robert but he's gone.

When Denise returns from the dentist she is surprised to see me crying in the road and when I tell her she says that of *course* Robert rang me from Seattle, he rang the office and our home, didn't Gloria tell me? Robert rang distraught to say his gran had had a stroke and he'd try and call when he could but it would be difficult. Denise says the third time he rang she took the call and wrote it all down but Gloria said *she'd* pass on Robert's message, which was, "I know you'll understand and wait for me." When she tells me this my heart crumples like an old tissue.

I left Crispy to pull up his tight trousers and I ran home and called Robert to explain but he couldn't forgive me. He couldn't forgive that casual lust, it was too cruel, it changed me for him, irreparably. I wasn't the woman he thought I was. I cried and begged but I understood because five days is hardly much time to wait for love, not when you've waited for seven years, so what was left for me but to do the thing that would most spite Gloria?

If you don't believe in happy-ever-after, Crispy isn't a bad person to be with. He's sweet if self-satisfied, but our sex life isn't up to much. Whenever he tries it on I see Robert walking in and the pain on his face takes me back all those years to when he first tapped me on the shoulder and said, "Ah, excuse me, but you're treading on my toe."

Males and E-Mails
Jessica Adams

When Hilary and I first moved from Sydney into this apartment together, we sat around the table eating Lucky Charms (yes, I'm afraid some women still buy breakfast cereal advertised by a spokes-elf) and we made up some house rules.

The first rule banned Hilary from stealing library books, which seemed important at the time, as she is a senior children's librarian. One year later, though, there is still a big pile of Harry Potter under her bed, and it shows no sign of being returned.

The second rule we made banned me from singing the theme song from *Fame* in the shower—particularly the part where they repeat the line "Ree-mem-ber! Ree-mem-ber! Ree-mem-ber!" For some reason, Hilary says she found this a little irritating. I can't think why.

Anyway…twelve months later, I am proud to admit that progress has been made—at least on my account. Not one line ever sung by the cast of *Fame* has crossed my lips, in all that time. To compensate, though, I do have frequent erotic dreams about Moby, which Hilary claims she can hear all the way down the hall.

Yesterday, a roommate summit was called.

"Victoria," Hilary began, "do you realize that if we were married, we wouldn't have to live with each other *at all*. Do you actually realize that?"

"Is that a proposal? And if we were married, I think living together would be a given."

"Very cute," she says. "Not married to each other. Married. Each of us. To the perfect husband."

"Is this about the noises I make when I have my Moby dreams?"

"No, it's about the fact that you go through the Lucky Charms and pick out all the orange stars and pink hearts."

"I'm sorry. They just look as if they have more protein in them."

"I go to the library every morning with nothing but yellow moons and blue diamonds in my digestive system!" she screams.

"I know, I know."

"And what's that stuff you've started putting on toast? It smells like old trainers. Is it some Australian thing?"

"It's our national spread of choice. It's called Vegemite. Hilary, it's the last piece of my old life I have. Please, take pity."

Hilary has a stressful job at the children's library. If there are no Harry Potter books on the shelves, the children become anxious, and they pee in the beanbags. After that, Hilary has to take them out into the library car park and hose them down. The beanbags, that is, not the children—but naturally, because the collected works of J. K. Rowling are hidden under her own bed, this anxiety reaction happens quite a lot. In fact, I'll be surprised if they don't have to order new beanbags throughout the entire San Francisco library system.

"I think you and I need to find husbands and get married as soon as possible," Hilary concludes, once we have finished with the contentious Lucky Charms issue.

"Honestly, Victoria," she continues, "I know marriage is a crumbling Western institution with a thirty percent failure rate. But it's also the only way we're ever going to get out of this apartment, and away from each other. No offense."

"Right. No offense taken. I love you, too."

"Anyway," she continues, "some guy at the library is having his thirtieth birthday party on Saturday night. Maybe we can find someone there to marry."

I stare at her. "Oh, I'm absolutely sure that will happen."

"Some guy with a beard, with paint all over his jeans, and a baseball cap, and a watch with a leather strap. That's the kind of man I think I could commit to," she muses.

"Oh, he'll be there for sure," I tell her.

"Yes," Hilary says, nodding her head. "I really think he will be."

The day before the party, though, something remarkable happens. Something that means I may not need to look for a husband at all.

My ex-boyfriend, Microsoft Mike, sends me an e-mail, with the subject header "????" and a picture of a confused duck sitting on a rock.

"This is big," I tell Hilary when she cranes over my shoulder to look at the computer screen. "This is very big. I think he wants us to get back together."

"What?"

"You know he has trouble communicating," I explain. "He's a computer help-desk guy. And you know he's been in therapy."

"Forget him," she says, eating Lucky Charms out of the packet.

"You know I can't."

"Victoria! You haven't even had sex! It wasn't even a relationship!'

"I know," I sigh. "I know."

Microsoft Mike and I spent most of last year seeing each other, in a relationship that was largely Internet based. Or, to put it another way, it began with us meeting in a chatroom, and then continued with him e-mailing me an attachment of a lovesick hippopotamus, with pink hearts floating around its head. More e-mails followed. About 46,000 of them. Not long after this, we broke up though—a sad but inevitable conclusion to our relationship, signaled (from his end anyway) by an attachment of an angry gorilla with lightning bolts coming out of its head.

Hilary stretches out in her chair and locks her fingers behind her head.

"I don't think you should continue to pursue a relationship with a man who can only communicate through free animal e-cards," she says. "You haven't even seen him naked. All you've ever done is sit around and drink four-packs of margarita minis together. No wonder you keep having erotic dreams about Moby."

"I'll get help. I promise."

"What happens in the Moby dreams, anyway? Why do you always make those moaning noises?"

"Because, Hilary, in my dreams, I rub his bald head between my naked knees."

"Oh my GOD!"

She leaves the room.

After this conversation, a few more e-mails from Microsoft Mike arrive, all within minutes of each other. When I fail to respond to the confused-duck attachment, he sends a picture of two flamingos whose necks are craned into a heart shape. When that doesn't work, he sends a computer-enhanced image of a harp seal, with big, shiny tears coming out of its eyes—but also a quote from Arthur M. Schlesinger Jr. that reads, "Everything that matters in our intellectual and moral life begins with an individual confronting his own mind and conscience in a room by himself."

I have no idea what this means, but this is twenty-one more words than I have ever seen in an e-mail from Mike before, and I feel like sending his therapist a note of congratulations. Her name is Helen, and he sees her every week. In fact, he sometimes sees her twice a week.

The next day—on the night of the party—I finally decide to e-mail Mike back. I feel sorry for him, after all; and I know that we never had sex, but we also had a lot of mutually satisfying back rubs while we were responsibly enjoying our margarita minis.

"What are you writing? What are you writing?" Hilary elbows me off the keyboard.

"Just some encouragement. Poor Microsoft Mike. He needs help."

"Ha! You're the one who needs help!" She twirls a finger around on the side of her head, and makes loco eyes at me.

Before Hilary can stop me, though, I press Send. And then, a few seconds later, I have my reply. An e-mailed attachment showing a laughing pig having a bath, while a porcupine is scrubbing its back.

"Ominous, deeply ominous," Hilary warns.

"How?"

"It shows what he really wants." She wags a finger at me. "This is a demeaning, patriarchal image, Victoria. Look at the smug expression on that pig's face as it reclines in the bath! Look at the submissive body language of that porcupine! Look at the way it's holding the soap!"

"Please don't do that," I ask her.

"What? What am I doing?"

"Don't pronounce patriarchy like that. And above all, *don't* wag your finger in that Bin Laden-ish fashion."

"So is this a new house rule then?" Hilary asks, wagging her finger again.

Soon after this, we make our way to Jim's party. He lives only a few blocks away but we decide to drive. We hear the sound of thumping bass before we even get to his street.

"It's Moby!" I look up at the window.

"It can't be," Hilary rolls her eyes as I park the car.

"I love Moby!"

"Yes," Hilary says, shaking her head, "I *know* how much you love Moby. You and your knees."

Once we go inside, we see that Jim has moved all the furniture in his apartment back against the walls, to make space for people to dance—but unfortunately, the only thing his guests are doing is sitting on the carpet, dipping corn chips into jars of salsa.

"My fellow librarians," Hilary says gloomily. "You can always count on them to sit on the floor."

Then I notice that Jim has hooked an iPod up to the speakers.

"Come on!" Jim pokes Hilary in the ribs, waving his arms around. "Join the digital music revolution! Let's dance!"

I quickly take a closer look at him, just to check if he has a beard, or paint-covered jeans, or a baseball cap, or anything else that Hilary desires of her future husband. But Jim is lacking in all these departments. Instead, he has a sprinkling of glitter on his cheekbones, a black mesh T-shirt and extremely tight jeans.

"That's the first time I've ever seen a man with a camel's hoof in his crotch," I tell Hilary as she takes off her shoes.

"Gay," she informs me, looking at Jim's mesh T-shirt. "Gay, gay, gay, gay, gay." Then, for extra emphasis, she adds *"Gay, gay, gay, gay, gay."* Then they salsa together, as The White Stripes start up on Jim's iPod. I guess his boyfriend is elsewhere.

After that, I go into the kitchen, which is what I always do when I arrive at a party and don't know anybody. Two children's librarians—both wearing floor-length gypsy skirts—are talking about Nancy Drew. One is drinking rum, and the other is drinking a straight bottle of piña colada mixer. One of them has also taken her shoe off and put it on the window. They both appear to be using it as an ashtray.

"The great thing about Nancy Drew is that she is titian-haired," the drunker librarian says to nobody in particular. "I love that. *Titian*-haired. Who has hair like that anymore?"

I check my watch. The party only started half an hour ago. They must have been drinking all day to have reached this stage. Then I notice the stubbed-out joint inside the shoe.

"The *really* great thing about Nancy Drew," the more sober librarian replies, "is that her boyfriend is called Ned

Nickerson. Which means, if she ever got married, she would become Nancy Nickerson. Nancy Knickers-On!"

"Rubbish," says a deep, male voice from somewhere inside the pantry, "she should logically become Nancy Knickers-Off, once marital relations have begun. Either that, or Ned should sue."

We all look toward the pantry door, and a dark-haired man in a towel walks out, dripping wet.

"I was looking for an egg," he explains, "to put in my hair. Bloody Jim's used up all the hair conditioner."

We introduce ourselves, and I discover that the drunker librarian in a gypsy skirt can't remember her own surname, and the slightly more sober one is no longer capable of pronouncing the letter A. This is tricky, because her name is Amy. The man in the towel, it turns out, is from London, and he is staying with Jim. He works in banking, and his name is Tom.

"May I ask a favor?" he says, suddenly staring at me.

"Sure."

"Can you stand guard while I have a shower? You look trustworthy."

"Thank you."

"The lock doesn't work—Jim's too lazy to fix it, although I've asked him a million times—and I don't want a lot of librarians walking in."

"Sure."

"I mean, that's not a slur against librarians, you understand—" he raises an eyebrow at me "—but the people that Jim works with are just a little bit…odd."

"I understand."

As I follow him into the bathroom I try not to look at his dripping back, or his dripping legs. Meanwhile, all I can think about are Hilary's words ringing in my head. *"Gay, gay, gay, gay, gay."* Followed by *"Gay, gay, gay, gay, gay."*

I sigh a little inside, as all women are inclined to do sometimes. Why is it that you can't meet a half-naked man in a pantry these days, without him turning out to be interested in homemade hair conditioner and other men?

"Do you want something to read while you stand guard?" Tom picks up a Harry Potter from the bathroom floor and hands it to me before he steps in the shower. It is a library copy. The only one that Hilary hasn't successfully stolen. Jim must have fought her to the death for it.

In the end, though, I don't get a chance to read anything because Tom decides to shout conversation at me through the shower curtain instead.

"I think this egg's scrambling in my hair!" he yells.

"Oh no!" I yell back.

"Oh yes," he says. "So who did you come here with?" he shouts a few minutes later.

"Hilary!" I tell him as he starts adjusting the taps.

"Is that your girlfriend?" he asks in a normal tone of voice, once the water is finally turned off.

"No," I say, wondering if I should hand him a towel or just avert my eyes. "She's my roommate. What do you mean, girlfriend? Do you mean, *friend,* or do you mean, am I a lesbian? Is that what you mean?"

"Yes," Tom says, sticking his head around the side of the shower curtain. "That's exactly what I mean. Sorry, I'm English. Nobody understands us. It's worse than being Japanese. I mean, is she your *girlfriend?* Are you a lesbian, Victoria?

"No. Definitely not. And you?"

"Oh, I'm a lesbian, all right." Tom winks as he stands in front of me, dripping wet and naked. "Actually, no. I'm—"

Before I can hear what he is, though—and I am fully expecting to hear the words *gay, gay, gay, gay, gay*—we suddenly hear an enormous bang, which makes us both jump. I peek out the door to see one of the inebriated librarians running past, tripping over her gypsy skirt and yelling at everyone to get out of the apartment because someone's just bombed the lobby.

"Shit!" Tom yells at me. "Quick, get out! Get out!"

And so I run down the hallway after him, taking my shoes off as I go, while he hangs on to his towel with one hand and grabs my hand with the other.

In the time since Hilary and I arrived at the party, dozens more guests have arrived—so the place is packed—and once we are all out on the landing, on top of the stairs, we find ourselves being squeezed into the walls.

"Victoria!" Hilary shouts across a row of heads. "Hey! Come over here!"

She is still with Jim, I notice, and he is holding her hand as well—although a good-looking black guy with a bandanna round his head is holding tightly on to the other one.

"I think she wants to talk to you," Tom says, letting go of my hand so I can push my way across.

"There's no way that was a bomb," Hilary says when I reach her at last—and she shoots an accusatory look at the drunken librarians in the gypsy skirts.

"It was a pretty loud bang outside," I tell her. "It could be a bomb. Are we still evacuating?"

"No." Hilary looks around her, still holding on to Jim's hand. "I think we're just standing here wondering what the hell's going on."

Then a tall woman—maybe the uber children's librarian of all Californian uber children's librarians—takes charge.

"It was a car crash outside," she yells. "Calm down, everybody. A car hit the traffic lights, and then it backed into a truck. That's all. An ambulance is coming. Go back inside."

"Terrorist attack!" yells someone else, who is still voting for the bomb. "Anthrax!"

But in the end, after a lot of jostling, noise and confusion, it appears that the tall woman has it right, and finally the super appears on the staircase to wave us all back into the apartment.

"So who was that guy you were with?" Hilary asks me once we are inside again, and the music has been turned back on. She has let go of Jim's hand, I notice, leaving him to dance with the man with the bandanna.

"I think he might be Jim's boyfriend," I tell her.

"But Jim doesn't have a boyfriend."

"Well, he's just a friend, then. He's from London. His name's Tom."

"And is he definitely gay?" she asks.

"Oh, I *know* he's gay."

"Oh well," Hilary says. "There's plenty of time for us to find our husbands yet."

"Yeah."

"I know he's out there somewhere," she says dreamily. "The man with the beard, and the leather strap on his watch, and the baseball cap, and the paint all over his jeans."

But although we dance, and talk, and drink—and drink some more—by midnight we are still without husbands.

"I'm bored," Hilary says, and I realize she is having the same problems pronouncing the letter B as the stoned librarian had pronouncing the letter A.

"Shall we go home?" I say hopefully.

"You just want to check your e-mail!"

"I just feel sorry for Mike," I tell her.

"New apartment rule, new apartment rule!" Hilary insists, thumping her fist on the mantelpiece.

"What's that?"

"You can eat any kind of Lucky Charm you want," she informs me, "as long as you SHUT UP ABOUT MICRO-SOFT MIKE."

Then, just as she is about to suggest that we pretend we are at Hogwart's, and play a game of Quidditch with Jim's vaccuum cleaner, Mike himself appears in the doorway—with his arm in a sling.

If this was a movie, I suppose the music would seem to stop—and the room would stand still. But it's not, so someone programs Queens of the Stone Age into Jim's iPod, and Hilary says she's going to the bathroom.

"Pig!" she yells at Mike as she walks past him. "Pig! Porcupine! Patriarchy!"

After she has gone, I touch his bandaged arm, gently, in case it hurts, and then realize he has a cut on his chin as well.

"I don't think Hilary likes me," he says.

"Never mind that. What are you doing here? And what happened to you?"

"I had to come. I saw your car outside. I heard the music. I knew you'd be here."

"What happened to your arm?"

"A truck ran into me outside," he says, sounding depressed.

"That was you? You had the car crash?"

"I just got back from the hospital. Oh God—" His face falls. "I think I should ring Helen."

"You can't have therapy now. It's midnight. We're at a party."

"Did you get all my e-mails?"

"Yes. Thanks, Mike."

He nods, and rubs his arm.

"I could e-mail her," he says after a while.

"Who?"

"Helen."

"*Mike.* Get over it."

And then I see him. Tom—in a white shirt and jeans—standing in the doorway, staring at me, while a pretty, pale woman with long black hair stands next to him, holding two drinks.

"That guy's looking at you," Mike says. "Do you know him?"

"He must be leaving," I reply. "I'd better go. I think he wants to say goodbye. Just stay here."

"I think I lost my BlackBerry in the crash," Mike says, sounding even more depressed.

Before I can go over to Tom, though—maybe that's his sister with him, they look a little alike—Hilary rushes over to me, and hurries me into the corner.

"What?" I sigh. "What now?"

"*Bi, bi, bi, bi, bi!*" she hisses in my ear.

"You're going?"

"No!" She sways around in front of me. "What I mean is—he's not gay, gay, gay, gay, gay, Victoria. He's bi, bi, bi, bi, bi!"

"Who is?"

"Him!" She points at Tom, who is now in deep conversation with the pale, dark-haired woman.

"Really?"

"I saw him kissing her! On the stairs!"

"Oh well," I say. And suddenly, I realize, I feel twice as disappointed as I did before. Is it worse that Tom belongs to a gorgeous brunette woman who isn't his sister, or worse that at one point I thought he was Jim's boyfriend?

Then, just as I am about to suggest to Hilary that we go home—and take Mike with us—the music stops, and the Queens of the Stone Age grind to a halt.

"Who did that?" I hear Jim protesting. "Who just pulled the plug on my iPod?"

"I think it was the guy in the doorway with the bandage on his head," says the man with the bandanna—who is still dancing, despite the lack of music. "That really angry guy over there, with the beard."

Hilary and I turn to look, and at the same moment the bearded, bandaged man spots Mike—and punches him, in his good arm.

"Lousy driver!" yells the bearded man. "You shouldn't be on the road if you don't have insurance!"

"You destroyed my car!" Mike shouts back.

"Yeah, well, you destroyed my paint truck!" counters the bearded, bandaged man—and it looks as if Jim's party is going to end like a cross between *Macbeth* and *How the West Was Won*—until something unexpected happens.

Maybe it's her cumulative intake of blue Lucky Charms, or maybe it's her overconsumption of alcohol, but suddenly, Hilary has decided to take charge.

"I may be inebriated," she announces, "and I may be unable to currently pronounce the letter B, but I have a proposition."

"Okay," I hear Mike whisper. He appears to be terrified of the bearded, bandaged man.

"*You* go back to hospital," she says in her most official librarian's voice, pointing at Mike.

"What?"

"You're far too ill to be out in public, Mike. In fact, I think you're concussed."

"Maybe," he admits, rubbing his head. "Maybe I am. Maybe I should."

"And *you*—" she turns to the bearded, bandaged man "—are a demigod of love, and you are coming home with me!"

And then she kisses him, and kisses him—until someone finally decides to put the music back on, and we all realize that, amazingly enough, the bearded, bandaged man is actually kissing her back.

"I'll send you an e-mail," Mike says as he heads downstairs to wait for a cab to take him back to the hospital.

"Okay." I nod. "I hope you get better soon."

"If only Helen was here," is the last thing he says before he disappears into the hallway.

"If only she was!" I yell back, wishing just for a second that the bearded, bandaged man had managed to break his other arm as well.

And then someone puts Moby back on, at the same time all the lights are turned on, too—it is nearly 1:00 a.m. after all—and I dance, and I dance—not caring who's watching, and not caring if anyone wants to join me or not.

Then, suddenly, I hear a man shouting something behind me. I can't hear what he's saying, but when I turn around, I see Tom—by himself, looking very tired.

"I've still got cooked egg in my hair!" he yells.

"I can't hear you," I yell back.

He is looking much older, now that all the lights in the apartment have been turned back on. And the hair on the back of his head does look oddly crunchy. But still. There's something about him. And I realize that all I want to do is stay next to him for a while.

"What happened to your girlfriend?" I yell as he starts dancing with me. My inhibitions seem to have left the building, along with Microsoft Mike.

"That was my ex-wife!" he shouts back, suddenly sounding very English, and very embarrassed.

Then, after a few more songs, the music is turned off again—though it is Jim pulling the switch this time.

"Enough!" He shoos people out of the room as if he is a farmer dispensing with hundreds of sheep. "Enough! Time to go! Ciao! Au revoir! Bon voyage! See ya later!"

"Well," I say as Tom finds his coat and I look for my handbag. "I'm not surprised she's your *ex*-wife, if you're sleeping with men as well."

"I beg your pardon?"

"You asked me if I was a lesbian, when we were in the bathroom. Don't I have a right to talk frankly about your sex life as well?"

"Possibly." Tom thinks about it as we wait for other people to pick up their coats.

"Well, then." I give him what I hope is a defiant look. "I'm glad we sorted that out. You use eggs in your hair, and you're bisexual, and your ex-wife has had enough. Frankly, I don't blame her."

"Well, she might have left me because of the eggs." Tom smiles at me.

"What do you mean?"

"I'm not bisexual. In fact, I don't even do it with poultry. Jim's just a friend. I've been staying with him while we were sorting things out with the lawyer. My ex lives here, too, now. She moved a few weeks ago."

"Oh."

"Exactly."

"Oh."

"And who was that man you were talking to?" Tom suddenly gives me a fierce look. "That cretinous fool with the broken arm?"

"He works for a computer firm. In Silicon Valley. I don't actually know him very well at all, really. And—I think he's in love with his therapist."

"Computer guy, eh?"

"Exactly."

"I thought so," Tom concludes. "He looked like a nerd."

Then something occurs to me. "Where are you staying tonight, Tom?"

"Why?"

"Because—because I just remembered I have a ton of hair conditioner back at our apartment."

"Oh?" He suddenly looks interested.

"Yes. Real conditioner. Totally egg free. And I don't think Hilary's friend with the beard is going to be using it…"

Before embarking on her writing career, Cecelia Ahern completed a degree in journalism and media communications. At twenty-one she wrote her first novel, *PS, I Love You,* which was sold to fifty countries, and movie rights were bought by Warner Bros. It went on to be one of the biggest-selling debut novels of 2004. In November 2004, her second book, *Where Rainbows End (Rosie Dunne* in the U.S.*),* also became an international bestseller. Her third book is titled *If You Could See Me Now.*

Find out more about Cecelia Ahern at www.ceceliaahern.ie or www.cecelia-ahern.com.

The End
Cecelia Ahern

Let me tell you what this story is about before I get into the finer details, that way you can decide whether you want to read it or not. Let this first page be like my synopsis. First of all let me tell you what this story is *not,* this is not an "and they all lived happily ever after" story, it's not about lifelong friendships, the importance of female relationships, there are no scenes of ladies whispering and sharing stories over cups of coffee and plates of cream cakes they swore to themselves and their weekly Weight Watchers class they wouldn't eat. Drunken giggles over cocktails do nothing to dry the tears or save the day in this story.

What if I told you that this story won't warm the cockles of your heart, it won't give you hope or cause you to blame escaping tears on the sun cream as you lie by the pool reading this? What if I told you that the girl doesn't get the guy in the end?

Knowing exactly how it ends, do you still want to read on? Well, it's not like we don't venture into things without knowing the end, is it? We watch *Columbo* knowing his misguided representation of himself as a foolish old man will help him solve the case, we know Renée Zellweger decides that she will be the one to go with Tom Cruise and the fish in *Jerry Maguire* every single time we watch it, Tom Hanks always sees Meg Ryan at the end of *Sleepless in Seattle,* James Bond always gets the girl, in *Eastenders* every once-happy marriage will end in death, destruction or despair, we read books knowing that the character will blatantly and predictably fall in love with the guy as soon as his name is first mentioned…but we still watch the TV shows and movies and read the books. There's no twist in my story; I genuinely mean it when I say it, I do not live happily ever after with the love of my life or anyone else for that matter.

It was my counselor's idea for me to write this story. "Try to keep an air of positiveness," she kept telling me, "the idea for this is to enable you to see the hopefulness of your situation." This is my fifth draft and I've yet to be enlightened. "End it on a happy note," she kept saying as her forehead wrinkled in concern while she read and reread my attempts. Well, this is my last attempt. If she doesn't like it she knows what she can do with it. I hate writing; it bores me, but these days it passes the time. I'm taking her advice though; I'm ending this story on a happy note. I'm ending it at the beginning.

I'll tell you, just as I told her, that my reason for doing so is because it's always the beginnings that are the best. Like when you're starving and it feels like you've been cooking dinner for hours, the smell is tickling your taste buds, making your mouth water, and it teases you until you take that first bite, that first beautiful bite that makes you feel like giggling ridiculously over the joy of having food in your mouth. You can't beat the first relaxing slide into a warm bath filled with bubbles before the bubbles fade and the water gets cold; your first steps outside in a new pair of shoes before they decide to cut the feet off you; your first night out in a new outfit that makes you feel half the size, shiny and new before you wash it, the newness fades and it becomes just another item in your wardrobe that you've worn fifty times; the first half hour of a movie when you're trying to figure out what's going on and not yet let down by the end; the first few minutes of work after a lunch break when you feel maybe you have just enough energy to make it through the day; the first few minutes of conversation after bumping into someone you haven't seen for years before you run out of things to say and mutual acquaintances to talk about; the first time you see the man of your dreams, the first time your stomach flips, the first time your eyes meet, the first time he acknowledges your existence in the world.

The first kiss on a first date with a first love.

At the beginning, things are special, new, exciting, innocent, untouched and unspoiled by experience or boredom. And so it's there that my story will end, for that is when my heart sat high in my chest like a helium-filled balloon. That is when my eyes were big, bright and as innocently wide and green as a traffic light all ready to go, go, go. Life was fresh and full of hope.

And so I begin this story with the end.

The End

...Feeling desolate, I looked around the empty wardrobe, its doors wide open, displaying stray hangers and deserted shelves as though taunting me. It wasn't supposed to end this way. What had only moments ago been a room overflowing with sound and tension of desperate pleas for him not to leave, of sobs and squeals, wails and shouts coming from both sides was now a chamber of silence. Bags had been thrown around, violently unzipped, drawers were pulled open, clothes dumped into sacks, drawers banged shut, and zips making ripping sounds as they closed. More desperate pleas.

Hands holding out and begging to be held, hearts refusing, tears falling. An hour of mass confusion, never-ending shouts, boots heavily banging down the stairs, keys clanging on the hall table as they were left behind, front door banging. Then silence. Stunned silence.

The room held its breath, waited for the front door to open, for the softer surrendered sound of boots on the stairs to gradually become louder, for the bag to be flung on the ground, unzipped, drawers opened, to be filled and closed again.

But there was no sound. The door couldn't open; the keys had been left behind. I slowly sat on the edge of the unmade bed, breath still held, hands in my lap, looking around at a room that had lost all familiarity with a heart that felt like the dark mahogany wardrobe, open wide, exposed and empty.

And then the sobs began. Quiet whimpering sounds that reminded me of when I was five years old, had fallen off my bicycle all alone and away from the safe boundaries of my home. The sobs I heard in the bedroom were the frightened sobs that escaped me as a child running home sore and scared and desperate for the familiar arms of my mother to catch me, save me and soften my tears. The only arms now were my own wrapped protectively around my body. My heart was alone, my pain and problems my own. And then panic set in.

Feelings of regret, gasps for breath in a heaving chest and hours of panic were spent dialing furiously, redialing, leaving tearful messages on an answering machine that felt as much as its owner. There were moments of hope, moments of despair, lights at the end of tunnels shone, flickered and extinguished themselves as I fell back on the bed, the fight running out of me. I'd lost track of time, the bright room had turned to darkness. The sun had been replaced by the moon that had turned his back on me and guided people in the other direction. The sheets were wet from crying and the phone sat waiting to be called to duty in my hand, and the pillow still clung to his smell just as my heart clung to his love. He was gone. I untensed the muscles in my body and I breathed.

It was not supposed to end like this.

And so I won't let it.

The Middle

…Oh sweet joy, the joy of falling in love, of being in love. Those first few years of being in love, they were only the beginning. Twenty phone calls a day just to hear his voice, sex every night until the early hours of the morning, ignoring friends, favoring nights in curled up on the couch instead of going out, eating so much you both put weight on, supporting one another at family dos, catching roving eyes as they studied one another in secret, existing only in the world to be with them, seeing your future, your babies in their eyes, becoming a part of someone else spiritually, mentally, sexually, emotionally.

Nothing lasts forever, they say. I didn't fall in love with anyone else, nor did he. I've no dramatic story of walking in on him, in our bedroom with the skinny girl next door, I've no story to tell you of how I was romanced by someone else, chased and showered with gifts until I gave in and began an affair. You see, I couldn't *see* anyone but him, and I know he couldn't see anyone else but me. Maybe the dramatic stories would have been better, better than the very fact that nobody and nothing, living in a state of lovelessness and heartbreak seemed more appealing to him than me?

We had one too many Indian take-aways on the couch together, had one too many arguments about emptying the dishwasher, I piled on one too many pounds, he refused one too many nights out with his friends, we went one too many nights falling asleep without making love and went one too many mornings waking up late, grabbing a quick coffee and running out the door without saying "I love you."

You see it's all that stuff at the beginning that's important. The stuff that you do naturally. The surprise presents, the random kisses, the words of caring advice. Then you get lazy, take your eye off the ball and before you know it you've moved to the middle stage of your relationship and are one step closer to the end. But you don't think about all that at the time, when it's happening you're happy enough living in the rut you've carelessly walked yourself straight into.

You have fights, you say things you definitely mean but afterward pretend you don't, you forgive each other and move on but you never *really* forget the words that are spoken. The last fight we had was the one about who burned the new expensive frying pan, that's the one that ended it. It stopped being about the frying pan after the first two minutes, it was about how I never listened, how his family intruded, about the fact he always left his dirty laundry on the floor and not in the basket, about how our sex life was non-existent, how we never did anything of substance together, how crap his sense of humor was, how horrible a person I was, how he didn't love me anymore. Little things like that…

This fight lasted for days, I knew I hadn't burned the frying pan, he "could bet his life" on the fact he hadn't even used it over that week and "of course he didn't, seeing as I was the one who did the cooking around here," which according to him was, "an admission to burning the pan." Years of a wonderful relationship had turned to that? He went out both nights that weekend and so did I. It was like a competition to see who could come home the latest, who could ring the least, who could be gone for the longest amount of time without contact, who could go the longest without calling all their friends, family and police sick with worry. When you train yourself not to care, the heart listens.

One night I stayed out all night without telling him where I'd gone. I even turned my phone off. I was being childish; I was only staying at a friend's house, awake all night, turning my phone on and off checking for messages. Waiting for the really frantic one that would send me flying home and into his arms. I was waiting for the desperate calls, to hear "I love you," to hear the sound of a man in love wanting to hang on to the best thing that had ever happened to him. As proof, as a sign that there was something worth holding on to. No such phone call came. That night taught us something. That I had stooped that low and that he hadn't cared or worried like he should have.

We had an argument and he left. He left and I chased.

You know those moments at the end of movies when people announce their undying love in front of a gasping crowd? When there's music, a perfect speech and then he smiles at you with tears in his eyes, throws his arms around your neck and everyone applauds, feeling as happy about the end result as you are? Well, imagine if that didn't happen. Imagine he says no, there's an awkward silence, a few nervous laughs and people slowly break away. He turns away from you and you're left there with a red face, cringing and wishing you'd never made that speech, took part in the car chase, spent the money on flowers and declared your love in the middle of a busy shopping street at lunch hour.

Well, where do you go from there? That's something the movies never tell you. And not only is the moment embarrassing, it's heartbreaking. It's the moment when your best friend, the person who said they would love you forever stops seeing you as the person they want and need to protect. So much so that they can say no to you in front of the gathering crowd. It's the moment that you realize absolutely everything you shared is lost because those eyes didn't look at you like they should have and once did. They were the eyes of an embarrassed stranger shrugging off the begging words of an old lover.

A man's face looks different when the love is gone. It begins to look just how everyone else sees it, without the light, the sparkle—just another face. And the moment he walks away it's as though the fact you know he sneezes seven times exactly at a quarter past ten every morning means nothing. Like your knowledge of his allergy to ginger and his penchant for dancing around in his underwear to Bruce Springsteen isn't enough to hold you together. The little things you loved so much about a person become the little things he is suddenly embarrassed you know. All the while you're walking away in that awkward, uncomfortable silence.

When you return home feeling foolish and angry to a

house that's being emptied, you begin to wish all those dark thoughts away. I began to wish that we were still together and feeling miserable rather than having to go through good-byes. He still felt part of me, I was still his, I was his best friend and he was mine, yet there was just the minor detail of not actually being *in* love with one another and the fact that any other kind of relationship just wasn't possible. I begged and pleaded, he cried and shouted until our voices were hoarse and our faces were tearstained.

Feeling desolate, I looked at the empty wardrobe with its doors wide open, displaying stray hangers and deserted shelves as though taunting me. It wasn't supposed to end this way.

The Beginning

He used to get the same bus as me. He got on one stop after me and got off one stop before. I thought he was gor-geous the very first day I spotted him outside after wiping the condensation from the upstairs window of the bus. It was dark, cold, raining, seven o'clock in the morning in No-vember, in front of me a man slept with his head against the cold vibrating glass, the woman beside me read a steamy page of a romance novel, probably the cause of the fogged-up windows. There was the smell of morning breath and morn-ing bodies on the stuffy bus, it was quiet, no one spoke, all that was audible were the faint sounds of music and voices from the earphones of iPods.

He rose from that staircase like an angel entering the gates of heaven. His hair was soaking, his nose red, droplets of rain ran down his cheeks and his clothes were drenched. He wobbled down the aisle of the moving bus sleepily, trying to make his way to the only free seat. He didn't see me that day. He didn't see me for the first two weeks but I got clever, moving to the seat by the staircase where I knew he would see me. Then I took to keeping my bag on the chair beside me so no one could sit down and only moving it when he arrived at the top of the stairs so he could sit down. Eventually he saw me, a few weeks later he smiled; a few weeks on he said something, a few weeks later I responded. Then he took to sitting beside me every morning, sharing knowing looks, secret jokes, secret smiles, he saved me from the drunken man who tried to maul me every Thursday morning. I saved him from the girl who sang along loudly with her iPod on Wednesday evenings.

Eventually on the way home on a sunny Friday evening in May, he stayed on an extra stop, got off the bus with me and asked me to go for a drink with him. Two months later I was in love, falling out of bed last minute and running with him to the same bus stop most mornings. Sleeping on his shoulder all the way to work, hearing him say he had never loved anyone else in his life as he loved me, believing him when he said he would never fall out of love with me, that I was the most beautiful and wonderful woman he had ever met. When you're in love you believe everything. We shared kisses that meant something, hearts that fluttered, fingers that clasped and footsteps that bounced.

Oh sweet joy, the joy of falling in love, of being in love. Those first few years of being in love, they were only the beginning.

Pamela Ribon is the author of *Why Girls Are Weird,* a novel based on her own experiences with her hugely successful Web site www.pamie.com. Her latest novel is *Why Moms Are Weird* (Downtown Press). She writes for television and lives in Los Angeles with three cats and a stee.

What Happens Next
Pamela Ribon

I walked into that video store knowing I was going to rent three movies and ask Peter out.

Peter made my thoughts jumble together. I had been planning on doing this for a while, but before a syllable would come out of my mouth, every possible scenario played in my brain like a demonic blooper reel. A terrifying cause-and-effect would unfurl in my head until I stopped myself from doing anything at all.

If I told him I liked his shoes, he'd look down at them, causing our heads to clunk together like a *Three Stooges* punch line. Then he'd back up, covering his head, wincing. This would make him step on the foot of the woman behind him, who would, inevitably, just have had bunion surgery. So the woman with the foot would wail, falling to the ground, clutching herself while screaming about a lawsuit. She would, of course, have some small dog that would yip and growl before peeing all over the carpet. Peter would be fired on the spot, and it would be completely my fault.

I couldn't put my finger on what exactly was different about tonight. It could still all go horribly wrong, but something about this evening made it okay to fail. It'd be worth it.

I had run out of microwave popcorn. While this may seem completely unrelated to video rentals at first, when I found the empty box in my cabinet, the first person I thought of was Peter. It wasn't only because Peter sells me this microwave popcorn due to its convenient location at the checkout line. When I didn't have any popcorn, I wanted to turn to Peter and say, "We're out of popcorn." I wanted to start a sentence with the word "We" and I wanted the "You" part of the "You + Me = We" to be Peter.

Peter + Maggie = We.

I left the house without closing the cabinet door. The next time I made popcorn, I had to have at least tried to make my life have a "We" in it.

I thought I'd walk into Happy Endings Video as if I had no intention of talking to Peter. I'd use a different checkout line for my DVDs. I'd find the girl he's always talking about— the skinny one with dreadlocks—and ask her to check out my movies. I'd seen her once but never talked to her. It'd be much cooler to finish my transaction with that girl before walking over to Peter and asking, "Can I get some popcorn?" Then, while he rang up my three-pack box of Pop Secret in Light Butter, I'd stare at the top of his head, looking deep into his dark tangle of curls, and ask, "Do you work Friday nights?"

It was a question I already knew the answer to, and he knew that. He'd smile, but I wouldn't see his smile because he'd be looking down, and he'd say, "Maggie, you already know the answer to that."

And I'd smile, but he wouldn't see it because he'd be still staring down at my popcorn, which by now he'd probably have put in a plastic bag, and I'd say, "I do. But I also have a question I don't know the answer to."

I'd end my sentence with a preposition like that because he once told me he can't let a sentence like that hang in the air. Peter was in graduate school for English, wanted to be a fancy-pants professor one day. I wanted to be the one who sewed patches onto the elbows of his blazers. I wanted to clean his monocle, polish his pipe, alphabetize his Twain. It all sounded so incredibly sexy.

"You have a question you'd like me to answer?" he'd say.

And I'd say, "Do you want to have dinner with me on Friday night?"

But I'd have leaned in to ask, to appear flirty, to appear irresistible, and I'd have accidentally rested my forearm on the intercom switch, so my question had boomed over the loudspeaker. The entire video store would have heard me. They would all be looking, laughing, judging.

And Peter would have to stammer, over the loudspeaker, "We're having a sale on Vin Diesel tonight. Don't miss it."

There'd be this agonizing silence as he turned off the switch, handed me my popcorn and kept his eyes averted from my face. I'd take the popcorn and leave the store, the city, and the state, forever.

So.

Maybe I'd start my video-store experience the same way I always did, marching right up to Peter and asking, "What have you got for me?" Peter had been helping me pick my rentals for the six weeks I'd been coming to the store. I'd have to start things naturally, act like it was all the other times I'd walked in, but then somehow work in the part where I date

him, make out with him, marry him and have his intellectually superior children.

I wanted to skip all of tonight and fast-forward to the part
where we'd already gone out and had a great time. Then the
next time I walked into the store I could jump up on the
yellow counter, dangling my legs over the returned disks, and
lean in for a kiss from my cute video-store boyfriend. He'd
compliment my T-shirt (which he'd bought me) that boasted
some ironic, geeky sentence, like "Don't mess with tech support," and I'd run my hand over the mess of brown curls on
his head. By then we'd have some kind of inside joke from
our fantastic date—a nickname he'd given his skinny female
coworker, perhaps—and I'd be able to be a part of his inner
world. "You working with Man-Hips?" I'd ask, and Peter
would laugh that warm laugh he's got, and he'd nod his head
in Man-Hips's direction. Then he'd wiggle his finger, warning me to keep his secrets quiet. I'd flirt back that he'd have
to do something to keep me quiet, like buy me something,
and he'd say, "Buy you something? You never asked me to
buy you something before." And I'd say, "Yeah, that part of
this fantasy is nothing like me. I was just going with it." He'd
frown and say, "I'm breaking up with you." Then I'd have
to jump off the yellow counter, but I'd miss, and I'd fall into
the returned-disks bin. Man-Hips would help me up but I'd
accidentally call her Man-Hips and I'd have to change my
video store, apartment and time zone.

So.

Peter knows more about me than I do about him, purely
through his knowledge of my past movie selections. He'd
hold up a DVD and say the movie's title. If I had seen it, I'd
launch into the story of when, with whom and what had
happened that night. Through Peter's game of Twenty

Movie Questions he'd found out the story of my best friend moving away to grad school (we'd stayed up all night watching her favorite movies—*Grease, Steel Magnolias* and, for reasons still unknown to me, *Taxi Driver*), the last time I had the flu (I had watched the first two seasons of *24*), and my recent breakup (I still haven't seen *Out of Africa*). Peter used his job to peek into my life. Now it was up to me to bring his life into mine.

I didn't want it to be my move. Peter had never asked me if I'd seen *Fight Club,* so he didn't know that I don't usually ask men out. My *Fight Club* experience was so awful I vowed to let love find me. I had asked out a guy named Terrence, which isn't a real name as far as I'm concerned, and he spent most of the date commenting on whatever piece of food I put into my mouth while simultaneously explaining how he was never going to get married. As soon as I purchased The Popcorn That Brought on Terrence's Most Disapproving Glare, I knew it wasn't worth putting myself through that.

It wasn't fair someone always had to make the first step toward progress. Someone had to be the brave one, or the stupid one, the one who was willing to change everything. I didn't want Peter to remain my video-store clerk; I wanted him to be someone I could see away from the glare of the fluorescent lights. I wanted to know what he looked like when he wasn't wearing a yellow vest. And because I wanted to know what he looked like in the dark, or in my bed, I had to be the one to put myself at risk, *in public,* and ask him if he thinks about me outside of the store, too. I had to see if he would eat a meal with me. That's the next step. *I flirt with you here in this store, and now I see if you'd like to eat food with me.* The dating ritual was truly bizarre. Why not: *I let you borrow my favorite sweater,* and now let's see if we have fun planting a rosebush together? It seemed just as arbitrary. *If I tell you what day it is now, will you then return a library book with me Friday night?* Dating was coupling up in new situations to see if people were still compatible. Why did it have to be the same series of steps—talking, eating, kissing—before we decided? Maybe I should throw Peter a curveball. He might prefer a girl who asked him to IKEA instead of a restaurant. Except then he might think I considered him hired help. *Now that you've chosen a movie selection for me, would you please grab that Allen wrench and help me put together this Skööl bookcase? Does this make you want to eat food with me?*

I pushed the doors of Happy Ending Video too strongly; they smacked against the wall with a clatter, making everyone in the store stare at me, wide-eyed. "Sorry," I said, my voice too quiet for the large room.

But I was in. I was one step closer to finding out if Peter would eat food with me. No matter what happened, once I did this I had earned the right to buy myself a burger and fries tonight. That was the reward I had decided to give myself. I could eat whatever I wanted tonight because I was a winner. I overcame obstacles. And winners ate cheeseburgers. Or I could order Chinese. Maybe some kung pao chicken from that new place, the one I've wanted to try. But if I ordered from there and it wasn't good, I'd have ruined my victory dinner with a risky new venture. Maybe my victory purchase shouldn't be something food related. That might look bad, when it comes to my self-esteem. I don't need food to be a reward. I'm not that kind of girl. How does a girl reward herself intellectually but still emotionally after a semi-shallow victory such as asking Cute Video-Store Boy out on a date? Let myself read an extra chapter of a book? Rent a foreign movie? Go for a long walk? Being a smart girl sure could be lame. I'd rather treat myself to a bottle of wine and an *Us Weekly*. I make progress in my life so I can judge the lack of progress in Cameron Diaz's.

I stood at the front of the store long enough for Peter to notice me. He waved at me from behind the counter. He was working an incredibly long line that weaved all the way back to the PlayStation games. I mouthed, "Busy!" and he shrugged back at me with a grin. I loved our secret communication, the shorthand language we'd acquired.

There was a time when I thought I had blown it with Peter, when I was sure I had disappointed him with our differences. We were wandering through the aisles, trying to find my next selection, and had just finished bonding over how terrified we were of *The Dark Crystal* when we were kids.

"Gelfling!" Peter screeched at me from behind the Academy Awards section.

"Stop it!" I shrieked back, tossing a copy of *Gandhi* at his head.

He caught the case, flipped it in the air and gave me one of those looks that said he was sizing me up. Then he announced: *"The Godfather."*

I was hoping this wouldn't happen for a few months, at least. I was going to have to confess something that would break the heart of any Movie Geek Boy. As much as I knew it would hurt, I needed to tell Peter the truth. I had to make sure he'd still respect me.

"I've never seen it." I kept my eyes closed so I couldn't see his immediate reaction. All I heard was the sound of Peter's breath escaping his body.

"How could you not have seen it?"

I was too busy blushing over the compliment to realize he was serious.

"Bad parenting?" I offered.

"Bad everything," he said. "Here," he said, handing me a DVD with Marlon Brando's face on it. "Wait." He handed me another case.

"This is the same movie."

"I want you to rent it twice."

He was right. It was wonderful. The only thing that would have made it better was if we had watched it together, so he could hold my hand during his favorite parts.

Peter was busy with customers, so if I wanted to impress him moments before asking him out, I was going to have to pick three killer rentals. What said, "I am an independent woman who makes her own choices, confident enough to let a man's taste influence her decisions but not be bullied into doing whatever he says"? Quite a movie; did it star Angelina Jolie?

I let my fingers dawdle on the plastic spines, listening to the quiet patter they created as I dragged my hand down an aisle. Perhaps I should start with an independent film, something made for next to no money, something with a good story behind it. I paused in front of Cult Classics, waiting for inspiration to strike.

"You see this one?" a female voice asked. A finger came over my shoulder, in front of my face, pointing at the words *El Mariachi*. "It's awesome. Rodriguez made it with the money he'd earned volunteering his body for medical experimentation."

I turned to find a skinny girl in a Happy Endings uniform.

The skinny girl. The yellow vest was baggy over her tiny frame, the bottom hitting her midthigh. She wore torn jeans with fishnet stockings peeking from behind the holes. Her hair, a dark blond tangled mess of braids, dreads and streaks of purple, was held in place on the top of her head by a chunk of plastic, making her look like a deranged genie. Her name tag read: "Zöe."

"What did they do to him?" I asked.

"It's this place in Austin. I hear they give you thirty grand if you let them cut off one of your toes and reattach it without any anesthesia."

"Wow." I pulled the DVD from the shelf. "Thanks."

"No prob."

Zöe moved to the other side of the aisle, but I could feel her eyes still on me as I made my way through the aisles, *El Mariachi* tucked under one arm.

I became distracted by a Sandra Bullock movie, something I hadn't seen before. I have a soft spot in my heart for her films. I always root for her, no matter how dumb the predicament. That girl could get herself into trouble trying to put on her clothes in the morning. I thought about a scene she was in where she was wearing a raincoat.

I was giggling when Zöe ripped the Sandra Bullock movie out of my hand.

"What are you doing?" she asked.

"Nothing!" I said, sounding like a kid caught with a stolen cookie. "I was just looking."

Zöe looked back at Peter. He was helping an elderly woman with her purchases. Giddy grandchildren jumped at her knees, cheering about a Japanese comic-turned-video-game she had rented for them. "He didn't see," Zöe said.

"Peter?"

"You're lucky." Zöe gave me a look, one that I had been dreading from Peter, one that said she knew I wasn't good enough. I wasn't the kind of person who got to date Movie Geek Boys. I didn't have a skinny frame or purple streaks in my hair or know random facts about filmmakers' private lives. I didn't grow up watching everything I could get my hands on. We didn't even have cable. I went to the movies on weekends with friends, which meant I was usually limited to the early works of Keanu Reeves.

Once I met Peter, everything changed. Foreign movies, old movies, actors I'd never heard of, films that were hidden, beautiful gems. He turned my television set into a nightly gift, this box that told me the most beautiful stories. Peter always knew what I'd love, and aside from one Vincent Gallo movie, he never made a bad suggestion.

Doing it on my own was different. I didn't want to do this without Peter, just as I didn't want to run out of popcorn without him. I didn't want to impress him; I wanted to experience things with him. He was my guide into this weird, wonderful celluloid world of DVD commentaries and extras and The Criterion Collection. If Zöe thought I didn't have the right to be his girlfriend, it was her problem, not mine.

"I'm sorry," I said, like a reflex, like it was what I was supposed to say. Zöe hadn't earned any kind of apology from me, but I had to say something.

"Wait here," she said before running off. Her belt made jangling sounds. A long chain that snaked from her back pocket to her knees bounced against her leg.

She tapped Peter's shoulder, beckoning him into a back room. An older man took Peter's place behind the register. The line had died down considerably.

So.

There I was, standing next to the collected works of John Landis, when I realized Zöe was tattling on me, telling Peter I was a Sandy fan, that I probably had *Miss Congeniality* on DVD, and it meant I also loved Julia Roberts, Jennifer Love Hewitt, or any movie for which Renée Zellweger intentionally gained weight. Zöe was telling him I was the kind of woman who cried at the end of a Topher Grace movie, who recited lines written by Nora Ephron, who loved Meg Ryan before all the plastic surgery, and Drew Barrymore when she wasn't in an independent film.

But so what if I was? There was nothing wrong with letting a film take over my brain, letting my life fade away to become a blurry murmur. A movie didn't always have to make me cry, or wish I'd joined the Peace Corps. Why did everything have to be so *serious* all the time with people like Zöe? Since when should taste in movies prove a person's worth? Sometimes movies should be silly, or even predictable. If my life could be as predictable as a Sandra Bullock movie, I could have walked in here tonight, delivered a perfect speech to Peter in front of all those people, executed a flawless pratfall on my exit and still found myself kissing Peter in the rain, living happily ever after.

Zöe and Peter were probably watching me on the security camera. I bet they were pointing and laughing their superior laughs, wondering what lame-ass movie choice I'd make next. I didn't need this humiliation. I just wanted a sweet love story. Zöe could have Peter. She was probably in love with him. Why wouldn't she be? He's perfect for her, with his sense of humor and his sweet demeanor. He's the perfect Movie Geek Boy. If I stormed back there right now, stopped their laughter by pulling the Sandra Bullock card, if I acted like these were the last ten minutes of my romantic comedy, I'd tell Peter I thought I had a chance with him. "A real chance between two people who just wanted to sit still and watch movies together," I'd say, because women always repeat themselves at the end of those films. Then I'd get serious, like they do, hurt with a hint of tears. "But I guess I was wrong," I'd say, because that's what they all say. And the music would turn sad, or if it were an indie romantic comedy it'd be something like The Postal Service, all bleeps and blips and a man crooning something about spaceships and love affairs. But this is my big-budget romantic comedy, so it would have to be something more predictable, like the Counting Crows. I'd wipe the one tear from my eye and ask, "You know what?" because that always precedes the really profound statement, the zinger, the punch to the mouth. I'd look Peter right in the eye and say, "I'm gonna go find my own happy ending." Then I'd walk out, grabbing a box of Pop Secret in Light Butter on my way out. Nah, fuck it: *Kettle Corn.* I was a new woman.

I wasn't going to put myself through this, in this garishly lit room where I wasn't cool enough. There was someone out there who loved me no matter what I wanted to watch on a big screen, no matter what preposition I ended my sentences with. Maybe he was outside that door right now. That's how some movies end. He'd be right outside, and I'd bump into him the second I grew a spine and the audience knew I was going to be fine on my own. I'd run out of the store, knocking into The One in my predictable, clumsy-but-cute-aw-shucks Sandra Bullock way. He'd drop his manuscript; I'd drop my popcorn box. We'd bend down together, catch each other's eyes, the music would start, we'd run to his place and the next time we saw daylight would be three days later when our bones were aching from how hot our lovemaking had been. That's how I would fall in love forever. I wanted a man who didn't giggle when I said "lovemaking."

Accepting my fate, I put *El Mariachi* on the nearest shelf, covering a Julie Andrews film. I pushed past a kid trying to sneak into the porno section. I reached the door. My hands gripped the bar and I pushed. Wind hit my face as I left behind the pressure, the anxiety, and Peter.

I immediately bumped into someone. A man. But he wasn't holding a manuscript. He was holding a yellow, plastic vest. Peter.

So.

"What took you so damn long?" he asked, shivering in the wind. He was in just a white T-shirt and slacks. He stamped his feet against the concrete, trying to kick warmth into his muscles.

"What are you doing out here?" I asked.

"I've been waiting for you to leave. I didn't want to do this in this stupid vest."

"Do what?"

"Did you get the Rodriguez movie?"

"No." I looked behind Peter, wondering if The One was over there, arms crossed at his chest, patiently waiting for his cue.

"Why not? Zöe said you were going to get it."

"She thinks I'm not cool enough."

Peter pointed over my shoulder. Zöe was behind the glass, inside the store. She was staring at us, biting her lower lip. Her hands were clasped under her chin. "She's been trying to get me to do this for three weeks," Peter said. He then pushed a hand through his hair and sighed. Breath curled in a pretty steam around his face. "I was hoping you like to eat food."

I was already smiling when he tried to explain. "My words get mixed up around you," he said.

Inside my head, music was swelling. I didn't feel like Sandra Bullock; I felt like me.

"I know what you mean," I said.

"I'm asking about Friday. For dinner."

"Peter, I would love to eat food with you."

New from the bestselling author of
Tales of a Drama Queen

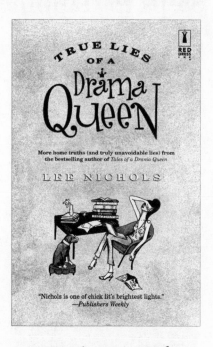

On sale June 2006.

Things just can't seem to get worse for
Elle Medina, but then again, maybe they can…. Join
Elle, the charming star of *Tales of a Drama Queen*,
as she discovers more home truths and truly
unavoidable lies!

**Visit your local
bookseller.**

**RED
DRESS
I N K**
™

www.RedDressInk.com

RDILN575TR

Are you getting it at least once a month?

Here's how: Try RED DRESS INK books on for size & receive two FREE gifts!

The Jinx
by Jennifer Sturman

Loves Me, Loves Me Not
by Libby Malin

YES! Send my two FREE books.

There's no risk and no purchase required—ever!

Name (PLEASE PRINT)

Address   Apt. #

City   State/Prov.   Zip/Postal Code

Not valid to current Red Dress Ink subscribers.

Want to try another series? Call 1-800-873-8635 or visit www.morefreebooks.com.